the woman who climbed trees

Celebrating
30 Years of Publishing
in India

Praise for *The Woman Who Climbed Trees*

"The Great Nepali Novel is here! I haven't read a better book in ages."

—PRAJWAL PARAJULY, author of *The Gurkha's Daughter*

"Smriti Ravindra's first novel is a magnificent tale of growing up as an outsider. Her protagonist combines a prickly individuality and a strange relatability. And this despite the brooding presence of a mother whose love is veined by her own demons. If you have loved and wondered why, you will want to read this book."

—JERRY PINTO, author of *The Education of Yuri*

"*The Woman Who Climbed Trees* is the achingly beautiful story of one family's search for fulfillment amid the deep psychological wounds inflicted by Nepali society. Smriti Ravindra is a gifted storyteller, evoking the many inner dislocations that Meena and Manmohan suffer as they move through Sabaila, Kathmandu, Darbhanga, and Janakpur to forge a family life together. Amid the instability of their cross-border identity, they and their children Adi and Preeti discover, by turn, that while a few of their desires can find expression, most cannot. With great empathy and skill, Ravindra captures the longing, frustration, and hurt that marks the Madhesi experience. This is a remarkable novel by an exceptionally talented writer, and an essential read for those interested in Nepal and its borderlands."

—MANJUSHREE THAPA, author of *All of Us in Our Own Lives*

"*The Woman Who Climbed Trees* is a searing tale of trauma, separation, and the circumscription of women's lives on either side of the Indo-Nepal border. This debut novel shines with vivid detail, weaving in folklore and modern cinematic references to create a portrait of heartbreak and maternal love."

—ANNIE ZAIDI, author of *Prelude to a Riot*

"A lyrical, furious triumph of a novel, mapping the marital journey of its protagonist, Meena, from girlhood to motherhood, from India to Nepal, from prosaic reality to magical madness. In the tradition of Salman Rushdie and Isabel Allende, Smriti Ravindra braids epic lore and myth to a narrative of claustrophobic domesticity, earthly damage, and incandescent love."

—MARIA DAHVANA HEADLEY, author of *Beowulf: A New Translation*

"Through a mix of ghost stories, myths, and songs, Ravindra examines the way that women are expected to reshape their lives for men and the pain that comes with leaving everything behind. When fourteen-year-old Meena marries a man from Nepal, she moves with him to Kathmandu and quickly grows to abhor him, despite their two children together. Meena's discontent is tempered only by the solace she finds in the women around her and their stories of being uprooted."

—HARPER'S BAZAAR

"Ravindra debuts with a stunning chronicle of an Indian woman's coming-of-age . . . . Many Indian and Nepali stories, songs, and myths anchor the narrative, and by the end . . . their meaning in relation to Meena becomes increasingly complex. This is electrifying."

—PUBLISHERS WEEKLY (STARRED REVIEW)

the woman who climbed trees

A NOVEL

SMRITI RAVINDRA

HarperCollins *Publishers* India

First published in India by HarperCollins Publishers 2023
4th Floor, Tower A, Building No. 10, DLF Cyber City,
DLF Phase II, Gurugram, Haryana – 122002
www.harpercollins.co.in

2 4 6 8 10 9 7 5 3 1

P-ISBN: 978-93-5629-623-7
E-ISBN: 978-93-5629-624-4

Designed by SBI Book Arts, LLC

Printed and bound at
Replika Press Pvt. Ltd, India

FSC www.fsc.org MIX Paper from responsible sources FSC® C016779

This book is produced from independently certified FSC® paper to ensure responsible forest management.

For my mother

AUTHOR'S NOTE

An image lives in me. It is a green and flat image. There is grass everywhere, and tufts of shrubs grow beside a stream. The day is transparent. Clouds swim like swans in the sky. On either side of the stream there is a horse. Each horse carries a couple, a man and a woman married to each other. The women are traveling with their men to inhabit their husbands' homes. At one point the horses stop for a drink and once they finish drinking, they cross the stream and exchange countries. One of these horses has crossed into Nepal from India, and the other from India into Nepal, but neither the horse nor the woman it carries realizes a transition has taken place. After all, not much shifts with the crossing. For an extended distance the landscape remains the same. The language. The customs. And the women are lulled into a happy security by this familiarity. But then the horses continue to move. The horse that is now in Nepal trots farther and farther into the new nation, and slowly the flat landscape is disturbed by budding hillocks that soon turn to soaring mountains and bottomless chasms. Beyond these mountains and chasms live additional languages, additional customs, additional expectations, all unknown to the woman who must make sense of them as the horse trots on.

The story of Nepal and India is a story of familiarity and dissonance. The countries share much—Hinduism for one, as well as saris, a love for food and festivals, a love for Bollywood. Nepali is spoken in parts of India, and Maithili is common to both countries where they share borders. But upon this fabric of similarities is printed the strong and garish pattern of divisive politics and political history, exacerbated by mistrust and misgivings between the two countries. The British, when they colonized India and manipulated the Nepali rulers into handing over Gurkha soldiers who would die in hundreds of thousands for their wars in Europe and Burma, fueled this mistrust; the kings—weak and greedy—stirred hatred and doubt in the minds of their citizens; and the politicians of today benefit from the ongoing suspicion that exists between those who see themselves as people belonging to the flatlands of Nepal and those who see themselves as mountain dwellers. A culture of suspicion and resentment simmers between the Madhesis and the Pahadis. The flatlanders, or the Madhesis, share stronger cultural bonds and closer physical features with Indian citizens. The mountain dwellers, or the Pahadis, consider themselves truly Nepali because their features don't always match those of people living across the borders in India. Instead, they share features with Tibetans and their Chinese neighbors. They are fair and creamy and dark-haired. Occasionally, the simmering comes to a boil and hearts are broken, lives are lost. But mostly, there is an attempt to live in harmony. Through all this, the horse trots on, the woman pines and seethes, the country—both a geographical marvel and a political construction—shapes and reshapes itself.

Smriti Ravindra

PROLOGUE

THE WOMAN WHO CLIMBED TREES

A man had two children and one day his wife died. So the man went looking for another wife but no woman would be burdened by the children and the man remained unmarried for some years. Then one day the man went to a neighboring village for some work and heard of a family that had a girl of marriageable age. After he had finished his work, the man went up to the family's house and made inquiries about the girl's age, color, and robustness. Satisfied, he offered himself as a groom. He had wealth, he said, and lots of youth left in him. He would take care of the girl, and the girl would take care of the children.

Show me the children, the girl said, and the man brought his children with him during his next visit. When the girl looked at the children, she fell in love with them. They were good children, shy and calm. They had beautiful sad eyes, like those of orphans, and they tugged at her heart and so the girl married the man.

For many years the girl was mother to the sad-eyed children, and eventually their eyes began to glow with joy. They learned mischief, learned songs and dances, played in the fields. They learned to chase after carts and birds. Eventually they forgot their birth mother and thought of the girl as their real mother. They grew up well, two handsome children.

One night the man could not sleep. It was a moon-filled night and the rays fell silver upon his wife. The tree outside knocked at the window, quiet and musical. The man stayed up, enjoying the night, and when, around an hour after midnight, his wife pushed aside the covers and stepped off the bed, the man was surprised. The girl put on her slippers. She made her way out the room and toward the front door. She stepped out of the house and disappeared. The man stayed behind, confused. The girl returned with the early hours.

She did the same the next day, then the day after.

The man was very disturbed by his wife's behavior and decided to follow her. One night, after much thought, he tied a thread to the tip of his wife's hair and held the spool in his hand. When she left the bed, the thread on the spool began to unwind and started a white path behind her. After a good interval had passed, the man followed the thread path. The thread went down the lane that crossed the fields and a cluster of huts. It went past the bazaar, past the temple, and followed the river. It stopped by a large peepul tree and climbed its bark. The man was puzzled. What could this mean? Why had the thread climbed the tree? He looked up and, sure enough, there was his wife, up on the tree, sitting on its branches, enjoying the wind and the stars.

The man hid himself behind some bushes and when he saw his wife readying to leave he rushed back home. For a month after that he followed her every night, and every night the girl climbed the tree and sat on its branches. Her feet dangled under her sari. Some nights she let down her hair and her hair fell like a waterfall upon her back.

The girl was beautiful and the man was severely in love with her, but despite all this he was also tormented. What could this mean? What could this mean? Finally, he began to talk about his wife with others.

He told his friends, his sisters-in-law, his brothers. Word spread. Ah, said the people, she must be having an affair. But after many nights of watching the tree it was clear there was no affair. She must be mad, said others, but all day the girl worked with such surety and skill that insanity had to be ruled out. Then someone said she must be a witch. Think of it, said someone, we cannot understand anything she does. Why did she marry this man, someone so much older than her? Why did she choose not to have her own children and raise somebody else's? Why do these children love her so? Why does she look more beautiful at night than in the morning? Why does she sit high in a tree?

Nobody could answer.

The man thought hard about it and decided it was time to let the children know.

She does not love you, he said. She is a witch.

That is not true, cried the children. She loves us. She feeds us sweets, stitches our clothes, gives us baths, sends us to school, strokes our hair until we fall asleep, and sings in our sleep so we dream sweet. She loves us.

Does she? said the man. Come with me and I will show you.

So he took the children along the next night and showed them the girl. She was upon the branches, light as a bird, her hair blowing in the wind, her skin without wrinkles.

Now, said the man, is that a woman or a witch?

The children stared. They had never seen their mother so lovely, so without worry, so far away, as though she cared nothing for them or anything they knew. She is a witch, they said, and returned home with their father.

The next night the man, the children, the friends, the sisters-in-law, the brothers, and the elders of the village surprised the wife by springing out of the bushes. When the wife fell off the branch, they gave her a good beating. The wife stared at her husband and said nothing, but when she saw her children, she began to weep. Save me, save me, she cried. But the children, who had never seen their mother look so beautiful, could not step forward. They looked away and stared into the distance in fear. They pushed their fingers into their ears so they would not hear her scream. Then the villagers carried her to the river. The children stared into the distance. They kept their fingers in their ears and did not hear their mother thrashing under the water, nor did they hear the silence when it came.

BOOK ONE

THE COLOR OF BIDAI

SPLIT ENDS ARE NOTHING BUT BAD LUCK

Meena was fourteen, standing with her sisters on the terrace of Darbhanga, shelling and eating roasted peanuts, when Kaveri, her mother, told her about Manmohan.

"A prize," said Kaveri. "Twenty-one years old and clean-shaven—not a mustache under his nose. A proper Romeo, I am telling you. Pukka Majnu."

In the picture Kaveri showed Meena, Manmohan wore dark glasses and had thick sideburns cut at a rakish angle. Standing with him were his siblings—one older brother, two younger brothers, and a younger sister. The photo, taken in Manmohan's ancestral village in Nepal, showed him posing in front of a bullock cart seconds before he got into it. The cart was the first of several vehicles that took Manmohan across the borders of Nepal into India, and finally to Varanasi, where Manmohan was receiving an education at the prestigious Banaras University.

"He is a big hero in his village," Kaveri informed her young daughter. "Imagine being the first from his family to study in India. The rest of the brothers will remain farmers only," she added. "Only this boy will become an officer, I am telling you."

Manmohan's older brother, Ashok, was married and had two sons, one-and-a-half-year-old twins who looked nothing like each other.

"I saw their pictures, too. What is the point of becoming twins if you don't look similar at all?" The twins and their mother, Kumud, were featured in another photograph, which Kaveri showed her daughter. "She is looking nice and plump in the picture. It is a house of butter and milk, that much is confirmed," said Kaveri. Meena stared at the picture. Kumud, already a mother, looked like a little girl. Her eyes were wide and darkly kohled. Her lips and cheeks were painted lightly pink and made her youth more apparent.

"She is pretty," said Meena.

Manmohan's mother, Sawari Devi, was a widow and worked the fields like a man. Kaveri had heard she was a severe autocrat. "That Kumud must be stealing from the kitchen to get as juicy as she is. I heard the mother-in-law is a naagin in the way she guards everything. But you can never be sure of anything. People always talk badly about mothers-in-law. But what good is being a naagin," asked Kaveri, "if she has to pull the plow like a man? Apparently she wears gumboots and goes right into the slush, working with the laborers. What good is that? God willing, she will be dead sooner than she should be. Fieldwork is not for women." Kaveri went on, "That son of hers, not the one you are going to marry, the older one, he can get gold from grass, I have been told. When your mother-in-law dies, there will be enough for all the sons. The sister is thirteen already so you won't have to worry about her. She will be soon married and become someone else's headache."

All through the month leading up to the night of the Mehendi party, Kaveri updated Meena. "Do you know only Janakpur has a train in all of Nepal? Can you imagine? Not even its capital has a train. Only Janakpur. How nice is that? You will be close to the only town that has a train station in it. That Manmohan can take you for rides. It must be some fancy village, that Sabaila, I am telling you, not like the one I come from. One bus from here to Jaynagar, five hours, yes? Then that one-and-only train from Jaynagar to Janakpur, three hours I have heard, then off to Sabaila, three hours also. Total, eleven hours. Only half a day. Not bad at all. And they have relatives in Janakpur. You can halt there for a night, eat there, all that. We can also come there any time. It is easier to get to you than to get to Dilli. Dilli is too far." That is when Meena started to sob. Eleven hours. Another town. Another village. Another country. And what about all my friends? she wondered. She played five stones and hopscotch with them after school. What would she now do in the evenings?

"What are you crying for?" scolded Kaveri. "Even Lord Rama traveled to Nepal to find a suitable consort for himself in Goddess Sita. And what a consort she turned out to be. One look at her in the gardens of Janakpur and Rama was smitten. What a love story!"

"No love story there," Meena said with a sniff. "Eventually, Rama threw Sita out of his palace, and Sita nicely killed herself."

"What nonsense," cried Kaveri. "Sita did not kill herself."

"No? So you think the grounds of the forest actually opened up like some donkey snake and swallowed the woman?"

Kaveri considered her daughter's statement for a few seconds. "You have a point here, Little One," she said. "But this Sita and Rama are only stories. No need to think too much about them. Think of me and your father. I am Nepal's daughter, too, and your father is from India. And we are married or not?"

"You are as much Nepal's daughter as a mango is a papaya," said Meena, weeping now. "You can't speak a word of Nepali, don't know a thing about Nepali food, can't sing a Nepali song or name a Nepali festival. It is thoroughly disgraceful."

"Disgraceful-misgraceful," said Kaveri in a huff.

Meena scowled at her mother's childishness, but her mother's lack of connection with her country suddenly caught in Meena's throat like a fish bone. Kaveri came from the fringes of the India-Nepal border, from a village that fell that side of the line, but that did not make her a Nepali. It just made her slightly more ridiculous. Kaveri had never lived with her parents long enough to visit Kathmandu or Janakpur or Sabaila, and the only times she ever evoked her Nepaliness was when she needed to scoff at her husband. “A citizen of a slave nation,” she liked to say about him every now and then. “He cannot help it. Now, look at me. A citizen of a nation that never bowed its head before foreign rulers. The land of Gurkhas!” All this though she did not have a single Gurkha friend and suffered severe motion sickness when she traveled up mountains.

All through the month leading up to the wedding, Kaveri consoled Meena. “Don’t worry about the village part, little one. You will not have to live in the village for long. Your husband is not interested in farming at all. He wants to be an officer. He wants to live in Kathmandu. Can you imagine,” she said, momentarily forgetting she was supposed to be comforting her daughter, “they don’t even have a video hall in that village, let alone a cinema hall. No electricity, no taps, only hand pumps, no roads, obviously. But their rice is fresher than fish,” she quickly added, “and their chicken younger than eggs. Eh? There is something to that or not? And they will dress you in silk and sleep you on mulmul. You should see the picture, how nicely round that Kumud is!”

“Nepal is like India, only,” said Kaveri, holding her daughter close. “It is like another state in India. Now, if you go to Madras will you understand a word they say there? No. But you can go to Nepal and still understand what they are saying. It is like that. It is the same country, just two different names.”

And now the wedding was here already. Meena was to get married the next evening and it was the afternoon of the Mehendi. The barber’s wife, a thirty-year-old woman who was much in demand during the wedding season, was in charge of Meena's hair and her mehendi and she worked with slow meticulousness upon Meena's feet, her fingers precise and steady, working the mehendi cone even as she chatted and gossiped. She scarcely raised her head to look at Meena, except when she needed rest.

Meena listened to the barber's wife and watched the patterns unfurl upon her toes. Within her, Meena's heart raced. The barber's wife talked continuously, her speech changing rhythm with the patterns she drew. When Meena's feet were done, the barber's wife took a break to style her hair. Meena's hair was long, touching her thighs, and the barber's wife snipped off inches where some hair had split. "Split ends are nothing but bad luck," the barber's wife said in her throaty voice. "There was this woman who got married without snipping the split ends and years later the husband found out she was not a woman at all! She was a chudail! A witch! They had to drown her in a river." The next morning the barber's wife would twist Meena's hair into a high bun and put a garland of jasmines around it. Meena, the barber's wife said, would make a very pretty bride. "You have nice big eyes," she said, "like the actress's, like Meena Kumari's."

By the time the barber's wife started the mehendi on Meena's palms the evening was already mature, and the barber's wife fell into her own trance. It was with a glazed stupor that she spoke about marriage and mothers and motherlands with Meena. "What-what these men say," she said, slowly shaking her head. "One can never change the mother and the motherland, they will say. Such nonsense. There is an incorruptible bond between child, mother, and motherland, they say, a loyalty that cannot be broken by will or act. Anything! My husband also lectures me sometimes"—and here she thickened her voice to mimic her husband—"'The mother and the motherland are not like the arms or legs of a body, which when decayed can be amputated. The mother and the motherland are the hearts and livers of the body. They cannot be removed. The mother remains, and the motherland, too, in daylight and in darkness.' Such babble of pearls fall from his toothless mouth. Just go and make some good money, old man, I say and push him away. But it feels like he has put stones on my chest when he talks this way. What is mother and motherland to a woman? They are impermanent dreams."

Meena and the barber's wife sat in the living room that had large windows on either side. Outside one set of windows was the balcony facing the inner courtyard, and outside the other window was the veranda facing the garden. On the veranda and in the courtyard were the men—Meena's father, her uncles, her brother, her many male cousins. They were getting their hair cut and their heads massaged. Two large halogen lamps burned upon the veranda to aid the haircutter. Soon these men would become strangers to Meena. Soon one man, one husband, would replace all. Soon she would belong to some Manmohan and no longer belong to her brother, Suman. Soon her brother would marry someone, too, belong to another woman and no longer to his four sisters. Soon Meena would not be in this room, looking out at him. Meena looked away. The pattern of henna upon her palms and feet seemed to confine her. She could not eat by herself, nor could she push a strand of hair away from her face. She had to stay still to make sure the patterns on her palms did not smudge.

Everywhere around Meena there was sound, and every room in the house was fragranced with the aroma of henna paste kept ready for mehendi. Girls and women sat around mehendi artists to get their palms and feet patterned, but these women were not getting married the next day so it did not matter if their designs were not perfect. It did not matter if they decided not to decorate their feet or snip off their split ends. No bad luck would befall them. Carelessness would not lead to accidents in their lives.

In another room her father had set up a projector for the absolutely lazy, and Meena could hear Dharmendra romancing Rekha. Children with sticky hands and mouths ran circles in the house, buzzing like flies with the sweets they had eaten. The balcony was crowded with neighbors and guests, most drinking lassi and buttermilk and talking loudly. It was a warm evening and Meena's blouse was damp with sweat. Older women sat in groups upon mats set throughout the house. They sang songs about marriage and sex. Kaveri was on the veranda, playing a dholak, and her cohort of singing friends were scolding the groom. *This groom is too fat*, they were singing. *He will eat my daughter out of the house.*

Oh, my daughter will suffer so
What a ravenous appetite!
Stop! Stop, you monstrous elephant
You hippopotamus mouth
You plump piglet
You swelling swine.
Oh, he will crush my delicate girl
Oh, how will she sleep?
Oh, she will say
Oh! Oh!

Meena felt a hush within herself, a nervousness that kept her still and silent, unable to enjoy her mother's songs, her brother's occasional glances toward her through the window, her sisters' unruly jokes, as they popped in and out the living room to check on her. "And so he pressed the bell, ding dong, only it was her nipple!" "The man said, can you hold the camel, please? . . . I can do this, can you? . . . And she fluttered around the room, wearing only her underwear, hehe." Every now and then her friends came into the room to check in on her. They came dressed in their best frocks, and a few wore saris for the first time. Two of her friends who were already married could not come because they no longer lived in Darbhanga. Those who came tittered and laughed as they looked at Meena's hands, but the tittering and their nervous, high-pitched laughter gave away their worry and curiosity. *Prepare us for what happens,* they were saying to her, though not a word about it was exchanged between them.

The barber's wife drew an intricate pattern upon Meena's palms: a lake with rippling water, curls of scorpion tails, flower buds blooming on vines, a peacock with checkered feathers, a mango-shaped ambi blooming into a lotus. Half the day passed and Meena was tired. She passed in and out of sleep, and every time she awoke she found a new pattern upon her, vaguely heard another clip of the story the barber's wife was still telling. "Once upon a time a barber sent his daughter to clip the nails of a ghost-bride," she said. "Such was the night that the wind howled and the water in the lake bobbed like a maddened animal . . ." When awake, when able, Meena watched in wonder. With what mastery the barber's wife drew and with what mastery she explained her art. "Marriage is a scorpion's bite," she said. "It will leave you hot and breathless, your throat burning for a glass of water. Marriage is an inverted game of chess, if you win, you lose. Marriage is a trip on a boat, up and down it goes, up and down." The lotuses, the mangoes, the flower buds on vines, these were the children. "Marriage is for children," said the barber's wife. "Many of them. Many, many of them."

Eventually, Meena fell deeply asleep, while the barber's wife continued the pattern until the forest of flowers and birds on Meena's palms were as involved as dreamscapes. All day the barber's wife drew and all night Kaveri and her daughters dabbed the mehendi with a mixture of lemon juice and oil, and so when Meena finally woke up the pattern flared like fire upon her skin. It would stay for three weeks, first red as fire, then fading slowly into a sunset, then to the color of an orange, then a blush, a hint thereafter, and finally it would disappear, become a memory. A bride's mehendi is her mother's house, it was how her mother's house sits within the bride's heart, first burning inside her, then lingering as a memory.

"What is he like?" Meena asked Kaveri just before Manmohan arrived at their door. "Tall or short? Fair or dark?"

But the pictures Kaveri had seen of Meena's soon-to-be spouse had been in black and white and Kaveri did not know.

PUKKA MAJNU

Though he had taught his friends at the Banaras University all the Nepali phrases worth knowing, Manmohan's friends could not consider him foreign or international and called him "foreign maal" only when they wanted to tease him. There was nothing of the outsider about Manmohan. Not his name, not his religion, not his habits, not his language. It was because of Manmohan that the boys at the Banaras University began to think of Nepal as another state in India. Was Darjeeling the capital of Nepal? They asked. Was Sikkim? Where exactly was Kathmandu? "Same thing, same thing," they said when Manmohan tried to impress his difference upon them.

"You don't have almond-shaped eyes," they said, dismissing him with a laugh.

"Fifty percent of Nepal does not have almond-shaped eyes," Manmohan protested.

"And you are a wimp. If you see a knife you will faint. There is nothing Gorkhali about you."

"And there is nothing of a man in you, you choot," said Manmohan, only half good-naturedly.

Some evenings, when his friends would allow him the time, Manmohan revealed to them the real reason he was at the university. "I am not here to get an education like the rest of you spoiled brats," he said. "I am here in hiding."

He went on to tell them that he had fled Nepal and come into India to avoid imprisonment by the king of Nepal, King Mahendra Bir Bikram Shah. "I joined the Nepali Congress Party four years back. The Nepali Congress Party," he expounded, his chest swelling with pride, "has been responsible for many political changes in Nepal. Back in 1951 it played a crucial role in the transfer of power from the Ranas back to the Shahs . . . Do you even know who the Ranas are, you assholes? You don't know anything."

"What? About the dot on the map you call a country?" His friends laughed, but they were intrigued, too. "Do tell us your story, O refugee," they coaxed. "Don't sulk like a woman, O warrior from the land of Gurkhas!"

And despite the teasing, Manmohan told them his story. "The true rulers of any country," he explained to his sniggering friends, "are not kings and prime ministers, but its people. No king, however rightful he may appear, should rule over a country. Though the Congress helped King Mahendra's father get back his throne from the treacherous Ranas, the Nepali Congress Party continued its fight to establish democracy in Nepal."

"Yeah, because that makes sense," said his friends. "Abolish monarchy by putting a king on the throne. A very intelligent party, I must say, this Nepali Congress of yours."

They enjoyed listening to Manmohan. There was something naive in his boisterous claims, in his boyish enthusiasm. "I fled in 1970," Manmohan confided. "In 1960, when King Mahendra took over from his father, he killed off several 'traitors.'"

"And it took you ten years to get here? You are a very slow runner, Manmohanji. At this rate you will surely be beheaded soon."

"Nobody is beheading me," said Manmohan, finally getting irked because his friends would not take him seriously. "Nobody knows I am here yet. But they will find out soon. I am not here to learn commerce and accounts. I am here to get in touch with the eminent Nepali leaders who live in exile in the gullies of Varanasi and other cities. I am here to scout them out. I am underground, my friends, underground," he said with a great flourish.

"Our hero here is a regular mole," his friends said, laughing.

By the time Manmohan joined the Banaras University, India's independence was almost twenty-five years old and somewhat stale, and the boys Manmohan spoke to had not been born when independence came to their country. They had, however, grown up wishing they had personally fought to push the British out of India. They dreamt of marches and protests and martyrdom. To bear the bullet for one's country, or to flee and live "underground" for one's conviction. They did not entirely believe Manmohan's claim that he was in self-exile and looking for renegades, but they were mesmerized by his dreams. They harbored similar dreams of adventure and espionage but had never thought it possible to voice them, and despite themselves, they were filled with envy, respect, and pride for their friend.

Of course, they also continued to ridicule him. Manmohan was too thin for hardiness and too studious for any real adventures. He spent too many hours worrying about exams and being buried in books and too many times he had let slip that he did not want to be a farmer like his brothers. He wanted to hold a position in some office. And despite having established so vehemently that he had fled Nepal to avoid political persecution, he inadvertently said, too many times, that he wanted to be an officer in Kathmandu, the city where kings and their kin lived.

"Well, you must be quite the daredevil if you want to run off to your own graveyard," his friends said, teasing him.

Also, they had not once seen Manmohan sneak away into the gullies of Varanasi to meet secret people who lived invisibly in small, dark rooms. However, despite the teasing and the leg-pulling, they did not feel too badly about what they thought were his lies. After all, everybody lied about such things. There were at least five dozen people that each of Manmohan's friends knew who either claimed their parents had been a part of the fight for India's independence or that they had played some crucial part in the plot. There was nothing malicious about this. It was daydream, a national fantasy of sorts lived by every oppressed citizen. And so, despite the rough-handedness and the mockery that defined life at the university, Manmohan could count on his friends to back him when he really needed them.

One of the most important favors Manmohan's friends did for him was to accompany his uncle, who had more or less adopted Manmohan after his father's early death, to Darbhanga to initiate talks of marriage between him and Meena. Three days later when they returned, they brought with them glowing reviews about Meena's beauty. "Like the actress Meena Kumari, ditto," they said. "If you are one percent, man, you will marry her. Large eyes, straight nose, a beauty, a beauty," as though life without Meena would now need to be an impossibility for Manmohan.

Manmohan could not drink a cup of tea anymore without his friends teasing and pestering. "Eh? Some tea she will make you, eh?" They nudged and elbowed one another and him, as though everything in life was now suddenly temporary and would be made permanent again only through this girl Manmohan was supposed to marry and whom he had not yet seen. And despite himself, Manmohan was smitten. When he lay in bed, the picture of the film star Meena Kumari—rosebud lipped, and dancing deer gaited—filled his room. He could barely breathe, barely sleep for the fragrance of this image. He took to watching one Meena Kumari movie after another, until his heart expanded and pasted itself upon the silver screen. His heart would not part from the large-eyed, straight-nosed beauty who looked back at him from the screen. He stared, wide-eyed with wonder, and even as he walked the streets, even while he slept, while he read, he saw her eyes, her fingers graceful as blades of grass floating before him. And just like that life did become absolutely temporary, hanging precariously around him, weightless and insipid. His days without Meena were listless, without destination. His world that had not yet heard Meena speak was cacophonous. His voice flat and expressionless. He could no longer study his books of accounts and commerce. Ambition was futile and tiresome. Life itself, bundled in temporariness, was tiresome. He sighed before responding to all and any queries.

"Is that your pen?"

Sigh.

"Are you ready for lunch?"

Sigh.

"Are you an idiot?"

Sigh.

"What the hell are you sighing for?"

Sigh.

"How could you not bring pictures?" he cried. "How could you not ask?"

"Yes," said his friends, shaking their heads, but also filled with amused sympathy. "And you think a girl's father would pull out a picture and hand it over to two goondas so you could go dancing the world with it? Are you mental or what?"

But matters had to be viewed differently once Manmohan, already on the thin and small side, could no longer eat his meals, no longer sleep at night or keep himself wholly awake during the day. He kept his friends up with jibber-jabber all night and dragged them down with his drowsiness all day. Finally, it seemed to his friends that Manmohan would not graduate that year.

"And no girl," they warned him, "marries a man who cannot graduate, understand?"

And so the three of them finally set off for Darbhanga. If setting eyes on his would-be was the only way to cure Manmohan of love, then so be it. The matter would have to be kept hushed, of course. It would mean nothing but trouble if Manmohan's guardians found out he had gone seeking his bride before he was married to her, and if the would-be's parents found out Manmohan was in town, "prancing around to get a glimpse of their girl," they would certainly call the wedding off. No respectable parents would give their daughter to a street-side Romeo walking the streets with his tongue hanging out. As for the friends, being accomplices to this treachery could mean the end of their own marital futures. Manmohan had to see Meena, but he had to see her on the sly.

It was decided the boys would wait outside the all-girls Jhansi ki Rani school and Manmohan would watch Meena when she left the school campus at four. The friends would point her out to him as she wafted by, light and nimble as a hint of perfume. Once they saw her, the three would hop on the next train and chug back to Varanasi.

The boys reached the all-girls Jhansi ki Rani at two and pasted themselves like lizards between the bushes that made them itch and the tall brick wall that protected the school bustling with girls, so many of them of marriageable age. The sun fell like rocks on the young men, hurting them and making them dizzy, but Manmohan could only stare at the bars of the iron gate joining the ends of the wall, and even the sun, angry and powerful, was no match to the heat building up within him.

His friends rested in the bush shade and came off ripe as red guavas at the end of the day but Manmohan stood away from the shade, in a spot where he could watch the gates. He waited for the sun to travel on, and for the day to halt at four o'clock. Finally, after volcanoes and fires, it was four and the red-hot bars of the iron gate screeched open and out came the undulating breeze of young girls in pale blue salwaar kurtas and pale white sandals.

"Which one?" Manmohan asked, his whisper hoarse and painful in his throat.

But the friends, itchy and beehived from the bush, could not point to a definite girl. "No, not that one. Not that. Not," they said.

One by one the girls came, each less appealing than the one who just left. In fifteen minutes the campus was empty. The boys remained suspended between bush and wall. Then the iron gate screeched shut. Manmohan turned to his stunned friends.

"You idiots!" he wailed and turned his head quickly back to the empty lane. There was, after all, still the possibility that Meena might squeeze out through the iron bars and come running soft footed toward him, her eyes glimmering with tears of joy, her lips parted but without words.

She did not come, of course, not even after the sun was fully set and there were more mosquitoes above their heads than there was wind. With every minute passing without Meena, Manmohan slapped his friends as much as he slapped the insects humming and drumming overhead, and the three of them, criminals and accomplices, howled at the misery of it all.

Manmohan married without having ever seen his would-be. His mother, Sawari Devi, gave him five invitation cards a month before the wedding. "Your marriage has been set for the tenth of next month, son," she said, smiling and stroking Manmohan's twenty-one-year-old head. "If there are friends you want to invite, go ahead."

The invitation cards, so unceremoniously handed to him, felt like sand between his fingers. And what would now become of his political career? he wondered. With a wife waiting at home for him, how would he sneak into the gullies and alleys of the dark world? But despite the misgivings that had begun to build within him, he dreamt of Meena Kumari, the breathtaking Bollywood actress who had so captured his heart.

CHECKERED FEATHERS

During the wedding ceremony, sitting beside Manmohan, her right hand caught inside his left, Meena was unable to turn fully toward her husband and look directly at him. Rumors, brought in by her sisters and friends, said Manmohan had seen Meena almost immediately after her wedding interview with his uncle and his two friends. Rumors said Manmohan had come to Darbhanga with the two friends and the three had hidden behind her school, waiting all day for the school to end and for her to come out of the gate, into the streets. It was possible, they said, that the three had followed Meena all the way home.

No man other than her father and her relatives had held Meena's hand before and sitting before the priest reciting the wedding mantras, Meena was conscious of Manmohan's palms pressed against hers. She wondered what he had thought of her that afternoon with his friends. Had he liked her when he saw her outside her school? Did he like her now?

She wondered, too, what she would have done had she known he was watching. Would she have stopped outside her school gate and turned around, taken a good look while he looked, too? Or would she have opened an umbrella and sailed past him, teasing him as women did in movies?

And through the ceremony, as the priest burbled on in his Sanskrit; as the fire in the hawan kund stretched tall and slender; as the pigeons, unable to land in the open courtyard, fluttered in and out; as children, spanked by their mothers, wailed and cried, Meena took sidelong views of her husband. She was happy he was not the hippopotamus, the elephant, the rhinoceros Kaveri and her friends had made him out to be. He was small, shy, and sweet. His lips were lovely, a little bruised, as though he had just returned from a brisk walk on a cold morning. His eyes, outlined with kohl, were quiet, but when he smiled, which he did when the priest made a joke, they lit up. Meena decided Manmohan was the shyest man she knew, and she enjoyed his awkwardness. She decided she wanted to tease him, to make him fidget and squirm, to make him happy but not comfortable. How tiresome was comfort! She decided she wanted never to be comfortable, never to relax. She wanted to be the bee, forever pestering the flower.

When the priest said they could let go of each other's hands, Meena looked at her husband's palms. His mehendi was not a twisting lattice of symbols like hers was. It was instead a simple declaration. Within a circle upon the hollow of his palms were two letters, M and M, and that was all. Meena decided she liked the directness of the letters but preferred the complications within her own hands. Manmohan would have to hold her hands long, would have to look long at them, if he wanted to study the rippling waters, the checkered feathers.

She repeated the vows after the priest. "With the gods as our guides," she repeated, "let us walk together so we can sow our food. Let us walk together so we can reap our food. Let us walk together so we can split and collect. Let us walk together so we can feed and give. Let us walk together so we receive many lives with each other. Let us walk together for companionship." She stopped after the sixth vow and listened to Manmohan in wonder. "With these seven steps you are my wife," he said, "half my soul and half my body. Let me never be severed from you, not in this life, not in the rest assigned to me. Let our lives be bonded by love, by children, and by wealth."

Meena nodded. "Yes," she said.

THE COLOR OF BIDAI

The morning Meena left her mother's house for her husband's she wore yellow, the color of bidai—of leave-taking. Yellow sari, yellow gold, yellow leather on her feet. Around her everything was yellow, too; clinquant leaves, bright flowers, the rickshaw with its yellow hood. It was spring.

The veranda was crowded with those gathered to see Meena off, and their voices rose in the wind and moved toward the street. Her sisters wept. Kaveri wept. Meena could not see her father, Bilash, in the crowd but she knew he too was crying. She knew his eyes were misty, a little pink, his voice scratched with effort. Her brother cried without shame.

There were two suitcases standing by the wooden compound gate. The other suitcases had already been dispatched, most carried away by Manmohan's relatives who had left earlier. When the first sob escaped, Meena gasped, struggling to pull back her cry, but it would not return. She stood for a while, trying to compose herself, but everyone continued to weep and finally Meena flung herself into the crowd, trusting someone would catch her. When her brother took her into his arms, she held him and wept. He wept, too, and passed her to her sister, Mansi. Mansi passed Meena to Kirti, Kirti to Shanti. Each one pressed Meena to their chest. Each kissed her hair. Each grabbed her swollen face and kissed her swollen lips. "Behave yourself," they said between cries and kisses. "Don't fight with your in-laws." "Write regularly." "Come as soon as you can." "Get pregnant right away. No need to be too modern about children." "Take care of your husband." "My baby! My daughter! My sister!" When Meena turned she saw her father, standing on the other end, his back toward the road, sobbing so hard his entire body shook. Meena pushed through the crowd, toward him. "Babuji," she called and he pulled her close to him. It was strange, that pull, foreign and sweet. Her father had never hugged her before, never held her so close for so long she could hear the sounds inside his chest.

When Meena finally got to her mother, Kaveri hugged her tight and stroked her hair. "There is no coming back, so keep yourself happy," she said.

Behind Meena, Manmohan was being passed from person to person, too, being teased and admonished, being asked forgiveness for all that might have gone wrong now or would later. "If anything was amiss, revered guest, please forgive us. Forgive us and forgive our girl. Our girl has a hot mouth but her heart is of gold, revered guest. Please don't judge too hard. Don't hit her, please."

He would forever remain the revered guest in Meena's house, until the end of his life, way past Meena's own life. Until the end of Manmohan's life, members not only of Meena's house, but of the entire neighborhood, indeed of the town itself, would raise themselves from whatever mishap, whatever lethargy, whatever commonness came to them and serve Manmohan, the revered guest, the daughter's husband.

When Manmohan came to Kaveri, she held his face. "Be kind," she begged. "Be kind."

Meena continued to cry in the rickshaw that pulled her away from her home. The joy she had felt during the wedding was now replaced with dread. With every turn of the wheel Meena felt her life enter the unfamiliar and the untried. She felt the threat of that entrance and its finality. She felt, too, her youth, the formlessness of her experiences. There had been nothing hard in her life until this moment, nothing uncomfortable. She had lived with people she had not yet learned to distinguish from herself. They had formed her eyes, her limbs, and with every turn of the wheel she felt herself evaporating, losing her form, felt she could not move.

She was too young for a strange man to be sitting beside her, too young to leave a town and enter a different country, too young to learn new manners, new lives. Meena wanted to be twenty-one, not fourteen. Twenty-one was fair. At twenty-one the milk in her veins would be replaced by blood, her father's tenderness replaced by the desire for men beyond her father, the need for sisters replaced perhaps with the need for children, the love for her only brother replaced with love of another nature. But now, at fourteen, the streets were still supple under her soles. She still wanted to play with her friends upon them.

The rickshaw pulled out of Urdu Bazaar and turned to Kila Ghat. The road was not a road. It was a broad lane paved with bricks arranged to form semicircular patterns, and the rickshaw vibrated upon its ups and downs. It passed the washerman's cottage and his children spilled upon the brick road. The children looked up from their game and waved at Meena. They knew her well. The washerman's two older children were behind a broad bench, ironing out the clothes piled before them. The heavy coal iron showed red dots of smoldering embers through the triangular holes built for smoke escape. Upon the floor was another heap of clothes—saris, kurtas, dhotis. Meena recognized her blouse, the orange one with puffed sleeves and a green band. She tried to think of the sari it went with, but the rickshaw moved on and the thought was lost.

She thought instead about what the barber's wife had told her during the Mehendi. For a girl, her mother and her motherland are temporary affairs, she had said. "A girl learns early on that her life is a tight bud waiting to burst into a flower." Her life is in limbo until she marries and changes mother, motherland, home, name, affections. Nothing she is born to does she belong to, and she must dream and prepare for the life that is permanent only after she has left the womb that housed her and the house that protected her like a womb. Her wars are never to be fought for the mother, nor for the motherland she is born to. Her wars must always be for the mother-in-law, who is her true mother, and for the marital land that gives her her name and dignity. Had a woman written the long history of change and conflicts, history would be the confusing path that forces one to unlearn the familiar and learn the new. It would lead one away from all that one loves to all that one secretly dreads.

"Would you like some juice?" Manmohan asked when they came to a fruit cart.

"Yes," Meena said and Manmohan asked the driver to stop and get two glasses of sugarcane juice.

Meena sipped gratefully through the straw. The sun was warm and the glass cool against her palms. "You will be all right. We have very good juice in Sabaila," Manmohan said. "There is buttermilk and yogurt and Mother will take good care of you." Manmohan continued to talk, to soothe her through tidbits of information, but Meena kept her face turned away. A strange man upon a familiar street, that was all he was to her.

The rickshaw slowed for a speed-breaker. There was the all-boys Tipu Sultan school, the one her brother went to. Farther down was the all-girls Jhansi ki Rani, the one Meena had attended, outside which Manmohan might have stood with his friends. Both schools had tall walls, whitewashed with chalk, and with rust-red doors and windows, rust-red patterns on the edge. Meena tried to memorize the patterns. When Kila Ghat joined the Market Road she tried to remember the shoe stores, the fashion shops, the shops selling plastic buckets and brooms, the rows of eateries, the food carts, the lassi, the chaat. She cried again at the International Cinema Hall, the one her father managed. The trusted vendor was outside, selling egg rolls, and Meena was suddenly troubled by the way she could not remember how that bread tasted or how it smelled.

A QUAINT TRAIN

When the world was still new and mysterious and miraculous, there lived a gentle king named King Janaka. He ruled over the land aptly named Janakpur—the city of Janaka. King Janaka had all the wealth he could desire but he was childless, and his palace, luxurious and opulent, was silent without the running feet of children. A grief, deep and shameful, and alive with desire, lived within King Janaka, and every evening, after having run the administrative tasks of being a ruler, the childless king sent silent prayers to Lord Shiva. Give me a child, O Lord, he prayed. How can I love my citizens, who are like my children, if I haven't learned how to love a child of my blood?

Lord Shiva, the ruler of the universe, but also a father of two sons and a daughter, heard King Janaka's daily prayers and was filled with tenderness. As a vagabond and nomadic god who had ultimately found peace as a family man, he recognized King Janaka's loneliness. He understood, too, that King Janaka would become a truly worthy king only after he had had children. After all, before Lord Shiva had married Parvati and had his babies, he had scarcely been able to see beyond himself. "Childless men," said Lord Shiva to his consort as he watched his devotee suffer, "rarely know the meaning of sacrifice and surrender, and therefore made poor leaders." And so, one evening, as King Janaka prayed, Lord Shiva spoke to him. "Care for your citizens before you care for yourself," he whispered into his devotee's ears. "Love your citizens as you would love a child. Only then will you be worthy of becoming a father."

King Janaka bowed his head in gratitude. Immediately, he stepped out of his palace and entered the world of his people. He was surprised to see that while he lived in comfort and lavishness, his citizens toiled endlessly upon a land, which though fertile with vegetation of all sorts, refused to yield that which could be consumed by humans. There were berries for birds and hard nuts for squirrels, but there was little for his people. Janaka was embarrassed and acknowledged that engrossed in his own shame he had not noticed his people's hunger. The sight of his thin, emaciated people shook King Janaka out of his grief and he vowed to bring relief to his land. He visited the strangely barren fields of Janakpur and stood watching the inedible berries and wild flowers that grew in such abundance that they spared no space for rice, wheat, lentils, and brinjals. He knelt down upon the obstinate land and stroked its unyielding body. "Bring the kodalo to me," said King Janaka to a farmer as he stroked and patted the earth.

The farmer, too famished to recognize the king, went into his hut and returned with a kodalo, and King Janaka, who had never wielded any tool other than the pen, held the kodalo in his hand and struck the land with it. "Feed your children, Mother Earth," he beseeched as he tilled. "Feed the children you have borne. What is a mother who cannot feed her children?" He labored all night, striking the earth, whispering to it, caressing it with his bare hands, until his hands bruised and drops of blood fell like carnelians upon the mud. The earth heaved toward the stroking hands and greedily drank the king's dripping blood.

For a year King Janaka lived a farmer's life. He woke early to milk cows, to herd goats, to till the land and spread seed upon it. Daily, the mud, wet with the king's sweat and blood, grew moister and was filled with yearnings to give to the king what he so desired. The earth turned within itself, its limbs coiling and uncoiling deep below the surface.

Janaka's sweat and blood went to its core and it held them like a heated lake in a bowl of burning gold.

It took a year for the bowl to fill and for it to ascend from the earth's core to the surface of its skin. Slowly it traveled upward, using the heat from King Janaka's body as a compass for its journey, and exactly a year after King Janaka had renounced his palace, his kodalo hit upon something hard and metallic in the land. He parted the mud and pulled from it the golden bowl. King Janaka held the bowl in wonder, and his heart filled with an indescribable ache. What could it be? he wondered, and he heard for the first time the soft cry of an infant. In his fright he almost let go of the dish, but he knew instantly, too, that he never could. Quietly, with a tremor, he untied the green scarf tied upon the mouth of the vessel and found his daughter curled upon the base of the golden bowl. The child looked at her father and cooed happily. "Sita," whispered King Janaka and scooped her into his arms.

This is the story of Sita, the daughter of the earth, the mother of fertility, the balm of aching hearts. The Nepali princess who later fell in love with and married the Indian prince, Rama. The Indian prince loved his wife, but only as much as the traditions of the time allowed a man to love a woman, or a king to love his queen, and so, despite the fact that Sita proved her loyalty and love for her husband over and again, the tradition-bound Rama ultimately abandoned his pregnant wife in the tropical jungles of the land. Alone in the jungles Sita gave birth to her twins. Amid lions and snakes, she raised her sons to be warriors and rulers, and when her tasks with her children were done, she knelt before her mother, Earth, and asked it to take her back into its womb.

And into this land of verdant fertility and aching womb, the land that birthed the epic tale of *Ramayana*, traveled Meena.

She sat in the train that would take her from the Indian town Jaynagar to the Nepali town Janakpur. From the train's barred windows Meena watched the changing scenes as the train, tortoise paced, pulled deeper into her new nation. The huts and houses remained familiar. The land was flat, and upon it were bullock carts and bicycles, men in dhotis, women in saris.

During the journey Manmohan gave Meena bits of information. Janakpur had a cigarette factory, a paper mill, and the Janaki Mandir dedicated to Sita. From Janakpur Meena would travel to Sabaila, Manmohan's village, and once there they would settle into the routine of married life. Meena marveled at this transition but felt no fear on its account. Villages had their fairs and marts, their theaters and Rama lilas. Villages were rich with songs and colorful with murals. Villages were for pretty women and hard men. She would enjoy its lakes and trees.

The quaint train endeared Nepal to Meena. As a child Manmohan must have looked forward to riding this train, she thought. This must have been the first train her husband sat in. As a child he must not have known that only very, very slow trains took three hours to cover a twenty-one-mile distance. He must not have known trains were supposed to run faster than people and bicycles. It was in the train, imagining Manmohan's boyhood, looking out at men in bicycles, birds flying along, children outside bursting into runs to compete with the train that Meena began falling in love with her husband. How green, how helpless was her husband's world. Meena had been on many trains, fast, efficient vehicles that whizzed past neighborhoods like visitations from the future. One had to be careful in those trains. You could not let those trains pull away without you. If the train left you behind, you were in serious trouble. There was this one time Meena's father had been left behind at the Lucknow station and it was almost a week before the family saw him next. But not so with the Janakpur railway. The Janakpur railway was a toy, a plaything that cared nothing for carefulness. In the Janakpur railway everyone was a child. Already Manmohan had stepped out of the coach several times. If the train pulled off from a station, he could simply run to catch up. Even Meena could run faster than this train. This train was just a silly madman on many wheels.

The train was crowded. The roof, what there was of it, had men sitting on it. Bicycles and slippers hung from windows, tied to the bars with drawstrings and gamchas. Towels and kerchiefs fluttered like flags declaring freedom. Hair ribbons flapped. The entrance to the coach was jammed with crowds of half-dangling men who occasionally stepped off to relieve themselves upon adjoining tracks. Behind these men children performed tricks and stunts, hopping and climbing over people until they got yanked and spanked. There was much bawling and screaming. Mothers, querulous and haggard, traveled with sacks of merchandise—firewood, potatoes, onions, mangoes. They seemed to flutter like birds, like crows, cawing at their younglings. Outside, men climbed the windows, their slippers, worn to shreds on the ends, slipping on bars and bicycles as they pulled their bodies to the roof. The coach smelled of onions and oil. It felt like the end of the world—hot, humid, full of bodily stench, noisy beyond belief. And all along the train chugged on at its mind-boggling speed of scarcely seven miles an hour. Beyond the train's noisy, smelly population was comforting land, flat, brown and green, spread like an enormous leaf, and within the train was Maithili, her father's tongue. Children were scolded in Maithili, occasional songs sung in Maithili, conversations in Maithili. Upon the dusty mud path outside walked dark and slim women in hot-pink and parrot-green saris. There were wheat fields and adobe huts with flat roofs. There were occasional Hero cycles and Mahindra motorcycles blowing dust clouds toward the walking women. There were oxen carts and dust under oxen hoofs. There were betel-nut and paan shops that sold sweets and cigarettes. There was nothing to be afraid of. Everything she saw was what she had known forever.

Manmohan sat next to Meena. And next to Manmohan was another pair of newlyweds, the bride with her veil pulled low over her face, just the way Meena had her veil pulled down. The groom had on a tall turban. Between them sat the groom's sister who looked exactly like the groom. Meena nudged at Manmohan and grinned inside her veil. She felt terribly sorry for the bride and the groom—a sister in between!

At the Khajuri station the train came to a slow stop—there were five stations between Janakpur and Jaynagar, each specialising in certain snacks. Khajuri was known for its hot and delicious pyajies, deep-fried onion fritters to be eaten with puffed rice. Even Manmohan was on his feet, seeking an opening to the door before the train had come to a full halt. The groom with the tall turban made his way out too. A little while later his bride whispered into the sister's ears and began to leave. The sister immediately took her sandals off and put one sandal each on her brother's and sister-in-law's seats. "If you don't watch, anyone will come and sit on the seats," she said to Meena, so Meena took off one of her sandals and put it on Manmohan's seat.

Under her window the Khajuri station bustled like a bazaar. Meena kept her eye on Manmohan. He was buying fritters and making small talk with a man next to him and when the train blew its whistle, he continued his conversation. The train began to pull away and Manmohan jogged slowly toward her, still talking with the stranger who remained at the station. Eventually Manmohan ran up to Meena's window and handed over the snack, a cone of puffed rice topped with fried onions, then he slowed to catch the coach's entrance. Somebody there pulled him into the coach, and once inside the coach Manmohan pushed his way toward Meena, grinning because he had caught a running train. Meena bit her lips. How handsome he was, like no other man she had seen, like Dharmendra, she thought, like Rajesh Khanna.

"Is it good?" he asked, but she had not yet taken a bite of the fritter. "We will eat together. Is that all right?" he asked.

Meena nodded.

The groom with the tall turban and his bride were not yet back and the sister, who looked just like her brother, began yelling out the window. "Bhaiya! Bhabhi!" she yelled. The groom was nowhere in sight, but the bride stood upon the station platform, small, petite, brighter than the sun in her golden sari, rooted to the spot, staring at the moving train.

"Run, run!" Manmohan shouted to her from the window, but she did not move.

"Run, run!" the sister shouted.

It was after the train was a good way away that the groom appeared suddenly under Meena's window. He was running, panting, and screaming to be heard. "The bicycle," he yelled. "Untie it, please! Please!"

"Go to the door," Manmohan shouted back. "They will pull you up."

"The bicycle, the bicycle," the groom insisted, so Manmohan untied the bicycle. The bicycle, free of the gamcha that had held it in place, fell too suddenly and Meena wondered if it had collapsed upon the ground and broken into a thousand pieces. She held the sister's hand and watched in suspense. They did not see the groom or the bicycle again for a while and the sister wept, and her panic made Meena laugh. How silly to cry over missing a train so slow. Then they saw the groom again. There he was, on the cycle, pedaling hard while his bride sat behind him, hands around his waist. She had pushed her veil back and was looking around with large, young eyes, smiling. They waved at their wonderstruck sister. Meena and the sister waved back. Manmohan laughed. The bride and the groom kept pace until the train pulled into the next station.

BIRDCAGE JHUMKAS

The river was almost dry at this time of the year and the bullock cart dipped in and out of its bed. There were no rickshaws in Sabaila, only occasional bicycles and carts pulled by sturdy oxen. The cart carrying Meena, Manmohan, and Manmohan's extended family, who had left Darbhanga a day before the groom and bride and were therefore at the Janakpur train station to welcome the newly-weds, had large blue wheels. The oxen's horns were painted orange, and the animals wore orange bells around their necks. The cart's roof was woven bamboo with a canvas sewn to it. The canvas was decorated with oval fishes with square eyes swimming amid triangular seaweeds under many yellow moons. When Meena looked up she knew she no longer belonged to an earth. She belonged to rivers and their skies.

Sabaila was not far. One could leave Janakpur in the morning and reach the village early that evening, and throughout the journey Meena looked eagerly around her. Once the river was crossed everything was brown: wide brown lanes, broad fields of brown wheat, brown barks under dusty leaves, lakes with brown water, brown cow dung, brown cows, brown walls on mud huts, brown thatch for roofs, brown women with brown brooms sweeping off dust. Against the brown were Meena's red sari, her gold jewelry; the diamond on her nose flashed and contrasted. Her toe rings twinkled.

She sat at one end of the bullock cart; Kumud, Manmohan's brother's wife, sat next to her; and her boys, Sitaram and Shyam climbed on and off her lap. Sitaram and Shyam were twins and Meena was amused by their intense difference. Sitaram was fair like the fresh grains of wheat, Shyam was the color of a tree's dark bark. There was Binita, Manmohan's sister, sitting beside Kumud. Manmohan's mother and his older brother were already in Sabaila, having left early to take care of affairs at the home front. They would be at the door to welcome the newlyweds, and when Meena thought about them, she grew anxious and worried. A mother-in-law after all was a mother-in-law, and Meena had watched enough movies and heard enough from her married sisters and cousins to know there was nothing like a good mother-in-law. What she had seen of her husband's mother during the wedding had not eased her mind. Sawari Devi was stern and quiet, and Manmohan's older brother, Ashok, had too much dignity for Meena's taste. He had barely smiled at her, and during the blessings he had placed his hand on her head for scarcely a second. She wondered what her housewarming ceremony would involve. With her own brother still unmarried, no bride had yet entered Meena's house in Darbhanga and Meena's two married sisters had gone through very different ceremonies at their marital doorsteps for Meena to form a coherent picture. Meena hoped Sawari Devi would have a tray of vermilion paste set out, that Meena would be asked to step into the tray, to step into the house so she left new footprints inside her new home.

In the cart Manmohan sat diagonally across from Meena, reading a book, and if Meena wanted to look at him she had to first look at everybody else, at Kumud and her twins, and at Binita. Manmohan was not wearing his groom's turban or the silk kurta he had during the ceremony and Meena was conscious of her own silk and her vividness. She was conscious of the vermilion upon her hair, new and bright.

Now and then the twins came to Meena and touched her jewels.

They played with her pendant and dangling earrings. They took her hands and shook them gently so the bangles jingled. Kumud, made bold by her children, touched her jewels, too. She touched Meena's mangalsutra. "Once the children come you can't wear anything," she said. Kumud touched her own sparsely adorned neck. She wore a simple chain around it. She looked slyly at Manmohan and smiled back at Meena. "I would tell you to wait with the children but I don't think Mohan will be willing." She smiled again and Meena grew warm. "These are lovely," said Kumud, flicking the birdcage danglers. "Mine don't have stones. These red stones are very nice." Slowly Binita came over, too. She pushed the twins away and sat before Meena, looking at her as though she was from another world. "You are so pretty," she said. "This sari is so soft," she said. "Can I wear this ring when I get married?"

Meena smiled. "What is the hurry for marriage?" she asked, conscious that Binita was only one year younger than she was. She wanted to put her rings, her necklaces, her bangles, her anklets into a box and bury the box under a tree so obscure, so deep in a jungle, she herself would never be able to get to the treasure again. She did not want to give the ring to Binita. Like her mehendi art, these ornaments bound Meena to her parents in ways she could not explain. Meena knew she would not visit her parents too often, perhaps once every three or four months, and then perhaps only for a few days. Once the children came, visits would become less frequent, depending always on school vacations. If Manmohan took her to Kathmandu, long mountain ranges would stand between Meena and her parents. The mountains, Meena had heard, were of immeasurable depths and turns. It was best, Meena had heard, never to travel upon them. The rivers were too fast, too white against boulders. When a bus fell, everybody died. No, visits would not be frequent.

After marriage, a foot between the mother's house and the husband's house becomes a kilometer, an hour becomes a day, and a lake an ocean. What would become then of mountains and rivers? The mother's house was distant and precious, and everything that came from it was precious too. This Meena wanted to explain to Binita. You will know when it is your turn, she wanted to say.

The gold was more prized than its price. It had, in all probability, cost her father a piece of land, or put him into a small debt maybe, or if nothing else, cost him more than he had estimated. She imagined her parents selecting designs. She imagined them more interested in the weight than the fashion of a neckpiece. The heavier the gold, the more secure Meena's future against unseen floods, and no matter how much they spent, they felt they had not spent enough. This Meena knew because she had seen her parents' struggle during her sisters' marriages. Eventually, after her father could no longer afford another bracelet, another nose stud, he took off the chain from his neck and added it to Meena's trousseau. This Meena knew because she recognized the chain. Kaveri took off her ring, the one she had altered twice to accommodate the years, and it became Meena's, worn amid other rings upon her fingers. It was this ring Binita asked for now.

"No hurry," said Binita. "I am only asking."

"You are too young, too young," said Meena, nonchalantly covering her ring.

The boys, Sitaram and Shyam, were bored and wanted a song. "Song! Song! Song! Sing us a song!" they cried, and Meena, who had indeed watched more movies than she could count and therefore knew countless songs, who sang along with radios and projectors, began one right away. To amuse her audience she picked silly tunes.

My name is Chin Chin Chu
Chin Chin Chu, baba, Chin Chin Chu
The night is moonlit

And it's me and you
Hello mister, how do you do?

At the "how do you do" she cocked a brow at Manmohan and half winked at him. He had been watching her, too, listening to her songs, and he was startled by her half-wink. Kumud laughed. The children giggled. Manmohan smiled, turned a page, and went back to reading.

STOLEN MOMENTS

It was a clean, effortless world Meena entered with Manmohan while she sat diagonally from him, singing popular movie songs to entertain the children. In the lane were women carrying firewood. They walked in single file, staying close to the fields, and when they saw a wedding cart they smiled, tittered as though a wedding cart reminded them only and always of their own wedding night, as though a wedding never went beyond its first night, or perhaps after its first night a wedding no longer remained a wedding and became something else, became firewood, became fields. Meena looked out, enthralled. She felt she knew these women. She knew the swing in their walks, the flirtatiousness of their smiles. She understood the lush, overgrown grass edging the lanes, the sudden fleet of birds overhead, the small hills of matted mud amid the folds of tilled land. However, despite the lushness, she was vaguely aware of the darkness that lurked beneath the swinging hips and the shivering grass, and her awareness made her a little wary of her surroundings.

Meena had discovered the honeyed center of pleasure in her body long before she discovered its pains. Early in her life she learned the secret dips and rises that scattered tremors of desire through her limbs. Even as a child who could barely focus on the world around her, Meena had been able to interpret the tingling in her palms and feet. She had understood the value of caresses and the relief that came only with rubbing herself breathlessly against the warp of warm bedsheets. She spent hundreds of nights trying silently to pleasure herself as her sisters slept unaware of her thudding heart, her taut calves that ached from being so rigidly stretched out.

It was slowly and through the years that Meena learned that her sisters, too, throbbed with the same longing that inundated her every night; they, too, burned and worked silently, noiselessly to fill themselves. It was through her sisters that she understood, somewhat partially, the meaning of her desires. The first time she witnessed a physical display of love was between her sisters Kirti and Shanti. Kirti was a few months away from getting married and one night, while she thought everyone was asleep, she had unbuttoned her shirt and put Shanti's hands upon her chest. Meena, nine at the time and awake because she needed, suddenly, to go to the bathroom, had seen Kirti's unbuttoned shirt and Shanti's hands and held her pee in, too afraid to be caught. Her heart banged and she knew something terrible would happen, somewhere in the world, and to her, if her sisters knew she was watching them. She opened her eyes only narrowly and had the presence of mind to keep her breaths long and deep. Kirti traced her nipples with Shanti's fingers and leaned in close, hovering her nipples like bees over Shanti's mouth. Involuntarily, though she knew this was impossible, Meena opened her mouth to take the nipples in, but she shut it instantly, feeling a loss she could not understand. She closed her eyes then, too afraid of the pain in her chest and throat, and when Kirti finally lay down beside her again, Meena could feel her quivering like a string against her body.

For the next few days Meena watched Kirti and Shanti for signs of guilt or togetherness, but there were no signs. It was as though the night had not existed. They continued chatting and working and playing with each other as though they shared no secrets, and slowly, because there was nothing there to confirm her memory of the night and because Kirti got married and left the house, Meena began to doubt what she had seen. Perhaps it had been a dream. Perhaps she was a bad girl, imagining bad things in the middle of the night.

And then it was there again, a few weeks before Meena was to get married, almost five years after she had witnessed Kirti and Shanti on that warm and terrifying night. Once again Meena slept at the edge of the bed, Kirti beside her, and Shanti at the other end. Once again, Meena, filled with nervous tension because of her marriage, was unable to sleep. And this time it was Shanti who slid her hands upon Kirti and Kirti who trembled and held Shanti close. Meena kept still, turned to stone with a sense of horror and shame. And yet, she wanted, so much, to be a part of Kirti and Shanti, to have those hands upon her, but she knew this was always and forever between her sisters. It was their guilt, their pleasure, and their story. Kirti breathed in ragged gasps, as though she was choking, and then she took her sister's hand and placed it between her legs. Meena shut her eyes and tried to block out the sounds, to pretend she was in a dream, but Kirti's breaths, hot and broken, Shanti's moans, soft like the mewls of a kitten, kept her up, and because her sisters were in a world where she did not exist, Meena put her own hand between her legs and with the other she clutched her breast.

And yet, despite the intimacy with which Meena knew her body, it remained alien and elusive in so many ways.

When Meena was seven and her sister, Mansi, thirteen, there had been that first day when Mansi had thrown the covers aside and leapt out of bed, uncaring if she stepped upon Meena's feet in her hurry, or upon Kirti's. Kirti was eleven. Shanti five.

Mansi had rushed to the bathroom and Meena heard the door slam behind her. Shanti slept through the sudden chaos because Shanti was born deaf and therefore could not hear, and because Mansi had not stepped upon her legs as hard as she had upon Meena's. And Meena, now awake, noticed the brown stain, oval and well-shaped, like a bird's egg that Mansi had left upon the sheet. She had noticed the brown shape of an egg, a smooth pebble upon Mansi's petticoat before she ran out. Her sari must have come undone in that hurry. When Mansi was gone. Meena looked at the twin spot upon the sheet. It was an old sheet, faded, and the spot was the only pattern upon it. It was a dark moon upon a light sky. Then Mansi was back, her face contorted somehow, as though she was angry with Meena. She must have been, too, because she looked at Meena and asked, "Was there any blood in your potty today? Your soosoo? Yesterday?"

"No," said Meena, taken aback.

There were no bees-and-birds talk in Meena's house. Kaveri, too busy with her many children, let the talk slip and fall upon Mansi, the first girl to get her periods in the house. Mansi dealt with her responsibility the way she saw her mother deal with it. She remained wary and silent.

The only cover for menstruation was secrecy. Being caught menstruating meant being allotted a separate room in the house and given a separate plate to eat out of. It meant restrictions, floating like dust in the air and settling on menstruating girls. Menstruating girls could not enter the kitchen, could not use the hand pump, could not watch television since the television was always in a public room, could not go on outings, could not touch their fathers and brothers. Once caught, menstruating girls could not escape. They had to speak with more decorum and manners during these days, as though for five days their personalities changed and became that of a woman's. It was from Kaveri that Mansi learned to keep her silence, and she was quick to notice that her mother seemed never to get her periods, that her mother was never quarantined, that she ate what she chose on all days of all months, that she went out and entered temples during all seasons. When Mansi asked her mother, Kaveri shrugged. "Just don't let anyone know," she said, and

Mansi, perpetually afraid of getting caught, extended her silence with such rigidity she kept even her sisters out of it.

Periods were complicated matters. They needed months of preparation. It was sewing sanitary napkins out of old cotton saris and stocking them away in boxes pushed deep under beds so the males in the family would not accidentally stumble upon them. It was keeping up spirits through fatigue and listlessness, never showing one's exhaustion. It was cooking meals, listening to jokes, serving guests, accepting challenges to games of gilli and gutti when one did not want to play. It was creating codes where anything from insects to slippers to floods could stand in for periods. Mansi, and later Kirti, turned down scooter rides offered by their father because sitting on the scooter seat was too uncomfortable. They were, despite their desire not to be, afraid of touching their father during these days. Perhaps there was a curse to touching your father with a menstruating body. Perhaps you took years away from your father's life if you did. They were ashamed of their secret and ashamed of themselves and too afraid to reveal their conditions, afraid of the banishment and the weeklong seclusions that followed these reveals. They washed and dried bloodstained cotton pads in fiercely guarded places. They kept themselves scrupulously tidy. They never complained.

Meena watched. "What are you doing?" she asked.

"Making mattresses for our dolls," said Kirti.

"Can you make one for mine?"

"Go sew your own mattress," said Kirti.

"Go away," said Mansi, "or I will tell Mother."

When Meena asked why their faces were so contorted, they said they were sick. When she asked what of, they said they were sick of her. When she asked why, they yelled. "Go away!" they shouted. "Leave us alone! Mai," they complained to their mother, "tell this girl to leave us alone."

"Leave them alone, you shameless girl," said Kaveri.

And Meena backed off, unsure of what she had done, why she was shameless, why she had been yelled at.

When at thirteen Meena did finally see blood in her own panties, she knew enough to know she was not dying, but not enough to be sure. She went to Kirti and Kirti gave her a doll mattress, then while Meena stood there, staring at the pad in her hand, Kirti burst into tears. "It hurts," she wept, overwhelmed by the years of tightly held pain, and by the terrible pity she now felt for Meena. Meena stood before her sister, who had burst so inexplicably into tears, and knew she was going to die, perhaps not that very moment, not that very day, but sometime, someday. The death disease was in her now, and day after day it would take away enough from her to leave her a little without life. She cringed within herself. She wanted to throw the pad down, to run away, become a child again, to remove every drop of blood from her veins so there would be no drops upon her panties. She stepped away from Kirti, perplexed and unsure of what it was that hurt. In the bathroom she pulled down her panties and stared at herself.

Periods came with all their severity and Meena could not fake energy during those days of the month. She stayed in bed until late, and when her brother came looking for her, she snapped at him. She could not relax. She hated the wetness and kept the muscles of her legs and her buttocks so tight she gave herself muscle cramps. She took small, ungraceful steps. She could not eat.

"I want to die," she said to Kaveri. "Kill me, Mai."

Kaveri patted her daughter's head. "Don't worry," she said. "It gets better after marriage. It pretty much goes away after marriage."

And that was how Meena started dreaming of marriage. It would take away the cramps, bring in ease, relax her body. She imagined herself with a man, strong, virile, filling her not only to pleasure her, but also to release her, to render her world painless and peaceful. Slowly, over time, Meena became aware of the waves upon which her body rode. There was the week of pain and cramps, and then, almost immediately after, the clawing, tingling need that locked her inside a fog. All she was awake to in that blinding fog was her own body, pulsating, seeking a relief she struggled against but also wanted to hold tight against herself. She lay on her bed, tortured by desire and haunted by imaginations of fulfillment. In all this there was the man, shadowy as of now, but real, out there in the world, patiently waiting for her.

On the way to Sabaila there were cattle crossing the lane—cows, buffaloes, goats—that refused order and created momentary traffic jams. The cart driver hollered, the herdsmen patted the behinds of their cattle, coaxing them to move, but the animals stood around, staring at nothing or chewing the cud. It was like a scene from a Manoj Kumar movie.

At one such traffic jam they stopped for lunch. It was high afternoon and they sat on the edge of the lane, their feet in the wheat field. Meena and Kumud pulled their veils low, Manmohan and the driver rolled up their sleeves. They ate out of the tiffin boxes. The children ran about. Occasionally Meena looked at Binita, young already but without marriage and without its veil, looking about her like a child would. For the first time that day Meena and Manmohan sat together. They sat so close she could feel her husband's shirt upon her skin. She thought of the night they had spent together in Darbhanga. They had not done anything. They had hardly spoken, and yet Manmohan had touched her everywhere. He had traced every piece of jewelry upon her, the jhumkas on her ears, the curled tika sitting upon her forehead, the ring on her nose, the kangans around her wrists, the mangalsutra around her neck falling between her breasts, the moonstone swan upon her fingers, the waistband circling her waist and resting upon her hips, her anklets, her toe rings. He had helped remove each piece, drop each in the bags meant for them, put them away in a box. He had kissed her only once, on her back, where a chain hung from the mangalsutra and made a straight line above her blouse. She had asked him to shut his eyes, to look away while she changed into her night sari, and she had closed her eyes and looked away when he changed into his nightsuit. In their cotton clothes they had played the games Kaveri had spread out in the conjugal room. How far away that seemed now. Manmohan had beat her in chess, she had beat him at snakes and ladders.

Now Manmohan turned to her suddenly, between morsels, and said, "Your eyes are like a bird's."

Meena laughed. "You cannot see through my veil," she said.

"I saw you last night," said Manmohan, and Meena felt herself blush.

In Darbhanga Meena and her sisters would sit in rickshaws and meander into the bazaar, following the little paths that led to cinema halls. These outings had delighted them; three hours of cinema, then hours again between the cinema and their house. They ate out, picked trinkets, visited school friends. The day slipped into dusk. Patriotic movies were Meena's favorites. She looked forward to the men who could till gold out of barren land, the magic of both the land and the man. She looked forward to the women dressed in their coarse saris, and their love for their men. She looked forward to the hardships that unfolded into successes upon the screen. She watched, rapt, her feet tapping to songs, but she was aware, even during moments when she almost forgot, that she was an audience, an outsider, and what she watched on the screen was not a reality in the world where she lived. Now, sitting upon the lane, imagining her husband's hands upon her skin, looking at the fields, at the women and the cattle, the cart, the orange-horned oxen, the brilliance of her sari, the nervousness within her, now Meena became a part of the screen, the hardship and the love.

WHORE

Meena stood partly behind the door and watched her husband. He was returning to India. He would be back in three months, after his final examinations were over. That morning Meena had followed her mother-in-law's instructions and packed a box of curry for Manmohan to eat on his way. She had packed it well, compacting everything into a small tiffin. She felt alone and followed her husband while he folded his blanket, his inflatable pillow, the underwear that had only just dried, and put them into a bag. She followed him to the hand pump and watched quietly as he washed his hands and feet. She went with him into the prayer room and when he bowed to the gods, she bowed, too, praying for his well-being and his quick return. She bent down and touched Manmohan's feet, lingering there because she was in tears. When Manmohan stroked her head and lifted her up, she let herself cry a little. And then it was time for him to leave.

Meena stood behind the wall and watched Manmohan haul his bags into the cart, the oxen at the yoke flexing their muscles. The parting made her tremble. What did married people say to each other? But they had only been married a week and she did not know. Meena was conscious of her newness before everybody else—the mother, the sister, the brothers, the sister-in-law, the twins—but she also felt closest to Manmohan, as though she had him trapped inside her. After the bags were all in, Manmohan came over and touched his mother's, his older brother's, and Kumud's feet. He nodded at Meena and his younger siblings. He patted the twins. And then he was gone. Meena stood by the door, half hid by the wall, listening to the cart wheels creak all the way until it reached the lake at the other end of the dirt road, and then she could hear it no more.

For weeks after Manmohan's departure Meena felt terribly fresh, terribly beautiful. She had spent their last two days together in a fever and ache that only Manmohan's young hands could soothe. They had stayed up nearly all night, having discovered suddenly that in the cover of darkness they could toy with each other, play endlessly, touch and caress. It was not Meena who played these games of fingers and teeth. She was too shy to initiate, too new to know what was allowed to her and what forbidden. She knew from movies and slyly read novels that hers was the role of coyness and faint shies. She was to be Manmohan's playground, laid expansively below him, letting him run himself over her skin while she herself stayed inert. And so she had stayed still while Manmohan, inexperienced and yearning, touched her, and apologized, and touched again, trembling, breathing hard. It left Meena dizzy, her throat dry, her body moist. She longed to taste him as he tasted her, but all she did, when the burning got too intense, was reach with her hands and pull him close.

And now, a week after their marriage, just two days after she had felt him with her palms fanned upon his back, Manmohan was gone.

Meena felt her tragedy and rejoiced in it. She rejoiced in her burning body, rejoiced that her new house was large and sprawling but the room where she had spent her night with Manmohan was small and tight, with only a bed and a shelf to brand it as theirs. She rejoiced that so many others lived in the house and yet she felt alone and lonely. She rejoiced that her mother-in-law was practical and business-like, living her life in the fields and speaking to Meena only when she needed to. She rejoiced in her new look, which was plain without her jewelry. When her mother-in-law had asked, Meena had handed over her jewelry for safekeeping, and she rejoiced in her ability to do so. She had kept nothing to herself save simple earrings and bangles, a small pendant, a thin anklet, small toe rings, and Kaveri's ring for daily adornment. With so little upon her, with so many chores to master each day, Meena was a hermit's wife. Her hermit had gone off into the jungles to meditate and pray, and she, the hermit's wife, was meditating, too, though her meditation was filled with action.

In three months Manmohan returned from India, a fresh graduate, Sabaila's pride, and a month later he left for Kathmandu in search of a job.

"Sabaila is the future, Meena," he said, breathing her in deeply. "We will return here to die in peace. But Kathmandu is the present; it is where our children will have schools to attend and we will have a house. There are roads there, built by China and India, bridges built by Japan, homes of Chinese bricks that you will not be able to stop looking at. Ratna Park is so big, you can walk around it all day. Then there is Godawari. There are more flowers and trees in the Godawari park than there is in all of Dhanusha's forest."

When Manmohan left for Kathmandu, Meena began her penitence again. It was not easy being a hermit's wife. Hermits traveled relentlessly, going places, living destitute lives and expecting their loved ones to accept their destitution. Didn't Gandhi subject his wife to seclusion and expect her to clean toilets because he was Gandhi? At least Meena was not Kasturba. At least Manmohan was not Gandhi. And yet, in too many ways Meena felt worse than Kasturba. At least Kasturba had a child the first time Gandhi left her behind for his struggles. At least Kasturba still visited her parents. At least Kasturba did not have to suffer her in-laws. And all of Kasturba's wars eventually took her to South Africa, had her imprisoned with freedom fighters, turned her into a symbol of struggle and greatness. Meena's wars, always fought with her mother-in-law, did not feel as grand as fighting for one's country, or fighting against foreigners and foreign ways. Meena had watched enough movies to know her mother-in-law would not be kind to her. In the tradition of things, it was the mother-in-law's role to be nasty and the daughter-in-law's to work hard for the benefit of the house, but even so, Meena was surprised by Sawari Devi's brusqueness. Every afternoon, when Sawari Devi returned from the fields, she walked around the house and shook her head. "Nothing to do all day, and still the house is a pigsty," she complained. "And just because this one's husband has gone off gallivanting again, this queen cannot cook her vegetables right, cannot make her rotis round. Oh, we were cheated in this marriage. So useless, this girl!" Within six months of marriage, Meena was alone, aching and unfulfilled, wanted but not taken, desired but left behind. And what use was Gandhi and his poverty-stricken ways in Nepal anyway?

After four months, when Manmohan returned to Sabaila after his trip to Kathmandu, Meena insisted that either he stay back or take her with him. "We have been married for seven months and I have hardly lived with you for ten days," she said. "We can stay in Sabaila. We don't have to go." But Manmohan had to go. He was not a village boy. He wore trousers with flaring legs, shirts with collars so wide they spread like wings from his neck, and dark glasses to cool his eyes. He did not belong to cattle and dung. He belonged to the capital where men wore shined leather shoes and contrasting belts to hold their pants in place. He brought with him health drinks and woolen socks for his mother. He brought identical saris for Meena, Kumud, and his sister, Binita. "I don't want to seem partial," he said. He brought identical clothes for his brothers, identical shirts for the twins. "No point getting fancy," he said, then he pointed to the saris and said, "You can choose the color."

He had brought along pictures of himself and his friends taken before the temples and palaces of Kathmandu. Meena looked at the pagodas with curling tips and gleaming peaks, and her husband smiling before them. She liked the pictures with the rows of long prayer flags rising from mists and vanishing amid thick vegetation and fragile-looking steps cut into hills and mountains. And there was one with the royal palace in the background. Narayanhiti Palace, where the king lives, Manmohan told Meena.

"Take me with you," Meena said, and Manmohan held her tight and shook his head.

"It's not time yet," he said.

That night when Manmohan finally consummated their marriage, he used a condom before he entered her body. "We cannot have children until I have settled some more in Kathmandu, Meena," he said. "Give it a few years, just two, just three, until I make everything ready."

Slowly, over the rest of the year, Meena realized she was not a part of Manmohan's life. His life was with friends, in cities unknown to her. She was destined to wake alone in dim rooms, the ceiling dusky, the blue curtains purple in the darkness, the orange flowers the color of rust. "Society is a great judge, Meena," Manmohan said as she packed his bags for him. "You cannot play foul and expect to be forgiven by the social structure. Women like my mother are too simple. Their life is between the house and the fields. They have seen nothing of the world outside this village. What do they know about the intricacies that keep the system going? But you, you Meena, you are an educated girl, at least you understand. You have to understand and respect the complex systems of interactions," Manmohan said. "It is not enough to climb the economic ladder. No. Money does not buy peace and happiness, but peace and happiness don't buy money, either. Ultimately, respect and pride come from knowing people, from talking to people, from well-wishers. Your books on finance and economics are not going to teach you any of this."

Nothing could stop her husband. He was the traveler, the kite that flew against the course and cut through the clouds. His body was designed to spend its afternoons on bullock carts, its nights in buses, passing flats and hills, speaking to those numerous people living between villages and capitals. He was a man of various workplaces and various homes, comfortable and efficient in each. Once he left one place and entered another, he did not let the former disturb him. Once away from Sabaila, Manmohan did not write to Meena. He did not think it necessary that she know his whereabouts. He returned at the end of the trip and told her briefly the things he thought she would understand. "I met Girdhari. He has had a grandson. Kapil's wife sent her greetings." Meena knew nothing about his work. She did not know who Girdhari or Kapil were. She did not know why her husband left—and left so often for so long. What did he do in Kathmandu? What did Kathmandu look like? She felt a pull to Kathmandu, an urge to follow Manmohan.

Then there was that one day Meena wanted to travel out of Sabaila on a snake's back. It was four in the morning and Meena could not sleep. The women were already waking up and she first heard the door to Kumud's room, then her mother-in-law's open and shut. The sky was visible in tiny dots through the thatch upon the roof. It was March, too early for roof repair. Roof repair would begin in April, a month before the rains came. Manmohan had left the previous day and Meena could not sleep. She listened to Kumud and her mother-in-law moving quietly, the hand pump in the courtyard creaking as they used it.

Soon Meena's mother-in-law would call for Meena. "Meena, daughter, Meena," she would say, standing at the door, and Meena would have to wake up at four in the morning because it was not decent to let men see a woman before she was completely dressed and ready. Every time Sawari Devi called Meena "daughter," Meena wanted to tell her she was not a daughter in this house. Binita was the daughter in the house and Binita spent her mornings sleeping. Binita was allowed to be seen by men as unkempt as she chose. Binita was not expected to take her baths before sunrise. Binita did not have to cook and clean and participate in the day's never-ending cycle. Binita did not have to suffer Sawari Devi's tongue, tart as lemon.

Meena stayed in bed, waiting in the dark for Sawari Devi to call out for her. She could hear the water gushing from the hand pump. She could hear it falling into the bucket. She waited still. Sawari Devi would call once Kumud was inside the small cubicle that served as a bathroom. But Sawari Devi did not call and Meena was surprised when she heard Kumud and Sawari Devi grow suddenly frantic. She heard their run, heard them shout against the hand pump that had gone silent. "Saap-Saap! Snake-snake!" Sawari Devi cried. But even as Meena heard the cry the danger did not register to her. She stayed in bed, still waiting for the cry to become her name. Then she heard the snake, too, on the roof, moving in and out of the thatch. At one point she saw its tail. It fell through a small opening in the thatch and hung there like a sickle. Then it was gone. Meena sprang out of bed and dashed out of the room. Kumud and Sawari Devi were in the courtyard, the iron bucket by their side half filled with water. Manmohan's brothers ran out their rooms, too, sticks in hand. They looked at the women, and Meena realized she was not presentable. Her hair hung loose upon her, her blouse had ridden up and her breasts showed like moons under it. Her sari was disheveled.

"Outside," Kumud said and the men went out to check.

"Whore," said Sawari Devi. "Is this how you come out of your room? One day her husband is gone and she is looking for another."

Meena started and stared at her mother-in-law. Sawari Devi's hair was white and wispy, her body thin, her teeth dyed with betel juice. She wore dark tattoos upon her chest and around her wrists. Her voice was hoarse and croaking in this morning hour. And as Meena stared, she became one of the men with the sticks, chasing the snake away from this house and into the fields. Meena ran alongside the snake, out into the fields and onto the lanes, taking a diversion here, missing the next one, slithering without minding the dust. She reached a lake, then another, one that belonged to another village, then another. She reached the Dhanush Mandir, went past the Dhanusha forest, and around the Parshuram Lake. She entered Janakpur. She climbed onto a rickshaw and returned to the train station. She waited for the slow train to speed, enduring its lackadaisical ways. She got off in her own town and came to the neighborhood of white and yellow homes. She turned at Kila Ghat and stepped into Urdu Bazaar. She opened a wooden front gate and entered, walked the short brick walkway, all the way to a house and a door. She knocked upon the door and Kaveri appeared before her, like a goddess, shining and smiling. She took her into an embrace and called her little one. Little one, said Kaveri, you have been away for more than a year and I have grown thin waiting for you.

Away from her mother, staring at Sawari, Meena fell in love with Kaveri. Why had she not noticed her own mother before? Why had she not seen how beautiful Kaveri was, how lovely her eyes were, how tuneful her voice? How far was Kaveri who was only a day's distance away. How impossible was a day's distance.

"Whore," said Sawari Devi, because that was how she spoke when angry. "Pull your blouse down, will you?" and Meena pulled her blouse down.

YOUR NAME ON MY ARM

Three years after their marriage, Meena was still in Sabaila and Manmohan in Kathmandu. In the three years, Meena had visited her mother once to attend Shanti's, her deaf-and-mute sister's, marriage. Manmohan had accompanied her and the couple had stayed in Darbhanga for three days before they had had to return because it was time for Manmohan to take the bus to Kathmandu, and because it was the harvest season and Meena was needed in Sabaila. Meena had cried when she had seen her mother and siblings and cried again just a day later because it was time already to leave.

In Sabaila the work never ended and all day, together with Kumud, Meena toiled in the large mud-caked kitchen. Together they ground wheat to flour upon a stone chakki and cleaned sacks of rice. Two flat dugra leaned against the kitchen wall and together they poured rice upon these cane baskets. They tossed the rice up and down, up and down until the husk separated from the rice and settled upon the floor and the rice upon the dugra was left clean, ready to be soaked in water. Meena fanned the wood inside the earthen hearth, coaxing the fire to burn, and cook the rice upon it. She made cottage cheese and tied it in a thin muslin cloth. She hung the cheese along with jaggery, garlic, and onions on hooks from ceilings so rodents would not get to them. She was not very tall and she had to stand on a stool. Sometimes, while still midair, one foot on stool, another off, she thought of Manmohan. He has a stove in his room, she mused. He could be boiling eggs right now, simmering chicken. Why should he return to me?

Springs in Sabaila were the easiest, when fields ripened but were not yet ready for harvest. Days were still busy with chores, but they could be managed. The winters were easy, too, because the fields were mostly empty and the days, despite the season, not too cold. The monsoons were the worst. In the monsoons the fields were sowed with rice. During the monsoons Sawari Devi turned savage, yelling at laborers who pestered her for advance payment, did not turn up, complained about the hours, and were never satisfied with their compensation. Every day, at all hours, Sawari Devi worked. Every day, at all hours, she was angry with the world that sat on its haunches, cleaning its buttocks, fat with the food people like her slaved to make. Meena spent her days in the kitchen with Kumud. They made big, flat rotis on strong iron tawas. They cooked rice in large patilas and boiled daal in the deep pots. Monsoons brought with them men—distant brothers, uncles, grandfathers, who sat down for meals on the veranda, facing the courtyard into which the rain fell in thick sheets, like panes of translucent glass, off the roof. Drops bounced off the courtyard and lined the veranda with a thick border of slippery wetness. Meena had to be careful running in and out the kitchen, ladling daal into bowls, heaping rice upon plates, keeping her eyes away from the young men she sometimes felt looked too intently at her. When the men finished the first serving, they asked for more. Then they asked for more. After lunch the men left abruptly. They did not carry their plates to the tub in which Meena would collect them later. They did not pick the morsels of sticky rice off the ground. They did not thank Meena or Kumud. A mountain of pots and pans, a hill of plates and bowls, glasses and jugs stared at Meena and Kumud. These they carried gingerly to the hand pump dug outside the house because the drainage in the courtyard was not good enough. They scrubbed the utensils clean with coal. Beside them, Kumud's twins splashed in the dense rain.

The twins gave their mother no rest. When not tending the house, Kumud tended her children. She bathed them under the hand pump, hardly able to distinguish which water she pulled from the earth and what fell from the sky. She massaged their backs with mustard oil, nursed their tired bodies so they would fall asleep, cleaned their perpetually leaking noses, ran out into the neighborhood when one of them did not return after sunset. While not away with neighborhood children, the twins skipped around their mother, holding on to her even as they played with each other. In the kitchen they played with vegetables, with rice, with each other, and with Kumud. They made a mess and left it for Kumud and Meena to clean.

"Why do you fuss over them so much?" Meena asked. "They are almost five."

"They are my sons," said Kumud.

"Even sons can take some care of themselves if you spank them good and proper," said Meena.

"Sons are delicate vines," said Kumud. "They will give you many fruits but you must take care of them. They are not like daughters. Daughters are trees, sturdy. You can let them be."

"You are a donkey," Meena said, irked by her sister-in-law.

Kumud lessened Meena's loneliness but also intensified it. Meena longed for twins of her own, boys who would cling to her sari, would despair and weep if she raised her voice, and be mended only by her smile. But three years after marriage she was still not pregnant. Three years after marriage Manmohan was still bringing home packets of condoms, which he got for free from His Majesty's Family Planning Center where he worked in Kathmandu.

To push away her loneliness, Meena played with Kumud's children, trying to be patient with them the way Kumud was. She hid behind doors and under beds and played hide-and-seek. She chased and ran from them. She fed them fruit and pieces of jaggery. But sometimes she had no patience and when Kumud was not looking she smacked or pinched their arms, convinced they were beginning to love her more than they did their mother because they did not seem to mind. "You both are donkeys," she said, laughing. "How you howl when your mother hits you."

"But you are not our mother," said the twins, pinching her back and running out to play in the rain-sloshed village.

In Manmohan's absence Meena fell in love with Kumud. She loved her sister-in-law's arching brows, the slim nose above a slightly bucktooth mouth, the timidity in her voice, the neck rising long from bone-thin shoulders. She loved how Kumud seemed not to love her husband, not to pine over his absence. Her husband left early each morning and came home late. He was involved in village politics and was the youngest member of the village panchayat. He was essential to his mother's fields and to the shops that sold their products. He took upon himself the responsibility of organizing festivals and fetes in the village because he was the president of the village theater that trained for and put up dramas twice a year. Meena fell in love with Kumud because she did not ask her husband for trips to the theater. She sent the twins and when they returned she asked them for details, which they never gave.

"I would die if he were my husband," Meena said to Kumud.

"You might as well hang yourself from a tree then," said Kumud, wiping her children clean. "Your husband . . ." and she did not complete the sentence and the sentence, half finished, took on frightful endings. Your husband will never return. Your husband does not love you. Your husband has another wife in the city. Your husband is dead. During one of Manmohan's trips, there had once been a short death scare. The bus in which Manmohan was traveling with his friends fell off the cliff and for a week it was believed all passengers were dead. It was believed Manmohan was dead. For that one week Sawari Devi wept and raged and when she saw Meena, she lunged at her. "This cobra ate my son!" she cried. "My son died before I did. This woman, always pestering my son, ate my Manmohan." Meena stepped away, aware suddenly that she indeed had killed her husband. She had thought of his death a day before the bus had tumbled. He might as well be dead for all he is worth, she had thought, and the bus had tumbled the next day. Meena stepped away from the weeping women, and the men who looked on seriously. She stepped away from the laborers who whispered to one another upon the balcony outside.

They were told later that Manmohan was not dead, that no one in that bus died. The bus was caught between trees, and the passengers, each one, had gotten out. They had scattered into the houses within the forests and had waited for help to arrive. When help arrived, in about five days, they had traveled on to Kathmandu. But despite the good news, a part of Meena had remained a widow.

It was Kumud who kept Meena sane. One evening, after all the work was done and the twins were asleep, after Meena and Kumud had spent hours waiting for Sawari Devi and for Kumud's husband to return from the monthly village panchayat meeting, Kumud took a needle out from a sewing box and gave it to Meena. It was dark, and the silver needle gleamed golden in the lantern light. "Here," said Kumud, "write your name on my arm."

"Why?" asked Meena, surprised and intrigued.

"Because I don't have a sister," Kumud said.

So, in the lantern light with the flame fluttering upon the bed where the twins slept, Meena took the needle and cut out her name upon Kumud's arm.

"Your turn now," Meena said, and Kumud took the needle from her.

Kumud's arm said Meena. Meena's arm said Kumud. The wounds bled and swelled and with the swelling, with the bleeding, Meena became convinced she would never need Manmohan again. She no longer cared if Manmohan returned or died. She did not care if she never saw Manmohan again, never had children, never went to Kathmandu and lived in a house of her own. She did not care if Sawari Devi abused her for the rest of her life. She stared at her arm, awed and frightened by the pain she felt. She could, if Kumud asked her to, jump into a well and die. She could set herself on fire if it pleased Kumud. She could walk out of the village barefoot and walk until there was no skin left on her. She could abandon her husband and live with Kumud instead, raising the twins so that the twins would eventually get confused about who their real mother was. She could become a twin herself, living within Kumud, indistinguishable, thinking Kumud's thoughts, getting the nourishment from the food Kumud swallowed, sharing a soul. At one point while carving Kumud's name upon her arm she touched her wound to her name bleeding upon Kumud's arm and watched their bloods mingle. Meena wondered if she would wake up the next morning half Meena, half Kumud. It felt possible.

And so she was not surprised when she did wake up half Kumud the next morning, feeling Kumud's frustrations, Kumud's moments of happiness. Kumud was neither sister nor friend. She was sister-in-law, a stranger inside a house where Meena, too, was an outsider, as neglected by her husband as Meena was, more abused by their mother-in-law than Meena would ever tolerate. She felt, suddenly, an intense hate for Manmohan. She now dreaded his presence, and for the first time in the three years that she had known her husband, Meena began to notice the things that were ugly in Manmohan. He had a pinched nostril. His eyebrows flared like grass above his eyes. His breath smelled of milk at the brink of turning sour. His hands were always rough. "I don't want him to come back, ever," she confided to Kumud, panicking at the thought that he would return.

In the evenings, after the twins had fallen asleep and all the chores were complete, Meena and Kumud sat on the terrace under the dark sky and spoke in shy whispers. They held hands and their fingers swam gently upon each other's. Meena was seventeen now, glowing, waiting. Kumud was twenty-four, young, well-formed, kind. On the terrace, under the stars, Meena's heart banged against her ribs with an intensity that threatened to break its cage. There were long moments when Meena wanted to crush herself upon Kumud, to smell the scent of her neck, to call her beautiful and to hold her close, but she held herself back. She knew this was wrong. She knew she could only hold hands with her sister-in-law. She could only love Kumud by working with her, by helping her raise the twins, by talking to her during stolen moments, by saving her from Sawari Devi.

For the first time Meena was truly angry with Sawari Devi. So far she had endured her mother-in-law by almost convincing herself Sawari Devi did not really exist. Among the first things Meena learned in Sabaila was that Sawari Devi respected nothing but hard work. There was no pity in Sawari Devi, no humor, no adventure. Her wrath, foulmouthed and crude, was seasonal, following the crops. If the fields were mellow, Sawari Devi's wrath was mellow, if the fields were heavy, her wrath was heavy, and Meena had learned to escape that wrath simply by having all chores completed on time, but Kumud, burdened by the twins and by her husband, often lagged.

The chores had been divided early. This Kumud was responsible for; this, Meena. And at the end of the day Sawari Devi did not care what got in the way of the work as long as the tasks were completed, and so Meena kept up for Kumud. When Kumud put the twins to nap, Meena folded Kumud's share of clothes. She washed extra dishes, chopped the vegetables Kumud would otherwise have to chop, put out water so Kumud could hurry through her bath, saved curry so Kumud could have a generous meal, but occasionally the stove would go unmopped, or the firewood become damp, then one evening there would be too much salt in the dinner, and Sawari Devi, already angry with laborers who thought they could be lazy and troublesome, who thought they could speak to her like she did not know her own business, who could be insolent and rude just because Sawari Devi was not a man, because she was a widow, flew at her daughters-in-law in her rage. Like that one evening when Meena and Kumud were eating their dinner and Sawari Devi kicked Kumud's plate away.

"Lazy bitch," she said. "Just sitting all day and not doing a grain of work. Look at that pile! Shameless whores, always walking hand in hand. And who will pay for what you eat? Your fathers?" She turned to Meena sitting by the stove. "And your husband thinks he is a star, living far in the sky. He has no concerns with the house but he leaves his wife behind for us to feed, and she eats like a buffalo, a pig!"

Meena spat into the stove and pulled back Kumud's plate. "Eat," she said and put the plate before her sister-in-law. She stared at Sawari Devi, and Sawari Devi, infuriated by the stare, kicked Meena's plate away. Meena pulled her plate back and continued eating and with every bite Meena took, Sawari Devi screamed louder. "Whore!" she screamed. "Piglet!"

It was a strange scene and it made Meena chuckle. Kumud sobbed beside her and cursed her fate, her mother-in-law, and her husband. Sawari Devi kicked Meena's plate again and again Meena pulled it back, eating on. "She calls me a whore," she said, biting into her roti. "This widow who chewed her husband to death. She calls me a whore. Who gave her all these children? The dead husband? Whose children are these, whore?" she asked, biting into a fleshy piece of mango pickle.

Kumud stopped sobbing. Sawari stopped, too, one foot slightly raised.

GOLD

When a girl turned two, her earlobes were pierced with gold wires. The nose was pierced, too, and a pin-size stick broken off the backs of incense sticks and pushed into the flesh. Each morning drops of dew were picked off grass and dropped upon the gold and the wood. The dew soothed the pulsating pain left behind by the piercings. Sweets were forbidden while the wounds healed—no sugar, no guavas, definitely no mangoes. Winters were preferred to summers as piercing seasons, but cold also meant tingling and smarting wounds. In the summer the wound hurt less but lasted longer.

Meena did not know if she really remembered the day her ears and nose were pierced or if the recollection was reconstructed from Kaveri's narrations about the day and what Meena had seen her younger cousins endure on their first trip to the goldsmith's. Sometimes she thought she remembered sitting before a woman who squatted beside a coal stove, needles lining a steel box. She thought she remembered bawling while Kaveri stuffed sweet balls of jaggery into her crying mouth. She thought she remembered touching gold wires encircling her lobes and the wood upon her nose. She remembered flinching at the pain. She remembered the dew, she thought, its first touch as Kaveri dropped it upon her sore nose and ears. Meena did not remember the hot golden needle that must have punctured her skin, only the crying, the treat of jaggery, and later the cool dew upon her tender skin. She remembered more definitely her first piece of jewelry, the earrings and the matching nose stud—simple circles each with little globes dangling underneath, ornaments Meena wore for years, until it was time for her sister's wedding and Meena was given longer earrings to complement her sari. When Meena married, the long earrings became part of her trousseau. When Sawari Devi began choosing and picking jewelry for her own daughter's dowry she picked these earrings out of Meena's trousseau and placed them with the small collection containing gold and silver that Meena and Kumud had brought along from their mothers' homes.

Sawari Devi took from Meena exactly as much as she took from Kumud, even though the dowry Meena brought was more stylish. Meena's collection had intricate whorls and ringlets of gold twisting together. There was a playfulness to them that Kumud's dowry lacked. The silver fish, the silver betel nuts, silver vegetable chopper—these were almost silly in their accuracy. Under the silver scales the fish had silver gills and their eyes were of pale gray moonstones. Had the vegetable chopper not had a silver blade and board it could have been used in a kitchen. For Binita's silver collection Sawari Devi chose the fish and the chopper. For gold she took what she knew Meena would not care to wear—the waistband, the neck piece so long it could only be worn once during a lifetime, and the dangling earrings that were old and needed cleaning.

Dowries were formidable expenses, and no parent could accumulate enough to marry off their daughters. The day the daughter was born the mother began the process of accumulating and collecting the child's dowry and upon marriage the daughter took the same to her husband's house and replenished what had been taken away from that house by the husband's sisters. This was the system, the links in the chain. Sawari Devi, too, had received from her mother and she, too, had sacrificed what she had received. But Sawari Devi knew not to engage with her daughters-in-law. She knew enough to know her daughters-in-law would not give up their gold and silver with any willingness. If Sawari Devi asked Meena and Kumud for their gold and silver, they would rebuke her the way she herself had rebuked her mother-in-law. This, too, was the system. This, too, was the linking chain.

And so Sawari Devi maintained the secrecy that had always been maintained between in-laws. As the head of the family all treasures were under her care, signed away in safes and lockers, and from these she took secretly. What Sawari Devi did not anticipate was Meena's hazy recollections preceding the trousseau—the piercings, the drops of dew. With every item Meena brought from her mother's house, she brought along a story, and it was the story Sawari Devi did not foresee. The waistband was fashioned on paper by Meena's sisters before it was fashioned by a goldsmith. The long necklace had not always been so long—Kaveri had added gold to it over the years. In not anticipating Meena's stories, Sawari Devi could not anticipate Meena's anger, the extent to which Meena's wrath could stretch, including within it not only Sawari Devi but everything that belonged to her—her son, her home, her good name.

Besides, even before Meena discovered Sawari Devi's theft, she was already angry.

Only recently, after Sawari Devi had formalized her daughter Binita's wedding, Meena had told Kumud the barber's tale and slapped her own head during the telling. "Is it the town barber's fault if he is smarter?" she had asked. "Is the town barber supposed to give up his business just so the village barber and his stupid daughter can keep customers? And what? Customers are never allowed to move to more modern hairstyles or what? They are donkeys, I am telling you." And was it Meena's fault if she was from a town? Was it her fault that she was more educated, more beautiful, more wealthy than the dowdy villagers she had married? Was she supposed to live in Sabaila's dull confines washing mountains of pots and pans, plates and bowls, glasses and jugs each afternoon? If Manmohan could afford a kerosene stove in his pseudo-bachelor room, why had he not brought the stove over to the village so Meena would no longer have to blow at the wood smoking in the chulha? "I am sick of scrubbing all this with coal here. Why can't they have soap?" she asked. She was sick of coating the pots with clay so the fire from the chulha would not burn the metal. "These are not my pots and pans," she said. "I will not clean a day longer, I am telling you."

And still Meena cleaned. There was no alternative. If the utensils were not cleaned, there were no utensils to cook in, and if nothing was cooked, there was no food to eat. All day Meena either banged utensils or wept in her room. When misery hit her most, she lashed out against her mother-in-law. "You thief! You fat buffalo!" And this even before Sawari Devi had taken her gold.

Had the wars between Sawari Devi and Meena begun earlier, Sawari Devi might have played safe by not promising her daughter, Binita, to a rich family in Patna through marriage. She had never taken Binita to the fields, just like she had never taken along Meena or Kumud. The open field was no place for girls to be prancing around in. Girls had to be protected, sometimes from their fathers and brothers, and at all times from the eyes of strange men. Within the house the girls were safe and out of harm, given they had adequate work to occupy them, and therein lay Binita's problem. Binita could embroider, she could knit and sew, but she could not mop a floor or stir large pots of curry. She could not grind chilies to a paste. She could not climb up and down the stairs carrying buckets of water. She could not even wash her hair without giving herself a headache. One doctor had suggested Binita was frail out of choice and a sound beating would cure all weakness and Sawari Devi had thrashed the girl with a broom but even as she had hit and slapped, Sawari Devi had felt fear within her. She hoped the doctor was right. She hoped her daughter was lazy and indolent but not sick. Sawari Devi had lost two children to sicknesses and knew the fate of the sickly types.

However, when at sixteen Binita was still not married, Sawari Devi, desperate and afraid, had begun to cast her net farther and farther away from home in her search for a groom. Finally, her net had reached Patna, the capital of Bihar in India, and there she had found a family that manufactured and supplied light bulbs for the Indian Railway. It was a family rich beyond Sawari Devi's means but it was also the only one that would accept Binita despite her indolence. The family's own girls, three of them, had married at the age of eighteen and they did not think Binita too old. They did not think it a disadvantage that Binita could not cook and clean. They had servants for the cooking and cleaning. They were delighted with the bedsheets and tablecloths Binita had embroidered. They liked Binita. She would travel free on trains. She would live in a capital city. She would live in India. She would have servants. The only thing the family wanted was a dowry large enough to maintain their social status. "It has to be sizable," they said. "People have to know our son is married to a wealthy farmer family. Farming has to be respectable."

And so Sawari Devi leaned back upon the system and took hold of the linking chain. After all, what was dowry if not a fund for further dowries? What were daughters-in-laws if not funds for daughters? What worth was gold piled worthlessly in safes?

What Sawari Devi did not anticipate was Meena's spite, petty and young and blown out of proportion with loneliness. Meena had decided she would outshine Binita during her own wedding. Meena would wear not only pendants and anklets, toe rings and bangles she had brought from her mother's house, she would also wear her waistband and the longest neckpiece she owned. She would bribe the barber's wife who would come in to decorate Binita and get her own hands as heavily decorated as Binita's would be. Meena would wear a red-and-gold blouse and a red-and-gold sari. She would make the groom wish he was marrying her instead. She would show Manmohan what she was made of!

"My papaya is moister than that Binita's can ever be," she said, giggling at Kumud, "and every man in that gathering will know that. And let Manmohan Chaudhary do what he can!"

It was with the intention of outshining every woman in the marriage room that Meena went to Sawari Devi. "I want all my jewelry," she said. "I want to wear all of it for the marriage, all of the pieces, each one."

"Why?" asked Sawari Devi, keeping her voice steady despite the sudden fear she felt. "Because you are a whore?"

"Yes, because I am a whore," said Meena. "So get them all."

"Get them yourself," said Sawari Devi.

Day after day Meena asked and Sawari Devi denied her her gold. Every day Meena's frustrations reached new peaks. She could not get the jewelry herself. She did not know where the bank was. She had never entered a bank before. She had given everything to Sawari Devi immediately after coming into the house as a new bride. She had signed what had been asked of her. She had not known to ask anything in return.

"Give it right away!" she shouted at Sawari Devi.

"I will not have you whoring around during my daughter's marriage," said Sawari Devi, always in a hurry to leave the house, always returning later than usual.

And so battles that had so far been fought within the house became public events, discussed and enjoyed by all. At one time somebody reported seeing Sawari Devi being dragged around the veranda by her hair, at another time it was rumored Sawari Devi had hit Meena with a ladle. And quite suddenly somebody else saw Sawari Devi at the bank and she had with her such men as would be required if she was hiding gold under her petticoat. And somebody's somebody was sure Meena had threatened murder. Give it back now or I will slit your throat when you are asleep, she had supposedly said. It was believed Sawari Devi locked herself upon the terrace so she could sleep without fear.

Those mesmerized by Meena's dark brows and dark eyes, those who liked the drama, sided with Meena. Could at least have asked, they said. How do you think that Sawari Devi got so rich, they asked. Her husband, excuse me, was not such a rich man as to leave her in such comfort. It is all this thieving that has done the trick. Have you seen her arms? She beat a man to a pulp once. Whore? Did her daughter-in-law call her a whore?

Those who had their own daughters-in-law to contend with sided with Sawari Devi. What is a dowry if not a fund for further dowries? What are daughters-in-law if not funds for daughters? What good are town girls in villages? No wonder her husband does not take her along. Who does she think she is? Whore? Did Sawari Devi call her a whore?

Others shook their heads. They were tired of these age-old wars and could no longer stomach this vulgarism. They hated all women, really. A woman is a woman's biggest enemy, really.

Meena fumed. She walked up and down the terrace, not bothering with the veil anymore, not bothering with village decorum, village ethics. She would show Manmohan, she fumed. She would show him. He would return every piece of jewelry his mother had stolen from her. She would poke his eyes out otherwise. He was a donkey. A cheating misleading donkey who had taken her life and turned it to hell. She would run away one day. She would never return. She would set it all on fire!

Now when Manmohan returned to the village he returned as a referee, forever evaluating quarrels between his mother and his wife, presiding over them, tamping them down. The first time Sawari Devi cried before her son, Manmohan pulled Meena into the kitchen and hit her hard, slapping her arms, her head, her thighs, and with every hit he looked at his mother and shouted, "Are you happy now, Mother? Is this what you want? Is this?" and he hit Meena some more while Meena struggled to free herself.

Later, in the bedroom, he held Meena close. "It is only money," he said. "Money is not bigger than family."

Manmohan came home regularly now. He liked Meena differently. He liked the way she struggled and pushed her plate away and would not eat. He liked the way her eyes grew large and dark with anger. He liked the way he could punish her, hit her body until his own tingled in response. He now saw his mother as old and obsolete and his wife as the volcano who could ruin his standing in the village forever, and this danger in her excited him. Now when he took Meena to their room she was the woman-child who melted his heart but hardened his penis. He held her raging body down with his own and felt himself grow hot with desire. She struggled beneath him and he fucked her till he grew dizzy with fatigue. Now he forgot his condoms, forgot the reasons he had wanted a career and a house in Kathmandu. Now when he thought of Kathmandu, those rooms in which he had so far lived like a king, he was gripped by loneliness. Now he wanted Meena with him.

A TORRID RIVER

Sawari Devi invited every relative and friend to her daughter's wedding. Kaveri and her husband, Bilash, were invited, as were Kumud's parents. Any other time her parents' presence in the house would have given wings to Meena's heart, but now, with her love for Kumud and with the terrible disgust she felt for Manmohan, Meena shrank from her mother and father. Since Shanti's wedding Meena had gone back to Darbhanga one more time to stay with her parents and to celebrate her brother's, Suman's, wedding. Suman's wife came from Calcutta and could read and write English. She, Suman had said to his sisters with a big smile, would transform the very walls of Darbhanga. All brides were meant to transform the landscape of the houses they married into, and standing before her brother's accomplished wife, Meena had felt hollow and worthless. Meena had transformed nothing. She was nothing more than a slave and a laborer in her husband's house. She was little more than a hardworking buffalo.

How could she explain her unease to her parents? How could she talk about Manmohan's child, now living within her, without revealing the terror she felt?

The house hummed with the sound of guests. Mattresses, rented from marriage organizers, were laid from end to end in almost every room, and the house was divided so women slept in the rooms and the men took up the balcony, the courtyard, and the terrace. Children slept where possible. The halwais were given space beside the cowshed to set up their chulhas and enormous cooking pots, and all day one could smell puris being fried and brinjals being roasted. There was pickle and papadum and tangy curd. Heaps of rice and daal fragranced with ghee perfumed the air. The room with mithai was kept locked and Sawari Devi carried its key tied at the end of her sari.

Manmohan went about the house, always important and Kathmandu-returned, and spoke to the pundits in grave, learned tones. He sat with his friends and cousins and ordered the halwais for snacks and cups of tea. "Some pakoda, too, Motu Halwai," he said with a laugh, and his friends laughed along. Meena could see the envy in their eyes as they looked at him. She could see, too, that even when he was amid friends, his eyes searched for her, though secretly. He did not want his friends to know that now, after nearly four years of marriage, he could not get enough of his wife. During the nights when Manmohan could get hold of her, Meena felt his deep and troubled yearning. She sensed it in the way he slid his hands upon her, in the way he made hot promises. "You will live like a queen, Meena," he whispered. "I will take you away from all of this." And now that the house was full of guests and he was forced to sleep with men on the terrace, he was restless and impatient, catching her in corners and laughing at her discomfort.

A few years ago Manmohan's impatience would have charmed Meena. This is what she had dreamt of—to be so wanted, to drive her husband mad with want—but now his fingers were repulsive, and despite the gold stolen from her, Meena was glad to have the wedding to hide behind. She kept herself busy with decorating the mandap, the prayer room, the courtyard. There was always some crisis like a missing ingredient for some ritual or a piece of jewelry that had slipped off a finger and fallen somewhere in the chaotic house, and Meena vanished within these emergencies, working so vigorously even Sawari Devi was impressed and hesitantly began to believe that Meena cared deeply for Binita. All day Meena was aware of Manmohan's eyes upon her. She could sense his body turning every time she came close to his radius. She could sense the hidden smile of invitation he sent her way, and she shrank from it. Already, in the few weeks that he had been here for Binita's wedding, he had taken her several times, and she felt a growing resentment at the ease with which he could have sex with her. It made her sore and dirty. It made her feel like she had forsaken Kumud. Even if they only held hands all their lives, she wanted Kumud to know she was dedicated to her and would never enjoy another person. I know I am having a child, she wanted to say, and I know it is Manmohan's child, but they mean nothing, not the child, not the man. Only you, only you mean something.

If only Meena could tell Kumud about the child, she could have relaxed. If only Kumud could assure her that they would raise this one together, just like they were raising the twins, Meena would have asked Kumud if they could run away. But Kumud was always busy. As the older daughter-in-law, she was the one responsible for most ceremonies. It was she who accepted the shagun sent during the cheka; she received the turmeric paste sent by the groom's family and she applied it on Binita's body first. As the daughter-in-law with children, all rituals of fertility were performed by her. Meena, childless and younger, stood silently, counting days since she had missed her periods and told no one. Kumud built the bamboo trellis that supported the marriage mandap, and when the mango leaves arrived in large baskets, Kumud spent the entire day weaving the leaves into garlands to decorate the bamboo pillars with. Sawari Devi hovered like a falcon, watching the work, nodding appreciatively or making suggestions. She assigned Meena menial tasks that kept her away from Kumud.

Finally, two days before the actual marriage, Meena fled to her mother.

Immediately Kaveri held Meena in her arms and rocked their bodies together. "Are you pregnant yet?" she asked, kissing her daughter's hair.

"No," Meena lied.

"But you could be," said Kaveri.

"No," said Meena.

"Why?" asked Kaveri, concerned. "Why aren't you still pregnant? Is your husband still bringing condoms from his office in Kathmandu?"

A dull fear settled inside Meena then. "No," she said.

"Then how do you know you are not pregnant?" Kaveri insisted.

"Because I don't want to be," said Meena.

"But that's not how it works." Kaveri laughed. "Besides I can see that he will only take a house in Kathmandu when he thinks there are enough members to fill it. You better do something."

"I don't want to go to Kathmandu," said Meena.

"What?" asked Kaveri, aghast. "And what will you do here? Till the lands like some man?"

"I don't mind," said Meena. "I just don't want to live with your son-in-law."

Kaveri frowned. "Look, little one," she said. "You have to learn how to be married. The only way to be married is to live like you have no husband. There are no married women in this world. We are all widows, but only the lucky ones get to set fire to their husbands and throw away the ashes in rivers. You understand?"

Meena stared at her mother. "Then why are all of us married. If we must all live like widows and widowers, why get married at all?"

"Eh? What will happen to the world otherwise? How will houses run? Where will children come from?"

"I don't want to be married, Mai," Meena said, quietly.

Kaveri sat Meena on the bed. "Is your mother-in-law evil?"

Meena nodded.

"You have to slap her around some more," said Kaveri. "I thought you slapped her around well."

And then it was the wedding day and Meena was more than a month pregnant.

Amid the crowd, in the corner room, Binita was locked with a group of women working to get her ready. The boy's wedding party would be at their doorstep in an hour and there was still much to be done. Binita, now seventeen, sat upon a tall stool while Geeta, a cousin, shaped her hair into a bun. Through it all Binita wept bitterly. Meena stood away from the crowd, dry-eyed and watching as Kumud spoke softly with Binita, stroking her hair and back, wiping away her tears. In the courtyard, Kaveri sat with Sawari Devi and added finishing touches to the wedding mandap with the last bits of flowers and paint. It burned Meena to see Kaveri with Sawari Devi, like it burned her to see Kumud with Binita.

What also bothered Meena was the unearthly glow on Binita despite the weeping and crying. Meena was convinced Binita cried only to attract attention and not because she grieved the loss of her home and her childhood. What was there to cry about when she was so decorated? Sawari Devi had outdone herself. She had decked her daughter from head to toe in stolen gold. Binita wore Meena's stolen waistband over her sari. She wore Meena's birdcage earrings on her ears. Her hands were ornamented with Kumud's set of kangans, and around her neck she wore the necklace Kaveri had so meticulously lengthened over the years and gifted to Meena. Sawari Devi had wrapped her daughter in the finest Banarasi silk. She had found her a handsome and healthy man from the richest family possible and ensured her daughter's escape from the village to a city. She would now go off to Patna, a capital city, and there, glistening in silk and gold, she would dictate over a house of servants. She, who had not worked a day in her life, would never have to work at all; while Meena was married to a village and abandoned, and just when she had found her comfort, she was yanked away to the city to live with a man whose touch made her skin crawl; while Kumud stayed with her too-important husband in her too-important role in a household that caged her like a prison. What did Binita have to weep about?

This was the thought Meena wanted to hold on to but the child in her confused her senses and Meena could not glare long enough at Binita to shame her into giving up the stolen jewelry. Instead she helplessly watched Binita who sat on her stool, crying as though she was soon to marry a beggar.

"What a donkey this girl is," she said to Kumud when Kumud came over to stand beside her.

"Why? Did you not cry when you got married? I remember you. You had Ganga and Yamuna flowing from your nostrils the whole time."

"I did not. And she is wearing your kangans and your anklets. Aren't you boiling looking at her arms and legs? May this girl have a rotten life."

"Don't be a bitch," said Kumud and walked back to Binita.

Meena continued standing away from the gathering. She wondered if the baby in her was a girl or a boy. She wondered if she would have twins. In sudden panic she imagined herself in Kathmandu with Manmohan. She did not want to live with Manmohan. She did not want to be confined in a house with him, raising his children, at his mercy. She wished the child would vanish and dissolve within her. It had not come to her when she had wanted a child, and now when she wanted nothing to do with Manmohan and his Kathmandu, here it was, swimming inside her. She wanted it gone. Gone!

I wish this Binita dies, she thought in a moment, and in the same moment she thought, I hope this donkey of a child dies too.

It was a day after Binita's bidai, after she left Sabaila for her husband's capital town and took with her more than half the guests in Sawari Devi's house and left behind only Meena's and Kumud's parents, that Meena crawled into Kumud's bed. Her feet ached with having stood too long and having held secrets within herself for weeks. Her head reeled with Manmohan's promise of big city and city life. A tired loneliness pressed her down, and she put her arm around Kumud with relief and fatigue. She had come to tell Kumud about the child, to ask her if they could perhaps start elsewhere, without the absent-yet-lecherous husbands, the hardened mother-in-law, the unforgiving village days, the unrelenting exhaustion. Please, she had come to say to Kumud, it's been four years since I have watched a movie. Can we go to the cinema, please? And please, after the movie, can we walk to the chowk and have some kachri-murhi by the roadside?

But the warmth of Kumud's body as she wriggled to make space for Meena softened Meena and she forgot about the movies. What she wanted instead was to sleep quietly and deeply. Even when she woke up, early, before the sun rose, she wanted to stay entwined with Kumud, listening to the twins asleep by her side. She did not want the sun to rise.

She cupped herself against Kumud and held her close, as she did so often now. She knew Manmohan was in the house, looking for her, upset that she had escaped. She knew Kumud's husband would return soon from wherever he was, but he rarely slept in Kumud's bed. Mostly he slept on the terrace. Kumud's bed was too small for a man, a woman, and two children, and this arrangement with her husband on the terrace while Kumud slept in the room would go on until the twins were old enough to sleep on their own. It thrilled Meena that though Kumud's husband could not fit in the bed, she did with such ease. It made her realize that Kumud and her husband did not hug so tight. They did not mold into each other, like tumblers stacked together, or like pieces of oranges under their thick peels.

For a few minutes Meena fell asleep, and when she woke up, with a start, from the dream she was having, her body was on fire. The room was dark. Kumud, turned to her, was asleep. The twins were at the other end of the bed and snoring softly, the way children sometimes do. Meena's throat burned and she swallowed for relief. And then, because there could be no other relief, she reached out and placed one palm on Kumud's chest. Instantly, she sensed Kumud wake up, sensed the change as she gently squeezed Kumud's breast through her blouse. Kumud's eyes flew open. She did not turn the act into a game, as Meena had so many times with her sisters. She did not keep her eyes shut and her breaths deep to mimic sleep. Instead, she stared at Meena, her eyes wide with questions, and in a frightened response, Meena closed her eyes. Her chest ached and the palm still playing with Kumud felt numb. She knew she had to stop, but she could not, and she leaned in and kissed Kumud, the way Manmohan had taught her to kiss, on the mouth, with a little sucking, a little biting. She pulled in a long breath, taking in Kumud's sweat-perfumed smell. "Please," she said at one point, though she did not know what she asked for. "Please," she repeated, but Kumud stayed still, like a sculpture beneath Meena's burning body, and slowly Meena fell away. She lay beside Kumud, cold with fear, the inch of space between them like a torrid river, and she and Kumud the banks meant never to meet.

Almost without moving, Kumud shifted away. "Go to your husband," she said, her voice flat and without emotions.

The next morning Meena dragged herself to Kaveri. Kaveri was on the terrace, drying her hair in the sun, getting ready for her journey back to Darbhanga that evening.

"Good you have come," said Kaveri. "Eh? All your jewelry that whore of a girl was wearing. How did you let that happen? Your father is beside himself with grief and anger. Is this what we saved everything for?"

"I am pregnant," Meena said. "I have been for a month."

Kaveri looked at her daughter and despite the anger she still felt at the lost jewelry, she braved a smile.

Meena started crying. "I don't want a child, Mai," she cried. "I want this child to die. I don't want this house. I don't want this husband. I want to go home with you."

Kaveri stared at her daughter, then she held Meena's shoulders and began pushing her along the parapet against which they were leaning. "You want this child to die?" Kaveri hissed as she pushed. "Do you know what you are saying, you idiot? Do you know what you will feel if the child dies? A woman only has a child and she has nothing else. Women who don't have children are ash."

Blood prickled up like glass beads where the parapet tore her skin, but while Meena had cried earlier, she now held her cry tightly in her mouth. Kaveri's anger, suppressed and distorting her face, terrified Meena and she could not cry. When Kaveri finally let go of her shoulders, Meena said in a hoarse whisper, "Take me with you, Mai, and I will raise a hundred children if you say."

"I have raised my children. You raise your own," said Kaveri and walked away. Meena followed her mother down the stairs to the courtyard where the remnants of Binita's marriage stood against Meena in defiant colors. For a few seconds Kaveri and Meena stood staring at the painted pots, the woven baskets. An otherworldly, singing sound filled Meena's ears and she felt she was somewhat drowned in it. When Kaveri spoke, her voice was distant, like Kumud's had been the night before. "This is your home and your graveyard," said Kaveri. "Make the best of it. All women have done it before you. You will manage fine."

BOOK TWO

MANMOHAN

THE HIGHS AND THE LOWS

When Manmohan was an infant, an old woman named Sukumariya lived in Sabaila. Sukumariya was Sabaila's babysitter and kept check on babies and tots by telling them stories: harmless tales if the children behaved well and stories with ghosts and witches if they did not. In return, families of these children rewarded Sukumariya with food, clothes, and sometimes with colors and dyes they made at home. Like others in the village, Sukumariya lived in a hut whose mud walls were supported by frameworks of bamboo grilles, and her walls were decorated with murals of fish, moons, banana trees, suns, and mountains. When she worked, she often started from the top of her mud canvas and a whistling sound escaped her gummy mouth as she created dense, magical worlds upon walls. The walls of her hut advertised Sukumariya as an artist, albeit a whimsical one, and she was often commissioned by the villagers to adorn marriage mandaps and angans with images of gods and goddesses. Every now and then she was summoned simply to decorate huts with her fanciful paintings. Sabaila was a village of brown mud, brown huts, and brown lakes—and Sukumariya's colors were welcome here.

By the time Manmohan was old enough to walk up to Sukumariya and listen to her tales, Sukumariya was so old she was almost blind, and the entire village called her great-grandmother. She was so old she painted by feel alone, and when she could no longer remember the order in which she lined her containers of color, she asked the children gathered around her to shift this bowl of paint, then that bowl of paint, toward her. She painted with trust in her heart, with the belief that the children would not trick her. It was a fanciful faith, though, for children will always trick the blind, meddle with colors, and change the way the walls of the world are meant to look. More than once Manmohan pushed forward a purple bowl when Sukumariya asked for green, and yellow when she wanted red, so that Sukumariya painted purple trees, yellow skies, green people, and blue horses. The results were startling, like alternate visions.

Mostly Sukumariya drew what was demanded of her: a bride in a palanquin and a groom upon a horse, goddesses upon symmetrical lotuses, geometric figures of cattle and men. But at other times she drew from inspiration and embellished the village with snippets of her dreams.

Sukumariya was so old she knew the now when it was the beginning. She was so old she sometimes cursed herself for being alive. "May destruction befall me," she sometimes sang. "May the blood that leaves my heart forget its way back."

"What will you draw today, Great-grandmother?" Manmohan asked one afternoon.

"The mountains," she answered.

"What of the mountains?"

"Its highs and its lows."

She patted the wall before her, felt for outlines of doors and windows, then she stretched her hand and began to paint. She bordered the base of the hut with a pink range of mountains and on the sky she drew a sparrow with lavender wings. The sparrow had its beak facing down and its feathers spread like tiny arrows on either side.

Sukumariya sang as she painted:

La Ho! A sparrow flew
From a grass to a branch
From a branch to a cloud
From a cloud to a moon
From a moon to a star.
La Ho! This star to that
And the world beneath his wings so small
Smaller than his beak
Smaller than sand
Smaller than the dreams of man
Was the world above which he flew.
La Ho!

"Which one is white?" she asked and Manmohan guided her fingers to a pail of rust-red paint.

"A sparrow looked down and saw the world," said Sukumariya painting rust-red snow upon her pink mountains, "and in that world he saw Nepal, small as his eyes were small, so small he almost did not see it. And then there were the mountains he could not miss, white and purple under his wings. Here the Himal snuggled with Tibet, her crests so tall she wore clouds like sandals upon her feet. Here, next to China, the mountains knelt on her knees and clouds played like children on her lap, and here she sat cross-legged and the clouds rounded her breasts and floated away to India."

All week, as Sukumariya drew, painted, and sang, Manmohan watched and listened. The mountains staircased upon the hut, high at one end and skipping down thereafter. There was snow on towering caps, trees and snow on the next, and flowers as the mountains lowered, and fields of paddy as the land flattened to become the Madhesi belt of Nepal.

"Here," said Sukumariya, describing her work, "in our Madhesh, the land is flat and looks up to the clouds as a child reveres her older brother."

"Tell me about an older brother," said Manmohan, referring to the mountains.

But Sukumariya was old and she confused his demand for something else. "Older brother?" she said. "There was no older brother. I was always the oldest of all brothers and sisters. Eight of us. I forget how many brothers and how many sisters. They died one by one, some before I was married off and some after. All of them but me. I live."

O ré, she sang, *this world is small*
Smaller than a grain of sand
Smaller than the dreams of man.
O ré, this world is a small, small world
For my big, big heart of pain.

"Tell me a story, Great-grandmother, about the small, small world and the big, big heart of pain."

Sukumariya laughed. "What can I say about pain? We all have our pains, do we not? Big and small, some like grains of sand and some like rocks upon our chests. Pain begins with death. It begins when we die for the first time, then die again after our second life, and so it goes, from one death to the next, skipping like a river, never the same, never too different. What can I say? When did mine begin? It began when my sister died. A snake bit her. Then the other sister died. A tiger ate her. Then another died. She fell into a gorge. My brothers died. One for no reason at all. Nothing ate him. He just died. All died. My pain began when I knew I would not die, no matter what happened. Animals went roving around other huts. Kings came from the capital and carried people away. Snakes crawled on our roofs, too, but I knew I would not die. I was fated to console my inconsolable mother, who also would not die. Then she too died. That is the worst pain. The mother's death. What is pain? It is death, that is all."

Over the week the mountain upon the hut's wall melted into rushing rivers and the rivers thickened to become land, and the land spread out flat, even as the sky, verdant with grass. Then Sukumariya drew a village, small and thick with trees so dense the huts were scarcely visible.

"This," said Sukumariya, "is our Sabaila."

"Were there tigers and snakes even during the day?" asked Manmohan, looking at his village with wonder.

"When I was young? When I first came here with my father and mother? Yes. Yes. There were snakes—vipers, kraits, cobras—that leapt and coiled like alphabets in the air. It was all so long ago. I cannot remember her age anymore. My sister's. How old was she when a snake bit her? How old was I? What does it matter? Let us say she was young. Let us say she died young."

She told Manmohan more through another morning.

"When we first came here, there was only me and the sister who died of a snake bite. And there was a brother. I don't remember how he died. I forget my brothers so easily, but I remember I had a brother and we walked for days and arrived upon this land—father, mother, one sister, one brother, and me. There would be more brothers and sisters later and they would all die, but that first time we walked for days, we were only the five of us. Before we came here, I had no country. I did not know there were countries in the world. I simply went where my parents went, and my parents went where there was food and shelter. We had begun our walk because a letter had come to us from a king of Nepal. It came to our father and to others like our father. At the time my father was a sipahi, a foot soldier in the British Army of India, and there was no money to eat with, no clothes to wear. The letter said: 'I am the king of Nepal. I live enclosed by mountains, in a city called Kantipur. The mountains are high and at its foot spreads a forest, wide and furious, but also lush and giving. A drop of its land is enough to feed a village, and a drop of its water enough to boil a pail of sweet rice. One day spent hunting there brings meat for a month. Rain falls and there is nectar. There is abundance. Come, fell the trees, till the land, sow the seeds. All you till is yours to keep. All you sow is yours. Build a hut, settle a family, and become a part of this abundant land.'

"This is what the letter said, and so we went, because we went where there was food to be had, and the British in India gave us no food, and so we left. We, and many others like us. We sang as we left our thin, hungry villages and marched toward the teeming forests of Nepal."

Le Ho! A home is made of husband and wife
A journey is made of strife.
A home is made of sons and daughters
Some are good and some are rotters.
Le Ho! We leave a home, a home we take
We make a pan, a pot we break.
A room we build, and walls and doors
And if wood is left, we build some more. Le Ho!

"We sang to keep fear away. When a fellow traveler fell, we heard the whoosh-whoosh of leaves and the thuk-thuk of branches, and we heard the dhadamp of his fall, and for hours we heard him moan.

"We sang because every burden was small after the burden of hunger we were leaving behind, and because we imagined a paradise, and because death had not visited us yet. You see, pain comes with death, and though I had seen hunger and poverty, though I had seen an uncle die of a strange addiction to a strange crop the British in India forced him to grow, I had not yet seen my siblings die."

"Tell me about the pahads, Great-grandmother. Tell me about the mountains," said Manmohan, growing afraid of Sukumariya's bleak tale.

"The pahads, the mountains?" asked Sukumariya, staring at her past and watching herself. "I don't know anything about the pahads. I have never lived in mountains. I draw from imagination and from the memory of what the king of Nepal wrote to us in his letters."

Sukumariya was so old her breasts were flat under the folds of her sari. Her nails, curved and corrugated, sat flat upon her thin fingers. Her hair was flat. Her toes, splayed with having walked all her life without slippers, were flat. Her eyes, thick and pearly, were flat. The walls she painted were flat, the color of earth. The earth she squatted upon was flat, the color of hay. The horizon, unbroken and faraway, was flat, the color of dust. Sukumariya knew nothing of mountains.

It was through Sukumariya's stories that Manmohan was first introduced to mountains and kings and capitals. Through her stories he first imagined the palaces of Kathmandu, and through them he first had a sense of his own place in the world. Sukumariya's stories were the unwritten, unknown history of the flatlands of Nepal. It was the story of the people that felled its forests and tilled its land. It was also the story of imperialism, of kings who summoned and families that followed in hope. If the stories were to be written, one could begin by saying—long, long ago, when the world was more animal than human, when amid thick trees lived beasts, when man died quickly of snake bites and slowly of malaria, then . . .

Then, somewhere in that beginning, Manmohan's ancestors, like Sukumariya's ancestors, had come to the flatlands of Nepal from the bordering villages of India. They had stumbled upon an expansive jungle where orange tigers rested under branches, and dark rhinoceros drank from streams. There were pheasants, monkeys, and vipers. The ancestors had wrestled with the jungle and its animals and cleared a space for themselves amid it all. Some had died of diseases they could not name, or of violence they had not anticipated. Those who survived had built clusters of huts to live in. Against the backdrop of jackal calls, they had domesticated cattle, begun a life of farming, and built a village where nothing human had existed before.

As he grew older Manmohan heard from relatives that his ancestors had been among the first to grow garlic in the village and its neighboring areas, and they had used the bulbs as much for medicinal purposes as they had to flavor their food. His ancestors were, therefore, both farmers and doctors. That was an era when all farmers were also something else, and when Manmohan thought of them he was filled with pride.

But despite the pride, despite the affiliation he still felt with those distant, glorious ancestors, Manmohan felt alienated from them. They lived only in the memories of old women and men. They were narrated about nostalgically, or with regret, during lax evenings and forgotten again when mornings brought with them tasks and pressures. No one had recorded the expositions and climaxes of these ancestors. Nobody had illustrated the conflicts underlying their decisions and victories. One could not enter a library and read accounts of their lives and deaths. One could only rely on people like Sukumariya—old, blind, and delirious with having lived too long. By the time Manmohan left Sabaila for Kathmandu, Sukumariya had been dead for nearly twenty years. She had died at the age of one hundred and six and made any history that had presided with her inaccessible and mythical.

As Manmohan grew older, these stories left him restless. When, as a child, he had asked Sukumariya to tell him about mountains, he had wanted to hear tales of kings living in expansive palaces. He had wanted to hear of Sagarmatha, the tallest mountain in the world. He had wanted to hear of people with slightly Mongoloid features, of buffalo meat steamed in pouches of flour, and of foreigners who flew in from distant nations to trek and hike upon snow-capped peaks. When Sukumariya had laughed and said, “I don’t know anything about the pahads. I have never lived in mountains,” Manmohan had experienced intense disappointment. Like the lavender sparrow in Sukumariya’s mural, Manmohan had wanted to fly high above the world and look down with equal insight at the dark, sharp-featured Madhesi, and the fair, flat-featured Pahadi populations cradled within hills and mountains. He was not satisfied with saying he knew nothing of the mountains. And so, here he was now, living in Kathmandu, the city of kings, breathing in the crisp air of the city they had built, heading out early every morning for walks, running to catch the buses that would take him to his office, making progress toward setting up a house with his wife and soon-to-come child. He knew, of course, that despite his job, his walks, his bus rides, and his conversations with vendors, he was an outsider in the capital. Though no longer required to fell forests to expand a king’s kingdom and to gain citizenship, he and his kind were still consigned to positions meant to ease the Pahadi population of its discomfort. This had been the relationship between the ruling Pahadi and serving Madhesi for centuries. It was a near miracle that men like Manmohan could now come seeking jobs in Kathmandu. For the likes of him were posts of teachers and clerks. They could grow to become doctors and engineers in their country. And some businessmen could make money. But Manmohan had to only look around to see that the poorest in Kathmandu mostly belonged to the flatlands. They went from house to house, collecting used bottles and stale newspapers to sell to junkyards. The more fortunate ones peddled vegetables on bicycles they pushed along the streets, singing out their wares like ghosts lost in foggy neighborhoods. The roads of Kathmandu were lined with

Madhesis mending shoes, umbrellas, quilts, knives, and pots and pans. They lived twilight lives, unknown, unappreciated, feared and mocked in the teeming city. It would be decades before Madhesis like Manmohan would be allowed significance in political forums, decades before they would be allowed to serve in the army. These positions of power and decision-making rights were dreams that men like him did not bother to hold.

Of course, Manmohan was astute enough to see that at least among the Madhesis he had the chance to rise. He was educated, confident, handsome, and already he had secured for himself one of the best jobs he could hope for. His job at The Family Planning Center, or TFPC, provided Manmohan with the much required stability in an otherwise foreign and sometimes hostile city. If he wanted, he could already have rented an entire house for himself, and if he currently shared a house with four other men, it was only because an empty house seemed redundant and useless to him. Once Meena and the baby joined him in the capital, Manmohan would move to a single house, not because he would have to but because he could afford to. Eventually, the perks of working for His Majesty's organization would mean a piece of land upon which he would build his own house. Already, working with TFPC had earned him recognition and respect and there were people at work who stood to attention when Manmohan passed them by. They called him "sir." Even those who did not address him as sir addressed him as Chaudharyji. Some in his office were addressed by their first name, but not Manmohan. No one in the office addressed Manmohan by his first name anymore. For everyone at his work, Manmohan was either sir or Chaudaryji, and Manmohan recognized it was no small feat to come from the Madhesh and have Pahadis stand to attention when he passed them by.

MARSIYA

On the day he woke earlier than usual for his morning walk, Manmohan had been living in Kathmandu for four years, and before setting out he glanced quickly through the announcement his housemate had left for him in the kitchen. The announcement was printed on a thin, yellow sheet and stated, in thick, round writing, that the Household Shop situated in Bagbazar, quite close to the Padma Kanya Campus, was shutting down and therefore selling off its wares at remarkably cheap prices. The pamphlet, cheerful and optimistic despite the obvious loss that had prompted it, welcomed all customers for the grandest sale they had ever experienced in their lives.

Randheer, Manmohan's housemate, had informed Manmohan about the sale the night before. He had stated rather matter-of-factly that his uncle, the owner of the Household Shop, was an idiot and a fool who could sustain nothing at all worth holding on to. The statement had surprised and amused Manmohan, but it also made him admire Randheer, a thin, reedy man from Hetauda, who, like Manmohan, was in Kathmandu to make a life for himself. "He spent all my aunt's money setting up this business," Randheer had said, scowling the entire time, "and now, only two years later, he has to shut it down. Before this he had started a business of canned food. Who buys food trapped in a tin box? Is this Amreeka or Vilayat? No, this is Kathmandu. We don't buy stale food hidden in boxes. And now this Household business. Who buys furniture? Tables and chairs? Are carpenters dead? Aunty had warned him, but who listens to women? And now Aunty will be sending desks and cushions over to our house, like she had sent over cheese and fish when the previous business collapsed. But you, Manmohan, you must make the best of it. Your wife will be here soon. You might as well begin to set up house."

Manmohan had thanked Randheer broadly for his thoughtfulness. Meena was currently with Kaveri in Darbhanga and two months pregnant with his child. However, once the baby was delivered and raised to about four months of age, Meena and the child would join him in Kathmandu, and Manmohan wanted to be ready to receive them with at least the necessities.

"There will be a rush at the shop," Randheer had warned. "It will be best if you get there early enough. Maybe by nine. If I happen to get in touch with my uncle, I will let him know you will be coming over, but even so, be early."

And so Manmohan set out early for his morning walk. In fact, when he set out, there were still a few stars dotting the purplish sky, and the morning was dark and misty. He had to be careful not to step on anything sharp or untoward when he left the house and started his walk. Manmohan's room was tucked inside a narrow lane in Maitidevi but once he got off the lane, the road broadened and red-bricked temples rose from the ground and stood duskily against the semidarkness. At a distance buildings stood in drafts and sketches, either hiding or partially hidden by gray fields that occupied most of the neighborhood. The atmosphere was scented with the fragrance of incense that seemed to have mingled permanently with the air. There were many temples and shrines along the path Manmohan walked and he felt a deep sense of calm within him. He wondered at the fact that any hour one could find lamps flickering before these numerous spaces of worship. Their fire was delicate and golden against the half-light and gave the morning an otherworldly feel. Varanasi, the Indian city where Manmohan had completed his bachelor's degree, had been a city of temples, too, and could claim better fame and a larger area than Kathmandu did, but there was a quietness to Kathmandu's streets, a gracefulness and beauty that Manmohan had come to treasure. He especially loved the mornings. He loved the cold air, the empty streets, the occasional morning walker, the people who stepped out early for packets of milk and crates of eggs. In these hours he felt both like a part of something large and insignificant, and he was touched by the beauty of both the emotions. He felt the presence of the gods most strongly before the sun made its appearance in the sky, and he appreciated the quiet devotion that was such an integral part of the people in the capital. In Kathmandu, the rituals of daily living were closely bound to the rituals of prayer and devotion and this living, Manmohan thought, was frank, genuine, and unaffected.

Manmohan walked briskly, aware of the way his body heated with activity and the way his heart rate went up. He felt good about taking care of himself. When he imagined his old age, he imagined himself with a spring in his steps, with a lean body and strong bones. He imagined himself ageless and agile, with his body supporting him until the day he died.

With these thoughts Manmohan stepped into the compound housing the Maitidevi Temple and rang the large bronze bell that hung from a sculpted frame.

Mahalakshmi Namastotay

Devi Mahalakshmi Namastotay, he chanted as he walked around the temple.

It was a tidy, tight, redbrick temple with intricately designed doors on its four sides. At this early hour the doors were still shut and the goddess, guarded by two ferocious lions, slept peacefully within. As expected, lamps lit by some early devotee flickered upon one of the long posts.

Ya devi sarva bhuteshu, shanti rupena sangsthita, Manmohan sang. He completed his round and stepped back onto the main street.

It was marvelous to pray, and to pray so early, to pray first thing in the morning, to know that one had prayed before one had drunk tea or bought milk or spoken to another person. He waited for the feeling of rest and wellness to make him kinder, more tolerant before he turned toward the road again and continued his walk. He now opened up to the people around him. He said Namaste and smiled at other walkers who also stopped at their favorite temples or shrines to pay homage to their gods and goddesses. Most devotees were regulars and Manmohan knew them at least by face if not by name, and he respected and acknowledged their daily endeavor toward good health and good habits. He raised his arm in greeting, but he never stopped or slowed down for conversation. After all, there was a time and purpose for everything. If he wanted socializing, he would do it with his colleagues or his peers during leisure time.

Manmohan walked up a slope and stood before a smaller shrine dedicated to Goddess Lakshmi. Here, too, he rang the bells and said his mantras.

Greetings to you, Lakshmi. Salutations to you, mother Lakshmi, the goddess of fortune and wealth.

The shrine stood beside a grocery store and when Manmohan finished his prayer and stepped out he smiled and waved at the men gathered outside the store for milk and whatever else they needed.

For the most part the roads and lanes were occupied by men during this hour. Other than the woman who manned the grocery store, he seldom saw women out and about in the darkness. They would, however, be coming out soon with buckets and other vessels to collect water in. Not all houses had an abundance of water, and many homes relied on the dharas built at varying intervals to satisfy their need. In this aspect at least Kathmandu was inferior to Sabaila. It was true that homes in Sabaila did not always have taps and showers, but every house, even those belonging to the poorest ones, had hand pumps dug in their courtyards and the pumps never ran dry.

And sure enough, the moment Manmohan completed his second round, the streets of Maitidevi were suddenly crowded with women and he had to zigzag his way through them. The women and their children moved like cantankerous ghosts upon the landscape, many carrying buckets of water and talking loudly to one another. Others were out to buy the freshest of meat or vegetables. There was even the exceptional woman in sneakers out for a morning walk. This was the woman who had servants at home and did not do a single paisa's worth of work in her home. This was the rich, nose-in-the-air Pahadi madam who liked to litter her Nepali with English words and sometimes appeared in public smoking cigarettes. Manmohan stayed away from all women. All women, irrespective of how they occupied the streets, were noisy. They yelled and shouted even if their addressee was as close to them as their own hand. "Ke chha? What's up? Oh, it's disgraceful, the water shortage is really something this year!" It was hard to imagine that these women belonged to the same household from which came the sedate and stately men Manmohan knew, and he had to remind himself that no matter how rich or strong these women were, they were uneducated and crass, often born and raised upon the raggedy corners of hills and mountains and married to the city and its privileges. After all, marriage did not erase or refine one's birthplace, nor did it erase or refine the woman.

One of the reasons Manmohan made it a point to finish his prayers in his very first round was that he did not want to be stuck behind a female devotee. At the temples the woman always took longer than anyone else. She rang every bell hanging from every door and every frame, she performed extra parikramas, muttered more mantras than were necessary, and spent too much time burning diyas and incense while her poor husband shuffled and waited for her to finish. It was torture and Manmohan knew he would never allow Meena to make such a fool of himself or other men.

He would have to train Meena. After all, Meena, too, was a near-uneducated woman from a town that just could not be compared to Kathmandu. Manmohan would have to educate her, set her on the right path.

By the time Manmohan finished his walk, returned to his apartment for a quick bath and a hot meal of daal-rice one of the tenants had prepared—Manmohan cooked the morning meals on Thursdays and Fridays—and arrived at the Household Shop, it was nearly nine o'clock. Thankfully the shop was only a short bus ride away from TFPC, but even so, it left Manmohan with scarcely a half hour to shop. Even at this early hour the streets of Bagbazar were already teeming with vendors selling everything from sweaters to hard pieces of cheese displayed on carpets and scarves spread upon the footpath. Manmohan's eyes darted around to find the Household Shop and he sighed in relief when he spotted it a few shops down from the Padma Kanya Campus. He walked over hurriedly. It was apparent the shop was shutting down permanently and Randheer's uncle planned on salvaging what money he could from yet another failed business. To attract customers, the uncle had placed a table set with his finest collections of bowls and plates outside the shop, and around the legs of the table were tied ribbons and streamers for color and festivity. Bracketing the ware-topped table were mudas and small stools kept out to display the quality of furniture buyers could find within the shop. Large placards announcing the sale were pasted on the walls of the shop and upon the young peepul tree that grew beside it. Cookware, said one placard. Bowls, plates, glasses. Gardening tools. Furniture! Beside the peepul tree a Madhesi tea vendor had set up stall and was beaming at the business the unfortunate uncle had brought to him. Manmohan looked quickly at and away from the Madhesi. He wanted to start a conversation, to ask the man where he came from and where his family was, but he was too much in a rush for that. Already, though it was still very early for any robust commerce, a few customers had arrived at the shop and were excitedly browsing through the samples of bowls and serving dishes. Soon the place would be crowded and transactions would take longer.

Manmohan peered into the shop and saw two Pahadi men manning the lower floor of the shop, and Manmohan nodded in their direction. The shop was long and narrow and Manmohan could see no furniture on the ground floor. What he saw instead were brass and steel cookware—thaals, tiffin boxes, chopping blades, spoons and ladles. What immediately impressed Manmohan was the order and festivity with which the wares were laid out despite the owner's apparent absence from the shop, and despite the fact that the shop was soon to fold. There was a sincerity to this effort that tugged at Manmohan. This dedication to work, he felt forced to acknowledge, was a distinctly Pahadi trait. If nothing else, the Pahadi were a hardworking lot, earnest, frank, and unafraid of labor. A Madhesi, for all his cunning, was often lazy and conniving. Had two Madhesis, instead of two Pahadis, been left in charge of this dying shop, they would have turned up with grouchy faces and put out the tumblers and thermoses with careless haphazardness. The lack of heart would be apparent.

Manmohan entered the shop and nodded at the older of the two salesmen.

"Where is the furniture, sauji?" he asked and the elderly man smiled broadly and said, "Oh, this is a very big shop. Here, there are only pots, cookers, and such. You go up those stairs and there is another room full of desks and benches."

Manmohan thanked the man and turned to a customer who was carefully inspecting some serving bowls. "Isn't it odd that the shop is shutting down? It seems like a fine shop. It is rare to have so much space right in the middle of the city."

The customer, a middle-aged, potbellied man in a tight, gray cabled sweater nodded. "But who opens a furniture store?" he asked. "And then who tucks away furniture in a dingy room on an upper floor? And wooden furniture? I can understand a store for cane furniture, or even metal furniture, but wooden furniture? Who does that? Would you buy a bed or a dresser from a shop? Or would you call a carpenter and get them made to measurement? Some people have no business sense. But I do feel sorry for the poor fellow. Now look at these bowls. They are rather fine. I think some of them are from Hong Kong!"

"Ah," said Manmohan, smiling. "I am a newly married man and haven't yet built my house. I suppose a wooden furniture store does well for me."

"A sale does even better!"

"Indeed!" Manmohan laughed.

Quickly, because he did not have much time, he chose a few plates, bowls, and glasses, half a dozen spoons, three spatulas, and two soap cases. He calculated the amount he owed the uncle as he made his purchases and was amazed at how little it all added up to. Manmohan wondered why the uncle had bothered with this elaborate morning for almost no profit. Did loss really drive people to cut such corners that they had to give away their goods, or did this mean goods were truly exorbitantly priced during better times? Such were the casual thoughts that occupied Manmohan as he selected items for the kitchen he would set up with Meena. He felt he was getting away with loot and his heart swelled with a sense of success.

While the salesman prepared his packet, Manmohan took the narrow steps to the upper floor. It was a rickety affair that, however, reached an expansive space in which were stacked tables, stools, chairs, and short mudas. FURNITURE! said a sign pasted upon the wall at the end of the staircase, as though without proper labeling a customer was bound to misinterpret tables and chairs for something else. Under FURNITURE! the placard stated, "Ask us if you want to check out larger items." A few balloons and streamers were stuck around the sign.

A woman salesperson was in charge of this floor and she asked him if he would like some tea. "You saw the Marsiya outside? Selling tea? We can always ask him for a cup of tea for you," she said.

Manmohan stilled at the word Marsiya. It was a derogative swear word used to address Madhesi people. He had heard the word only after coming to Kathmandu and he still did not know what it meant or why it was an insult, but he knew it was used to remind people like him that they did not belong to the capital. It stood in the same category as kale—darkie—and dhoti, and most Pahadis saw nothing difficult in using it. For a second Manmohan considered reprimanding the woman, then he gave himself a mental shake and said, "I had tea just before I left home. Besides I have to be at work soon. I came in early because I did not want to miss out on the best part of the sale, but I don't really know if I can buy anything after all. How will I carry them home and still be able to get to work on time?"

"Not to worry at all, mister," said the woman. "Why don't you make your purchases now and you can return later in the evening and take your things. I will have them stacked in the corner for you."

"You can do that?" asked Manmohan and pushed the tea vendor out of his mind. "Will you not need space for other items?"

"We will manage, mister. We are not keeping space for new things," she said and laughed.

Manmohan laughed, too, both perplexed and overwhelmed by the woman.

He walked about the room inspecting the items. Clearly, the furniture did not match what a carpenter would make on order, but they were not altogether bad. In fact, he thought some of the tables with their colorful sunmica sheets were rather fancy. Manmohan's room in the house he shared with Randheer and the other tenants was not small, but it was not big enough for large pieces of furniture. He could not as yet purchase beds, for instance, but he could certainly buy a table and maybe a couple of folding chairs.

"How much for the chairs, bahini?" he asked.

"The all-wood ones are fifty rupees each. The cane ones are thirty rupees each."

"And the teapoy?"

"Which one? The green is sixty, and the brown, fifty."

"I will take the green one."

"Will you take it alone or will you take it with the side tables?"

"How much with the side tables?"

"A hundred and ten, total."

"And you can keep them for me? I can come back in the evening for them?"

"Yes, yes." She laughed.

And so Manmohan paid the woman a hundred ten rupees for the tables and ninety rupees for the cane chairs.

"I have never been late for work before," he said as he handed over the money. "I suppose this is what marriage is all about, no? Getting late to work?" He grinned. The woman grinned back. And Manmohan left the shop in a hurry.

Outside the shop the tea vendor called out to customers. "Hot tea. Masala tea. Tea with cardamom in it. Tea however you like yours."

When Manmohan returned in the evening with an open-backed autorickshaw to carry home his table and chairs, the streets of Bagbazar were crowded and the driver had to honk several times before he could find any space to park. The shop, too, was swarmed with customers and Manmohan chuckled at the thought that Randheer's uncle was finally able to do business.

A tight and sudden excitement filled Manmohan. He realized that despite having been married for so many years, despite yearning and craving for Meena some nights, he had never really felt truly married. In the four years since he had first held Meena's hand, he had not spent any real time with her, and now, pushing through crowds, mingling with people who milled around him inspecting cups and thermoses, thinking of stools and side tables, Manmohan suddenly felt married and was overcome with the desire to write a long, detailed letter to his wife. He had never written to Meena before and he realized suddenly that the months of silence between them that were broken only when he visited her in Sabaila had left him lonely in Kathmandu. He had enjoyed the freedom of living like an adult in rented homes with men whose concerns were mature and responsible. He had enjoyed not living in hostels, under supervisions of wardens and teachers, but he recognized now that he had never really been an adult until this moment. He was twenty-five years old, Meena was eighteen. They were going to have a child. He was in Bagbazar, in a shop, buying durable goods at throwaway prices, being thrifty and responsible because he was truly an adult. His job was more important now than it had ever been before. Meena would be a mother and run a house. They would bring in more children. Manmohan ran his eyes over the items in the shop. Practical items made of steel or wood or iron or brass, meant to last decades, and the significance of this took Manmohan's breath away. All of this Manmohan wanted to tell Meena. He wanted to write to her about the students of the Padma Kanya Campus walking toward the autorickshaw stand, now that all their classes were over. They were fresh and young in their uniform of brown khaki sari and red blouses. He wanted to tell Meena these girls reminded him of the day he had stood outside her school, hoping only for a glimpse of her face. How far away that day now was. What children they had been. He wanted to tell Meena about the tea vendor who was still standing under the peepul tree and doing great business. He wanted to tell her about the pinch he had felt when the saleswoman inside had called him Marsiya. He wanted to tell her he had been lonely without her. He wanted to tell her about the houses he found himself looking at, wondering what kind of a house he would ultimately build for the family. It would have a balcony, of course, but would it also have an angan? Were angans completely impractical structures in the cold of Kathmandu? He wanted to discuss this matter with her. Manmohan knew, of course, that he would not write such a letter. Such a letter would show him in a weak light and she would lose the respect and fear he commanded, but even so, for several moments he was gripped tightly with the desire to talk to Meena, then he shook it off and entered the shop.

He went straight up the stairs to the furniture room this time. The saleswoman was still in charge. The long day had made her haggard, and strands of hair stood out comically from her head. She sat on a chair with her brows raised and looked both perplexed and exhausted. Her feet she kept up on a stool. She was a queen surrounded by her population of wicker and wood. The furniture was no longer as orderly as it had been in the morning but the disarray enhanced the feeling of festivity, and the balloons and streamers that had been a little incongruous in the morning now felt well integrated with the room.

When she saw Manmohan, she recognized him immediately and waved her hands at him happily. Manmohan walked over with a smile.

"I will not take much of your time, bahini," he said. "I will take my things and be out immediately. I can see you are busy."

"Oh," she said, "it has been busy. Why were people not buying all this before? Everybody wants a stool and a muda now. Let me ask Gopi to help you with your things. The teapoy is big. Gopi!" she called and a young boy, scarcely a teenager, came up the stairs and stood waiting for instructions. "Take out the mister's teapoy and chairs," she said. "Help this mister load his rickshaw."

Gopi walked to the end of the room and Manmohan followed closely. The boy was young but stout and had a mischievous expression that made Manmohan suspicious of him but also drew him to the boy. Together they carried the green teapoy down the narrow, rickety stairs and loaded it to the back of the autorickshaw. The act of carrying a table down the stairs, of feeling its sturdiness in his grip once again left him aching for Meena and once again he laughed at himself mentally. How silly he was this evening, how juvenile. What he wanted was to collapse time. How would he endure another year without her?

He returned with Gopi for a second round of loading his wares. This time Gopi picked one chair and Manmohan the other and they carefully descended the stairs. Then Manmohan returned to the furniture room and picked up the side tables that came with the teapoy.

"Are you taking the side tables, too?" asked the woman.

"These are the last items. They are small enough, but maybe Gopi should help me with one. It will be faster that way."

The woman frowned and pulled her legs away from the stool upon which she was resting them thus far. "But you paid for only the teapoy. You did not buy the side tables. How can you take them?"

Manmohan stopped. "No, no," he said. "I paid for the teapoy and the side tables."

"Not at all. Here, look at the register. I have marked down all the purchases. Teapoy sold to the Marsiya, it says."

Manmohan stilled. "Marsiya is not a good word, bahini. My name is Manmohan."

"What has happened?" asked Gopi.

"I paid for all the three tables but bahini here has made a mistake and is giving me only one," said Manmohan, trying to avoid the word that still hung in the air and was recorded in the register.

"Look here for yourself, Gopi. What does the register say?"

"I cannot read and write. What does it say?" asked Gopi.

"It says he paid for only one table and now he is saying he paid for all three."

For a few seconds Manmohan stood reeling, then he wondered if he had indeed bought only one table, though he had meant to buy all three. Perhaps he had made a mistake after all.

"Never mind," he finally said. "I will take all three. I will pay for them now."

Gopi laughed, the mischief in his eyes dancing. "I see what is happening, Kavita didi," he said, his laugh turning into a guffaw. "Do you see what is happening? I see what is happening." He looked at Manmohan with an appreciative glint. "It is a clever thing to do. You, Marsiya, you are a clever thing. You win this way and that way. What is the harm in trying? It is a clever thing." He continued to laugh, but his eyes burned and Manmohan's mouth filled with the taste of filth.

Sukumariya was so old she knew trees when they were seeds, fields when they were jungles, and men when they were beasts. And sometimes she told stories about those times . . .

Well, she said, now that I am so old, I have my doubts. Did I really see him? Did I really see a king? Or did I see a boy, young as I was, on an elephant? What did I see? I wonder.

He came on an elephant and many others came behind him, on horses and on foot, with dogs, spears, and guns. When they came they hunted. There were white men with him, people either so colorless they were ghosts or blotched red with heat. Even in January, when the rest of us covered ourselves with wool, the white men were blotched. It was never cool enough for them. The king looked from his elephant. He called upon this one and that one and asked them how it was going and if there were women to be had. He called on my father and said, "You, you must have a daughter that can be had," and my father began to shake.

"I did, Your Highness," Father said, "but they died, each of them eaten by tigers or bitten by snakes."

"Each one?" asked the king.

"Each one," answered my father.

And there I was, alive the entire time. I was at the fields when I heard a king had come asking about women. A joy, unbearable and painful, made me stop my work. To be had by a king! To be a king's playmate! To be a queen!

I began to run, asking whomever I could about the direction in which I should run.

"Don't go that way," people said. "The king is that way, don't go. He is looking to have women. He has already had a few. Some he gives to the white men, some to his men, some he has for himself. Don't go."

But I went, running all along the way. I had heard such things about the mountains. The birds and the flowers that grew on branches. I had heard such things about the capital where the king lived. Palaces and roads and fairs. I had heard such things. If the king would have me, I thought, if I could do a good, pleasurable job, please him without resisting, I could go to the capital.

I ran until I ran into my father and my father stared at me. "Where are you running off to?" he asked.

I hung my head and would not answer. He caught my hand and dragged me away. "Stay here and don't you dare move," he said. He locked me in the shed with the cows and the buffaloes.

And there I stayed, locked with animals, while the king went from house to house, eating meals and having women until the entire settlement became suddenly quiet. I wondered what had happened. I peered from the gaps and saw nothing. When I came out, I was the only woman who had not been had.

There were some who had thrown themselves into the gorge and disappeared. There were some who were had and looked around with big, dark eyes. There were some who cried. Some who laughed. Some who banged their heads. There were women, married and with children, who could neither cry nor laugh. My mother stared at me. She opened and closed her mouth but no sound came out, not ever again. I held her hand but she did not have the strength to hold mine back. Father and I carried her back to the hut and laid her on the bed and I did not know how to hold her again. She cried quietly and I did not know how to ask her to stop crying. All the while I thought of my whore heart that had wanted to cross the forests and mingle with the mountains. All the while I looked at my mother and thought of the king, so young and beautiful on the elephant, with a heart so black, with such intentions as a devil might have.

SILVER-SCREEN GODDESSES

For all her pregnancies, miscarriages, and deliveries Meena stayed with Kaveri in Darbhanga. This was the tradition of marriage. It was understood that only in a mother's house did a woman have the right to rest. In a mother's house a woman could sleep in late, eat as much as she pleased, and be pampered and cared for. Following tradition, too, for each of these events, Manmohan stayed away.

During the first pregnancy he sent her a letter letting her know that he was no longer living in the dera he had so far shared with other men, all immigrants like him who lived in the capital and focused on making money. He had rented the upper story of a tight, somewhat obscure house at the edge of a quiet road and furnished it with a few chairs, a teapoy, a cupboard, and a bed. He had bought a kerosene stove and a few utensils. "If something is missing," he wrote in the letter, "you can tell me when you get to Kathmandu." Most of the letter was dry and informative, but at the end he slipped in a shy sentence. "I hope you like the house," he wrote. "I am waiting eagerly for my wife and child."

Meena's hands shook as she read the last line. She tried to block the tone in which that sentence spoke. She tried not to let the image of the house and its teapoy build within herself. She tried not to think of Kumud, awkward and evasive before Meena left Sabaila. "Find peace with him," she had admonished at one point, looking away, focused on a mundane task. "There is no other way." Meena's house in Darbhanga had changed. Her sisters were married and lived in other towns and villages, and the only people in the house were her parents, her brother, and his new family. His wife had already given him two children in three years and though the house was silent without the sisters, it was alive with the noise of children and the adults who fussed over them. Meena tried to keep to herself, to remind herself daily that this was not her house. This was her mother's house, and Kaveri had explicitly said to her that she was not allowed to haunt the members of this house. Meena kept herself tightly apart.

Then, when Meena was three months pregnant, she bled in the bathroom and lost the baby.

Manmohan came a few months after the miscarriage and took Meena to Kathmandu.

Her journey from Darbhanga to Janakpur with Manmohan was almost identical to the one she had undertaken after her marriage, except that this time in Janakpur Meena boarded a night bus that would take her to the city she had come to dread.

All night she leaned her head against the cold glass of the bus window and stared at the night-bleached world mysteriously passing her by. She felt the bounce and roll of wheels under her. She tried to sleep but sleep would not come and she watched the landscape, dark and vast; then, as the sky slowly lightened with dawn, she was caught unaware by the wraps and folds of dark green mountains upon which she traveled so precariously. Above her hung a mirror-blue sky against which, like a momentary mole, dangled an almost immobile bird. Astonished and breathless, Meena stared at the green, viscous river bending and stretching like a yawn below her feet. *Look*, she wanted to say to someone, but there was no one to talk to. She felt her aloneness then. Her baby was dead, Kumud had refused her, Kaveri had abandoned her. A fear that Manmohan would attack her for having killed their child, or that he would try to show sympathy by embracing her left her restless. She opened the window wider and breathed in the cool air. She drank skies and river. Her dead baby floated languorously, heavily in her body, and in the early hours of the morning, surrounded by a pristine world and exhausted by the guilt and loss she carried like a skull in her chest, she fell back upon her seat and slept.

Among the first things Meena noticed from her new, sparsely furnished house in Kathmandu was the Boudha Stupa across the road. Kathmandu, with its temples and hills, soothed her and from her bedroom window she gazed at the golden pinnacle of the stupa and the strings of prayer flags whispering with the wind. After Manmohan left for work, she sat by the window and watched people going to and coming from the Buddha's temple. She tried to imagine the lives of these people, their desires, but they seemed strange and distant to her and she gave up trying. Instead she watched them as one would a movie, enjoying the aesthetics they lent to the streets and to the day. She conceded there was something beautiful in the red saris and the gold nose pins the women wore, and the beige kurtalike garment of the men. Some evenings Meena walked over to the stupa and sat on the broad steps skirting its bulging belly. Some evenings she leaned against the cool, round body of the temple and fell asleep. She woke to lamps lit by strangers and to rust-orange monks smiling and talking quietly beside her. From high above, the eyes of Buddha looked down at her, somewhat sternly, reminding her to go home, and she walked back to her new house. In the house, almost absently, she cooked on the green-and-gold stove Manmohan had presented to her with such a flourish on her first day. Two months after she had arrived to the calmly pious, coolly distant streets of Kathmandu, and the hot, bothering demands of her husband in their bed, Meena got pregnant again and had to be sent back to Darbhanga.

For her first two pregnancies Meena decorated her room at Kaveri's house with pictures of gods and goddesses. The radiant blue skin of baby Krishnas looked upon her from all four walls. She found an iconic painting of a baby Saraswati on the lap of a wise Brahma, smiling beatifically at the world, and this she hung on the wall that supported the bedroom door. Beside baby Saraswati, Sita strolled in the jungles with her sons, Luv and Kush. There was baby Ganesh riding a mouse, though Meena tried not looking at the elephant god too often. She did not want an elephant-headed baby. There were no Hanumans or Garudas. Upon the door Shiva sat on the Himalayas with his family. Right below Shiva was Buddha, his eyes gently closed and unlike the stern eyes that had looked at her from the stupa. She was surrounded by tens of gods, but it was to Buddha that Meena spoke. Please, please, please, she pleaded, scarcely able to voice her fears. Don't let the baby die. Don't let the baby die.

After Meena's second miscarriage, Kaveri held her daughter to her breasts and rocked her gently. "It does not matter, my dove," she said, gently rocking. "There will be more, many more. What do gods know of motherhood? They themselves are a barren lot. Don't worry about them."

"I did not mean what I said," Meena said, returning again and again to the day she had wished her child dead. "I was foolish. I did not know what I said."

"Hush, my baby. Hush. Hush," rocked Kaveri.

After her second miscarriage, Manmohan waited for six months before bringing Meena back to Kathmandu. This time he rented a house closer to his workplace and added a radio to his collection of furniture and stove. He gifted the radio to Meena and left early for work. All day Meena listened to the radio and in the evening she stepped out to buy vegetables and grains. Sometimes she took the lane that branched off the main road and went to the Pashupatinath Temple. The lane sloped down, then leveled, then rose, and was lined with trees and shrubs dotted with a hundred monkeys. There were monkeys crossing the lane, monkeys sitting on the short wall that seemed to exist just so monkeys could sit on them, monkeys eating bananas and sweetmeats they had stolen off devotees. Meena sat on the short wall and watched the monkeys grooming one another. Sometimes, when she watched mother monkeys carrying their babies on their backs or their stomachs, Meena turned away from them toward the lane where women clad in bright red saris made their way to the Shiva's temple, each hiding their offerings to the gods under their shawls. The monkeys watched her curiously but said nothing. They were not used to humans sitting so casually with them.

It was after her second miscarriage that Meena began to dissolve and, for little moments of the day, become air. The first time she turned into air, the morning was bright and her uterus, so full only a few hours earlier, was clean and empty. She lay in a hospital bed trying to focus on her parents. Kaveri and Bilash sat across from her on hard, metallic hospital chairs and at one point Meena raised her hand to call to her parents but she could not see her hand. She looked hard, but she could not see her fingers or her nails. She called out to her mother but realized there was neither voice nor silence in her mouth. And there was nothing in the world out there that she could call or not call to. For a second she wondered if she had fainted, but knew she had not. It was just that she was no longer associated with her body. She did not know where exactly she was. Perhaps she was with her babies, her dead ones, in that place invisible to the living. I am sorry, she said to her babies. I did not know what I had prayed for. She tried to pull herself back from the invisible place and when she could not, a slight panic entered her. Where was she? She could not see her hands, her thighs, her feet. She noticed with a start that she could now see her parents clearly, but they looked through her. She did not exist. She had dissolved and become air. I am sorry, she said again to her dead children.

The next time she became air, Meena was on the wall with the monkeys. A young monkey sat beside her, casually drinking from a water bottle. The young monkey made Meena laugh, but when she opened her mouth, no laugh emerged. And then, once again, she had no hands or fingers or toes. It was only after the young monkey threw the water bottle, now empty, on the lane, that Meena's body returned to her, and Meena wondered if the monkey had trapped her body in the cheap plastic bottle, like the genie in the story. "Don't think I will do some magic-shagic for you now, Mr. Monkey," she said to the monkey. "You can trap me as much as you please, but once I am free, I am free." The monkey wrinkled his nose at her and jumped off to the tree behind them.

For her third pregnancy Meena decorated the room where she had lost her first two children with Bollywood posters. Sensual, fertile, corporal, voluptuous Bollywood to oppose the barren, lifeless, and materialistic gods. Where Buddha had once lived, she pasted portraits of Madhubala and Dev Anand, and between the door and the ventilator above it she pasted cutouts of Dharmendra and Amitabh from *Sholay*. If this child lived and was a girl, Meena decided, she would be as beautiful as Madhubala; a boy would be Dev Anand, or maybe Rishi Kapoor. Meena's heart fluttered for young Rishi, fresh like a girl in *Bobby*, smiling at her from the wall that had once belonged to Saraswati and Sita. No more Krishnas for her now. Now Hema Malini, Dharmendra's *Dream Girl*, floated in the room like soft mist.

Now, Meena prayed to Geeta Dutt and Rajendra Kumar. She confided her fears and hopes to Dharmendra and to Rekha. All afternoon, while she felt the baby within her in half jubilation, half dread, she listened to songs on the radio Manmohan had given her and which she had carried with her to Darbhanga, soothing the child within with melodies of love. *I cannot live without you*, one song went. *If you do not come, I will live no more. I will know nothing of love if you do not come.* She abandoned incense and divine calendars and took up film magazines and song lyrics.

And indeed, what the gods of heaven failed to gift Meena, the gods of the silver screen gave to her with ease. Adi was born to her quietly, without fuss, and Meena's father, the first male to hold the infant in his arms, wept with joy. "Aditya," he uttered between sobs. "He is our little Aditya."

When Adi was four months old, Meena returned to Kathmandu and began a furtive and stealthy search for sinful cinema. Her third home in Kathmandu was as surrounded with temples and stupas as had been her first two. At every few steps rose a temple, elaborate or simple, greasy with lamp oils and smoothed by the touch of devotees. One had to be careful on pavements, which were sometimes decorated with mandalas and diyas. There were incense sticks pushed into bananas and potatoes and left before trees, stones, doors, and roadside gargoyles spilling water from their mouths under which women dressed in petticoats tied high above their breasts washed clothes and took baths. The air smelled of oil and perfume. Barks of trees and faces of stones were dotted red with vermilion. In the compound of one of the temples lived two colossal tortoises believed to be a thousand years old. They walked their slow, imperceptible walk and chewed on cabbage leaves. All around women, wrapped inevitably in their red saris, walked briskly and decidedly, chanting Shiva's name and bowing before temples, trees, stones, doors, and statues, as they made their way to shops or relatives or offices.

Meena ignored them all—gods, tortoises, praying women. Every morning she waited for Manmohan to leave for his work at TFPC, and after his departure she rummaged through his pockets and bags for money. Manmohan did not give money to Meena because he brought with him groceries and eggs in the evenings. Long-lasting products like oil, sugar, spices, soaps, and creams were delivered to the house once every fortnight, and rice and legumes often came to Kathmandu in big sacks all the way from Sabaila. If there were months when rice and wheat could not be delivered from Sabaila, then these items were added to the fortnightly list. Once a week Manmohan brought along chicken or mutton with him. He enjoyed mutton liver and the gizzard of chicken and when he could find them in good condition, he bought two hundred and fifty grams of one or the other. Once a month, during the correct season, he brought fish. Once, since Meena had begun living in Kathmandu, he had brought home a quarter kilogram of prawns.

Money, according to Manmohan, was of no use to Meena. She did not shop for clothes for herself or Adi. She was not expected to leave the house for films or restaurants.

It was over time and through diligence that Meena discovered Manmohan's hiding places. His pants, crafted by the tailor above the Tik-Top Samosa Shop, always had chor pockets, or thief pockets, stitched to the inner side of his waistband. His coats and blazers had pockets in the inner side of their lapels, and these pockets were secured with zips and buttons. If Meena was lucky and Manmohan had not already deposited the money in the bank, and if he had not decided to put the pants away for wash, if he had not worn a particular coat to work and emptied it completely, she could find occasional twos and fives in them. She pulled out a few notes and stashed them in her own hiding place. These discoveries and profits were rare and Meena was careful about how she spent her money.

Once Manmohan left, she picked up her baby and walked the city of temples in search of cinema halls and private screenings on small televisions. She found them tucked behind shrines and shrubs, and she entered dark auditoriums filled with the sounds of fantasy and lost herself within the hushed and excitable crowd. Oftentimes she was the only woman in the auditorium, and always she was the only woman with a baby in her arms. To keep her child quiet, she carried a small box of honey into which she dipped her finger and offered it to her son to suckle on. Once the movie was over, she returned home without turning to the gods. What did they know? The barren lot.

Meena neither knew nor cared about what Manmohan did in his office. He never spoke about his work with her and she never asked, though she did meet several of his colleagues over the years. Manmohan liked to have his friends over at their house. He liked showing off his pretty wife to his friends. He liked the effortlessness with which he could ask Meena to make tea for them. He took pride in showing Meena his friends, all urbane and erudite, speaking Nepali, Maithili, and Hindi with equal ease. He laughed when Meena tried to speak Nepali. "You stick to Maithili," he said to her. "What do you need Nepali for?"

Away from the movies, in her alien house, Meena left the radio on as she worked through the day. It was on the currents of music that she visited her dead children, momentarily vanishing from the world of the living to soothe her other babies. Inhabiting both worlds was exhilarating, now that the journey no longer filled her with dread.

When Manmohan returned in the evenings, he found his wife in the kitchen, tunelessly humming the latest Bollywood craze. Even after the third miscarriage, which happened a year and a half after Adi was born, Manmohan came home to a humming wife. Some days he found her music brave. On other days the songs annoyed him. "Do you have no heart?" he asked her. "Singing, singing. Your child is dead and still you sing?" When Manmohan spoke, Meena turned to look at him absently, then she turned away, as though she had forgotten who he was. What she saw where Manmohan stood was a garish puppet making incoherent sounds. Sometimes his absurd existence reduced her to laughter and it was only through singing that she could control this laugh.

"Look at your father," she whispered to the two-and-a-half-year-old Adi as she tickled him. "Isn't he ridiculous? Only you are a real monkey," she said, kissing him all over. "You are my potato bony butts. Oh, you taste like oranges and apples, my mad sack of sugar." Adi would break into giggles.

And then she was pregnant again and the old dread of death, the guilt of misspoken words and murderous thoughts, the anxiety of childbirth even as she prayed for its safety had Meena shivering again. Let it be well, let it be well, let it be well, she prayed, and in a soft, hidden corner she hummed a different song. Let it be a girl, let it be a girl.

MANMOHAN MEETS MR. KAJRA

Manmohan's problem was his indelible tie with India. His skin was dark, and he had sharp features. He looked Indian. He spoke the language of his Indian ancestors, ate the ancestors' food, enjoyed the distant ancestors' music, adopted his ancestors' customs, and married a woman who came from the ancestors' land. Despite the national anthem he was taught in his school, despite the fact that his village followed the Panchayati Raj (panchayat system) laid down by the royal Nepali rulers, despite the fact that he traded with Nepali rupees and celebrated holidays marked in the Nepali calendar, he was tormented by the loves and fears that had marked his Indian ancestors. Like his ancestors, Manmohan was distrustful of the Boy on the Elephant, who, under the guise of rule, had plundered, looted, and raped the land his ancestors had tilled. Occasionally, he forgot the ancestors and became the Boy on the Elephant, became king—the high and mighty ruler who looked down from his seat—and during these moments Manmohan felt infused with power and authority. During these moments he felt he could walk the streets of Kathmandu and take on his Pahadi neighbor with strength and virility, but these moments were brief and unsatisfactory. Eventually, the image of Sukumariya's mother, raped and bruised, looked back at him with her mute eyes and Manmohan became a young boy running from a careless, cruel king.

It was during a time when Manmohan felt most stifled by his situation in Kathmandu that he met Mr. Kajra. Preeti was two then. Adi five. The meeting was accidental and took place in one of the New Road shops that sold imitation jewelry made of Tibetan stones. It was a spring morning and the two men stood before shop number 43 and surveyed the items on display. As Manmohan inspected, he wondered how such a shop was even possible, and who would possibly buy such chunky and laborious pendants and rings. Beside him, Mr. Kajra contemplated which neckpiece he could pick for his wife. And quite by chance a conversation began between the two men. Or perhaps the conversation was not so accidental after all. After all, what triggered the conversation was not the Tibetan necklace of blue and maroon stones, but the fact that the two men shared a history. Mr. Kajra—dark, thin, sharp featured—spoke in a broken Nepali that revealed immediately that he was a foreigner to the city, and Manmohan, because of his affinity and abilities with Hindi, immediately became the translator between Mr. Kajra and the shopkeeper. For fifteen minutes Manmohan translated, pointing to pendants Mr. Kajra wanted to check for his wife.

"Metin has strange tastes," Mr. Kajra said, chuckling, "and at least sometimes I like to be able to get her exactly what she will like."

Mr. Kajra was Manmohan's foil. For instance, Manmohan too spent time buying things for Meena when he went off on trips. Almost all the saris Meena wore were ones Manmohan had bought for her. It had never, however, occurred to him that Meena might have tastes and preferences that were unlike his or, as Mr. Kajra put it, were strange. He bought what was cheap, what was durable, and what was brightly patterned. That Meena might have preferences for strange designs never occurred to Manmohan. And though Mr. Kajra's shopping habits did not consciously make Manmohan reflect on his own relationship with his wife, he was struck by Mr. Kajra's romantic ways—his agony over clunky jewelry, his amused chuckles as he inspected first this then that stone, the openness with which he talked about his wife—all this struck Manmohan as deeply frivolous and boyish and within minutes Manmohan ascribed Mr. Kajra's boyishness to an ease of life. Mr. Kajra was clearly rich, and men with rich, easy lives could afford to never grow up.

In the fifteen minutes that Manmohan worked as a translator between Mr. Kajra and the Tibetan store shopkeeper, Manmohan learned several things about Mr. Kajra.

Mr. Kajra, he learned, was from Gorakhpur, a city close to the border between India and Nepal, and his father had supported his family by driving a taxi in Bombay. He had sent money home each month so his three sons could get strong educations, strong morals, and a strong sense of self. Mr. Kajra's brothers were ashamed of their father's job, but all Mr. Kajra ever felt for his father was love and respect. "Love and respect, Manmohan," Mr. Kajra said, "conquers everything. If your actions are propelled by love, success will come to you. If your actions are actions of fear or struggle, you will fail. You might make money, but you will fail."

And so, even though, unlike his two brothers, Mr. Kajra was no good at studies, he eventually succeeded where his brothers failed. Mr. Kajra's father took him to Bombay and there Mr. Kajra learned his father's trade and drove a taxi in the nighttime. During the day he apprenticed with a cook and learned everything there was to learn about making sweets and frying fish. Three years later, Mr. Kajra started his eatery in Bombay—a small, clean, stylish, and immensely successful food-on-a-cart arrangement under a sprawling banyan tree. Two years after his success he returned to Gorakhpur to get married. He married a girl from Nepal because his mother was a girl from Nepal and he loved his mother.

"Like I said, Manmohan, everything motivated by love leads to love. My Metin is a pearl."

Mr. Kajra went on to open and run several restaurants in Bombay—some in rooms, some in open spaces, always near trees. Then, after Metin had delivered two children—one girl, one boy—he opened his first restaurant in Kathmandu. "Kathmandu is a gold mine," he said. "It is blessed by Pashupatinath and all seeds grow to sturdy trees here."

Now, Mr. Kajra's restaurants in Kathmandu were his pride and were visited by the people of all pockets. Mr. Kajra visited Nepal four times a year to sort out accounts and records, and on the fateful day he met Manmohan, he was on a lookout for an accountant for one of his restaurants. "You are smart, Manmohan," he said, "and with time you could be my chief accountant. What do you say?"

Manmohan's heart swelled. Mr. Kajra was not a friend, not a prospective boss. He was an ancestor, and when he asked Manmohan to look after the accounts of his restaurant, what Manmohan felt was a deep sense of homecoming. What Mr. Kajra wanted, Manmohan understood without having to try, and so when Mr. Kajra asked, Manmohan gave with trust. When Mr. Kajra patted his back, Manmohan grew warm with pride. He did not have to like Mr. Kajra to love him.

And so it was that Manmohan agreed to meet Mr. Kajra and his wife over a meal at Koyla.

"So, what do you think, Mohan?" Mr. Kajra asked, showing Manmohan his restaurant. Manmohan nodded enthusiastically and genuinely at everything. Finally, when they took their seats, Manmohan ate a dish of pork chili, poking his fork deep into the chunks and watching the fat that oozed. Mrs. Kajra drank a green, minty, frothy drink from a fat glass. Mr. Kajra ordered momos. "Nepalese don't appreciate their momo enough," he said. "When in Kathmandu, I eat nothing but."

Mrs. Kajra sat beside her husband and smiled at his enthusiasm. She had a way of smiling with the straw still in her mouth. She wore a blue sari and a thin string of pearls round her neck. Manmohan wondered if they were real. Did rich people only and always wear real jewels? Mrs. Kajra made Manmohan somewhat uneasy. It seemed to Manmohan that she was too quiet, too dismissive of everything around her. Even the minty, frothy drink was drunk dismissively, without care. It was a very foreign way of drinking. Manmohan had seen tourists drink their drinks that way, without deference, drinking not for taste but for benefits, for rehydration and keeping fit. He was somewhat ashamed of enjoying his own dish of meat so much. He ate carefully, digging his fork deep and taking his time chewing.

"So the plan," said Mr. Kajra, "is to start a chain. Have you been to America, Mohan?" Manmohan shook his head. "It is a place worth going to," Mr. Kajra said, "though not a place worth living in. I cannot understand people who go and never return. That baffles me." He spoke as he chewed, relishing his momo. "But there is much to learn from them. Hard work. Now that can be learned from them. Honesty. Business. They have chains and franchise and societies and clubs for everything from outdoor hunting to indoor picnics. That is the kind of place it is. Like a machine. Thoroughly organized." He popped another momo into his mouth with his fingers. "I am mesmerized by them. I want to start a chain, Mohan, a food chain that will provide top food at low, affordable prices. A chain that is in some ways a social equalizer, one with enough reputation to attract the rich, and affordable enough for the needy. You get the picture?" Manmohan nodded. "Metin thinks it an excellent idea and Metin never thinks wrong. Everything we have ever achieved we have achieved through her intuition." Mrs. Kajra smiled her smile.

"I like Kathmandu, Mohan," Mr. Kajra went on, smiling and relishing his food. "There is a newness to this city despite its ancient temples. The people are somehow new here. They like the global, the international. They particularly like the American. They like new experiments and new ideas. To them all things new are challenging. Look at the fashion among the young; it's jeans and T-shirt, jeans and T-shirt. Look at the music. I don't even know what the Nepali dress is. I love the curls on the older women's heads. You don't have to be a society woman to grow curls on your head here." Manmohan still waited. His fork stayed in his hand, unused. He listened. "I want you to be a shareholder, Mohan," Mr. Kajra said and Manmohan put the fork down. It clattered on the plate. "You understand the market better than we do. We will give the service, you keep the books, analyze the market. We need someone we can trust, someone a little bit like us." There it was—the little bit like us—the shared language, the shared history.

Manmohan took a bite of his pork. He felt the piece travel down his throat and pause fractionally in his chest before pulsing slowly toward his stomach. He took a sip of water. "I don't have that much money," he said.

"We don't need the money. We have the money, and the rest the banks will provide. We need a different kind of support, one entirely on paper. We want you to stand in as collateral with the banks, but only and only if you want to. Metin wanted me to ask you first only because both of you are fellow villagers. There are other people we can ask and we will hold no grudges. You will continue to handle our accounts."

Manmohan looked at Mrs. Kajra. A fellow villager?

"Metin is from Mojendranagar," Mr. Kajra said but it still made no sense. Mojendranagar was the village next door to Sabaila.

"Haan kahi deyu," Mrs. Kajra said. Say yes, said in Maithili. Manmohan felt a cool, soft breeze inside him, like a fan on a hot, stifling day. He scarcely spoke Maithili and when Meena spoke it, he cringed a little, and yet here it was, Maithili, spoken by Mrs. Kajra, who had not said a word so far. The entreaty, made with a smile and without a hint of the city in it, caught Manmohan and put him almost in a daze. How was it possible? This simple pride in her small, poor village that had nothing but cows and buffaloes to boast of? This unyielding perfection. His own tongue felt tired now, speaking Nepali all day, never letting the Maithili climb up.

"Kenake na chinhechiyau hum ahan ke?" he asked. How do I not know you?

"Baud duniya hai." It's a big world.

"Kanka ke duniya hai ab." It's a small world now. And they laughed. The world had indeed shrunk, become small and comfortable.

And so the deal was made over another round of dinner and drinks. The waiters sensed the change and were elevated, too. They turned the music up. They came smiling. They bowed. They addressed Mr. Kajra with a familiarity they had not displayed so far. "After so long you have come, sir and madam," they said.

Because Mr. Kajra was an Indian, Mr. Kajra explained, he could not start a business in Nepal without a Nepali citizen's backup. A Nepali citizen was required to stand as assurance to the banks. The citizen was to assure the banks the businessman was of good character and smart mind, and that if something was to go wrong the citizen would take the blame upon himself and give up his own property to cover any and all losses caused by the businessman's conduct or misjudgement. Because Mr. Kajra was an Indian, the banks could not take over his property in case of loss or fraud.

"Everything I have started in Nepal has a Nepali's backup," Mr. Kajra explained. "Until recently it was my father-in-law, but the man has passed away now and Metin has no relatives she knows or trusts enough, and she herself became an Indian citizen once she married me. No person who has ever stood as backup for me has ever suffered any loss. On the contrary, there has always been profit. You know the Jains?" Mr. Kajra asked, and Manmohan nodded. "They were my backup for my bakery at the Annapurna. Nothing will go wrong. I would never take any risk to jeopardize you. But it is after all a fluctuating world. I cannot foresee earthquakes and floods, I cannot see catastrophes." Again Manmohan nodded. He knew the Jains. He had always wondered at their sudden growth.

And so Manmohan left his job at The Family Planning Center and started an accounting firm, first with only Mr. Kajra as his client, and then, with Mr. Kajra's initial support, he added a few more. In a few years Manmohan spread his wings and either began or became a part of a few small businesses in Kathmandu and in Janakpur. When Mrs. Kajra's brother, Swaroop, joined Mr. Kajra as his business partner, Manmohan was no longer required to stand as collateral and the small threat of bank capture that had existed in Manmohan's life vanished. He was a free man, an accountant for Mr. Kajra and several other businessmen. He was successful. He was settled. He bought land in Ganesh Basti. He built a house. Meena started a garden.

BOOK THREE

PREETI

JAI SANTOSHI MAA

I was born three years after Adi. Two years after my birth, Rajkumar Kohli's horror fantasy, *Jaani Dushman*, hit the theaters in Kathmandu. In India, the movie was a raging success and Ma heard much high praise about the film from her sisters (plot: murdered newlywed husband turns into a ghost and avenges himself by killing newlywed brides) and so, during a week when Papa was away, Ma took Adi and me (already displaying some fear of the dark) to a dark room full of ghosts and screaming brides. While Ma and Adi ate Wai Wai straight out of the packet, I wept and cowered in fear.

For the next three years Ma watched no movie on the big screen. She spent these years trying to coax me into the theater, but terrified by sounds and images buried deep within my subconscious, I refused. Images of bloody mouths and dripping eyes surfaced in my dreams, and when I woke, unnerved with fear, I saw ghosts in the room, stuck to walls and hidden within coats and jackets hanging from pegs. A particular woman, fluttering inches below the ceiling, caught my attention and I could not escape her. If I closed my eyes, she clung to the bottom of the fleshy pink of my eyelids and writhed there as though experiencing demonic convulsions. Even after I had forgotten the details of the movie, I dreamt of hairy ghosts and tainted brides. I would wake with a start and turn to Ma for comfort. Some nights I found her beside me. Some nights she was nowhere. Some nights I was convinced the person asleep by my side was a ghost and I squeezed my eyes tightly shut.

What finally saved me from the horrors of the cinema was a reshowing of the movie *Jai Santoshi Maa* (plot: Goddess Santoshi Maa loves her devotees) the year I turned six.

Now, at forty, I no longer remember scenes from *Jaani Dushman* but I carry in me some clear images of *Jai Santoshi Maa*. I remember, too, my mother groveling before Jeevach Uncle, our only Christian relative, living with us while he trained with my father to become an accountant. He was sweet, down-to-earth, and eternally thankful to my parents for allowing him shelter in the city. When *Jai Santoshi Maa* was back in the theaters in Kathmandu, Ma recognized an opening in her rapidly closing world. If the ghosts of *Jaani Dushman* had crazed her daughter, then perhaps the gods of *Jai Santoshi Maa* could exorcise them?

"Just take her, please!" she implored Jeevach Uncle, near tears. "Do whatever you have to. Drag her there! Please!"

Dear Jeevach Uncle, of whom I was inordinately fond because he bought me sweets and doughnuts at a time when sweets and doughnuts were luxuries, relented before my mother's heartfelt plea.

I, of course, had to be tricked. Bribed with extra sweets and extra doughnuts. Promised a ride around the market on Jeevach Uncle's bicycle. Flattered and entertained. And I, a lovely duped child, perched upon Jeevach Uncle's cycle, and pedal-pedal-pedal, trinn-trinn-trinn, we went around the market, harmlessly passing Jai Nepal Cinema Hall a few times before I understood the trap set out for me and began a screech to rival a witch's shriek. There were a few policemen out on their tall horses, lackadaisically patrolling the streets, and any other day their handsome sight would have mesmerized me to an awestruck silence, but this day, suspended on my own high ride, I paid them no heed. A line of women selling corn and berries sat against the wall before the cinema hall and they scowled at my cacophony and clicked their tongues disapprovingly. "Lau, lau," the one bundled in a blue shawl said. "What is there to cry so hard?" And one of the policemen, finally distracted by my crying, stopped to look at me and his horse did a little trot-dance in place. "I am taking her to the cinema," explained Jeevach Uncle to the policeman. "She is afraid of the movies," and the two broke into a laugh. I cried louder.

"Lau, lau," the blue-shawled woman said again to her companions, "what is there to cry in that? In our days we had no cinema halls to visit. And our fathers took us to no movies."

And that is when the policeman looked fully at me and told me a little secret about Jai Nepal Cinema Hall. "Do you know," he said conspiratorially, "long, long ago, before even I was born, the Jai Nepal Cinema Hall was not a cinema hall." I listened, albeit disapprovingly, because I had no choice, but also because the policeman was kind, smiling, and handsome in his strapping blue uniform, and because his horse was dark brown with white patches, and because I could sense a story coming on. "It was a crocodile hatchery," the policeman went on, still with the tight secret in his voice. "Do you know what a crocodile hatchery is?"

I shook my head. I did not know what a crocodile was. "A crocodile hatchery is a place where pet crocodiles hatch out of their eggs," said the policeman, assuming I did not know what a hatchery was. "The Jai Nepal Cinema Hall was where the Rana rulers kept their crocodiles. They took the baby crocodiles to the rivers of Chitwan and trained them for crocodile fights. Now is that something or not? Not everyone knows this, but now you do." Had he not been seated so high he would have tickled my chin, but he was perched high and he could only smile proudly at the knowledge he had imparted to me. I suppose, had I known what crocodiles were I would have begun to cry again, but in my ignorance I imagined little wrinkled baby birds peeking out of their fragile eggs and was momentarily cheered. I smiled back at the handsome policeman and he trotted off to join his friends.

And that was how I was placated enough to enter the stuffy interiors of the crocodile-breeding cinema hall, though when the curtains rose to reveal the screen, my fear of ghosts came rushing back to me and I turned to Jeevach Uncle and bit him hard on his arm.

Poor Jeevach Uncle! How he fought my fear. How he kept me down on my seat. He stuffed thick doughnuts into my mouth when I bawled. He held me tight when I tried to run away. When the lights in the hall went off, he was truly heroic, simultaneously holding me down and stuffing doughnuts into my mouth. The movie began and I cried louder, but no ghosts floated out the screen, no sounds of susurrating wind, haunting, singing, disappearing brides, possessed bodies. Instead the world filled with images of sprawling skies upon which the celestials nimbly walked. On earth lived pious devotees who overcame all obstacles simply by the force of their faith. There were songs and dances. Rifts and crimes and redemptions. But mostly there were gods and goddesses, beautiful beings, granting beautiful fates to those who served them.

Surprised and intrigued, I stopped crying. I fell in love.

Jeevach Uncle and I watched *Jai Santoshi Maa* eight times in all, and I watched it an additional two times with an ecstatic and deeply grateful Ma. I have watched no other movie ten times. Jeevach Uncle left our home shortly after *Jai Santoshi Maa* was replaced by another movie and I never saw him again—I heard later that he joined an NGO that cared for abandoned children and I like to think his success with me had something to do with his decision. When I think back to those days I taste sweets and doughnuts. I mouth cheesy, god-filled dialogues. I cry "*Jai Santoshi Maa!*" with my Christian uncle at the end of the reel. I feel touched by the divine. I lose my fear of ghosts.

I have grown up strangely devout and so much of my knowledge of gods and goddesses I owe to the screen—*Ramayana* and *Mahabharata* on TV on Sunday afternoons, *Chalo Amarnath* in the theaters, this despite the fact that I lived in a city surrounded by pagodas and stupas and lamps of devotion. I am embarrassed to acknowledge my faith, and will, to hide my belief, commit extreme actions. I have, for instance, nonchalantly thrown icons of goddesses into dirty, filthy dustbins without wincing. These pretty icons are just rubbish, my actions say, no different from potato peels and plastic packets. These are manifestations of our irrational fears. It is at the moment when the statuettes hit the bottom of the bin that I believe most fervently.

When Ma began her Friday fasts for Santoshi Maa ("Why not? The only useful goddess I have ever met . . ."), I was delighted. Santoshi Maa with her eccentric dislike for all things sour was my favorite goddess and I wholeheartedly endorsed Ma's newfound piety. For almost a year, Fridays were for sweet prasads and sonorous prayers ("Pray loudly. It gives you a clear throat and a good singing voice") and Saturdays for parathas and pickles packed into steel tiffin boxes that went with us to Jai Nepal Cinema Hall where we indulged in three hours of fantasy. After a year Ma got bored with her fasts and prayers and gave up on Santoshi Maa, but we held on to our Saturday ritual.

Every Saturday, for several years, we sat in the darkness of the auditorium and shouted and whistled when the hero appeared on the screen to save the day (ah, Jackie Shroff!); we booed at villains, and despite ourselves, wagged our fingers at them and said—*khucching taala paitala, paanch paisa ko suntala*—the meaning of which evades me even today. Who knows what *khucching taala paitala* means? And *paanch paisa ko suntala* translates to "oranges worth five paisas." It makes no sense, but wagging our fingers and threatening villains with oranges left us heady with excitement. Here, in the dark cinema hall, Adi, Ma, and I echoed fight sounds—*dhisum dhisum*—and fought against bad men with Jackie Shroff and Amitabh Bacchan. We danced with Meenakshi Sheshadri and Neelam, and wept, noisily and shamelessly, at life's every tragedy.

THE QUEEN'S LAKE

Rani Pokhari, or the Queen's Lake, so named because of the gleaming, white temple that stands in the middle of a green, shallow lake, was about seven kilometers away from our house.

Legend speaks of a queen. In one version, the queen, also a mother of an eight-year-old child, is so haughty people break into sweat when she passes them by. In another version, she is a rich and ugly toad and the king tolerates her only because her father is powerful. In both versions her child, a son, is trampled and killed by an elephant. Both versions insist that the day her son died, the queen was sitting under an umbrella in the garden, watching her boy at play, when the elephant emerged from the hedges, gray and large like death, and killed him. As the elephant approached the child, the queen remained on her seat, petrified by suspense, but after her son's death she fell in a faint. The elephant disappeared as unhurriedly as it had appeared.

For years after the son was killed, the queen was unable to tend to herself. She found it difficult to wake up, to bathe, to put her hair in order, to smile at the day-to-day happenings of life. It was not only that she missed her child, it was also the guilt of having done nothing to save him. Over and again she recalled the slow-moving elephant and wondered why she had not shouted; why had she not dashed across to her son and plucked him off the ground? The morning her son died the sun had been bright and blissful in the sky. Its warmth had drugged her. Thereafter the queen was tormented by the feel of sunrays upon her skin and refused to step out of the palace.

The king tried everything to cure the queen's grief. To appease the gods that had cursed him and his queen, he set up prayers and yagnas. He organized games and entertainments. He invited other little boys to play in the garden. He had all elephants slaughtered and all images of the animals banned from the kingdom. He criminalized all mahouts. But nothing cheered up the queen—after all, a queen is not a king. A queen cannot lose herself in rituals and intrigues. She cannot devote herself to laws and murders and systems of justice. A queen, like other women, raises children as correctly as she can. A queen, like other women, dreams of her children, and this queen, haughty or not, ugly or not, had only one child, dark eyed and elfin. And then she had nothing.

After all else failed to resuscitate the queen, the king ordered that a mausoleum be built to commemorate the boy—a white temple standing midlake. The temple had come to the king in a dream, and in his dream the temple had gleamed nobly under misty beacons of light.

Once the temple was built it stood lonely under the sunlight, simple and direct like a plea, the waters at its base glittering. With the temple the king found his peace and let the child go. With time he touched other women, more beautiful than the queen, and with them he had other sons who lived beyond eight years of age. He offered these boys to the queen but she refused the substitution. These boys too were dark eyed and elfin, but they were not the boy she had lost in the gardens.

The temple was constructed thus that the queen could see its luminous body from her windows. The constant view was meant to soften her grief, but became instead the reminder of her loss. Each morning the queen's heart hardened a little more against the gods to whom the temple was dedicated and she drew her curtains against them; then she shut the windows, then she left the chamber and shifted to another wing in the palace. Here she leaned against the walls and replayed, again and again, the afternoon she had dozed off under the sun and the elephant had squashed her child's head. The temple stood helplessly outside the shut windows.

As the years passed, the temple, dull with neglect, began its own slow mourning and the water in the lake began to dry an inch each day, its level dipping until eventually one could see the lake's slimy green underbelly.

Ultimately the king tired of the queen and left her alone. What else could he do? The dignity of a king lies in his ability to rule effectively even under suffering. And so he focused on ruling his kingdom. He focused on agricultural developments and military expansions. He sent men and boys, some as young as eight years old, off to wars, so national coffers could be secured against droughts and famines. Many men and boys died in these wars, and their women, those who were widowed or those who lost their sons to the king's battles, moved slowly toward the drying temple lake. The lake whispered to them. Come, it said. Stand here. Look at me. The women drifted to the lonely temple, to its slimy green lake, and stared into its water. A quiet vine, like a cord, grew from their bodies and disappeared into the sinking, emerald base. All around the nation water bodies began to dry. Wells turned into blind eyes, and parched rivers lay exposed like bare arms upon the landscape. On these arms dead fish were scattered like inert babies. Despite the king's dutiful eyes on the kingdom's fields and borders, the kingdom began to shrivel.

The king was distraught. How long will this go on? he cried. How long will I loot other nations to fill the coffers of my own? How long will I let the grief of one citizen be the death of a million others? Finally, he understood that it had never been about the nation or its people. It had never been about rivers and fishes. It had always been about the child, the elephant, the king who thought all could be substituted, and the mother who would not be consoled.

It had been years since the king had communicated with the queen, years since their son had died. The king pulled in a long breath and sent for the queen.

You must die, he said to her. How else will the kingdom live?

But what about the other mothers? the queen asked. Those who linger by the lake because you have killed their sons?

The king tilted his head and listened.

You are the elephant, the queen said. You trample life under your feet. You are without thought or feeling. You are consumed with yourself. If the land is to be cleansed, you must die first. One grief the nation can bear. But a thousand? How will the nation bear such grief?

Let all mothers who grieve for their children die, too, then, said the king.

And so it was that the queen and all the mothers lingering by the lake jumped into its water and drowned themselves. What else could they have done? The dignity of kings lies in ruling; the dignity of queens and mothers lies so often in death. Their death released the kingdom of its curse and the temple of its sorrow. With a satisfied breath the waters rose around the temple and the fish came alive once again.

The legend of the Rani Pokhari is not make-believe, a false tale meant to attract tourists into its body. The truth of the story has forced the government to build a tight fence around the lake. The fence holds sad, despairing women away from the water. In the afternoons the fence leans in slightly under the pressure of women pretending to watch fish.

They pretend they are there only to feed the fish, but what they want really is to throw themselves into the lake. They pretend to enjoy the sun, though sunrays burn their skins. The fence is strong, tall enough to make climbing difficult, especially in open-toed sandals and saris; it forces the women to head home at sunset, dreaming of death and goldfish. But even so, every now and then, news of suicides surface from the lake and linger over the city.

When I first heard the story I was confused by this sadness, deep like centuries; then, later in my life, when I lost my own babies I felt a terrifying kinship with the leaning women. But perhaps I did not grieve truly, or with any intensity, because as a mother I never went close to the temple or its lake. I stayed away from the place, kept my eyes away from it. The only times I ever touched the fence around the lake was as a child with Ma who would invariably stray toward the lake, as though pulled by the quiet temple, and while we threw fish food into the water she narrated bits and parts of the legend to Adi and me.

"A woman who throws herself into the lake no longer becomes a fish now," she once told us. "Now she becomes the Kichkandi—a magnificent, bloodsucking, man-grabbing witch. She takes on the form of an irresistible woman and wanders these streets around Rani Pokhari. She wears chiffon saris and has long, soft hair. Her eyes are large and helpless. Her skin glows in the moonlight. She targets boys on motorcycles because she likes to wrap herself around them the way creepers frame themselves around trunks of trees. During the motorcycle ride she draws the boy into her body and he falls in love with her. Slowly she leans in and gently sucks his blood, preferably from the back of his neck. Her lips are like silk on his skin and the more she takes from the boy, the more he loves her. She sends the boy quietly to his death.

Death with the Kichkandi is slow and languishing. It is a dream death. Death with the Kichkandi is so exquisite it makes life look vulgar and garish. When the Kichkandi wraps herself around you, you want to die. In fact, you want to watch yourself die because the more you die the more the Kichkandi glows under the moonlight and at this point of your death all you want is beauty."

Ma, the teller of horror stories! Adi was perhaps eight then, the age of the queen's dead child, and he began to cry. Ma shook her head. "No need to cry, Mr. Adi Chaudhary. Just know you will never get a motorcycle. And no staying out until late at night with your lafanga friends. And no moving around with strange girls as though you are some movie actor. And if you keep on with this crying-shrying I will beat you with a stick when we get home. Come now, let's buy ourselves some roasted corn."

Did my mother cultivate still lakes of death within her each time her babies died? Did her madness come from her longing for death? Women, I have learned slowly, are fond of death. They dream often of dying. Even those who are vengeful, who curse, accuse, manipulate, hide; even those who exploit children and starve the old; those who speak in dirty, filthy languages, even they are exhausted by life and long for death. Did my mother go mad because she was forced to live, always, always for those alive around her? Would she have preferred being with my other siblings, unborn but living within her like still pebbles at the bed of running rivers?

"Your father," she told me once, "was never there. I held two dead babies in my palms, and one I never saw, but your father was away each time. He left me with my mother in Darbhanga and waited for me to recover before he came to take me home. He could not deal with the headache of having me around while I still cried. And I cried so easily then. All of you were born in Darbhanga. All my five children."

When I was older Ma told me about her other babies, the two she lost before Adi, the one after him. "My body is a graveyard," she said.

When Adi was born, three years after Papa and Ma settled in Kathmandu and two years after her first miscarriage, the doctors assured her the fault lay not in her body but in the timing of her pregnancies; they revealed her body to her, the nature of its lunar cycles, its ebbs and flows. "Tell your husband to stay home more," they said. "Plan it out."

"Children are revelations of time," Ma said to me. "They are products of that split second when the universe comes together, the body touches the moon, the blood thins, and a life stirs."

Adi's birth, almost unexpected after the miscarriages, transformed and bewildered Ma, filling her with a tight joy that sometimes kept her from sleeping. She stayed up, even when exhausted, just so she could look longer at her child's broad-browed face. She leaned close to him and pulled in deep breaths, filling her lungs with his talcum-scented smell, holding her breath, wanting her baby back inside her womb where she could count his turns, his kicks and hiccups. She wanted so much for there to be only him and only her.

But despite Adi, the pregnancy after him failed, and this time the doctor cautioned her against more children. "Enough," he said. "You have one and he is enough. You don't need a room full of them." He turned to Papa who, ironically, worked at The Family Planning Center at the time and said, "Manmohan, this has to stop. This is enough."

"But I never mattered to your father," Ma told me later. "He would not let me be. Months I would stay alone in the house while he traveled to villages, educating villagers about family planning and condoms and carefully planned ejaculations. He came home from his villages, having spoken to ripe, young women, and wouldn't let me go."

Adi and I grew up watching Ma as one watches the sky. Our souls were tethered to hers and like vast seas rose to her closeness with an expanding of our spirits, and to her distance with melancholy. After Ma died, Adi performed a certain ceremony in which he momentarily became Ma. He wore white cotton clothes and lived in Ma's room. Everyone around him was supposed to pretend he was Ma; pretend that if we sat beside him, we could be with her. I sat with Adi all day, pretending hard. For almost ten days Adi was served Ma's favorite food, played Ma's favorite songs, told stories about her. This was supposed to soothe him and lessen the pain of her death, but I could see how traumatized he was. He could not rest. He could not eat. He missed her with an intensity only I could understand.

When my son was born, I immediately wanted a sibling for him, not because I was afraid he would otherwise grow up lonely and sad, but because I knew only a sibling would understand his grief when I or my husband died. I imagined my son in a room, alone, longing for his dead parent, and then I imagined him with a sister. If he had a sister, he would make it through. But my body, too, turned out to be treacherous and I lost two babies after my son was born. And frightened of the graveyard within me, I gave up.

I think about grief sometimes; I think about the ways grief is different for different people. My grief, when my babies died, was momentary, like a feast, something I indulged in, fell sick from, recovered from, and recalled fondly for the rest of my life. When grief came to Adi, he wore it like a garment that was too long for him. His eyes took on a focused look, as though concentrating on the heavy folds of sadness he dragged along the floor. When Papa was sad, his sadness ballooned inside him and escaped him in heavy, audible sighs that demanded attention and cure.

When I think of grief and Ma, I think of insect wings hardened beneath layers of resin, undetected. Loss, I think, is the plot of a woman's life, and madness is grief's younger sister frolicking on eager toes. She dangles from lamps and ceiling fans, awaiting her moment. She lets go and lands on grieving shoulders at the opportune time. She fits onto the shoulder, like trees onto grounds. She sings, always of loss.

THE SMELL OF HARVEST AND HAY

We moved into our own, brand-new house at Ganesh Basti when I was seven. Our furniture had already been shifted, and on the final day of the move we boarded a blue bus and rolled off to live a new life. Perhaps because it was a Thursday afternoon, a working day, the bus was not too crowded and Adi and I got seats for ourselves in the bus. Adi promptly took the window seat and I pinched him to get him to move. "It's my turn," I reminded him. "You sat there last time," but he pretended he could not hear me and I hit him hard on his thigh.

"If Papa was not here, you would be dead," he muttered in warning.

"If Papa was not here, you would be dead," I mimicked.

"Sit quietly," Papa said from the aisle, where he stood with Ma because there were no seats available for them, and Adi and I stilled for a moment.

Outside the window, parts of the city jogged along with us for short distances before falling away, and slowly the older side of the city gave way to the posher, central space that was now our home. The wide expanse of the road was almost magical and tall lampposts grew gracefully from the sidewalks and lined the streets like thin, elongated beings. I craned my neck at exaggerated angles to get their complete view and groaned in discomfort to emphasize the wrong being done to me by Adi.

The tall lampposts alternated with shorter posts that held His Majesty's portraits high above our heads. His Majesty, Shri Panch Birendra Bir Bikram Shah, leaned against the blue-gray sky, bespectacled and smiling, and spoke softly and lovingly to us almost all the way to our new home. Love your country like you love your gods, he said from one portrait. An act of kindness to your brothers and sisters is an act of kindness to our nation, he said from another. Nepal is a fragment of Lord Vishnu's dreams. We must tend and care for it like a gardener tending to flowers. I read every quote, and the image of His Majesty expanded within me and filled me with a peculiar ache. Had it not been for Adi sitting between us, I would have pushed my head out the window and smiled directly at our king. Had it not been for Papa, I would have yanked Adi's hair and sat by the seat that was rightfully mine. Do not quarrel, said His Majesty. It bitters the sweet drink of life. Despite His Majesty's admonishment, I pulled Adi's hair when Papa was not looking and we got into a fisticuff, and so, when we finally got to our new house, Ma tied us each to a bench and left us out in the sun to bake.

"This is a nice way to start your life in a new house," Ma said, tying us down. "Once you are nicely cooked we will eat you for dinner, and then there will be some peace and quiet in this world, yes or no?"

Though I threw terrible tantrums during the first week of our life in the new house ("This is such a dull house. The walls are not even painted! I will not live here!"), my tantrums were temporary and fake, thrown for effect. A few days after beginning in my new school where I met Sachi; a few visits by Shanta Aunty and her sons—Uddip and Prajwal, both of whom I would one day dream of kissing; a few intricately coiled sweets gifted by Thapa Aunty (and one day she would die and I would realize I had loved Thapa Aunty's spacious home as much as I had loved my own); a few movies watched in Bhandari Aunty's house before Papa bought a television (for the longest time I did not know why Neelam, Bhandari Aunty's daughter, was so thin, and why Bhandari Aunty was so thin, and why her son was so thin, then I realized disgrace, like famine, could make people thin, wiry, and incapable of eating a good meal); a few adventures with Adi; and a few tight slaps from Ma cured me of my bad mood and I became a part of our new neighborhood, Ganesh Basti, in love with all its houses and all its fields, and all the carefree wind that tousled the smell of harvest and hay.

Ma was in love too. She wore her shortest-sleeved blouse and sat on the star-studded floor of our new veranda and grew ecstatic over the quality of the morning sun. "Isn't it lovely, Pirti?" she asked, the sun sliding on her bare arms. She frowned as she thought of our earlier homes, each rented, each unaccommodating and tyrannized by a series of fat, untidy landladies who refused to fix broken taps and ripped off floors. "No balconies even! So dingy it used to be. And no land to plant anything, not even chili-shilly."

Adi and I played Pen Fight on the pistachio-green teapoy Ma placed on our new veranda, and pens knocked each other and flew off tables as we jumped from one end of the teapoy to the other, shouting war cries: "Haaai! Haaai!"

"Why are you mooing like cows?" Ma asked, but she laughed as she watched us and we knew we would never need to stop playing.

In this new house with its copper taps, its starry, sunlit veranda, and the long strip of land running from its feet, Adi and I were invincible, and Ma was always on our side.

Soon, upon that long strip of land, Ma grew chili-shilly, corn-worn, and beans-seans in abundance. Soon, trees laden with fruits lined its edges. Butterflies visited flowers in our flowerpots. Bees hovered. Later came trouble and grief. But that was later. For now, Adi and I flew in the air and Ma laughed.

Initially our land was bare and Doctor Uncle's land, which was separated from ours by a line of slim peepul trees and bottlebrush flowers, looked like a lush piece of paradise beside ours. Every morning Papa looked at Doctor Uncle's land and said, "We should plant peepul trees along our boundary, too, Meena," but Ma shook her head.

"With fruits, Chaudharyji," she said. "We will border our home with fruits."

A few months after we settled into our new house, Ma, Papa, Adi, and I took a trip to Paat Ra Haanga, a small nursery where saplings and trees were neatly arranged in tight columns and where sweet peas nodded in the wind. I walked with Bhimsen, the nursery gardener, looking at flowers growing out of small plastic bags of dirt. Every time I stopped too long before a plastic bag, Bhimsen frowned and clicked his tongue. He checked the plant I halted at to make sure I had not destroyed anything. Finally, because he was so distrustful of me, I broke a snapdog when he was not looking and stuffed the flower into my skirt pocket.

"Duita lapsi," Papa ordered. Two lapsi trees. "Euta rato umba," one red guava. "Euta seto umba," one white guava. Two red plum trees, one apple, one Asian pear, two oranges, one lemon, and one mango.

"Mango? No mango," said Bhimsen. "They will die by next week. I don't know why the Sauji keeps mango saplings here. Mangoes only grow in hot places, like in your village. Not here." For a second I wondered how Bhimsen knew where our village was. I was still too young to know the complex structure of the valley we lived in. I had not yet learned to notice differences between people.

"Lots of sun and water for this one," Bhimsen said when he loaded the shrub of lemon into the cart. The leaves were dark and curly and Bhimsen turned to Adi and said, "Be careful of the thorns. Tell your sister to keep distance. The poor plants have to protect themselves from her." Adi laughed and I huffed away. But the truth was I liked Bhimsen. I liked him because his face was like tilled land, full of furrows and crevices, and when he laughed eddies of wrinkles spread upon his face.

Once all the trees were loaded, Ma bought a dozen clay pots and instructed Bhimsen to load those in the cart, too. Then Papa and Ma held each of my hands and said, "One, two, three, wheeee," and flew me up in the air and perched me down on the cart, amid all the trees and pots. I was so startled by my parents' lightheartedness, so taken aback by their sudden levity that I laughed all the way back home.

I had never seen my parents so infatuated before, never seen Ma so coy, scolding Papa for being silly. I had never heard Papa ask questions neither Adi nor I knew how to answer without helpless giggles.

"Isn't your mother the most beautiful woman in the world?" he asked.

I giggled, unsure of what was going on. The unexpected flight into the air, the ride down the road on the cart, the smell of leaves and clay—all this made me shy of my parents.

The next day Bhimsen came over to help us plant the first few trees. Mostly Bhimsen and Ma worked with the plants. Papa and Adi were in charge of placing the plants at required spots. I was asked to remove weeds, dig out small stones, and bring water to those who were thirsty.

"Farming," Papa said as he distributed the plants, "is in our blood. Do you know, Adi, your father is the first man from his family who is not a farmer? We were among the first Madhesi families called over from India by His Majesty Prithvi Narayan Shah in the early 1700s.

That far back, yes, three hundred years back your ancestors were invited to clear out the jungles of Sabaila and create a settlement. And why do you think His Majesty did that? Because your ancestors were such great farmers! And as rewards they were given so much land, from this corner to that. Real zamindars they were."

"What happened to all that land?" Adi asked.

"Oh, well, land reform and all. But we still are healthy landowners."

"Put your eggshells and tea grains into the dirt," Bhimsen said as he dug. "Number-one-style fertilizer. Where do you want this chap, Sauni?" he asked Ma, and after Ma indicated just where she wanted which plant, Papa and Adi lifted off the "chaps" and brought them where needed. The apple and guava were placed by the water pump, the lapsis beside the tap, one plum tree straight outside the bedroom window, the other by the main gate. The lemon and oranges were lodged in the water tank where their roots soaked while they waited to be planted.

Over the course of the day the land turned into careful rows of craters behind which stood exclamations of thin, young trees. Bhimsen had brought with him two large sacks of cow dung and poultry poop and by the end of the morning he had fed the fertilizers to the open craters.

I moved around, weeding, cleaning.

"A mug of water, baby," Bhimsen called out to me, and I ran to do his bidding. "Another mug. One more." When the bucket emptied, I went to the pump to fill it again and my body flew high on the pump's iron hand. It was an intoxicating day.

At noon Ma served lemonade and oranges mixed with yogurt.

"You know," Papa said after he put a piece of orange into his mouth, "orange achaar is your mother's speciality. Remember, Meena?" he asked, and suddenly, without any warning, Ma and Papa burst into a laugh.

I stared, mesmerized. Adi stared too. Only Bhimsen, who did not know our parents, joined their mysterious laugh.

Throughout the day as we dug holes and made heaps of stones and weeds, as we wriggled our fingers through the dirt to make airway tunnels, as we measured the roots of trees and dug the holes deeper, as we poured water into the cavities, as we filled empty flowerpots with the mud we dug out, as we fertilized and planted, Papa told stories.

"When my father died," he said, "his sister, my aunt-mother, adopted me. In those days people did such things. They raised each other's children. There were so many children in those days no one missed one or two."

"What foolish talk," Ma said, laughing. "You were only four of you."

"So? It only means everyone I left behind in Sabaila wanted me back home. They missed me no end."

I had seen my parents not fight before. I had seen weeks and months when they sat together telling each other what had happened to them during the day, not once raising their voices, Papa not hitting Ma. I had heard them reminiscence about a time when neither Adi nor I were a part of their lives, but I had never seen them this way—shy, apprehensive, lifting their eyes to watch each other, speaking in riddles, almost as though they were secretly holding hands.

And yet, even then, even on this fairy-tale day, I knew this holding of hands was temporary. It had to do with the new house we inhabited, the land we were digging, and the plants we had lowered into the earth. It had to do with the dirt on our fingers and the dream of fruits and vegetables dangling from branches. I knew, though I did not understand, that I worked harder that afternoon than I had ever before so the fruits my parents anticipated would be sweeter than their expectation.

"When I came home from my aunt-mother's house, your uncles and I always made a dash for the lake," Papa said. "There was a small fishing lake a little away from your grandmother's house and it was still as a sheet of mirror until I and my brothers rippled it with our bodies. We were great swimmers and we caught fish like a bunch of cranes! We kept your grandmother busy in the kitchen with all that fish."

When it was time for lunch, Papa went to Chakrapath and returned with momos and we sat on the veranda and ate dumpling after dumpling. This too was new—the picnic. Ma gave two of her momos to me and Papa gave two of his to Adi and when Ma brewed tea for the adults, Adi and I were allowed to take sips. I was full with the momos and the sun, full with the plants and my parents' happiness, and I slipped slowly, slowly, sliding from my sitting position until I was lying on Ma's lap, soft and mellow like the sun, but even as the wind soothed me to sleep I was aware of an unease, of something unbalanced.

My unease was not unfounded. After that Saturday, Ma became erratic once again. And once again it seemed to me that my mother lived in several worlds, and not all worlds were places where I could follow. Sometimes, when Ma thought she was alone, I found her on the terrace talking to an invisible someone with a broad smile on her face. She walked along the parapet, immersed in a fantasy conversation, sharing details I could not always understand. There was a flirtatiousness in her voice, a tinkle in her laugh as she walked, round and round, never tiring of her ghost. Sometimes I stood at the edge of the terrace, waiting for her to notice me, and I was always amazed at how long it took her to see my body. When she did, she stopped suddenly, a little surprised. I expected her to be embarrassed by being caught in her play but she never was. For a few seconds she frowned in concentration, then she smiled again and called me over. "Want a sip?" she asked, offering me her cup of tea, and I shook my head. I had a feeling she was pushing me into some danger, perhaps testing my resolve, and when I held my own, she was both impressed and disappointed.

Ma and Papa returned to their routine soon enough, and some mornings she would not come to the door to see Papa off when he left for work, and some mornings, while he sat on the muda to put on his socks and shoes, she paced within their bedroom, hands tightly crossed, while Papa grumbled loudly about Ma's inability to hold any meaningful thought in her head, and her loud, crass language. "Worse than a villager," he said.

"Stuck in this jungle," Ma cried out from her room.

And other days they sat beside each other, watching TV until Papa suddenly switched channels. "Time for news," he said, and when Ma fled the TV room, he shook his head. "Like a frog in a well," he said.

Papa lapsed into his erratic self, too, and was not around when Ma began the vegetable patch. He was not there when Ma, Adi, and I sowed corn, beans, potatoes, spinach, onions, garlic, mustard into the ground. He was not there when Adi asked if we could keep the left side of the land bare so he and his friends could play on it. He was not there when Ma said, "Of course we can, my fuzz bucket," and left a patch bare. He was not there when Adi and I made plans for a badminton court and a futuristic swimming pool complete with color-changing lights illuminating its base. He was not there to see the abundance we created. He was not there to see Ma bloom in that abundance, like yellow petals of mustard flowers. He did not see Ma pack that abundance into small packets and gift them to people in the neighborhood. A bag of beans, corn ears, and plums for Bhandari Aunty, a bag for Thapa Aunty, some guavas for Sunna's parents. Papa did not see Ma become a part of the neighborhood.

Ours was the best vegetable patch in Ganesh Basti. Maybe Thapa Aunty's vegetable patch was the richest, yes, but she had gardeners who tilled and harvested for her. Even Doctor Uncle had gardeners who tended to his roses and dragon flowers. But Ma did all her gardening herself. In the storeroom behind the house she stored hen poop fertilizer, cow dung fertilizer, and nitrogen fertilizer in separate sacks, and when she was ready to feed the soil she mixed the fertilizers in varying quantities to suit various plants, and the vegetables and fruits that came from these plants were always plump, always the best in the neighborhood. Ma was not, by nature, lavish, but the extravagance of produce in our garden expanded her, made her generous, and her bounty in turn made the neighborhood generous. And so it was that Bhandari Aunty and Thapa Aunty and Sunna's parents sent over little tokens of appreciation as return gifts for Ma. So it was that if they saw Ma on the streets they stopped to start a conversation. So it was that they sometimes came over for evening cups of tea.

Of course it was not always easy, this giving to and taking from the neighborhood. There were competitions sometimes. Sometimes insecurities. There was that one time, for instance, when Doctor Uncle, who rarely engaged with the neighborhood, sent over a cucumber for us. The fruit was so large it must have weighed eight kilograms if not more. Ma stared at the little boy who carried the cucumber to our door and did not know what to say. The boy, no older than me, eight, maybe nine, sank under the cucumber, his eyes large with panic. I had accompanied Ma to the door and when I saw the boy and the cucumber, I felt a tickle in my stomach, a desire to burst into a laugh, but I held back. Ma took the cucumber from the boy and nodded at him.

"Sit in the kitchen, little rat," she said to him, "and I will make you some tea."

She sat him down on a mat in the kitchen. I jumped up on the cooking counter and carefully studied the boy. What a wasp he was! Thin waisted and large eyed.

"What is your name?" Ma asked as she poured milk into a pan.

"Gadahawa," the wasp squeaked.

Ma turned around.

"What now?" I asked, convinced I had heard him incorrectly.

"Gadahawa," the boy repeated.

And so the little tickle I had been holding within me ever since I had seen him spread like cream upon me and I burst into a laugh.

"Gadahawa?" I asked jumping off the counter. "Your name is Gadahawa?"

"Stop it, Pirti Chaudhary," Ma scolded, "or I will give you a hammering."

But I could not stop.

The boy stared at the floor.

Then Ma started to laugh too. "Never mind Gadahawaji. Never mind," she said, trying to control herself. "This Pirti is a donkey and nothing else. Here is a cup of tea for you and a cup for me. Nothing at all for this donkey Pirti, and all the biscuits are yours!"

We laughed while the boy slurped his tea, laughed while he stuffed his mouth with so many biscuits, laughed when he finally ran away.

Later, when Adi returned from school—he came home later because he was older—Ma told him about little Gadahawa.

"How can a person literally be named Donkey?" she asked, wiping her eyes. She mimicked a mother holding a newborn baby in her arms and said, "Ah, you are such a lovely, my little Flower of Rose, I shall therefore name you Donkey. There, there, my Donkey, have some milk!" She guffawed.

Adi laughed, too, though he could not bring himself to approve of our behavior. "You are hideous," he said, trying hard to appear stern.

Of course, Gadahawa's disappearance from the kitchen did not solve the problem of the massive cucumber. The beastly thing was larger than my head, larger than my head combined with Adi's head, and it was clearly not meant for salads. A monster so large needed pickling. But cucumber pickle was one Pahadi dish Ma had no appetite for. "They smell like Hajmola farts!" she complained every time she was offered cucumber pickle, and so the mutant sat upon the kitchen counter like an ancient, reprimanding rock.

"What will we do with this madness now?" Ma sighed.

It was only the next day, after both Adi and I had returned from school, that she decided to send "the thing" over to Thapa Aunty's house.

"Give the thing to Thapa Uncle," she instructed, then she narrowed her eyes and added, "Tell him the thing is from our garden only. Don't tell him anything about Doctor Uncle. Just say Ma sent it, understand?"

Understand.

And off we set, Adi and I. Because the vegetable was so large, it was obviously Adi who carried it like a pot over his head. I had nothing to do other than trot beside my brother making horse sounds until Adi glowered and threated to first kill me then slap me blue. "Neelai padchhas!" he growled, but with the mutant cucumber sitting on his head Adi was about as dangerous to me as were the distant mountains, and so I trotted and galloped and neighed all the way to Thapa Aunty's house.

Perhaps it was because I had harrowed Adi with my equestrian talents during our short trip to and back from Thapa Aunty's house that he told on me when we got home.

"You know what Preeti did?" he asked the moment he saw Ma.

"What? Did you again go and fall down somewhere?"

"No," I said and pinched Adi, and, before he could respond to the pinch, I added, "It happened by mistake, Ma. By mistake only everything came out."

Ma frowned. "What came out?"

"By mistake, god promise, Ma," I swore.

"What came out, Adi?"

"The moment Thapa Uncle opened the door," Adi answered, "Preeti told him Doctor Uncle had sent the cucumber for us yesterday but because you think cucumber pickle smells like Hajmola farts you wanted nothing to do with it, and you wanted Thapa Uncle to take the cucumber. And then she said, actually the cucumber is from Doctor Uncle's garden and he sent a boy named Gadahawa to deliver it to our house but Ma told us to tell you the cucumber is from our garden only. Then she said she was telling Thapa Uncle all this because it was wrong to lie."

I stared at my brother in disbelief. A terrible panic paralyzed me as I watched Ma's eyes grow larger than the accursed cucumber and her nostrils flare like fire. Even in a state of paralysis I knew I needed to run away from home, to never return to it, to vanish forever, but I could not move.

"Is that so, Your Truthful Highness?" Ma asked.

I could not shake my head. I was paralyzed.

And it was only when Ma removed her slipper and swatted me like a mosquito that I began to wail. And it was almost a whole week after the incident before I spoke to Adi again.

LOVE

In popular imagination, it is always the brother who protects the sister, but there is a story, celebrated every year on the day of Bhai Dooj, in which a sister protects her brother.

The sister and brother, living during a time when humans could eavesdrop and listen to what the gods had to say, were severely close to each other. They played together, ate from the same plate, fell asleep with their hands held, were wide-eyed and innocent. And then, one day without warning, it was time for the brother to get married. The sister, in her innocence, was overjoyed. She did not know that marriage would take her brother away from her. She thought of marriage as another game, something one indulged in for days and emerged from unchanged.

My brother is getting married, she announced to all her girlfriends as she went to the riverside with them. There will be new clothes, plates of sweets, days of music, and a hundred relatives to play with. Brother and I will eat and dance all day, she beamed. Her girlfriends, all of whom had, at one time or another, fantasied about the girl's handsome brother, tittered.

While this simple drama unfolded by the riverside, the many gods and goddesses sat on clouds and watched with seemingly bored attention. The truth, however, was that every god sitting on the clouds and filing their nails was jealous of the bond between the sister and her brother. They were so engrossed in each other that they had little time for prayers and rituals. All day the boy and the girl played among trees and huts, and when they spoke, they spoke of matters so personal, so private, that the gods felt entirely left out of their lives.

Finally, one of the gods could take it no more. "I cannot stand this brother and sister duo," he said.

And at this precise moment, the sister, who was filling a pot with fresh water, stilled. She heard distinctly and clearly, as though the god had spoken straight into her ears, what the god had said.

She continued filling her pot, and when it was time to return home with her girlfriends, she matched her steps with theirs, but she kept her ears tuned to the sky.

"I cannot stand them, either," said another god. "They are arrogant, self-centered, and rude."

"Let's kill them," suggested another god, perking up.

"Oh no. They will come here together and keep up with their ways. What a terrible nuisance that will be. Let's kill only the brother."

"Hah!" said god one, loving the idea. "Let's kill him on the day of his marriage. We will show this mite of a girl what feasting and dancing awaits them."

"Hah!" agreed all other gods, squealing with delight.

It was decided that during the first round of the marriage rituals, the gods would throw down a shower of invisible arrows that would pierce the boy and kill him. If that failed, then during the second round, when the boy and his bride circled the marriage fire, a snake would climb up his back and sting him to death. If that did not work then, while the groom slept with his bride, the roof of their room would collapse on the boy and crush his bones to powder.

"Hah!" said the gods in unison and clapped their hands.

The girl continued walking, balancing the pot of water carefully on her hips. She smiled and nodded when her friends spoke to her, but her heart beat hard and her limbs felt heavy.

On the day of the marriage the girl went into her room and emerged from it dressed like a boy. When the priest announced that it was time for her brother to sit beside his bride and hold her arm, the girl threw a terrible fit. "I will do it first, I will do it first," she cried like a petulant child. Everyone, including the girl's mother, was upset and angered by the girl's ridiculous ways. "What nonsense is this?" they demanded, but the brother, forever indulgent, smiled and said, "Let her sit here and enjoy the ritual first," he said. "What does it matter? Come, sweet one, sit beside my bride and hold her hand."

The sister promptly sat beside her brother's bride and held her hand, and no sooner had the priest begun the mantras when a shower of invisible arrows rained down from the sky upon the girl's body. The girl smiled, for against the girl's soft skin, the arrows were harmless. They melted like air upon her.

Once again, just before the brother circled the sacred fire with his bride, the sister stamped her feet. "Me first, me first," she insisted. Once again family and relatives clicked their tongues in disapproval. "What a spoiled brat," they said, but the brother smiled and said, "Let her circle the fire with my bride. What does it matter?"

And so the girl circled the sacred fire with her brother's bride and when the snake slithered up her back and stung her neck, she felt its venom turn to nectar within her veins.

Finally, it was time for the groom and the bride to retire to their nuptial bed, and now too the girl wept and howled. "I want to sleep with her first," she pleaded. By now everyone was thoroughly fatigued by her and simply said, "Oh, do what you have to do. What does it matter?" And the girl slipped into the covers with her brother's bride and waited for the roof to collapse. When it did, it turned into a soft sheet and enveloped the two girls.

And this was how a sister saved her brother.

Ma told us this story every year on the day of Bhai Dooj. On the morning of the ceremony she had me wear the most festive dress available at home, then I was led to the garden and asked to break off a few thorns from our rosebushes.

"Prick your tongue with the thorns, lightly but firmly," she said, "and as you prick, say, 'I will cook my brother and I will eat him, too.' All day today you are allowed to have terrible thoughts about your brother. Today you fool the gods so they think you cannot stand the boy at all. But only today, understand?"

I nodded enthusiastically. Adi frowned. "When can I have terrible thoughts about her?" he asked.

Ma shook her head. "Never," she declared.

"I will cook my brother and I will eat him, too," I repeated all day. All day I followed Adi until he came near to knocking me down. "I will cook my brother and I will eat him, too," I proclaimed loudly.

Later in the evening, Ma and I sculpted brothers out of mud and cow dung. "This is Adi, the brother I cannot stand," I said with a big smirk on my face and placed one of the dung brothers upon a platform.

"You are in for such a kick on your bum tomorrow," Adi said and left to play football with his friends.

"This is Suman, the brother I cannot stand," said Ma and placed the other dung brother upon the platform.

Together we said, "I will cook my brother and I will eat him, too," and pricked our respective brothers with fresh thorns broken off our rosebushes.

"Such donkeys these gods are," said Ma, shaking her head.

I was ten the year Ma held a rose thorn in her hand and frowned at the dung brothers sitting upon the altar we had made for them on the terrace. "Do you ever wonder what happened to the girls in the story?" she asked.

"What girls?" I asked.

"The girls who got married."

"Which girls got married?" I asked, surprised.

"Didn't the sister marry the brother's bride? She went through all the rituals first."

I stared at Ma. "That is true," I said, amazed.

"It must have been very confusing for the brother's bride, no?" Ma asked, now contemplatively pricking her brother. "At least the sister knew why she was behaving so strangely and performing all the rituals. But what must have the new bride felt? Here she was, getting married. Here was the priest with his mantras, and here was the fire, and here was the bride, holding her husband's sister's hand. She walked around the fire with the sister, and she slept her first night with the sister. She must have thought the sister was her rightful husband, yes or no? How terrible for her that she had to live with the brother when her true husband was really the sister."

I stared at Ma. I could scarcely look away from her face at that moment. There was something in her expression I could not read. "Girls always love girls before they love anyone else, isn't it true?" she said. My heart began suddenly to bang inside me then, and for the first time I recognized my aching, yearning love for Sachi.

HOW MANY CHILDREN DO YOU WANT?

I met Sachi almost immediately after we shifted to our new house in Ganesh Basti. She was not my immediate friend. My immediate friend then was Sunna and I spent most of my days with her, away at the neighbors' houses, playing eternal rounds of House-House in which I was invariably asked to enter fake kitchens to boil fake tea and fry fake snacks for fake guests who were perpetual protagonists of these lengthy performances. It was Sunna who trained me to balance half a dozen cups and saucers upon a small tray and walk the length between the kitchen and the living room without rattling the dishes. When the fake guests arrived, mostly led by Sunna's friend Sachi, who was two whole years older than me and who loved being served, I greeted them all with a brilliant smile and sat them down in the living room before I ran off, as modestly as I could, to the "kitchen" to boil the "tea." Once every few rounds of House-House, Sachi and her troops announced they would be arriving to "my house" as a "groom's party"—a groom's party, Sunna revealed to me, was a group of people coming to inspect a girl and to decide if the girl would make a good bride for the dashing young boy in their family. When guests decided to arrive as the groom's party, then a lot more groundwork than mere tea-making had to be covered.

I was, somehow, always the possible bride during these afternoons, and I had to prepare thoroughly for my role. My face was cleaned and caked with turmeric face mask for five full minutes, which in playtime represented five full days. I had to learn to wear heels, to smile without showing my teeth, to take at least a fake hour to finish a cup of fake tea, and to not speak until spoken to. My lips were colored with real lipstick and a sari was wrapped over my pants. There were bangles and eyeshadow to match. When the groom's party finally arrived I looked as pretty as sweetmeat—my face yellow and white with the left-behind turmeric and excessive talcum powder, my lips bursting with cherry-red lipstick. I limped and struggled beneath the five-yard sari and the oversize heels. I sat before Sachi, the taciturn "groom," careful and quiet, never once lifting my very green eyelids. I smiled only so much as to not show my teeth. And I never frowned, and never let my discomfort show. When the groom's father, the groom's uncle, and two of the groom's best friends began the interrogation I answered only in yeses and noes.

Did you really make all the samosas and the sweets, too?

Yes.

Do you know any painting? Embroidery?

Yes.

Do you want to learn computers?

Yes.

Are you ready to get married?

I don't know—this said shyly, to convey coyness, not indecision.

And finally the dreaded question.

Do you know English?

I nodded.

The groom's father smiled gently and asked if I could write a letter addressed to Sachi. Just for the fun of it, he said. Just to take something back home so the groom's mother could see it.

I nodded again and began the letter, my heart like wings inside me. I wrote:

Respectable Sir,

How are you? I am well and hope you are fine too. By the grace of Lord Pashupatinath, and all the other gods, the weather is very good, and you should be able to get to our house without difficulty.

I am very happy to be married to you. I can cook very well and my mashed brinjal is very good. I am good at embroidery and can knit good sweaters.

I am not afraid of traveling on buses over the mountains.

Thanking you,
Sincerely,
Preeti

Do you want to go to Bumbai for a honeymoon? the groom's father asked.

Yes, I said, shy again.

Do you want many children?

Five? I asked, uncertainly.

By the end of the play Sachi and I were married and I was irrevocably and permanently in love. Sachi was very impressed with my letter to her and after one of our weddings, we held hands as tight as we could and we had lots of sex, and once, when no one was looking, we kissed. Another time Sachi pulled her pants down and showed me hers, and I shook my head and said I did not want to show mine to her, and then for the rest of the way back home, we did not know what to say to each other. I was nine then, already in love, already married, already sleepless, and finally one day I pulled my pants down and showed her mine, too. We never talked about it.

THE ROYAL PROCESSION

It was only with Sachi that I lost all my fears. Without her I would never dare sit by the gorge, the one that divided Ganesh Basti from Chundevi and was inhabited by the most ancient creatures known to mankind. Without her, I would never dangle my feet into its abyss as though nothing ever frightened me—not the dark trees below our toes or the darker flowers. Between the gorge and the lane that rolled away from it, dipping then rising into Ganesh Basti, lay a thin strip of land woven and dappled with shamrocks, and the year I turned ten, the gorge seemed to burst with flowers. The sun, washed with days of rain, was luminous, and women and men idled upon the grass and sang folk songs that promised eternal love and unending happiness. A group of schoolboys kicked around a deflated ball, but nobody other than Sachi and me, and crazy Kanchi Aunty, who was pregnant with her third child and needed as many walks as she did rests, ventured too close to the gorge. There were stories not only of human ghosts but of animal spirits trapped in its bottom and of creatures that, unable to crawl out into the sunlight, had morphed into unrecognizable beings.

"There are snakes," said Kanchi Aunty, staring into the deep chasm, "larger than the earth, blacker than the night, and fiercer than rivers. Lord Vishnu sleeps upon the largest of the snakes. Lord Shiva wears the curliest one around his neck. These snakes protect the gods. They protect cities and nations. They protect those who worship them and they swivel out of the earth to slay those who will not pray and will not bow and will not believe."

As always, Sachi rolled her eyes and repeated Kanchi Aunty's words.

"Swivel out of the earth!" she mimicked and I giggled behind my palms. But the truth was Kanchi Aunty's sandlike voice, her swollen stomach under the cotton nighties she wore at all times, and her short, sudden sentences filled me with dread. I stared into the gorge and imagined endless snakes slithering at its bottom, waiting patiently for unbelievers to fall upon them.

"Do you think we will be able to climb all the way down if we try?" Sachi asked loudly, only to irk Kanchi Aunty who snorted at us. I found her defiance both heroic and brainless.

"Of course," I said, loudly too, almost fainting with tightly held in fear.

Snakes were common in Kathmandu and especially common in Ganesh Basti with its gorge, its paddy fields, and its untarred lanes. I saw more snakes in Ganesh Basti than I saw toads and frogs in its waterlogged fields, and even when I saw the toad, I thought of the snake in the waters, ready to open its oval, elastic mouth and swallow whole its prey. I worried about the toad, imagined it suffocating in the tight pocket of the snake's mouth. I thought of the amphibian, its bones cracking and mangling under the snake's teeth, and imagined it blind inside the snake's belly, unable to breathe, alive for many painful hours, the snake's stomach wringing its defeat like a piece of wet cloth, and juices—acidic and pinpointed—rupturing the skin upon its prey. I hated the snake and feared it. And yet the snake, glowing with stripes and crosses, left me exhilarated; and I imagined it under the crops, beautiful and easy, swimming like lightning in the murky waters.

I stayed close to Sachi and listened attentively to Kanchi Aunty. The universe, she said, sat upon a snake's head, and when the snake moved, the universe trembled and quaked. The snake was born before the earth, and at the birth of the earth the snake's body mixed with dirt and it became impossible to tell where land began and where the snake ended.

"The snake," said Kanchi Aunty, "lived in Kathmandu before people did." Once upon a time, went her tale, all of Kathmandu was a gigantic lake, a bowl with walls of mountains, and snakes lived in this lake like noodles in soup. Then came the demigods, powerful but not strong enough to tame the near-eternal serpents. The demigods slashed the mountain walls and cut gorges through them so the water would drain out of the lake. The water gushed away and took with it most of the snakes. The valley evolved then, fresh and soft, filled with dreams and hardships, and ready to welcome people within it. But they belonged to the snakes, too, and some of them never left. They only burrowed deep into the city.

"Now don't go jumping into this gorge, you stupid girls," said Kanchi Aunty, suddenly glaring at us. "Step away from it. Just looking at you I feel giddy and sick. Is it not enough that I am pregnant? Must I also have to babysit stupid girls like you?" Then she got off the ground and walked away.

Sachi rolled her eyes again. "Hormones," she whispered to me.

I giggled again, though I had no clue what hormones meant.

Around us flowers were furious upon trees. The ground was green and marigolds grew accidentally along the lane that followed the gorge for a bit before turning and leading us away from it. Marigolds reappeared and disappeared as the lane unrolled upon Ganesh Basti. Wisps of clouds sailed the clean sky. The moon still floated, pale like china.

The new school year had begun and Sachi and I had our satchels with us. Sachi's was new and bright orange and though mine was not, mine, too, bulged with crisp copies and textbooks uncontaminated by ink. We had decided to cover and label our books here, and behind us, leaning against shamrocks, was a roll of brown papers held together with a rubber band, a pair of scissors, a wad of cellophane sheets upon which we had placed a good-size stone to keep the plastic from fluttering, and a band of Scotch tape.

Sachi sighed. "Let's jump down and kill ourselves," she said.

"Let's," I said, because what else could I have said.

She sighed again. She sighed so much because she was going through her periods, and during the days of her periods everything either made her roll her eyes or sigh dramatically. Everything took on a tragic tone and so, because Sachi had periods, she and I stared dolefully at the gorge. Its walls burst with morning glories and coneflowers, and bachelor buttons were intensely blue, like stars.

"Our frocks will get caught in the trees," Sachi said, "and we will be hanging like kites from the branches."

"All torn."

"Completely tattered."

"No point jumping."

Behind us the cellophane rattled in the wind. The Scotch tape, standing on its side, rolled an inch forward. My satchel, precariously balanced, fell on its back with a soft thump.

"Let's just cover the books," I said.

My blood still hummed with Kanchi Aunty's stories and with the lushness of the dark gorge, but I pushed down the strangely intoxicating buzz in my head and crawled up onto the grass where our satchels lay and took the books out from our bags. Sachi continued to sit by the gorge.

"If nobody marries us by the time we are twenty, let's marry each other," she said.

"Yes," I said and piled the books into two stacks. The taller one was Sachi's because she was already in grade seven, two grades higher than me, and had more books and copies to go through. We had decided to be systematic this year. We would cover one of Sachi's books, then one of mine, then one of Sachi's, then one of mine. Whatever was left would be covered the following week, but Sachi didn't step away even after I had finished stacking the books, so I shuffled my pile and placed my favorite text, *The History of Nepal,* on the very top. It had the prettiest cover, one I wanted to preserve better and longer than the unlaminated, black-and-white covers of the math or the English or the moral science books.

The cover of *The History of Nepal* showed a painting of His Majesty, King Prithvi Narayan Shah, Nepal's first Shah ruler, who in the 1700s had won several wars and gathered the hitherto scattered kingdoms into a single Nepal. He stood stern and straight before Nepal's rectangular map. In his left hand he held a sword, slanted down upon the ground. His right hand was raised and a ringed index finger pointed toward the sky. He wore a crown filled with emeralds and topped with the white plumes of the bird of heaven. Behind him, his throne, thick, golden, and coiled upon itself, rose like fire. His throne was imaged after Sheshnaag, the thousand-headed cobra upon which Lord Vishnu, the creator of cosmic destiny, reclined in the oceans of heaven. For a few seconds I stared at the throne, disarmed by the sudden epiphany that King Prithvi Narayan Shah, and all the kings after him, were closely related to snakes. Why had the royalty's proximity with reptiles not stirred apprehension in me before? Though what I was apprehensive about, I did not know. I knew kings were reincarnations of Lord Vishnu, but their close relationship with snakes came to me as sudden realization now.

"His Majesty Prithvi Narayan looks so funny in this picture," I said, and finally Sachi moved away from her perch and came over to me. "He looks like he is wearing a frock."

"King Birendra would never wear a frock," Sachi said, looking at the cover.

"But if there had been no King Prithvi Narayan Shah, then there would be no Nepal, and had he not had some sons, and those sons had more sons, and some more sons, then ultimately there would be no His Majesty King Birendra, and if there was no King Birendra, who knows what would happen. There would certainly be no Royal Procession going down the Ring Road today. And it would be so boring without the Royal Procession."

"Should we cover the history books first?" Sachi asked, and we settled down to cutting brown paper to size, to pressing down the paper upon the books and taping their flaps into place.

"You know," Sachi said as we covered our books, "you should never shape your palms to the shape of a cobra's hood. It attracts the cobra. The cobra is always looking for a mate. And never whistle after dark. Better never to whistle at all, it is hooliganism and nothing else. But never whistle at night. Snakes come out at night and they might mistake your shrillness for the shrillness of a beena. And never kill a cobra. They are always in a pair, even if one is away hunting. Theirs is an unending love story. The survivor will click your snap and save your photo in her eye and she will make it her mission to find you and bite you to death, even if it takes her forever. A vengeful lot they are."

"Anything you will say," I said and joined Sachi in her laugh, though I knew everything she said was true. There were enough stories written and movies made about she-cobras that went hunting down people who had deliberately or accidentally killed their mates.

We continued to cut and fold, to cover and stick, but our hearts were not in the task. All week we had spoken of nothing but the Royal Procession and now that the morning was here we were restless, though occasionally Sachi complained about cramps in her stomach, aches on her back, and the tightness in her thighs. I never wanted to get periods.

"I am sick and tired of it," she said.

"Me also," I said, though what I wanted to say was, will you come home and talk to Ma? Will you bring your mother, too, with you? We could all have tea together.

"Why couldn't the procession come some other day?" Sachi said. "This is a conspiracy against me, I am telling you."

Sachi's history book lacked the glamour of my history book. Her history had no monarchs and maps on it; instead it showed the national symbols—a cow, a rhododendron, a danfe, all in beige and badly photographed.

"But what if somebody does marry us before twenty?" I asked.

"Then what is there to think about? We will be married."

"Do you think Prince Nirajan will be in the car with His Majesty today?" I asked when we began covering our math books. I hesitated before adding, "I think I am in love with Prince Nirajan." I glanced swiftly at Sachi but she was engrossed in securing brown paper as neatly as she could with tape. "I think it is all right to love Prince Nirajan. He is only thirteen, only three years older than I am."

"He is only a year older than me," Sachi said.

"That is not a big enough age difference. There should at least be three years between husband and wife. Besides, Prince Nirajan looks so much like Ritvik. Last month I saw the prince playing football on TV and I had to look a long time to make sure it was Prince Nirajan on TV and not Ritvik. You cannot fall in love with Prince Nirajan. That will be like falling in love with Ritvik." Ritvik was Sachi's first cousin.

Sachi pulled two candies out of her pocket and gave one to me. We sucked on our strips. When I stretched back and lay on the ground, there was a perfectly shaped cloud in the sky and a fleet of swallows swept past it. "I could not fall in love with Prince Dipendra. I liked him before but he is too fat now, no?" I said. "Besides, Prince Dipendra is ten years older than me. My parents will never agree to our match.

Or maybe they will. What do you think? It is not a joke to be married to the Crown Prince. If I marry the Crown Prince, I will be the next queen of Nepal. That is no joke. It already makes me nervous, even though we will not be getting married for quite a few years."

"Of course," said Sachi. "That will be a very big problem, Your Highness."

I laughed. "When I am queen, I will assign five maids to you who will massage you day in and out when you have periods."

"You are very kind, Your Highness."

We finished covering our books and went back to sit by the gorge, but Kanchi Aunty, who was taking rounds a little way away from us, sent a yell at us. "Do you want me to get sick right here?" she yelled. "I have enough vomiting with this morning sickness. Come right away from that ditch, stupid girls. Do you want to fall into that hole, Miss Daredevils? Do you have no consideration for your mothers? Right away or I will vomit in a second."

Sachi and I gaped at her and Sachi yelled back, "You were sitting here nice and pretty all morning and now you are shouting at us."

"I will give you such a hammering for talking back, Miss Sachi, and I will complain to your father immediately," said Kanchi Aunty.

"I have had enough of this," Sachi said. "Let's get away from here. I cannot stand that woman."

We watched Kanchi Aunty leave the patch where she had been taking rounds and head for the lane that led back to Ganesh Basti. Her head disappeared as the lane dipped, then reappeared with the marigolds.

"That woman is mad only," said Sachi.

We inched back to the grass and put away our books. We stuffed the remaining brown paper covers into my satchel. We put the scissors into Sachi's. The Scotch tape had rolled off a little away and we forgot to pick it up. We rose and dusted the sleeves and the grass-stained backs of our frocks. Sachi pulled out two blocks of fruit-bursts from her frock and we chewed the gum as we made our way to the Ring Road to watch the Royal Procession. We were a few yards away when I turned and saw the Scotch tape. It shone like a transparent bracelet upon the ground.

We did not stay upon the lane. Instead, we cut through the fields, balancing upon the dikes. The fields were heavy, scented and deliberated with ripe panicles and the air smelled of raw rice and raw leaves. Sachi and I were similarly dressed in frocks with contrasting bodices and patterned slippers, but I was untidy in my longish skirt and my flying hair, and Sachi was very neat. We were mindful upon the small, low walls. Sachi stepped accurately, I tried to hop. We were like tightrope walkers, aware of the dangers of lagging into the water-logged paddy.

"Does everyone have periods at twelve?" I asked.

Sachi plucked a grain and gnawed out a single seed of rice with her teeth. "You are too thin. Yours will probably come at thirteen. Mine came at twelve because I am healthy."

"Why does it hurt you so much if you are healthy?" I asked.

Then Kanchi Aunty, who was still on the lane, saw us in the fields, half hidden by the thick paddy, and yelled out again.

"Do you girls want to die today?" she yelled. "Get out of the fields. There are frogs there, and toads, and probably snakes."

"Pregnant women are tedious," Sachi said and we continued to walk, but from the corner of our eyes we could see Kanchi Aunty waving her arms so we got out of the fields.

"I hope we get to see Princess Shruti," I said, "even though I heard mean things about her."

"What things?"

"When Princess Shruti was in St. Mary's School, she forced her dormmates to drink a whole glass of water out of peanut shells. That is mean."

"That is not even possible," said Sachi. "That is just stupid rumors."

We walked quietly after that until we came to the Dimple Kapadia Video Store and Sachi started talking again. "Last week," she said, "I was on the terrace and I saw some guys on the other side, you know, where that sewerlike stream from Chundevi gets into the gorge, and I was like eww, that is disgusting, you know? There were like six of them. I wasn't looking or anything, or even really thinking about them. They were pretty far off, you know, but I could see them. I guess I was kind of blank in the head, you know?"

"What about the boys?" I asked.

We looked around for Kanchi Aunty and cut through a small field and emerged at the Ganesh Temple. We did our namaskars without stopping or turning fully toward the gods. "Nothing much," Sachi said. "They were there and I was watching them, just like that, without meaning to or anything, just to have something to do while hanging out clothes. Then these guys started going into the bushes, and I was like ewww, why don't you just pee in the sewer? I mean, what is the point of going behind bushes if there is a river of pee flowing right in front of you? But then I noticed they weren't going into the bushes to pee."

"You could see all this from your terrace?" I asked.

"Believe it or not, your wish," said Sachi.

"What happened then?"

"They were not peeing. They were plucking leaves," Sachi continued. "I was just watching them casually, without meaning to or anything. The boys plucked leaves, crushed the leaves upon their palms, and ate them, like tobacco. You know how it is? I figured I could see them from my terrace but they could not see me."

We stopped before Thapa Uncle's house, the oldest slant-roofed house in the area, the house with bougainvillea arching over the main gate—the same Thapa Uncle because of whom Ma had swatted me with her slippers a few years ago. Thapa Uncle's house had the best flowers in Ganesh Basti. “Sure they could not see you,” I said. “Not clearly enough at least.”

“Yeah,” said Sachi, walking on. “Besides, they were a bunch of cheapsters and what did I care if they saw me or not?” She spat out her gum and pushed her hand into her pocket, fiddling for another piece. “They were doing drugs,” she said. “Siksha says there is poppy growing by that sewer. Isn’t it disgusting to be anything by the sewer? I wouldn’t eat anything from there, not for a million bucks.” Siksha was Sachi’s older sister who was studying medicine in India. Sachi had two older sisters and both studied in India. When Sachi was older, she would probably go off to India to study too.

“Yeah,” I said.

“You remember when Uddip broke his arm and he said he broke it because I pushed him?” Sachi asked.

I nodded. “That was mean of him.”

“Well, I did push him. He tried to kiss my mouth so I pushed him and he fell and broke his arm. How stupid is that?”

“It’s yuck,” I said.

We saw Kanchi Aunty again, now sitting with her husband on a wall and watching one of the new houses being constructed. Of late there was always at least one house under construction in Ganesh Basti.

Kanchi Aunty called out to us. “Have you seen Edna?” she asked. Edna was Kanchi Aunty’s daughter.

“No, Aunty,” we said in unison and walked on.

We passed Sachi’s Chinese brick house with its green windows.

“He was there, too; Uddip, with the boys at the sewer,” Sachi said.

“How do you know it was Uddip? Weren’t they very far away?”

“Oh,” said Sachi, “I would recognize Uddip if he was sitting on the moon,” and she giggled.

“How can you see so much from your terrace? I can’t see all that from mine.”

"If you don't believe me, I don't have to tell you," said Sachi. "Besides, your house is not tall enough."

We came to Kanchi Aunty's house after that. It was three storied and each story had balconies supported by ornate English columns. Then, two houses later, it was my house and though my house was not built of Chinese bricks and though it was flat-roofed and only one story high, I swelled with pride. Ours was the greenest house, surrounded by trees and without any boundary walls. Ours was the only compound not enclosed within bricks and stones, and its openness gave our house a brave and fragile look, like houses one saw in postcards.

"Let them eat drugs by the sewer," I said. "What is it to you?"

"They were a bunch of goofers, that is what. So, I am watching and thinking that they can't see me. Then someone starts pointing at me and I think, oh, what does it matter? I must look so small from so far below. So I keep spreading out the clothes. And you cannot even imagine what happened next. This one guy—his hair was all long and all, this guy, he pulls something out of his pocket and starts looking through it. I think it was a pair of binoculars."

"Oh?"

"Yup! These guys must be watching women through windows, movie style."

"Yuck!"

"I know." Sachi giggled. "It's totally eww, isn't it? Then they passed the binoculars around and I was so embarrassed about being in shorts. Thank god my shirt was a loose one. Whosoever heard of binoculars being so readily available?"

I had never seen real binoculars in my life. "Next time don't wear shorts to the terrace then," I said.

"You are an idiot," Sachi said, still giggling. "They were so irritating I stuck my tongue out at them."

"What?"

"Yes. Then I gave them the finger."

"What?"

"The middle finger, idiot. I gave them the middle finger, and they gave me theirs, and I gave both of mine back to them. Now," Sachi went on, barely able to speak. "Now, every morning they sit on the stairs of the Dimple Kapadia Video Store and when I pass by they stick their tongues out at me and call me their morning glory. I hate it that I was wearing shorts."

I stared at my friend and adjusted the weight of the satchel on my shoulders. "You are mad," I said.

And we were at the Ring Road.

The lane so far had been all brown, all dust, snaking through the neighborhood, but the Ring Road was tar, briefly curving around Ganesh Basti like a deep gray carpet, graceful and attractive, the asphalt twinkling. On its one side, bordering the neighborhood, was the greenbelt with tall and light trees, and soft violet mimosas. Here and there, within the greenbelt, were kidney-shaped ponds choking with thick purple lilies and fat leaves so dark they were almost as black as the waters underneath. We had never seen what lay in those waters. If we went complaining to our mothers about lost balls, our mothers told us to play with something else. "That water is surely poisonous," they said.

That morning the Ring Road was like a dream, quiet and without a single vehicle upon it. The air wrapped around the mimosas and came off fragranced. Policemen stood on both sides, lined upon the sandy sidewalks. They stood at regular intervals, some at ease and looking ahead, others working to direct transportation away from the street and into smaller, branching lanes.

I wondered where His Majesty was going this morning. The Royal Procession mostly passed our neighborhood when His Majesty was headed to the airport and there had been talks about His Majesty flying to India for something but I was not sure.

It was a dangerous thing to be king. Being a king meant being blessed and cursed, and I was wary of the people, the gods, the animals, the temples, and everything else that seemed to rule His Majesty and his family the way they did not rule me. I was not cursed. I could go where I pleased, when I pleased. But His Majesty and his family were cursed. They could not go to certain places. Certain temples were forbidden to them, as were certain gods. They could not perform certain rites and rituals. If they ever went into the Budha Neelkanth Temple, for instance, they would be bitten by the most poisonous cobra in the world and would die before they could ask for water to soothe the fire in their throats. This was a curse all kings had to live with. The curse had come to a king in his dreams long before His Majesty Prithvi Narayan unified Nepal, and the curse had stayed with every monarch who ever ruled the nation. There were stories of several members of royal families who had tried to defy the curse and set foot into the Budha Neelkanth Temple only to be found poisoned to death. It baffled me, this complete vulnerability with which all royal families lived, and I wished His Majesty luck in his travels. I had heard Papa say often that His Majesty was a pure and gentle soul, but there were other souls, not pure and not at all gentle, who would ruin His Majesty and his Nepal at the first chance they could. "They are swarming under the palace," Papa often said.

"Let's go," said Sachi, and we moved to cross the street.

A policeman blew his whistle at us. "Stay where you are," he said. "It does not look any prettier from there." He looked at Sachi and smiled.

Sachi rolled her eyes. "Men are just eww," she whispered.

People were gathered all along the sidewalks, waiting for the procession, and their noisy chatter had the policemen frowning and blowing their whistles at everyone. Two policemen were mounted on very tall horses, one on each side of the road, and the horses trotted rhythmically in place.

I thought of Nepal and His Majesty as I thought of trees and their fruits, of skies and their birds, mountains and their clouds. I thought of His Majesty as molded into the land, as Nepal herself. I adored the pictures hung upon the walls of houses, offices, and shops, amid oleographs and calendars of gods and goddesses, behind diyas and incense sticks, reverentially garlanded with strings of marigolds and amarnaths. The royal portrait in my school auditorium was in a circular frame with His and Her Majesties seated in deep chairs; His Majesty wore the traditional daura suruwal while Her Majesty sat serene in a green-and-gold chiffon sari. Princess Shruti, the Crown Prince Dipendra, and Prince Nirajan stood behind their parents, their hands folded before them as though they were members of a choir. The royal portrait in the school canteen showed His Majesty in an army outfit, sash across his chest, multiple badges and stars upon his shoulders. Her Majesty wore a sash, too, and the badges, but there was nothing militaryesque about her. Her smile was gentle and she looked shy, like a little girl.

My favorite portrait was the one that came on TV before the programs began. His and Her Majesty were fully majestic on the screen—silver cape, silver crown topped with plumes of the bird of heaven, emeralds fringing their foreheads, heads so high up it made me dizzy. This was the portrait I had once bought off the sidewalk from a woman who also sold candies and dried fruits. Under this picture of His and Her Majesty was the quote: "The universe is woven and interwoven in Vishnu. From him is the world, and the world is in him."

It baffled me that none of the walls in my own house had pictures of the royal family. When I handed my purchase to Ma and asked her to hang the portrait on a wall she said she would not because there was no reason to go banging nails upon the walls. "Look, nails everywhere. There is no need to crack the walls with more."

"We can Scotch tape it in place," I suggested.

"The glue will ruin the paint nice and proper, leave square marks upon it."

I looked around. The paint was already ruined in many places.

"We have all the gods on our walls," I pointed out, tilting my chin toward the many calendars showing images of gods and goddesses hanging from nails driven into our walls.

"King Birendra is not a god," Ma answered.

"He is. He is Lord Vishnu."

"Lord Vishnu," Ma said, emphasizing every word, "is a nuisance. He reclines and rests on his useless snake and his useless snake swims all day in the ocean and your Lord Vishnu gets properly blue with pneumonia and stiff with rheumatism. Poor Lakshmi has no other job than to massage his legs day in and day out. If he stopped sleeping on a snake and started doing something more useful, it would be better, no? Chronic pneumonia and severe rheumatism, that is all it is. And that Lakshmi is an idiot. What is the point of being a goddess if you do nothing but press your husband's feet? Donkeys!"

I stared at Ma, my mouth open. There were two Lord Vishnu calendars in the prayer room and one in the bedroom where this conversation was taking place.

I went from Ma to Papa. "Papa, hang His Majesty in our house," I said.

"No way!" said Papa, laughing until he nearly choked. "You are in a mood to get us killed."

But I did not care about my parents now. I had never seen His and Her Majesty in person, and the possibility, however remote, that I might see them for real today made me doubly anxious. I held Sachi's hand

and stared at the street, unaffected by the policemen treet-treeting their whistles and scolding people around them.

"Aren't they handsome?" Sachi asked, forcing me to look.

The policemen were handsome in their glowing, creaseless, light-blue uniforms. Navy blue caps hid half their faces, and only their lips and their chins showed under the helm of their caps. The sky shone on their boots and guns.

One of the policemen saw me looking at him and said, "Heavy bag you are carrying."

"We have to have the books covered for class," I said.

"Why don't you put it down? Nobody will steal it. There are policemen everywhere."

Sachi smiled and put her bag down, even though the policeman had clearly been speaking to me. I hesitated. I realized that no matter which frock I wore, I would always be shabby before a policeman.

"Put it down," the policeman coaxed and finally I removed the satchel from my back.

"When will he come, dai?" Sachi asked.

"Any moment now, any moment. So keep it quiet and full of respect, won't you?"

We nodded. My heart fluttered in my head. Any moment now.

The Royal Palace started at Durbar Marg, the King's Way, and ended at Maharajgunj, the King's City, which meant the palace was two and a half kilometers long. Just the statistics mystified me. How could any residence be so long, and how could a family of just five people live in all of it? "His Majesty will have to take a car simply to get to the dining room," I said, talking aloud, and Sachi, who always understood everything I said right away, rolled her eyes. "Imagine him in his silk nightsuit, Sachi," I went on, "driving his Rolls-Royce to breakfast. Of course, His Majesty does not drive his car himself, and there are many, many, many people living in the palace who drive him around.

His Majesty's breakfast is probably brought to him in his bedroom, probably in the Rolls-Royce too! But still, imagine, what must a king's Rolls-Royce look like?"

"You know what a normal person's Rolls-Royce looks like?" Sachi asked and I scrunched my face at her.

I had read in one of the Casino Royale magazines at Sachi's house that His Majesty was the only person in Nepal to own a Rolls-Royce. I had sat on Sachi's bed and flipped the magazine from the first page to the last, looking for an image of the car, but there had been none and I had tried to imagine it all: the insides of the palace, the insides of His Majesty's car, the lives of the many, many, many people within these insides. It was the difficulty of the imagining, of trying to count the "many" that confounded me—how many? A hundred? A thousand? I imagined millions, but that would have meant the entire country!

"Do you think His Majesty will roll his window down and smile at us?" I asked. "And maybe we will see Her Majesty, too, no? It will be so sweet."

"His Majesty," said Sachi, "is probably in his palace right now, drinking whiskey. Daddy says His Majesty drinks whiskey without any soda." Sachi's father worked at the Casino Royale at the Hotel Yak and Yeti and had spoken with almost every member in the royal family.

I was suddenly annoyed with Sachi. Sachi had her periods and rolled her eyes at everything, said "ewww" and thought of nothing but boys, and was forever making comments about His Majesty. Last week she had said His Majesty was a really nice person but his brothers liked to bully him and he let them. She said his brothers were smugglers, which meant they were soon going to sell Nepal to a European nation, though when I challenged Sachi and asked how anyone could pick a country and take it all the way to Europe, Sachi had had no answer. And now I was more annoyed with Sachi than I could bear.

"I am only your friend out of pity," I said. "Edna thinks your legs are so long you look like a mosquito."

And I picked up my bag and moved away. I walked toward a small crowd and as I walked I heard the far-off rumble of motorcycles. I felt the tickle of their vibrations in my soles and I started to run. I ran so I could stand near the mounted policeman and his horse. I had never stood near a mounted policeman before and I laughed a little as I ran, my anger toward Sachi vanishing as suddenly as it had come. Everyone else seemed to be laughing too. The motorcycles were at the turn for the Ring Road and their growls were still diffused but I could hear them getting closer and when I turned around I saw them emerging, two at a time, and I threw my hands up and jumped, unable to contain myself.

A man before me said, "Oho!" and clapped his hands. Other people clapped too. Some whistled. One cried, "Ayo, aayo!" Another slapped his thighs. "Right here!" he said.

The policemen stamped their feet and from the "at ease" transformed to the "attention." They raised their hands in a smart salute and the sandy sidewalk clouded under their boots. Even the horses stood still. I held my breath.

"He is a god," whispered the woman beside me and held her son's hand. The son had long hair, almost touching his shoulders. He looked like someone who would eat drugs by a sewer and I felt my anger against Sachi return.

The motorcycles passed two by two and I faced the road and shouted out the national anthem, gloriously crowning His Majesty, praying for more glory, more success, more land to befall him. I shouted out the tune, and all the while I kept an eye on the long-haired boy, all the while I dreamed of kicking him, of throwing him on the ground and breaking his arms the way Sachi had broken Uddip's.

The boy pulled away from his mother and ran off into the crowd.

"These motorcycles are like no other motorcycles in all of the world!" he said. He kicked one leg and shouted "bha-ta-ta-ta-ta-ta," in imitation of the motorcycles. A few adults whacked him on his head for being a nuisance but did not stop him.

I looked around for Sachi but she was nowhere.

The motorcycles really were like no other in the world. They were very big and very blue-black with red and blue lights blinking and dancing in circles on their heads. The riders, mysterious and unknowable under large, all-enclosing helmets, had to bend low to hold the handlebars. Their hands were hidden in black leather gloves. They sat upon their vehicles like men from the future. They did not speed past us and were surprisingly slow, as though they, too, were looking at the crowd as the crowd was looking at them, but they were not really looking either. The motorcycle men did not turn once toward the sidewalks. They never looked any way other than straight ahead. The engines roared like beasts upon the road.

Somebody caught my hand and I jumped up in surprise. "Oy!" I cried when I saw it was Sachi.

"Hello," she said, smiling. "Want to race the motorcycles?"

"No," I said, and then, "I hate you." When I turned back to the road, I had missed the last of the motorcycles that went past. "You just come and disturb me," I said.

Cars followed the motorcycles. "The Rolls-Royce!" I cried. "There will be the Rolls-Royce!"

A policeman turned around and shushed me. "Don't be so noisy," he said.

The cars were black, but they looked blue under the sky. They had thin, silver antennae upon their hoods and they lulled the street with their soundless speed. The motorcycles had been so flamboyant—lights and sound and dark blue men in snow-white helmets—that the cars in their polished blackness, in their monotone, were dangerous and somewhat terrifying. The steel antennae shivered in the air and sparkled like swords.

"Are you mad? His Majesty does not sit in any of these cars," Sachi whispered into my ears. "Men with long guns sit in these cars so if anyone tries to do fishy things they can shoot you right there. Dhickchiyaun!" She shot me and I glared in return.

"Why are you making gun sounds in the middle of a procession?"

The motorcycles had varied and some were green and white, but the cars sliding by were identical, black with those silver antennae.

"It really is quite possible that His Majesty is not in any of these cars," Sachi said, keeping her voice low. "Daddy says that it is possible that His Majesty is not in the country at all, that he has disguised himself as such and such and taken the local transport to the airport. Anything is possible, my little candy. It is possible that there really is no His Majesty and the pictures and the movies, the speeches on the radio, all of this was invented because we cannot invent anything else and because we like interesting topics of conversation. Anything is possible, flowerbud."

"It is possible, dear cockroach, that you are mad and know nothing," I said.

Sachi snorted. "I know everything, dear housefly. My daddy works in the casino and plays cards with His Majesty. I know everything."

"Well, then, dear flea on a dog, if His Majesty plays in the casino with your daddy then he has to exist, no?"

"That too is possible, dear earthworm," Sachi said.

The long-haired boy came back to stand with his mother and I glanced swiftly at Sachi. Sachi was looking at the road but I felt the change in her. Sachi was different now. Her hair was longer, straighter. Her frock was shorter; her skin, scented like wood.

More cars and then more motorcycles passed before me and though I refused to believe Sachi's periods induced boredom, refused to be disheartened, I realized, quietly, that there was going to be no Rolls-Royce on display, that Sachi was right, that perhaps there was no His Majesty in the world, that even if there was, I would, in all probability, never see him in person. He would not risk his life for me, would not roll his window down just to wave. I thought of the boys with their binoculars, and of Uddip trying to kiss Sachi's mouth. I imagined Uddip at the Dimple Kapadia Video Store, sitting with his friends on the staircase, slumped, sprawled, taking up almost half the narrow lane. I knew that one of the boys played the guitar, and another had long hair, and one of them looked like Rishi Kapoor when Rishi Kapoor was very young, and that when Sachi passed them she twirled around, like that girl in the Cadbury advertisement, and her dress flew out and her polka-dotted panties showed, and she was their morning glory. I knew Sachi would not marry me. She would marry one of those boys. There wasn't enough age difference between me and Sachi. We were only two years apart and there needed to be three.

"We will never see His Majesty," I said finally.

It said in my grade four history book that centuries ago, before Nepal was a nation, His Majesty's ancestors had fled the flat deserts of India and come to the hills of Nepal in search of a better, safer life, and now, standing before the passing procession, I realized that what I had expected from His Majesty that morning was for His Majesty to recognize the story that tied us together. Like His Majesty's, my ancestors, too, had migrated from India to Nepal, and as with my family, His Majesty's family, too, returned to their ancestral country looking for brides and grooms for their children. What I had expected was for His Majesty to step out of his car and talk to me. I wanted to tell him about Ma. She is just like you, I wanted to tell him. You should talk to her. I wanted to tell His Majesty that some nights the monster sleeping inside Ma stirred, and Ma made a gurgling sound in her sleep. Some nights she woke up with a start and had to walk up and down the small corridor of our house to shake away her nightmares. Nobody knows, I wanted to tell His Majesty, because all day she is fine. The monster visits only at night. Nobody knows, but surely you must know. You must feel the same way too.

As the cars moved past, one after the other like a string of dreams, replicas of each other, I recognized the futility of the fiction I had built in my head. The king was nothing like me, even though history books and traditions said he was. He would not step down to ask me what was wrong with my life. He was a vain and effectless god, like all gods I knew. He was his own country, locked in dark cars and living in television screens and pages of books. He would not roll his windows down and send a smile my way. I touched, accidentally and permanently, the distance between me and the world I lived in. The king was gone. Sachi would never belong to me. My childhood was temporary. And something would take my mother away.

That night I curved my palms and wriggled the shadow of the cobra hood upon the wall. The shadow swished and leapt at me, flicking its wire tongue, but no cobra—black and moist—came.

I went to the terrace and when the sky—boundless and gleaming with stars—filled my blood with songs, I began to first hum then to whistle tunes and in the middle of the whistle I remembered the cobra, now out looking for a mate, and stopped. Then I started again, afraid of my adventures and yet too curious to let go. I whistled tentatively, with my eyes everywhere, ready to run, waiting for my tryst with the deity.

A snake's tongue is forked, I sang,
One part is here, one part is there.
A snake's back glitters,

One stripe is here, one stripe is there.
A snake slithers its body,
Its head is here, its tail is there.
A snake sheds its skin,
And it mixes with the soil.

In my dreams that night I saw snakes mounted upon one another like wrestlers. They fell and slithered upon the ground in big heaps. They turned into stockings and strung themselves from trees. They plopped, noodlelike, upon the floor. The next moment I was walking on a thin wall, a poised tightrope walker. If a snake tried to climb my wall, I took out a knife and chopped the nosy, long, juicy cucumber into perfect fifty paisa coins and ate them with salt and pepper. They were delicious, like fish, these snakes.

BOOK FOUR

NANI

PIGEONS AND PARROTS

I came to the kitchen to give Ma the radishes I had pulled out of our garden. They were to be chopped for the dinner salad, but in the kitchen I found Papa by the sink, turning on and off the tap from which not a single drop of water fell. Ma was by the kitchen counter watching over a pot of milk, and Adi sat leaning against a wall, pretending to read a textbook. When I put the radishes on the counter, my parents turned to absently look at me, then turned away to face each other. A small storm of panic began to build inside me, and I squatted down beside Adi.

"What do you mean not well?" Papa asked.

And from the conversation that followed between Ma and Papa, I gathered that Suman Uncle had called to tell Ma that my grandfather, Bilash Nana, was not doing well. Nana, Suman Uncle had told Ma, was near death, and Ma wanted to leave for Darbhanga right away, though she did not quite believe her brother's account about her father's health.

The first time Suman Uncle had called Ma with the news of Nana's approaching death, Adi and I were not yet born. That first time Ma had believed Suman Uncle and taken the earliest bus she could to rush over to Darbhanga. When she reached Darbhanga, Ma found Bilash Nana irritable and excitable but not sick, and certainly not near death. What she found instead was a sick and helpless woman in Suman Uncle's wife. It was her health and her life that was at stake. Her health had deteriorated after her latest childbirth and unable to come to terms with his wife's condition, Suman Uncle had called all his sisters over to Darbhanga under the pretext that their father was dying. "I cannot bear it if something happens to her," he had wept before his sisters. "You are all women. You understand what is happening to her. Make her well." That first time the sisters had taken turns caring for Suman Uncle's wife and caring for Suman Uncle, but despite all their efforts Suman Uncle's wife had eventually died.

"After his wife died," Ma told Adi and me several times over the years, "Suman forgot to feed his children, or clothe them, or educate them, or marry them, or welcome them home after marriage. He became a regular donkey and nothing else." After his wife died, Suman Uncle's older children looked after the younger ones while Suman Uncle crowded his balcony with neighbours who gathered each morning, gurgling and cooing like pigeons and drinking sweet tea through the day. Kaveri Nani and a servant she had hired to run the kitchen slogged all day in the kitchen while Suman Uncle's half-dressed children played in the famished garden behind the house and ate what they could find and prepare in the meagre kitchen. "They looked like stale food," Ma said, "unwanted and scowled at. Poor things." Without a mother they were hooligans, and though there was some intelligence in the sons, the daughters were regular donkeys, without skills or ambitions, and with either too much or too little temper in them. "No good," Ma said, "especially that Ruby. That Ruby is a Ruby-phuby-kuby and nothing else."

Ma's interest in Ruby was special because it was after Ruby's birth that Suman Uncle's wife had died. "The poor girl never knew a mother's love," Ma lamented, and for a brief period after Suman Uncle's wife died, Ma became Ruby's mother. She brought a motherless five year old Ruby with her to Kathmandu with the intention of raising her to adulthood. It had seemed then like Suman Uncle would never live again and that Ma would never have a child of her own, and adopting and raising Ruby had seemed like the best solution for everyone. Then two years later Ma had had Adi and returned Ruby to Suman Uncle. "The poor man," Ma said about her brother. "He was so devastated by his wife's death. It is a lucky wife who has a husband who will mourn her. Suman lived in a fog for years after his wife died, but all grief must settle with time, and his did, too, and when he emerged from his fog he wanted his girl back. It was only right that he should want her back, except that he was a donkey of a father. He did not know what to do with her. He did not know what to do with any of his children."

Suman Uncle came to rely more and more on his sisters to help him with his children. He had them come over when he needed to get them married, he had them come over when one of them went through childbirth, he had them come over when they cried because they did not have a mother. And each time he used their father's health as an excuse. "It is because we are not always free to attend to his majesty," said Ma. "Sometimes when he calls, we cannot go. He has become smart, though, and arranges all events and ceremonies over summer and winter holidays. That way most of us can go to him. But if something happens outside of the holidays, your grandfather begins to die. Which heartless daughter will not go running to care for their dying father? Which donkey husband of ours can keep us from going to our mother's house if our father is dying?"

And so it was that though Suman Uncle had called with the information that Bilash Nana was dying, neither Ma nor Papa believed him, and Papa did not want Ma taking off to Darbhanga when Adi's exams were so close.

"Maybe he is well," Ma conceded to Papa now. "Maybe nothing has happened to Babuji, but you know something has definitely happened."

"Yes," said Papa, "one of his children has a stomachache and you should just go running off to Darbhanga because of this drama. Tell your brother to be straightforward if he wants people to stop their lives and hop over to him."

"You cannot stop me from seeing my family," said Ma and this infuriated Papa.

Papa did not like Ma's family. He thought Suman Uncle was foolish and Ma's many sisters vain. He did not like Nana because Nana would not die and would instead live on, year after year, failing slowly, first the ears, then the teeth, the limbs, the hair, and Papa did not like anything that failed. He did not like Nani and called her a heroine, a character from some movie. "Had Nani not been your father's mother-in-law," Ma had once told me, "he would have called her a camel, an elephant even, though there is nothing of a camel or a bull in your nani. She is much too petite for such comparisons, wouldn't you say? She is a bird, really, a grasshopper, a miniature monkey wild in the neighborhood." Ma had paused for a second and swatted a housefly with the ends of her sari. "Of course your father sees nothing wrong in his own mother, that soulless widow. That woman robbed me of everything, my dowry, my status in the family, our village property, but your father is nicely blind to that, my sack of sugar. Only your father's father was worth anything in that family, but he died too many years ago, my lovely. Even I haven't seen him. I don't know how he must have tolerated that whore of his wife. He must have been a very patient man, a saint, really."

Papa paced about the kitchen, stepping over Adi who continued to sprawl. He lifted lids off pots and stirred the contents in them with the spoon he held firmly in his hand.

"You just want to run off to your sisters," he said, stirring the daal. "I don't like them one bit. Shanti is all right, but there is something of a horse about the rest."

"And your sister," Ma snapped back, "is just the most astounding beauty, what with her buckteeth rising like hills from her mouth."

Papa walked over to the counter where Ma stood before the pot of boiling milk and slapped her. "Your mouth runs like scissors all the time," he said.

Adi scrambled off the floor and put himself between Ma and Papa. He picked the pot of milk off the fire and poured the milk into the sink. We stared at him, stunned. Then Adi emptied out a packet of sugar into the dustbin. He watched Papa the entire time, his eyes burning. I did not breathe. Papa hit Ma often, but he had never laid a hand on Adi or me, and I wondered if that was going to change this afternoon. I was suddenly jealous of Adi, jealous of Ma's startled attention on him, jealous of the way Papa had stepped back, confused, jealous even of the hand he raised now to hit Adi.

"If you touch him," Ma said to Papa, her voice flat, "I will finish your job for you later. I will chop him up and bury him with the beans."

I stared at Ma. Only she could make such threats.

The next day Ma, Adi, and I left for Darbhanga.

Suman Uncle's house in Darbhanga was always crowded with his numerous friends who liked to hang around on the balcony. For their benefit, chairs were neatly and perpetually arranged under the windows lining the balcony wall and Suman Uncle's friends came in early, chewing their toothbrushes, their shaving kits tucked under their arms, and holding tight to jugs they would later send the children off to fill. Some came in their vests and lungi, flapping their bathroom slippers upon the cement floors. Most brought along their own tea and stood the short glass tumblers upon the windowsills before beginning their morning chitchat with comments about one another's beards and choice of mustache for the day. They discussed marriages and familial problems. They were especially hard on a particular person, Kedarnath, and his wife, who was hoping to become the president of the Ghar Sudharo NGO. She wanted to do amazing things for Darbhanga and its female population, but the men shaving and brushing on Suman Uncle's balcony believed it would be better if she did some amazing things for her husband. "He looks quite like a scarecrow, poor fellow," they said.

Below the balcony, where Suman Uncle parked his scooter, I played hopscotch with my cousin, Shikha. Shikha was Kirti Mausi's daughter and the same age as I was. We often exchanged clothes and shoes but mostly Shikha just gave hers to me because Shikha had more clothes and shoes than I did, and better ones too. It was from hanging out at the balcony and playing hopscotch there that Shikha and I learned about the two groom parties that had come to see Ruby but had not proposed marriage. "Why are they called parties?" Shikha asked, and I responded because I had played enough House-House with Sachi to know exactly what a groom's party was.

"Because," I said, "when the groom's party comes you have to make sure your house is very clean and the food you serve has been ordered from the best restaurant."

The groom's party remained a party even if the intended groom did not accompany it. The intended groom was not the important person. The important persons were the groom's father, the groom's uncles—at least one from each side—and the groom's best friends. Together, they were the party, and it was the intended bride's job to impress as many of them as she could. However, the two parties that had come to see Ruby had not proposed marriage, not because she could not impress them, but because on the eve of her first marriage interview, at dinner, Ruby had put the last roti on her father's plate and announced "Love." She was, Ruby had said, in love with a boy who visited the neighborhood every summer. She had been in love for two years and would not marry anyone else. So when the groom's party arrived the next evening, Suman Uncle did not even bother with ordering any food from a restaurant, and the interview that followed was more or less a charade to keep Suman Uncle's reputation from going down the drain. Then two months later Ruby came to her father and declared "Unlove." She was no longer in love and would marry any man of her father's choice. Almost immediately Suman Uncle invited another prospective groom's party to his house and despite the anger he felt against Ruby, he also felt the pride a father can only feel over a child who turns a corner. But a week before the second interview Ruby once again fell in love with the boy who visited the neighbor, and she briefly ran away from home to live with obscure friends. For once in the history of a marriage interview, it was the intended bride who was missing during the party. All this was six months ago. And now Ruby was declaring Unlove again, swearing by her dead mother that she wanted nothing to do with the boy who visited the neighbor, that the boy was as good as dead to her, that she wanted, like she wanted nothing else, to get married.

"Except," said Suman Uncle, lathering up a thick foam on his cheeks, "there is not a single groom's party anywhere willing to interview my Ruby anymore."

Word had stepped off Suman Uncle's balcony, walked into the streets, and wafted into every house in every neighborhood, and from there into other towns. Ruby was no longer marriage material.

Below the balcony, by the scooter, I jumped a hop. "Everyone knows now that she is nothing but a Ruby-phuby-kuby," I said to Shikha. "She is simply a complicated matter and nothing more."

Shikha shook her head. "She will get married," she said. "If she leaves her hair open during an interview, she will get married. Open hair is a miracle, my mother told me."

"Don't you worry," said Suman Uncle to his friends. "Now that my sisters have all come together, they will fix this hole. Women can fix anything. My wife, she could fix anything."

It seemed to me that my uncle was right. My mother and aunts would eventually make it all right. They were always whispering, taking Ruby out shopping and returning home with bags of creams and clothes, making phone calls and writing letters. Eventually the whisperings would work. The creams and the clothes would remove the phuby-kuby from Ruby and leave behind only Ruby, twenty years old, five feet three inches tall, a red stone on her nose, and big eyes that seemed always to have a sheen of tears on them. Without the phuby-kuby, Ruby would be beautiful, would leave her hair open during an interview, and be declared everyone's favorite. Not that I begrudged Ruby a wedding. Weddings were fine things to attend, packed as they were with sweets and new clothes. It was the attention Ruby would receive, the ease with which Ma would then forgive her, would perhaps comb her hair and kiss her forehead, that troubled me.

Already, within a week since Ma's arrival to Darbhanga, a prospective groom's party had been spotted. It was not an ideal party. The family was too steep, so high in the scale of steepness that the chances of the family marrying Ruby, daughter of Suman Uncle, who was rich only in heart, was rather negligible. "The boy is a chartered accountant," Suman Uncle told his morning friends, "and the family desires polish, class, that kind of bamboozling from a girl."

Shikha and I were playing gitti on the stairs when Suman Uncle asked Shikha to go into the house and fetch her mother. Shikha looked at me and I nodded. What else could be done? When Shikha brought Kirti Mausi to the balcony, Suman Uncle gave her a letter. "The chartered accountant wants a bride who can speak and write English," he said. "He wants a wife who is willing to go out and be taught computers, keep her hair down and her heels high during family gatherings. Someone with polish and sophistication. Someone who can learn to drive a car."

"Drive a car?" said Kirti Mausi, rereading the letter Suman Uncle handed to her. "Drive a car?" she repeated, shaking the letter. "Come girls." She snapped her fingers at us and we put away our stones under the papaya tree and followed Kirti Mausi into the house.

Kirti Mausi was an almost-fat-almost-thin woman. She had a large stomach and thin legs and thin arms. She had multiple chins but her cheeks were sunken. There wasn't a single gray hair on her head because she used hair dye as often as she could. Some days her hair was dark brown, other days it was red, but on all days she smelled of chemicals that wafted off the hair on her head and the polish on her nails. She did not like bright nail polish and kept it sober with pastels and browns.

"I tell you," said Suman Uncle behind us, "my Ruby will be flying rocket ships to the moon if I leave her to these women. These women will make minced meat out of chartered accountants."

"A car," said Kirti Mausi shaking her head and the letter as she led us into the house.

This was a large house, built the way houses were in old days, with an open courtyard at the center and rooms on all four sides—bathrooms and toilets on one; prayer room, storeroom, and kitchen on the other; guest room, "dining area," and TV room on the next; and all the bedrooms on the fourth. A veranda ran along the rooms and there were several stools and chairs upon it for people to sit on. All day pigeons swooped into the courtyard from the open sky, and all day the parrot Nani had recently bought screeched from its cage. Only my grandparents, Nana and Nani, had their bedroom away from the courtyard and were not disturbed by the pigeons and parrots gurgling and fluttering at all hours, but now that Nana was so sick he could hardly walk, Nani had banished him to the dining area and I heard his soft groans when I passed the door. In the courtyard, the parrot's cage swung from an oversized clotheshorse pushed to one end, and the parrot screamed for an audience.

"Dawn shows her breasts," it screamed. "Wake up. Maitri, wake up. Wake up, wake up, wake up. Out pop her breasts, wake up. Wake up, wake up, wake up," until its croaky voice turned shrill with impatience. I wondered who Maitri was. I did not know anyone named Maitri. Nani's name was Kaveri, not Maitri.

From the terrace Nani yelled back, "I am coming, you foulmouthed chicken!"

"Drive a car," Kirti Mausi said after every few steps. "A car." She stopped on the last step and read the letter once again. It was written on a blue aerogram. "A car," she said and burst out laughing.

All the women were on the terrace. Ma and Mansi Mausi were leaning against the parapet, throwing peanut shells at boys playing cricket on the street below. Behind them Ruby sat on a cot pushed under the awning for shade, folding clothes she had pulled off the line. Shanti Mausi was on the cot, too, reading magazines and looking as beautiful as the women on the magazine covers. Earlier that morning Kirti Mausi had also spread corn and lentils upon the mats, and the terrace was a patchwork of rice and parched paddy, beans and lentils, dried chilies and dried spinach, all spread out like galaxies. Kirti Mausi was always spreading things, always working, always busy. Even Nani, whose house this really was, did not work so much. She was now sitting at the foot of the cot, carefully oiling her legs, her sari pulled up to her thighs, talking about her parrot with Ruby who hardly seemed to listen. "Had it not been for me someone would have plucked out every feather from the beast's wings," she said, massaging oil into her skin. "They would have snipped off its irreverent beak, too. They would have cut its throat and drowned its haughty eyes in that bucket." She pointed in the direction of the bucket sitting beside the hand pump in the courtyard down the stairs and giggled. Her skin gleamed with oil. "Come sit with your nani, Shikha Jaiswal," she said when she saw Shikha.

"No," said Shikha and walked on with her mother.

"You come then, Preeti Chaudhary."

I was already standing with my mother but Ma looked at me now and said, "Go sit with her, Pirti," so I went back to sit down beside Nani.

"What an untidy girl," Nani said and slapped my head. "Playing in the mud like a loafer! What will people say? That Nani's granddaughter has come all the way from Kathmandu, Nepal, but look, she is such an urchin." She poured out a blob of sticky mustard oil in the hollow of her palms and began a rough massage on my hair.

"Nani!" I protested.

"If it was not for me, someone would have plucked out every feather from your wings, too," Nani said to Shikha, who was watching and laughing from the parapet. "Do you have lice in there? Lice?" she asked me.

"No," I shouted but Nani raised her buttocks and pulled a thin-toothed bamboo comb from under her and ran its sadistic edges into my hair. "All these lice crawling like kings on your scalp. If you grow too many lice on your head they will tow you to the well when you are sleeping and push you into the cold water. Understand? That is what lice do to untidy girls after drinking the untidy girl's blood."

"Let her be, Mai," Ma said. "She does not have lice."

"That is what you think," Nani said and held me tight, but I wriggled out of her grip and ran off to Ma. Sometimes I could not bear Nani. Sometimes I wished it was Nani and not Nana lying in the dining area, slowly dying in the dark.

"But here I am," Nani went on, continuing her conversation about the parrot with Ruby, "and his lordship receives seasonal breakfast all year-round. Eh? It is mangoes for summer now. Raw guavas in the spring, green hot chilies in the autumn, and chane-ki-daal mixed with jaggery all winter. What do you say? Good life or not?"

"You drive me mad," Ruby said.

Ma turned fully away from the parapet and stared at Nani. "Babuji is very sick, you know," she said.

"Who knows," said Nani.

From the floor below came the parrot's screech again. "Maitri, Maitri," it cried.

"Now that your father is so ill he cannot even walk," Nani said, "I was thinking I will sleep till late, like this duffer Ruby and everyone else does, but I can't. That poultry bag down there keeps screaming and shouting. Nothing to do in the mornings now, other than feed his highness. Earlier I had to make tea for your father, boil those beans for his breakfast. I was always worried about his breakfast. He made such a fuss over it. Now he is on soft diet—roti soaked for a half hour in milk and a spoonful of mashed potatoes to go with it." She giggled. "These are the holidays!" she said.

"Mai," Kirti Mausi and Ma cried out at the same time.

"You are too much," Kirti Mausi said. "You say anything. And you, Ruby," she said. Ruby looked up from her clothes. "Do you even know how to ride a bicycle?" Ruby did not answer and Kirti Mausi shook her head. "Cannot ride a bicycle and has to drive a car now."

"And this Suman," Ma said, leaning upon the parapet again, "he wants to give the bricks of this house away for charity. Look at all those people sitting on our balcony, like crows on a wire. Lined up nice and proper for Suman to throw grains at them, though where he will get grain from, I cannot say. And him like a king among them, and his father dying in the house too."

"Let father die for today," said Kirti Mausi. "You look at the letter." But Shanti Mausi, who had since left the magazines behind and come to the parapet, pulled it out of Kirti Mausi's fingers instead.

One of the men on the balcony stepped out onto the street and looked up. He was on his way back home and was holding too many things in his hands—shaving mirror, toothbrush, toothpaste, jug. When he saw Ma and her sisters on the terrace he half waved his cluttered arms and shouted out, "Meena!" before walking on, and Ma shook her head.

"As though he is my husband," she said. "Look at him shouting my name. Shameless!" But she was smiling and I knew Ma had already become contradictory. She always became contradictory in Darbhanga. In Darbhanga she smiled and frowned together. She was simultaneously angry and happy. Visible and hidden. When I went looking for her, she seemed to be nowhere; just when I gave up, there she was, on the bed with Nani, their legs balanced upon the wall, mulling over muddlements I was not privy to. Or she would be feeding the parrot. Some mornings Ma would feed the pigeons and I would mistake her either for my grandmother or for one of my aunts.

Darbhanga was a gathering of lookalikes. Ma looked like Nani. Kirti Mausi, Mansi Mausi, and Shanti Mausi looked like Ma. Ruby looked like Ma. They had the same face, the same hands and feet. Their faces and hands resembled Nani's face, hands, and feet. Their faces were oval with sharp widow peaks, and their hands and feet were small, with small nails. When Ma grew old she would look more like Nani and when Ruby grew old she would look more like Ma. When each of Ma's three sisters grew old they would look more like one another. When their daughters grew old they would remind people of Nani, too. There were great-granddaughters in the family who reflected their mothers and their grandmothers and their great-grandmothers. The few granddaughters who did not resemble Nani, the few like me, were oddly distinct, like rocks in a river.

In Darbhanga I did not understand what my mother meant to do, or what she meant, or what I meant to her. Ma left me behind with cousins and went out for movies with her sisters. She threw me out of the room and played crude games with her sisters, in which they chased one another around with Coca-Cola bottles and bottle gourds and laughed so loudly I felt my face grow warm with embarrassment.

Ruby had told me I was a foundling discovered on a park bench, wrapped in a newspaper. I no longer believed that story but sometimes in Darbhanga I still felt like a newspaper child and when I felt like that I also felt alone, as though nothing at all in the world was mine, not even my mother. Especially not my mother.

Now, again, I could not understand Ma, could not understand her indifference toward the letter Kirti Mausi was so eager about. Shanti Mausi held the aerogram firmly between her fingers, her eyes bouncing back and forth like table-tennis balls as she read. At the end of the letter she burst into a series of grunts and hiccups. Kirti Mausi laughed, too. Ruby left off folding the clothes and looked at them. The shadow of the awning shaded her face and just for a second I felt so sad for Ruby I wanted my aunts to stop laughing. I wanted to take the letter away and maybe burn it so Ruby would not have to see it again.

"Is it from a party?" Nani asked.

"Yes," said Kirti Mausi.

"Show," said Ma and finally took the letter from her sister.

"Girls nowadays want to become butterflies," said Nani. "That is why they don't get married. Men want caterpillars, littlelings that bloom into butterflies in their arms, not women with ready-made wings." Then she recounted a story about her own wedding, which I had heard at least a hundred times before. "What a wedding!" She clapped her gleaming thighs to emphasize the event. "Fourteen years old I was and oho, sooo pretty. Husband, venerated husband, he had not imagined such a pretty thing in his dreams. And I was a landowner's daughter. We could have been the lords of Nepal. My father had land from this corner to that corner. Husband, what did he have? Nothing. My palanquin was placed on an elephant. I still remember the elephant. Oho, so beautiful! I sat in the palanquin and looked at everybody from inside it, and then I got tired and I slept. Such a queen I was in those days. And husband, he came on a horse. A horse! I came on an elephant, he came on a horse!"

Shanti Mausi took the letter and read it again. When Shanti Mausi was a child, Nana had sent her to a school for the deaf and mute and Shanti Mausi could sign well. She could also read and write, and comparisons between Shanti Mausi and Ruby were inevitable. "Now look at this Shanti," said Kirti Mausi. "Look at her, and look at this Ruby!" Shanti Mausi was a vociferous fan of books and magazines that taught the skills of decorating a house with the smallest expense, of cooking three absolutely delicious snacks in thirty minutes, and turning old saris into new and fashionable skirts. She was now sitting on the parapet, slowly swinging her legs, and the blouse she wore was one she had crocheted herself. And here was Ruby, who was not deaf or mute, and who had been sent to the same school all her other sisters had attended, but she was no good with needle and thread and was always the worst student in the classroom. She had somehow learned her Hindi alphabets but was almost illiterate in English. Her cooking skills were not outstanding, either, and no one had ever seen her wear heels with any grace.

Ruby's real name was Kavita, poetry. "Ruby" did not mean anything, not in the scriptures, not in the dictionary. It was one of those names which, according to Kirti Mausi, was like Dolly and Molly, a Western name that was supposed to do crazy things to the wearee. "The Rubys of this world," Kirti Mausi said, "are supposed to be smart. They are supposed to speak English, wear trousers, drive cars. Even if they are loose, characterless whores holding hands with boys and speaking casually about the matters of the heart, they are supposed to have class. This Ruby"—Kirti Mausi looked up at the sky, which seemed to be turning darker—"this Ruby is a headache. I asked her the other day to clean her grandfather's bed and what does she say to me? She says, you are his daughter, you clean it. Stupid girl."

Shikha and I looked at each other. I wondered if I should tell Kirti Mausi that Ruby was not that stupid. She was full of nonvegetarian jokes about boys, about first nights and subsequent nights after marriage, about carrots and oranges stuffing pants and blouses. Ruby kept a notebook under her mattress where she pasted pictures of Bollywood stars and some nights she unbuttoned her kurta and pulled down her pajamas while she stared at Jeetendra and Chunky Panday. I knew because Shikha knew and because we had spied many times on Ruby through the gaps between the curtains of her room.

"This man wants more than just some woman who can cook and clean," said Kirti Mausi, still staring at the sky. "And, Mai, there is no point just lotioning your legs now, is there? Go down before the rain comes. This man wants a tutor at home, someone who can teach his children and keep up with the bills. The sun was so perfect only a second ago and look now! Accursed weather!" cried Kirti Mausi but Ma,

Shikha, and I did not move away from the parapet. Shanti Mausi remained on the wall, still swinging her legs. Ruby looked like she would cry soon. Nani listened to the parrot. Only Kirti Mausi moved away. "You think it will rain immediately?" she asked everyone. "No? Not right away? Ruby," she called out. "Come, beta, come help me pack the grains back into the sack. Be a love and hurry, will you. Stitch the sacks up again, come."

Ruby jumped off the cot. I moved to help. It seemed to me like Kirti Mausi would begin to cry any moment. "Will you move now?" Kirti Mausi asked because though Ruby and I had moved, we did not do anything. Shikha was with her mother already, helping with the spinach. "Why are you just standing and looking like an idiot?" Kirti Mausi asked. "Why are you not packing? Here, pack that one. That one we did not empty completely, pack that one. Why are you not stitching? Pick up those scissors and cut that rope thread. The needle is next to the scissors. Good Lord!"

Ruby picked up the scissors. "These are the heaviest scissors I have ever seen," she said.

"So?" asked Kirti Mausi.

Ma turned around to see what was going on. Shanti Mausi stopped swinging her legs. Even Nani paid attention.

Ruby shook her head. So nothing, her head shake said. She cut a foot-long rope thread from the spool and bent her head to better align the thread with the huge needle eye. "Good Lord!" Kirti Mausi cried. "It will take you all day that way. Just cut one long piece and hurry up. The screw in your head is loose or what? Such a wobbly head, really, all messed-up brains! Hurry, it will rain!"

"Let her be, Kirti," Ma said.

Ruby stood with the thick thread and the needle and when Ma spoke she turned around and glared at her. "Just because I don't have a mother, don't act like you are mine," she said. She put the spool back on the floor. "This is my house, not yours. Your father is dying, and all you are worried about is daal and tilauri. Your father is dying, and all you want is to be with your sisters eating peanuts. This is not a charity home for all of you to come waddling in with your pathetic marriages and your pathetic griefs. And nobody asked you to rescue our house. As though nobody eats in this house until you come swishing in your saris." Then she turned around and left the terrace.

Ma stayed at the parapet, her back to the wall.

"Come back, you!" Kirti Mausi called after Ruby. "Come back, you brat. If I don't catch you later and beat the living life out of you, my name is not Kirti Jaiswal. Come back." But Ruby was laughing from the staircase. I managed to catch a glimpse of her as the stairs turned and I saw Ruby's head bobbing up and down. Kirti Mausi stood akimbo, maddened by Ruby's bad manners. She could barely speak. She looked at Ma and asked, "Why did you not say anything? There is a devil in that girl. That is what it is. And what is the matter with the sun? Where in god's name did these clouds sprout from? Good Lord, Meena, stop looking so glum and pack these grains. Good Lord. Come, Preeti darling, come help me. That Ruby is going to get it from me when I catch her. Come, darling."

Half an hour later, after the sacks were hurriedly packed and pushed under the awning, after their mouths were stitched so the grains would not get soggy, Kirti Mausi, Ma, Nani, Shanti Mausi, Shikha, and I sat on the cot, sulking. Not a drop of rain had fallen. The sun was silver once again. Nani alternated between oiling her legs and commenting philosophically on life. "These daughters are very dangerous!" she said.

"Daughters are very dangerous, are they?" Ma snapped. "Your daughters come from every corner the moment you call but that you will not see. Your son has ruined everything, is on the verge of selling the bricks of this house to his vulture-friends, but that you will not see. Daughters are very dangerous!"

It was on the cot that the plan was shaped, the one Kirti Mausi hoped would get Ruby closer to marriage. "She might not marry the chartered accountant but it might hook someone else. Might hook the chartered accountant, too, who knows. He might be an ass after all." I was to write a letter in English, addressed to a groom, a decent, simple letter with the least number of grammatical complications. The letter was to convey that Ruby was not very proficient, but also not entirely unlettered in English, and that though she was Hindi medium educated, she could understand and write English to a manageable degree. "You are ten years old, are you not?" Kirti Mausi said. "Your English is perfectly of that kind." Once the letter was written, I was to read it aloud before the family, translating the contents when required, and when the letter was approved, Ruby would memorize it, both verbally and through writing it numerous times each day, and reproduce the same before the prospective groom's party. "If Ruby can produce a letter, it might be all the needed proof," Kirti Mausi said.

"You can do that? You can write a letter?" Ma asked, and when I looked at her, I saw that her smile was different. It was not playful. It was serious and sad and I knew Ma would always love Ruby. It would not matter what Ruby did, how many plans she ruined, how rudely she spoke, how badly she did in school. It did not matter that Ma had Adi and me. Ruby would always be Ma's first daughter, one she would have raised to adulthood if Suman Uncle had not asked for her back.

I nodded. I wanted to write the best letter in English there was in the world. I wanted to get the chartered accountant groom excited about Ruby's red nose ring and her long hair. I wanted to see Ruby married, to see her gone, to see Ruby belong to a different house so she would stop belonging to my mother.

Behind us Nani giggled. "This will not work. I tried to teach that crow some poetry, but crows don't learn, do they? Parrots do."

"Mai!" scolded Ma, glaring at Nani, and it was decided that I was to make this marriage possible.

In the stories Ma told me about herself when she was a young girl, still unmarried, Nana-Nani-ghar was filled with Nana. Even when he was not inside the house, when he was away, as he mostly was, managing the cinema halls for which he worked, he was within the walls of the house. When he returned home, late at night, after the last shift of movies was over, he did not speak much and yet all day long Ma and her siblings repeated Nana's words and answered to him, as though he was sitting right before them. They lived for him, Ma, her siblings, Kaveri Nani—they lived to see Nana return home, to take his walking stick and his coat away from him, to hang those behind the door, to run to the courtyard to fetch him a glass of cool hand pump water. When Nana was not home Ma, Suman Uncle, and their sisters listened to the radio Nana listened to and read the books he left dog-eared on the pillow. The food they ate was the food he preferred. The colors of their saris and their shirts were selected to please him. The movies they watched every week were movies he chose for them. There was no animosity over this in the house. There were few fathers then who would allow such clothes, such food, and any movies at all to their children. There was only gratitude.

And yet now that Nana was always home, groaning behind the curtain hanging over the dining area door, I could see that Ma had to force herself to remember him. She had to force herself and Adi and me into the dining area twice every day to check on him, to stand by the leg of the cot, waiting for the moment we could eventually escape.

Nana lay on the single bed pushed against the wall, under the built-in china cabinet that still held cups, saucers, and dinner sets. On another shelf were jars of pickles and preserves. The dining area was partitioned off from the guest room with a long, heavy, maroon curtain, and there were no windows. Even before Nana had taken ill and was banished to this corner, nobody other than distinguished guests, such as families of prospective grooms and families of Suman's Uncle's deceased wife, had ever eaten in the dining area. And now nobody would ever eat in it. The room smelled too dirty for guests. It reeked of urine and dirt, pickles and medicines. It did not smell of the Nana I knew, who was always scented with hair oil and kerchief perfumes. I stood close to the bed and held my breath against his stink. In the room's darkness, his body was yellow and small and his eyes were enormous behind his thick glasses. Some days Ma began to cry. Nana was bones and skin. It was hard to imagine he had once been tall. It was hard to imagine anyone had once been afraid of him or had once loved him. It was hard to imagine people reading the books he read and cooking meals he liked to eat. Ma said he had once been the most handsome, the most dignified human she knew. All of it was hard to imagine.

"The sun hurts his eyes in the other room," Nani said, peeping for a second from the door. "And he just complains. You know how much he likes to complain. And I snore and fart at night. Is that disturbing or not?" And then she was gone.

I stared at Nana and he stared silently back from the small, unmade bed. There was a stool beside the bed with a pitcher of water, a steel tumbler, and nothing else. Leaning against the stool was Nana's walking stick, its metal head worn with time. That, too, had been handsome once. And the leather shoes, shaped like juttis and curled at the tips—they had inspired fashion among his friends.

"It's me, Babuji," Ma said. "It's Meena." She poured some water from the pitcher into the tumbler, then poured it back.

I stood behind her, gripped by a fear I could not understand.

The parrot screeched and screamed outside, calling out for Maitri. I heard someone fiddling with the television in the guest room behind the curtains. I heard the pigeons beginning to flutter from the sky into the courtyard. Everything smelled sour. Then Ma turned around and walked out, and Adi and I followed a little too fast.

Nani was on the veranda, looking up at the square sky above the courtyard, listening for the pigeons. They came every day, punctually at seven, and Nani had her bag of grains ready with her. The sky was turquoise and teal, and when the pigeons flew in they blocked the sky out. A momentary shadow fell upon the courtyard and upon the house, a coolness came upon its warm walls. The birds flapped down, fanning the wind, quivering as they hovered for seconds above the floor, before descending to scratch the courtyard with their claws, their feet slipping upon the cement floor. They fell upon one another and Nani dipped into the bag and flung the feed toward the birds. The grains hurled out, rolling in space, unfurling before they fell rainlike upon the floor. The pigeons gurgled in response, cooed and warbled, oh-oor-ed. I could hear the tick-tick of their beaks as they pecked at the floor. They shat as they ate, their shit like white paint mixed with spinach. The parrot went crazy then, trying to greet each pigeon—"Good morning, bird. Good morning, bird. Good morning, bird."

"Mai," Ma said. "He will die soon."

"Just drama it is," Nani said. She flung out another handful of grain. Her bangles jingled as she darted about in hurry, making sure each bird got its share. "You know how he likes to do drama." Then she began to sing an old wedding song:

Sun Ré Dulha I might even curse your day and say
Oh, you no-gooder, your boss will never promote you to a better position
Oh, you no-gooder, I would rather that you be dead than that I wed you tonight
Oh, you no-gooder, may your hair stick out and your pants fall off and a hundred other misfortunes befall
Oh, you no-gooder, the bed will never creak and the pots will never bang and perhaps this night will never pass

I was drawn by the irrepressible joy in my grandmother, but Ma was trembling with anger.

"Do you have no shame?" Ma hissed. "Sleeping all alone in that big bed?"

"If you have so much shame," said Nani, "then you sleep with him." And she carried on talking about her parrot, and her visits to the temple, "That new priest is from South India, imagine, as though there are no Brahmins in Bihar," and about her daughters, "You just come when you please. Nice." And her grandchildren and her great-grandchildren who were already more than she could remember. "There are just too many pests in the world," she said.

Sometimes, if the afternoon was warm, Suman Uncle helped Nana out onto the veranda. He sat him upon a chair that had a rail around it so he would not slip off. Nana sat limp and drooling from the mouth, watching. He was afraid of where he sat. He was afraid of the parrot that would fall asleep and then awaken suddenly, screeching "All my life! All my life! All my life!" Nana was afraid of every visitor who came and said Namaste and asked after his health.

The maid came to sweep and mop and when she reached Nana, she lifted his feet and mopped under them. On his right, inside the kitchen, Ma, Kirti Mausi, and Shanti Mausi sat surrounded with staggering piles of bread and heaps and mounds of gourds and potatoes waiting to be stuffed into breakfast sandwiches. Shikha and I played in this strange setting of life and death. Suman Uncle called out for another cup of tea every half hour. The parrot mourned for Maitri. The pigeons, the latecomers, trickled in one by one, cascading and descending into the courtyard. Everywhere there was sound, and thick smells, and the ceaseless undying feeling of a feast in preparation.

I tried hard to get Ruby to memorize the letter, but Ruby was slow and impatient and twice she hit me for pestering her too much.

"Being able to write in English is not everything," she said.

"But at least it will get you married," I argued.

"We will see about that," Ruby said. She was wearing a green salwaar kurta, the kurta cut low, almost reaching her ankles, and I saw that it was made from one of Ma's saris. Ma used to wear the green sari occasionally until she stopped wearing it about a year ago and now Ruby had made a dress from it.

"It's a nice kurta," I said.

"Yeah," said Ruby.

My heart sank at my cousin's tone. I was convinced Ruby would not get married this time around, either. Ruby would refall in love and rerun away. There would be no wedding. I tried telling Ma Ruby was not participating, not following orders, but even amid the preparations for Ruby's future marriage, even amid the outings, the movies, the jokes, there was a silent, unspoken preparation for Nana's death, a sort of distraction I could not overcome, and sometimes Ma would not listen to a word I said.

"If you really tried, you could do it," I persisted with Ruby.

Ruby was painting her toes, a bright red polish, and she stopped painting. "Your mother and your aunts are only playing with you, you know. Only showing you off. A letter cannot get me married. Only I can get me married," she said.

"Then why don't you?"

But Ruby did not answer and in that silence I recognized the gap between me and my older cousin. I caught a glimpse of the world within Ruby and though I could not understand what that world was, I knew it was a world created not by circumstances but by age. Certain worlds were born with age and those younger than that age could do nothing to change them. It became clear to me then that Ma and her sisters were indeed playing with me, were only showing me off to make Ruby feel bad, that I could not change anything. I could not get Ruby married and belong to someone else. If Ruby wanted to remain unmarried, she would remain unmarried.

The day Nana definitely started dying, Shikha and I were in the neighborhood playing with friends. When we got home, Suman Uncle and his friends were on the balcony and he jerked his head toward the door. "Go in, go in," he said, shaking his head.

Ruby was on the balcony, standing by the stairs that went to the terrace. She was holding her shawl bunched like a ball over her nose. The parrot was squawking inside its cage, "Eeek, eeeek, eeeek." The thick air closed around my neck and I gagged before quickly holding my shawl over my nose too. "Nana shat all over the bed," Ruby mumbled behind the shawl. Ruby's forehead was covered in small, pimplelike eruptions and her eyes were slightly pink, as though she had cried some time ago.

"What happened to your head?" I asked, but I already knew the answer.

Ruby had thick eyebrows that bloomed like flowers over her eyes. Her father's eyebrows were thick and frizzled, too, and when the wind blew, the hair waved like wipers on his forehead, and sometimes Ruby's eyebrows looked very much like his. The beautician had said it would be best to thread and pluck her brows a month before the groom's party came over, and then again two weeks before the visit, and then finally three days prior to the interview. That way Ruby's face would not pucker up in pimples from the hairs getting pulled out and I guessed just by looking that Ruby had been through the first round. So a date for the groom's party's arrival had been set a month down the line.

Ma was at the hand pump but when Shanti Mausi, who was with Nana, started to scream, Ma stepped off the courtyard and waved to Ruby. "Come, come," she said and Ruby followed hesitantly. I watched from the door, holding my breath but unable to leave. My nana looked so old, older than any age I knew and I felt the sadness of his age. I knew everyone was waiting for him to die. An old person was supposed to die. An old person was supposed to die despite medicines, despite prayers and good wishes.

His bowels had rebelled and his buttocks were caked in crusty shit, and yellow shit, and his dhoti, his kurta, the sheets, the mattress, everything was filth. Shanti Mausi waved her hands in exasperation and made guttural sounds before screaming in that shrill way that brought goose bumps upon my arms. Ma took over after that and Ruby ran out of the room. I remained standing by the door. Ma rolled Nana's spindle body on the bed, first this way, then that, and the sticky garments peeled off the thin skin. She lifted his body and I stepped away so Ma could carry Nana to the hand pump where Ruby had filled a bucket. The parrot started to scream right away. "Wake up! Wake up! Wake up!" I wanted to stand with Ruby, but I felt strangely afraid of my cousin.

Nana sat flat upon the cement and he was small, no bigger than a five-year-old. His stomach sagged like a pouch over his hips and his chest leaked toward his stomach. His buttocks hung like a rag skirt below his hips. I kept my eyes away from his old genitals, soft and hairless, hidden by folds of loose tummy skin, but when Shanti Mausi lifted the folds and Ruby poured the water, when Ma rubbed the sparrow that looked like a bell, I felt like I had swallowed a blade and its thin metal sliced my throat.

Ruby poured mugsful of water over Nana and his dhoti. Nana sat on his haunches and moved slowly, this way and that way.

A week later Nana died, and during Nana's last week alive I saw healthy Nani fly toward damaged and decaying Nana like a corrupt, debased witch, screeching dreadfully at his petrified body. She hit him with full flat palms. "Die, you swine!" she shrieked. "Die! Die! Die!" until Ma pulled her away and locked her outside the house.

The morning after Nana's death Ma looked at the trough of sand that had been left at the gate for Nana's spirit to leave footprints of its afterlife. "Oh," Ma said, peering into the box of silver sand. "Babuji will be a bird, a parrot maybe."

Nani, resplendent and dry eyed in widowhood, flew around the house in glee. The priests were afraid for her soul and immediately began the mantras, but Nani flapped her hands in grotesque pantomime and squealed around the house. "Parrot! Pa-aaa-aaa-aaarot! Parrot!"

All day, while the priests performed the death ceremonies, Nani teased with wedding songs.

Sun Ré Dulha you will blush at my shamelessness
My bawdy words
And my slang
My dirty jokes will send hysterics up your spine
And my revenge will make you weep!
Sun Ré Dulha I come to you veiled
As a snake hides beneath the grass.

That was when Ma stepped away from the ceremony and slapped Nani so she would stop singing.

After the ceremony, Adi came looking for me. He was tired and stayed with me for the rest of the day. During lunch he coaxed me to eat, but he himself could scarcely put a morsel in his mouth.

"What will Ma do now?" Adi asked at one point and put the puri back into his plate.

"We will all go home," I said, pointing out the obvious.

"She hates Kathmandu."

"Ma does not hate Kathmandu," I said—and knew instantly that she did.

How strange it was to feel suddenly empty, in the middle of a meal, to understand clearly that the house we lived in was not Ma's home. Her home was here, in this chaos of sisters and brothers, in lives and deaths that mattered to her, in this place that sometimes felt so familiar and so alien to us, like it was built on the moon.

Ruby ran away from Nana-Nani ghar two nights later. It was a hot night and I could not sleep. Every bone in my body hurt. I sat inside the mosquito net, twisting my neck this way and that to crack the bones within. "Your bones are going to turn to powder one day," Ruby said from the door.

I threw my arm forward and cracked the bones of my elbows. "It hurts," I said.

"If you slept, you would feel better."

I crushed my ankles under my thighs with the hope that the weight would dislocate my joints. "All that water you sprinkle on the bed, that is what is giving you these aches. You had better sleep," Ruby said. "I'll turn off the tubelight but if you don't mind, I will keep the zero-watt on. I want to pack for a while."

"Are you running away again?" I asked.

"And I should tell you so you can go tell everyone else?"

"I won't tell anyone else," I said.

Ruby vanished under the switchboard and flicked the switch off, and everything, Ruby, the room and its content, everything disappeared and reappeared in monochromatic outlines.

It was an unusual room—almost oval, almost hexagonal, with Ruby's bed under one of the two windows opening toward the backyard.

Ruby climbed a wooden chair to noiselessly transfer shoes from the top of the cupboard to the floor. Then she pulled down a small suitcase. She climbed off the chair and took the kurta hanging from the peg behind the bed.

"So you are going for sure?" I asked.

"I won't run away for long. There would be no one for Papa if I did."

"Maybe you could just tell everyone you don't want to get married," I said.

Ruby spread a towel at the base of her suitcase. "I want to get married. You think I want to live here?"

"Oh," I said, at a loss.

"I just don't want to go crazy in the end, like everyone else," she said. "Like our nani, and Kirti Mausi, and your mother."

"Ma is not crazy."

"She will be."

We were quiet for a while. A lizard flashed out from behind the tubelight, then disappeared.

"Why doesn't your boyfriend ask for you in marriage?" I asked at last.

"I don't know," Ruby said. "I guess, sometimes someone sees you too much and so he does not want to marry you. Do you have that stupid letter with you? Give it to me."

"It's in my pants pocket, behind the door."

Ruby took the letter out. "I am only going to my friend's house. Pretend like you don't know anything, okay, but if they get too worried, if things are really bad, you know, I am only going to my friend's house."

"Okay," I said. Then Ruby picked up the suitcase, no bigger than a satchel, and left.

It was a miracle that the house still slept, that the sun did not suddenly flare out upon the sky, that the door did not open one more time to let Ruby back in.

I lay inside the net, feeling the wash of the fan upon my sweaty face, listening to the house sleeping, listening to the birds outside, and trying to listen for Ruby. Then I, too, fell asleep and trees and houses caught the moonlight and their roofs glittered at a distance. The moon was large and the cornfields bleached. The river came in slowly and curved under the bus and as the bus rose, the river was silver, then dark, then black, far down. The road was narrow and there were stories about buses that fell off. The road twisted and knotted, and the slightest error, the slightest fatigue, a second of dozing off, could send the bus tumbling down the cliff. When buses fell, they hit rocks, roots, branches. They tumbled, they tumbled, they tumbled, endlessly, hitting animals and clouds, logs and rocks, tumbling, the people within dead and broken, the sacks of grain tied to the bus top ripped open so that the grain fanned into the wind, flapping down, scattering along the sides of the mountains. The bus tumbled and once its fall was broken by bushes, and once by a large pigeon, then the bird itself broke and the bus tumbled on, abysmally, perhaps into the thick river. The grains established their own fields within the jungle of trees, and lush corn and paddy fields grew where no one could visit.

LOVE IS A THING OF THE CITIES

On our way back from Darbhanga to Kathmandu, we stopped for a few days at Sabaila. Ma never allowed us to stay for too long a period in Sabaila, but perhaps due to the infrequency of our visits there, for most of my childhood I was intrigued by my ancestral village.

I loved the landscape, so unlike Kathmandu's. I liked the daily routine of waking up before dawn, bathing before the sun was out, and praying to gods as though they really could hear my words. Despite her Friday fasts, Ma had raised us with little reverence for gods and goddesses and I found the clear grace with which my uncles, aunts, and cousins prayed beautiful. The only thing I did not like in Sabaila was Ma. While in Darbhanga Ma grew supple and light like a new blade of grass; in Sabaila she was hard and sharp. Everything pleased her only at the superficial level, and she was quick and sarcastic with everyone, especially with Kumud Chachi who visibly shrank before Ma.

In Sabaila I stayed away from Ma and spent most of my time with my grandmother, Sawari Devi, helping her with tasks like drying fruits, chilies, and vegetables on the terrace. It seemed to me she knew nothing about fatigue. She worked tirelessly. Even in her old age she went to the fields to supervise farming and when at home she was busy washing, chopping, drying, gathering. Mostly she worked alone but sometimes she called out for me and created little tasks I could carry out for her. "Help me with the rice," she said and passed on the flat basket that held the rice for the week. I sat with my grandmother and removed twigs and husks from the rice. At another time she asked me to spread the tilauri upon a sheet.

And this time, perhaps because Nana had just passed away and her own husband was on her mind, Sawari Devi told me a story.

"At first I did not know your grandfather was my husband," she said. "I thought he was a cousin, a playmate. I was eleven. He was fifteen. I did not pull a veil upon my face then, and your grandfather and I played all day in the fields."

She paused and looked at me. I wonder now if there was something in particular she was trying to tell me that day. I was so young then, I couldn't have grasped all her meanings.

"I played with him and with the other wives in the family. At night my mother-in-law slept between your grandfather and me. I did not mind. I did not know there was anything to mind. Besides, my mother-in-law was the closest thing I had to a mother. After your grandfather died, it was she who looked after me and my children. Eventually, she left off sleeping with us and I remember crying for her and I remember your grandfather running out of the room to bring his mother back so I would not cry. But she could not come. There was another bride in the house now, a younger one, who missed her mother and needed comforting, so she slept with her.

"With time I got used to sleeping with your grandfather. I had recently started my periods and all the rules had begun—the veil, the hours when I could talk to your grandfather and the hours I could not, the hours we could be seen together and the hours we could not, all that. The last time I looked directly at your grandfather in broad daylight was when he was seventeen. I was thirteen. I got pregnant at fourteen and your uncle was still so small in my stomach I did not know

I was pregnant, but every other woman in the family did. The face I remember of your grandfather's is his seventeen-year-old face.

"After the rules came in," she said, placing one tilauri behind another at regular intervals, "I went to bed first and your grandfather remained outside for an hour or longer, waiting for a decent interval before he could enter the room. In the mornings I left before the sun rose, and he followed a couple hours later. It was understood that all the women in the village were to be ready before the men stepped out for their baths and so when I came out of my room all the other women would be coming out, too, and we would go to the well to wash up. There was something nice about that." She paused, remembering. "The rooms were always dark after sunset. I don't know what I saw of him in that dim light, only that he was my husband. I knew him by his sounds, his voice, his shuffles, all that. I don't think I would have recognized him in the streets if I saw him."

"Do you miss him?" I asked.

"Oh?" she said, taken aback by the question. "I don't know."

The sun was strong, but we did not move. We sat on a mat, playing with its weave.

"I did not know the man," she said. "I knew the boy. He was a happy boy, always ready to play. I remember his boy face. He was a sweet boy. He must have been a handsome man. He must have become very handsome."

She laughed, embarrassed by her imagination, then she looked at me and smiled. "I have never spoken of him this way," she said.

Sawari Devi was a lean, tall woman. I couldn't tell her age, perhaps because she seemed to have more energy than any other person I knew. She was twenty-four when my grandfather died. My grandfather was twenty-eight. There were no pictures of my grandfather in the family. I had not seen my grandfather in any form and had no memory of him, not even imagined ones.

"Oh, I am probably exaggerating," my grandmother said, as though apologizing. "I probably did see him many times and probably knew his face very well, too. But it has been a long time. Even if I had seen his face every day for every second of those days, I would still not know his face today."

"You must have loved him a lot," I said because I had learned the word *love* from the movies. The movies had taught me that all wives love their husbands.

"Love," she said. "Love is a thing of the cities. In the villages love is a little bit like god. You don't see it or feel it. You just know it is there and go about living your life." Then she patted off the dried lentil from her palms and got ready for the next chore.

ONE STEP, ONE STEP, AND A LIMP

Kaveri died six months after she had danced at her husband's cremation. But before Kaveri started to die she lived briefly like a flowering cactus, all thorns and ablaze with colors. She sat on her balcony in bright saris, the sequins glowing in the sun, and shouted out to the vendors and neighbors passing the street outside her house. There was a new emerald on her nose and new bangles upon her wrists. The anklet, which she should have removed the day her husband died, peeped pink under her sari. She refused to wear white or pastel. She was a poltergeist, emancipated and wild, turning the house upon its head, breaking every rule of widowhood. Already children were beginning to gather around her, and she, no taller than the children at her height of four feet and eight inches, went off into the market to play gilli-danda and marbles with them. She bought trinkets for herself—leaf-shaped earrings, eels that wound around her fingers to become rings, cheap chokers. She bought the children sweets. She bought fruits for her parrot, basmati rice for the pigeons. She sat on the crowded market-sidewalks with the children and threw paper airplanes at customers. She tried to chase bicycle tires with sticks, the way the children did. On good days she followed the kids to their terraces and flew kites. At home she sat on a cot and rocked on her haunches. From her new throne she gave preposterous orders. "Fish curry!" she commanded. "Baingan bharta!"—culinary delights denied to her newly widowed tongue.

The day Kaveri started to die was also the first day of Dashami, the ten-day festival dedicated to Goddess Durga, and Kaveri found a mouse under her bed. On the second day of Dashami her hands shook slightly as she lifted food to her mouth. On the third day she saw Bilash in the moving shadow behind the fan. On the fourth day she went to the bathroom and had to stand outside, waiting for Bilash to finish his business. On the fifth day Bilash hid her slippers so she could not find them when she really wanted to go out to the streets. Kaveri did not take any of this too seriously. It had always been this way between Bilash and Kaveri, and on the eighth day she and the children set off to join the celebration by the temple even though a pigeon flying in for breakfast had died midair and fallen upon the courtyard earlier that morning.

Darbhanga was out upon its streets for Dashami, dressed for the occasion in bright saris and brighter shirts, loud in the praise of Durga, semidrunk with festivity. Kaveri and the children could scarcely keep a straight path or speak a complete sentence.

They zigzagged their way through people, some on trucks painted in tiger stripes to emulate the goddess's vehicle. There were people with skins coated bright with abir, as though it were Holi, and others carrying cardboard weapons and wearing cardboard crowns. Little girls dressed as Durga were so somber, Kaveri giggled. The makeshift Durga temple was like a little palace behind the crowd. The roads were jammed and devotees rode carousels and giant wheels, screaming in excitement. Hundreds were paying homage to the clay sculptors of gods and goddesses planted almost everywhere. Kaveri and the children got pushed around and found themselves in unexpected places:

stalls selling ribbons and handkerchiefs, toys and pins, parandas and bras, a Bilash, all hanging from nails banged into wooden frames; the rump of a content cow chewing on paper cones; a couple—a ten-year-old Lord Ram and Goddess Sita—having a conversation about school; a group of dhoti-clad pundits reading from *Devi Mahatmya* to an oddly serene crowd; and then a row of women with kerosene stoves selling onion kachries and dal kachoris to too many customers.

Kaveri ignored her husband who hung from a nail driven into the flanks of a cart and spoke to the fritter woman instead. "Durga never married," she said to the fritter woman while she unknotted a wad of money from her sari. "Did you know that? Here, give me ten rupees worth of kachries and ten rupees of moorhi."

All across the bazaar tall bamboos were stabbed into the ground—poles for loudspeakers tied high up, from which blared cries and pleas of children and wives who invariably got lost in the dissonant crowd.

Mohan, Mohan, please come to Ram Puri puree bhandaar. Your wife is waiting for you.

Giridhari of Mahendar Bazaar, Giridhari of Mahendar Bazaar, where are you, Giridhari of Mahendar Bazaar?

Gareeb Das, you will come to Imirti Dukan, yes, you will. Gareeb Das!

And so on and so forth.

Kaveri sat under a tree and grumbled. "Mad women," she said, "wanting to be found. What nicer luck than to be lost in a fair, eh? You tell me?" The children ate. Kaveri did not look up from her paper cone.

A man sat before the fritter woman, perhaps in his early thirties, thin and squirrel-like, shoving as much puff and as many fritters as he could into his mouth. He chuckled through it all. One of the loudspeakers was calling out for Raju ke Pappa, and the squirrel man promptly covered his mouth and giggled. "She thinks it's like a telephone!" he said, as he heartily munched the rice puffs.

"And you are an ass," said Kaveri, spitting out a small pebble that was in her fritter. "Eating away, are you, while your wife and children are lost?"

The woman in the loudspeaker sang another tremulous and tentative "hello" and went on, "Raju ke Pappa, I am sitting here lost and crying, and you are not even coming to look for me." The squirrel man looked mischievously at Kaveri but she was not impressed.

"I have no time for your monkeying around," she said.

"Raju ke Pappa, should I jump into the ocean now? I swear on my mother, I will jump into the ocean and die if you don't find me immediately." This threw the squirrel man into hysterics.

"She will have to travel at least three days in a train going the right direction before she touches the ocean," he said, laughing with delight. He ordered four more fritters—two potatoes and two onions—and giggled until the fritter woman shooed him away. He tottered off good-naturedly and sat down beside Kaveri and her children under the large tree. There was a giddy confusion of balloons and streamers hanging down the branches. Kaveri looked up and saw Bilash amid the ribbons.

The loudspeaker began to sing again. "Okay then, Raju ke Pappa . . . (here the squirrel man clapped his thighs and chuckled until he coughed) . . . I am now going to beat Raju. See!" and a sudden smacking sound followed by a slow whimpering cry drawled out the speaker. There was then another stinging slap and the whimper turned to a loud bellow. The children stopped eating. Kaveri's kachri hung midair between the paper cone and her mouth; others stared at the bamboos and the speakers. The squirrel man stopped eating and stared, too, his eyes big with disbelief, his potato-filled mouth open. Then there was another round of rigorous spanking and a riotous wail shook the speakers. "See, Raju ke Pappa, I will beat Raju till you come find us," sang the sweet voice, while another voice, that of a child's, cried, "Pappa! Pappa!"

The squirrel man spat out the potatoes, threw down the rice puffs, and wiped his oily hands on his dhoti. "What a bad mother," he said, scrambling to his feet and almost falling in his hurry. Raju was still howling when his father shot into the fair to look for his missing wife and son.

All around the crowd cheered. The children cheered the loudest. Kaveri clapped her hands and laughed. She jumped to her feet and did a small dance. She twirled and when she came back to position, Bilash was there, tall and lithe, like a movie star, foregrounded by streamers and balloons, smiling. "Hello," he said.

Kaveri did not speak to her ghost-husband. She stayed in the fair, pushing her way through until the gathering began to thin, the singers stopped singing, and the vendors began to leave. The children left, too, one by one, and went back to their homes. The sun faded and the air that had been heavy with oil and sweat began once again to smell of mud, of dung and wood, and of the night quickly coming on. All around sculpted gods and goddesses shone. Kaveri walked home in the dark and behind her Bilash, handsome and tall, walked with a limp.

One step, one step, and a limp, his rhythm went. One step, one step, and a limp. One step, one step, and a limp. He tagged along, not too fast. He kept a good distance and when Kaveri reached the gate of her house he was far but still behind her, one step, one step, and a limp.

OLD IRON TRUNKS

Two weeks after Kaveri died, Suman pulled out a dusty iron trunk pushed far under the large bed upon which Kaveri had first slept with her husband and then slept alone. Inside the trunk were silk saris; fashionably sleeveless blouses with strings on the back; lac bangles with fishes and leaves etched on their red circumference; a sandalwood sindoor box with a peacock on its lid; two gold rings; one gold pendant embedded with a moonstone swan; an old newspaper wrapped around a collection of notes ranging from one rupee to five hundred rupees; a tie-string bag full of coins; a geometry box, the type Preeti used for her classes, filled with flat cubes of silver; and a pair of soft velvet sandals, royal blue in color.

Kirti recognized the sandalwood sindoor box with the peacock on its head and cried out, "That damn thing is mine!"

Her sisters recognized other items—combs, soap covers, tikas. Mansi pulled out a shawl. "Mine," she said.

Kirti, Mansi, Shanti, Suman, and Meena did not know what to make of their mother's chest of stolen treasure, but slowly they concluded it was a hoard belonging to a woman who had once been wealthy but was eventually reduced to being a penniless, thieving housewife. "Imagine what a woman whose palanquin came on an elephant must have brought with her," they said to one another. They theorized that over the years Kaveri must have exchanged her loot for necessities such as money, or sweets and firecrackers. “How else,” they said, “could she have managed to feed us all and our children when we came swarming into her house?” Perhaps Kaveri was an active member of the pawn market, exchanging silk for cash, leaving behind gold and coming out with lard and butter.

But at other times they wondered if the cache had been driven strictly by vanity, if the pendants and the rings had served nothing but Kaveri’s narcissism behind locked doors. They imagined her standing before the mirror, wearing backless blouses and royal blue sandals, red lipped and kohl eyed. “You know,” Kirti said, “I dreamt of her once, and she was wearing a skirt, like one of those Goan secretaries they show in movies. Can you believe it? She was wearing a skirt, a short one.” And they felt strangely like castoffs, abandoned by their mother for worldly goods, neglected for silk and silver.

It was agreed the money in the newspaper, adding to almost ten thousand rupees, was stolen entirely from Bilash, though why they felt convinced their mother had not stolen money from them they could not say.

Throughout the day Suman crossed his arms across his stomach and laughed. “Look at that,” he said, meaning everything about the day, and hit the insides of his thigh in glee until his sisters hissed at him. “Behave yourself, Suman!” they said.

And Mansi, who had loved her father with more tenderness than she had loved her mother, paced up and down the terrace, tortured by the image of the bulging trunk and the arrogance the items in it hinted at. “How can you laugh?” she asked her brother. “That woman, first hitting that sick, dying man. His wounds filled with pus, did she not see? And now this? This dacoity!”

“Oh, stop the drama,” said Meena with a half smile. “What are a few slaps between husbands and wives? Husbands are always slapping wives, and no one goes jumping around like monkeys for that. What?

Will you not slap your husband nice and proper when you finally can?" And Mansi stared at her, aghast.

Meena's half smile was the smile of joy. For days after the trunk's excavation Meena felt a glow within her, a child's pride for a mother who had owned objects, was not poor, and had kept secrets. Meena fed Kaveri's birds, the pigeons and the parrots, and kept her mother's room clean, mopping it twice a day, once when the sun came in silver through the barred window, and once when it left golden. There was mystery to the room now, like there was to her mother. There was something mysterious about her father, too, Meena thought, but it was a simple mystery, created only by absence. A woman's mystery, a mother's mystery, was exquisite, guarded in a world where no space was allowed or allotted to her. Meena knew her father through absence, through the fact that the day would slip on without him, that life would go on without communication with him, that her father's role was godlike in its invisibility. And Kaveri, through her intense presence while raising children, grandchildren, birds, and animals, had sometimes blinded the eyes and was sometimes lost in the blind spot, but she was always present, was always everywhere. The house, used to Bilash's absence, did not change after his death. It grieved for a week, momentarily forgot its routine, briefly became sullen, but soon picked itself and resumed the movements of life. Soon it invited neighbors, went to the market, made three meals a day, watched television, and fell asleep. But Kaveri's death rendered the room Meena mopped unreal; the floors grew hard under her palm, the walls thinned, the rooms widened to unbearable spaces, the courtyard shrank and became small, infested with the poor mourning parrot and the pigeons that swept in and out from the open sky, scratching the cement floors. With Kaveri's death the house changed and Meena knew she was no longer a daughter but a visitor to this house, this city, and this nation. All things that had belonged to her while Kaveri lived were now alien. Meena could no longer come, luggage in hand, rest and sleep in mind, when the hardships of her everyday life in Kathmandu tired her and left her restless and angry. She could not come here on a whim, taking a bus and a train, scaling the mountains, chugging through plains. She was forever now a part of a different nation, a different city, like a frog stuck in a drying puddle.

YELLOW FROCK

I was eleven when Nani died and Ma could not take me along for her cremation because my midterm exam retake for mathematics was due in a week and our principal ma'am said that unless there was a medical emergency, I could not be excused from it. Perhaps, if Ma had let my principal ma'am know that my grandmother was dead, I would have been granted leave, but Ma refused to let ma'am know. "Why should I tell her I am without a father or mother? So she can click her tongue and shake her head and call me an orphan? I will go and your father can take care of you for once." And so she went to Darbhanga with Adi and left me behind with Papa. "And you," she said to me as she packed her suitcase the night before, "if you fail your math exam again and have to repeat your class like some donkey and cut my nose in the neighborhood, I will beat you blue when I come back, do you understand?" Then she collapsed upon the bed and began swaying back and forth. "My poor Maiya," she cried. "My poor, poor Maiya, trapped in that burning house like some moth."

The next day Papa and I went to the bus station to drop off Ma and Adi, and I felt paralyzed with terror. Home had taken on wheels and was about to roll away. It would be the first time I would sleep in a house without Ma. Even though I was eleven and Adi fourteen, there were still nights when the two of us slept with Ma and all night we fought over her body, forcing her to lie flat upon the bed with both her hands extended straight out so we could each lie on her shoulders until she grew sore and smacked us on our heads. There was an open competition between Adi and me, and now he had her all to himself and this left me nervous. I stood in the bus aisle, waiting for Adi and Ma to settle into their seats, reliving Ma's strangled cries from the day before, imagining she would not return. She would stay back in her favorite place in the whole world, with a son she loved, and her sisters and brothers.

Once out of the bus, I stood on the platform, wanting to cry Stop the bus, stop the bus!, but instead I stood stoically on the concrete. Papa stood helplessly by my side, perhaps finally comprehending the gravity of the situation.

Papa had never taken care of either of his children before. The one time he had had to care for Adi, my grandmother, Sawari Devi, had come over from Sabaila to help. But this time there was no one to help him. This time he was responsible for my actual food and sleep. He had to look into my homework and my hygiene. He had to ensure I was prepared for my math reexam.

For the first day, Papa came to school on time to take me home. The second day I waited for half an hour after school was over, then walked back. When I reached home, I found a lock upon the main door. I sat outside the door, forlorn, as though the stars had fallen off the skies and all trees grown barren. The house, so familiar and loved, became just that—first a house, then a building, and then something else, something foreign and frightening. And it wasn't just because there was a lock on the main gate. It was because Ma was not there and in her absence the world turned hostile and altered my life.

On the third day Papa took care of the situation by hiring Shankar, who he introduced to me as a house cleaner. "Your mother has taught you absolutely nothing," he said. "Otherwise a house with four people in it, and two women at that, is never dirty." He was not really sure how old I was and therefore did not know how capable or not capable I was in terms of housework.

I was delighted. I had a playmate to while away time with until Ma returned and once Ma returned she would have someone to help her clean the house. She could spend more time in the garden or with Adi and me.

"Now," Papa said, "I should be able to get a decent cup of tea in this house."

"And now," Papa said the next day, "you will have someone to look after you if I am not home sharp at three. Shankar will come pick you up from school."

I nodded.

Every day for the ten days that Shankar stayed in our house, I found Shankar at the school gate waiting for me. He was older than me, thirteen or fourteen, thin and dark to the point of near blackness, and he alternately wore the red shirt he had worn the first day he had come to our house and the green shirt he had worn the next day. When I stepped out of the school gate, he took my satchel and held my hand while we crossed the road. He was careful with me and my belongings, making sure the roads were clean of vehicles before we took our first step. Once home, he warmed a glass of milk and served it to me with a plate of snacks he prepared carefully. He helped me with my clothes, pulling out skirts and frocks from drawers that were too tight for me to pull. Once I was fed and clothed he played with me, making toys of wet mud and turning household chores into games. In the games I was the wife and Shankar the husband. I boiled make-believe tea for my make-believe husband, and during make-believe nights, Shankar lay me down on the bed and rubbed himself on my body, tickling me all the while so I laughed uncontrollably beneath his weight. On Shankar's eighth day in the house, he laid me down and showed me how babies were actually made. It was painful and Shankar assured me it would get better with time and practice and for the next two days, before Ma returned from Darbhanga, we practiced after school. We started playing at half past three and were done by four, an hour before Papa got home.

When I think back on those days I am surprised at my own serenity. Was I angry with Shankar then? I don't remember. I remember the yellow frock I wore the day Ma returned, but I remember little else. I cannot remember what Shankar had cooked for snacks that day. I cannot remember the details of his face, though his red and green shirts stay like fields in my memory.

Like always, I told Ma everything I thought was relevant to my life. I told her about Shankar, detailing the day Papa had brought him home. I related to her what he was meant to do in the house, how he had cooked slightly wet rice and vegetables one day and Papa had made a fist and hit him hard on his back. I told her what Shankar played with me and how. Ultimately I told her about the babies Shankar had taught me to make. And so it was that even before Shankar had helped Ma scrub the floors, before he helped the house become what Papa wanted it to become, Ma pulled out a bamboo broom from the nook behind the door and beat Shankar with it. First the broom, then an iron ladle, then flat, forceful palms, while I tried to protect the boy, who put his hands up to stop the blows from falling upon his head and face. When Ma would not stop, I started crying. "Let him be! He is my friend!" But Ma would not stop. Shankar screamed. "Aunty! Aunty!" he howled. Threads of blood trickled down his face.

It was because of the way Ma beat Shankar that I never talked about him with anyone. I said nothing to my friends, nothing to Adi, nothing to Sachi, nothing to the man I married, nothing to my son. I was forty when I finally told Ruby, who remained unmarried and in Suman Uncle's house forever, running it like the butlers I had read about in English books, looking after the dozens of men who continued to flock under Suman Uncle's veranda, gossiping about the day. I had rarely visited Darbhanga during my twenties and thirties, but now, with Suman Uncle not keeping too well, in my midforties, I felt a pull toward it and I went often, where I found an oddly cynical, and oddly resigned, sister in Ruby. We spent many evenings together on the terrace, as Ma had done with her sisters, shelling peanuts and munching on rice puffs sprinkled with mustard oil. Now that her father was not well, she worried about him constantly, though every now and then she called herself foolish and shook her head.

"My screw was loose, Preeti Chaudhary," she said, chuckling at her own naivete. "I thought it was essential to live a drama-filled life. How many times I ran away from home. I should have just stayed away, shouldn't have come back, but I am sure I would just have ended up a nice and fat prostitute on the streets of Calcutta then. What else could have happened? No education, no nothing that I knew how to do. That boy, for whom I ran away so many times, he grew terrified of marrying me, and he snuck away to Gorakhpur one night and married some nice and sober girl there. He was married a whole month before I found out, and when I found out I slashed my wrists here, there, everywhere. There was blood all around the hand pump, and I felt no pain, no pain at all. There were strings of blood, wriggling like worms in the water. That is all I remember. And Papa eventually came running to me and washed my wrists and bandaged them, and when I cried, he cried too.

He went out in the evening later and came home with full-sleeved blouses for me to hide my wounds behind. Enough of this, my Ruby, he said, holding my head. Enough of this. From now on it is me and it is you, and there is no one else in the world. And so, since then, it has been him and it has been me, but really, it has only been me in this room, and him on the veranda with those men who scarcely know I am the daughter of this house. They think I am the servant and Papa the generous master who provides such a room, such a life for me."

And so, over several such evenings, I told her about Shankar a little hesitantly, as though experimenting. And even then it was not Shankar I wanted to talk about. What I wanted to talk about was the monster in Ma's chest. My mother had a monster in her chest, I wanted to say. It had a blunt head and bright soft hair. It had no claws. It had a few teeth, mostly rounded like a cow's molars, but two of its teeth were long and sabered. I saw it often, clearly, when I slept next to her and woke in the middle of the night with a fright.

I wanted to tell her about the fights between Papa and Ma. There was, for instance, the fight over the sweaters, the patterns for which Ma learned from *Manorama Magazine* and knit for Adi and me.

"When did you make this?" Papa asked, appreciating how the sweaters fit on our bodies. He was having his dinner and he stopped eating to admire us. "I never saw you ever make this." And then that dreaded question. "Where did you get the wool from?" Ma stood with Adi and me, staring into the long mirror before us, and said nothing. I heard, as accurately as Ma did, Papa's real question. Where did you get the money from?

Finally, Ma nodded, more to herself than to Papa. "I sold some of the corns and some of the plums."

Papa considered this for a few seconds. "What do you want to do?" he asked. "Start a business?" He shook his head. "What will people say? What will your brother say? They will say I sold my wife off in some market because I wanted your money." He pushed away his dinner plate. "Too much salt," he said. "Too oily. You don't focus on your duties. You are a Chaudhary's wife, behave like a Chaudhary's wife. You are not some Gurung merchant, some chicken-slaughtering butcher."

Mostly Ma's reactions to Papa's various tirades was silence. But every now and then she lost her patience. "When I sweep the floor," she said, her voice guttural with rage, "the house gets clean. When I knit, a sweater is born. If I watched so much news, I would become the next prime minister of the country. But this man"—she went on, dropping a roti on his plate—"he watches news like it is water to him and yet nothing at all happens." Some days Papa finished his meals with measured leisureliness, then he got up and slapped Ma across her face.

On other days Ma carried on as though Papa had not spoken, as though she did not notice him humming like a bee, soaking up the last bit of curry even as he complained. Later, when she sat down for her own meal, Ma stared at her bowl of curry, then, still silent, she picked up the bowl and emptied it in the dustbin. She did not eat, my ma. She went to bed hungry, and Papa never knew, never found out that some nights Ma went to bed hungry.

I wanted to tell Ruby that Papa did not know anything. He did not know when I was growing up if I was seven, or eight, or nine, or ten, or eleven. He did not know which grade I was in ("Are you in class three now? Or in four?"). He did not know when I got my haircuts, or that I found math difficult. He did not know that sometimes, after she had walked on her terrace, or in her room, or in our corridor, Ma would begin to hit either Adi or hit me, and then suddenly, as though she remembered who we were, she would stop and hit herself instead. It was when she hit herself that I began to cry.

Some days she could not sleep and would pace the corridor of our house, up and down, muttering to herself, muttering to the walls that caged her in. Once, in the dead of darkness, she let out a loud scream. It was the howl of an animal. Adi and I had fallen asleep together and we woke with a start, frightened by the sound. He took my hand and we stepped out to see what it was that had rent the night and found Ma sitting and shaking on the muda we kept in the corridor near the shoe rack so we could put on shoes easily. Adi took her to our room and we laid her down. We slept on either side of our mother, holding her in an embrace that slowly calmed her, slowly evened her breath. She fell asleep quickly then, fatigued by her anger.

I wanted to confess my guilt to Ruby. I never really paid attention, I wanted to say. Blocks of time must have passed between Ma's transformation from a woman who chased Adi and me around the house in play, to a woman who chased ghosts in empty corridors. The transition must have been slow, imperceptible, because I did not notice the change—unhurried and insidious, like a bud slowly blossoming, quietly, without sudden movements, without attracting attention.

We slept through it all, unaware of the monster that had begun to slither along the corridor of our home, that climbed over Ma some nights and took over her body.

Ma eventually turned into a monster, I wanted to say. She howled and screamed and hit people with flat, angry palms.

All this I wanted to say as we ate our puffed rice. Ruby was in her early fifties. She had gained weight everywhere and fleshy arms oozed from her blouse. It pained me to know she had been so beautiful once. It hurt me that I had not helped her enough. Perhaps, if I had had the sense and the generosity, I could have helped her marry that boy, but I had envied her so much then, had hated her almost, and my efforts were soured by the hate I had felt. I had married and I had rejoiced too often in her loneliness, as though she deserved punishment, as though she deserved to live forever in the room where she had once hidden Bollywood magazines under her mattress, masturbated to handsome actors, and dreamt of a life of freedom.

Her room was small, comforting, despite the paint peeling off walls. Perhaps it was the austerity of the room—iron bed with frayed cotton sheets, a trunk labeled "saris," curtains constructed out of discarded bedcovers—that finally broke me. "I am sorry," I said and my words hung uselessly in the dark air because Ruby did not ask for what. Later that night I said, "I don't know how to reconcile Ma. She was like two women in one. One of my mothers was fun, like a child," I said, and because Ma was already dead by this time, I felt my stomach fall inside my body and bunch painfully below my navel. "She played with me. She and I went to the movies. The other was cruel. She hit so hard—not me, but others. She was cruel to anyone she could hit. You remember Rita?" I asked. "The girl who worked for us? Was she around when you visited us that one time?"

Ruby nodded.

"Ma used to hit her. That girl came to our house just before Adi and I had left for the hostel. She used to do everything in the house. She woke up at five to fill water in buckets and hauled them up stairs. And do you know how it freezes in Kathmandu? Water is like a knife in winters. And Ma would hit her with whatever she could, all the time. That girl would break out into blisters."

It took me a while to get to Shankar, the first person Ma had hit.

I related what I had to quickly, avoiding details, ending suddenly with, "It was nothing really," and realizing with a start that it was true. The incident itself had always been nothing to me. Shankar and his act I had forgotten. What I remembered were Ma's eyes—large, filling her face, her grunts as she brought her hands down heavy upon the boy's cowering body. "Haramkhor! Haramzada!" she screeched as she slapped and hit, panting with the effort.

"You know," Ruby said, "when I slashed my wrists, Papa called your mother over to spend some time with me. She was the only one Papa trusted with my situation. She couldn't come right away, but she came a month later and fed me guavas and chikkies and told me funny stories to make me happy. You and Adi had come along too—it was your summer holidays, I think, but she slept every night with me and protected me from everyone. And she told me about her special love affair with your chachi." Ruby looked at me at this point and laughed, a gentle, nostalgic laugh.

"What?" I asked, assuming I had misheard her.

"Her love affair with Kumud Chachi," she went on. "She held my crisscrossed wrists and said—who knows why it feels so right to cut one's hands in love. Then she told me about Kumud Chachi and her, and how they cut each other's names on their wrists, and how much after your chachi rejected her, she wanted to kill herself. My children saved me, she said. That Adi and that Pirti, they saved me. Or else I would have burned myself alive."

The night, after the beating, Shankar ran away, but before he fled he broke one of Ma's suitcases. He also broke the trunk in which she kept her jewelry. He took with him whatever money and gold he could find in those boxes. Papa, who came home late that night and knew nothing about the beating, nothing about what had caused the beating, was furious. He was furious with Shankar for stealing but also furious with Ma for having secured her things with no care. "No wonder I don't give you money," he said. I tried to explain to him what exactly had happened but Ma glared at me and I grew quiet. For months after that night I was haunted by my mother's cruelty. I hated Ma for the violence, for driving Shankar away, for having no one left in the house to help her clean and scrub.

A year later Shankar's family came looking for Shankar. "We have come to take our son home for Dasserha," they said. "Where is he? You said you would bring him over at least once a year but you have not brought him even once. And he never calls."

The father, a small shriveled man, asked, "Is he away at school?"

Ma stared at him like she had seen a ghost. "School?" she spat. "Your son was a thief. He ran away from this house with all my money and all my gold. School indeed."

"But where is he, malkain?" the mother asked. She was thin and shriveled, too, and nearly toothless. "Where is our son?"

"How would I know? He ran away. How do I know?"

"He is thirteen years old," the mother said, helplessly. "Where is he?"

A pit began to form in my stomach. Where was he? That thirteen-year-old boy?

The old woman began to cry. "Where is my son, malkain? My other son is dead, and Shankar is my only son now. But where is he?" She rocked as she cried.

The father looked bewildered too. "Did you inform the police?" he asked. "Did you tell the police our son is missing?"

Ma stared. Then she pulled in an unsteady breath and said, "Be thankful I did not tell the police about that donkey of your son. If I had, he would be behind bars right now. He did terrible things in this house, and he ran away with gold. Do you want your son behind bars?"

"But where is he?" the parents asked. "Where?"

"You know," I said to Ruby, "that question kept me awake at nights."

Where? Where? I imagined him on cold, icy streets, falling off slippery overpasses, crushed under cars, electrocuted on poles. For years after that I would look at children on the streets, wondering if one of them could be Shankar. But I always looked at boys who were twelve or thirteen and never saw him anywhere. And then, very suddenly, without any incident, I forgot him. I forgot how he looked, what he wore, how he prepared vegetables. The ten days he had been in our house became a blank in my memory. I went about my life. I had my share of crushes, felt up boys in dark night buses, invited calloused hands of grown men upon my body, all of that, without any memory. But I remember now, I don't know since when, but for many years now I have had his memory in me. I wonder if he got back home to his parents, if he survived the streets. I don't like to watch movies in which these boys get lost, grow homeless, are never found.

BOOK FIVE

THE TRAGIC MEENA KUMARI

GREEN SUITCASE

Radha, a neighbor with whom Meena had briefly dreamt of starting a sweater workshop-cum-shop, visited Meena one September, and in her two-hour stay walked around Meena's house like a bipedal lizard, hands clasped behind her, commenting upon decorations and chairs, and upon Meena's choice of teacups. That particular day, because Meena had forgotten to add sugar to the grocery list, the house was out of sugar and the women drank bitter black ginger tea from teacups Radha did not approve of. Radha sprinkled her chat with information about Asha and Pramila and how their knitting was progressing at the NGO. She made observations about the rooms in Meena's house. She thought the furniture mismatched, the curtains dismal, and the bed on which she sat a poor substitute for a sofa.

"You have such taste in patterns, Meena," Radha said after she had finished her tea. "Such borders you come up with; then why are your cushions all here and there? Asha says we really should all get together, all four of us. We really could start a business. It could work, it could fail. But you know how that Pramila is. Fat and lame and senseless. She has no sense of design, but she can look after the accounts. What do you say? Why don't you want to work? You are growing too rich, is it?"

She walked around the house and stopped before a fish-patterned square of knitting Meena used as a coaster. The fish's left end dipped lower than the right and it swam on a blue, geometric sea. "Is this yours?" Radha asked, frowning. "You are too good to have one fin wrong and one fin right."

Meena smiled. "It's Pirti's," she said. "I am teaching her."

"At ten? And what? You will marry her off at thirteen with a big dowry of beds and televisions? Really, you Indians are too much."

Meena did not answer. She waited, as she always did, for the moment to pass. She stared at the fish and wondered why Radha thought Preeti was only ten. At twelve, was her daughter too small for her age? How optimistic was the pattern of this fish. How conscious she was of the teacup she still held in her hand. It was made of steel, practical and safe. She knew shelves in Radha's house would be lined with teacups that were of fine china. Radha had once told her she was distantly related to the queen, and all relations of the queen, however distant, must drink out of fine china.

Meena shook her head. "I am not an Indian," she said and led Radha away from the woolen fish. She walked Radha to the bed that also served as a sofa and explained herself. "I am from the plains, from the Terai. I am a Madhesi, from Sabaila, really," she said and instantly the Indian in Meena dwindled to a point and caught in her chest like a pinprick, painful and pinching. Instantly, her discomfort with Radha turned to hate. She wanted Radha gone from her television room, away from the handicrafts upon the wall and the furniture on the floor. She wanted never to see Radha again.

And yet, a month later, when Radha called once again to announce yet another visit to her house, Meena felt a nervous excitement build within her. A fickle rain fell outside the window and Meena watched it as she listened to Radha.

"Such a lovely morning, no, Meena?" Radha said. "My mister is not in town and the children are away. I am quite bored at home. Should I come over at two in the afternoon, just for a chat?"

"Of course," Meena said, surprised.

"And," Radha laughed, clearly reading the surprise, "maybe try dragging you back to the Knitting House." She had been too busy in the last few months, Radha explained. Her new and sudden post as the president of the Knitting House demanded more from her than she had planned for, but now, finally on a Saturday, despite and because of the cold drizzle that had fallen in the morning, Radha hoped for an hour of gossip and tea, sugarless and bitter as it might be. "The Knitting House is an opportunity to change lives, really," Radha said, "and you are fantastic with all the artwork you teach your children. I was thinking of all those fish and flowers at your home."

Meena held the receiver close to her ear and while she listened she watched Adi on the bed, intently working on his Pen Fight logo, frowning and obstinate. How taken he was with this mad game he was playing. He had turned it into a rage in the house, gathering all pens and pencils he found, scattering them on whichever raised surface was available, and beginning loud, rambunctious wars among them. It amused her, his earnestness, his passionate pen-fighting.

In the early days when Adi had begged Meena for pens—"Please, Ma, give me that pen. Please, Mamma, buy me that heavy pen"—Meena had felt a strange resistance within her. "Stay away from your father's pens!" she had said to her son, but now she wanted to lavish him with stationery. He had won her over with his dedication. There was little she could do other than marvel as he filled notebooks with strategies, rules, diagrams, possible logos for imaginary world tournaments, and various names for absolutely similar-looking pens. Now when Meena passed by any shop, she immediately began to scan their stationery for bulky, ungainly looking pens, because she had learned that ugly, heavy pens made the best fighters in her son's mad world.

"Let's set the shoe rack straight, my orange," Meena said to her son when she replaced the phone. The cushions needed fluffing, the wood oiling. The bedsheets needed to be pulled taut upon the beds. "Radha Aunty is coming for tea. She will be here at two."

It was a sweet moment. It was sweet of Radha to call. It was sweet that the morning was only just beginning, that Doordarshan was airing Sridevi's superhit movie *Nagina* in an hour, that Adi worked with such diligence on something so silly. It was a sweet moment, a moment to change lives, Meena thought, only half mocking her caller.

Adi did not stop drawing in his notebook and Meena got busy gathering cups and saucers forgotten around the house. She dusted beds and divans and straightened the pillows. Hers was a house of few tables and chairs and many beds and bed-likes. When people from the plains stumbled into Kathmandu, looking for jobs or hospitals, it was to her house they came to stay and rest, sometimes for a night, sometimes weeks. Manmohan liked the village to come to him. He hoped to join politics one day.

Back in the television room Meena wiped the chairs, taking care to wipe above and under.

During the first commercials on the television, she dragged in the clotheshorse from the adjoining bedroom and folded what clothes she could while keeping her eyes on the TV. "Radha wants me to join the knitting NGO. She is its president now," she said in Adi's direction. "And what will I do? What to say to your father, you tell me. It is a good thing he is going out soon. I don't like him in the house when I have visitors."

Manmohan would leave for his office in an hour. After he left, Meena could get some soft drinks and biscuits from the shops, but until then she was trapped within the house, waiting. She looked at Adi. He was sitting cross-legged on the bed that also served as the sofa, now staring at the TV, his eyes widening and narrowing, his face reflecting the colors on the screen, the Pen Fight logo abandoned by his side.

In an hour Manmohan had finished his morning in the study and was in the bedroom. He transferred an envelope from his briefcase into a black folder, and at that precise moment Meena leaned a little forward to look through the door between the TV room and the bedroom. From the bulge in the envelope Meena knew there was enough money in the folder and when she looked away she saw Adi leaned a little forward, too, and she knew, just like that, that the day had become a day with many tasks. A movie would be watched, a logo completed, the house set to order, money stolen from a folder, Radha entertained.

They stole often. Stealing was not difficult. It was a simple, repetitive process: Years ago Manmohan had lost one of the three copies of the keys to the cabinet in which he kept the black folder. The morning Manmohan lost the key, Meena found it. The key now sat between Meena's saris, the ones she kept preserved in one of the many boxes stacked in the storeroom. The box of saris was under the box used to hold towels and bedsheets. The key to the box of saris was in the green suitcase standing against another pile of boxes. The boxes and suitcases in the storeroom rose so high they blocked any light coming in through the ventilators. The key to the green suitcase was at the very center of Meena's bed, under the heavy, sagging cotton mattress. The path was serpentine. There was no way Manmohan would figure this configuration.

On the television screen, Sridevi, a snake-woman with incredible powers, married Rishi Kapoor, a mortal man, who knew nothing about the powerful and bizarre world he inhabited due to his wife. In the bedroom, Manmohan shuffled between the cabinet and his briefcase, muttering along the way.

"People who don't ever work never know what labor is," he said, his voice loud enough to be heard above the newlyweds on the silver screen. "People just sit, waiting for food to appear before them. If it wasn't for me, there would be no foundation to this house. I came to Kathmandu with nothing but a bicycle and a twenty-rupee note and now that I have put up a castle, people think they can play in the garden, swim in the lake, and have servants bring out their meals."

"Servants!" Meena scoffed and pulled a blouse off the horse.

Even in the catastrophic disarray upon the clotheshorse, Manmohan's clothes were neatly piled, as though they had folded of their own accord, while Meena'a clothes climbed one on top of the other—the arms of her blouses tangled with the end of her saris, the hooks of buttons dug into pockets of sweaters, causing small tears. "There is nothing in the house to serve a guest and he talks of servants. Give me some money, Chaudharyji," she said. "Radha is coming today and what prestige will be left for you if I cannot offer her even Coke and chips? Tell."

"Last week I gave you a hundred rupees," said Manmohan. "What did you do with it? Eat it?"

"Eat it? Yes, I ate it." She turned to Adi. "This father of yours," she said, "he gives a hundred rupees and thinks he has opened a world bank for me. What a man! And the water-motor cost more than that to repair."

Manmohan peeped into the television room. "What is this, Adi?" he said. "When I was your age, I and my brothers bathed and said our prayers and started our studies with the sun not yet out. Don't you have homework? Go do homework."

"Homework-shomework," Meena snapped. "It is holiday time for him but you don't know what a holiday is." She looked back at the screen. Sridevi stung a villain to death.

Meena could not understand Sridevi. Here was Sridevi, bristling with powers. She could teleport, time-travel, read minds, live for centuries, vanish, fight villains, sense evil, and yet throughout the movie she did nothing but sweet-talk and dance for her husband. Had Meena had half the powers she would change the world. She would make money from leaves, fabric from sleep, and water from air. She would give the world enough gas and light, petrol and water, soda and chips to keep it content and without complaints. If Meena had in her cohort two fat cobras deployed as henchmen for her protection, she would teach the citizens of the world some manners. If Meena had in her custody the mani, a jewel of such strength it could be used for world domination, Meena would dominate. She would melt every mountain and create instead fertile and luxurious land. There would be bridges to cross rivers, wheels to scale heights, and machines to fold distance. She would not sit worrying and mulling and sweet-talking a useless husband. She could not understand why Sridevi fought so hard to appear ordinary, why she slithered in guilt, hiding her authority from those so obviously below her.

When Manmohan returned to the bedroom, Meena shook her head. "It is very annoying, I am telling you," she said to Adi. "I like this movie and your father will not let me watch." She watched her husband put the black folder into the belly of the cabinet and frowned. "Look how pointy your father's feet are," she said. "His head is big for his small body, no? Look. He is like a lamppost, head all big and golden like a light bulb. I tell you, your father might look all important but he is just a half-boiled egg, just a donkey."

Manmohan was a careful man. The cabinet held not only the folder but also records of all transactions and paperwork. It held files arranged alphabetically and stood straight so their fat, yellow spines faced him without confusion. He had separate files for Adi and Adi's school records, separate files for Preeti and Preeti's school records, separate files for electric bills, phone bills, water bills. Green spines showed rents that came in from the house he owned and rented out in Janakpur, profits and losses he gathered from the two paper and stationery shops he owned in Birgunj, and amounts earned through shares and policies maturing and multiplying not only in Nepal, but also in India, and adding to the annual revenue. There was a file that kept record of the accounting work he did with Mr. Kajra—his gains and losses, the tax Manmohan managed to save for his employer. "Distribution and decentralization," he liked to say, "amount to value." His major income came from grateful companies within the valley whose tax handlings he carefully disguised in his audit ledgers. "But," he liked to say, "the valley can be tricky," and so he branched out, spreading his many legs to many cities. "Congregation of everything in Kathmandu is the reason Nepal is the junkyard in the world's backyard," he liked to say. "All schools, all industries, all hospitals. What? Are people outside Kathmandu not people? Are people in Janakpur cows and buffaloes?"

Meena pulled a sari off the horse to fold and was defeated. If Meena had had Sridevi's powers, she would have taught herself the art of turning and turning a sari until its six-yard fabric folded into a neat square that fit perfectly into shelves.

"Look how jumpy he is," she said, though Adi, lost in the movie, saw nothing. "He likes people, especially me, to think there are problems only he can solve. As if! Last night I came right out and told him there are many wives in this world whose husbands are dead and still the wives go on. Eh, Adi, do the wives die? Do you think your mother would die? Some wives go on more successfully, I tell you. And there are many sons and daughters without fathers and they do just as well."

When Manmohan was ready to leave, he gave Meena some money. "Here is fifty rupees for you," he said. "Now be careful how you use it." It had taken him a few years to trust Meena with money, to let her go to the shops to buy daily requirements, and he was proud of the way in which he had groomed her thriftiness.

He looked at the television and huffed. "Show all this trash to your son and he will grow up without any brains. Eh, Adi, you are enjoying this very much, aren't you?"

Adi did not answer. Meena held the money tight in her hands. "What if I joined Radha and Asha in their business, Chaudharyji?" she asked. "Radha is going to ask today. I am good at the work, you know that."

"You knit for us, Meena Rani," said Manmohan. "You are a queen. Why do you need to work?"

Back in the bedroom Manmohan stood before the dressing table and pulled a watch onto his wrist. He plastered his hair neatly upon the head with a little oil and trimmed his mustache with a pair of folding scissors. How did a man so small, so thin voiced, have the energy he did? Meena wondered. How did he, without a mani, without any powers, manage so well?

And quietly, during another commercial, a song started in Meena's mind. It was single worded and soft tuned and clashed with the wide, invincible world playing on the television. While Sridevi conquered all, while she stung and bit, shifted shapes, danced, revealed and concealed, the tune within Meena grew into a monotonous, hypnotic song. India. India. *Bharat.* The word was magical. Bharat, went the song. Bharat, like a heartbeat. One could never simply walk and walk on Kathmandu's streets and hope to leave the city behind. There were too many rivers, too many sharp angled mountains. The land, seductively flat in sections, was an illusion, and fell into gorges and valleys at sudden turns. And its width was not enough to last a run.

After Manmohan left, the house relaxed. The mattress softened, the air expanded, the bricks behind the plaster grew warm and liquid.

The television came alive with the twisting music of the beena. Meena waited for the air to yield.

When she asked Adi, "But what will you do, my orange?" he shrugged, not comprehending what she meant. She did not know what she had meant by the question either.

Meena made a list of all things needed for the week. "Let me see," she said. "Powder milk is finished. Get me some paper and pencil, my fuzzy orange," and when Adi handed her his rough notebook and a pencil, she turned the notebook to its last page. "Powder milk, vegetables, rice, eggs, yogurt, mustard oil, coconut oil, belt, bathing soap, washing soap, and you know how many rupees your father gave me to buy everything? Fifty rupees. Fifty rupees! Rice is twenty rupees a kilo! What a man!" How excessive this inventory of necessities was! "Your father wants the best of everything. He wants chicken every week though he will give no money, which reminds me! Chicken. And I think your father has run out of hair oil. Do you think prawn chips for Radha Aunty? And Coca-Cola?" she asked, more to herself.

During the next commercial Meena went from mattress to suitcase to box to box, opening and shutting lids with this and that key.

She twisted the last key twice to open the cabinet. "Come here, little monkey," she said and when Adi did not move, she said, "Please, baba," and finally Adi went to his mother.

Inside the cabinet was the safe, small and square, and Adi rolled the rows of numbers upon it until he hit the right combination. "Nine. Zero. Two." Adi first memorized the incorrect order. The door of the safe opened with a soft huff, as though letting go of breath held too long.

The black folder was in the safe and there were other envelopes stacked on it. Meena could not steal from the envelopes. The money in them was counted and rubber banded together, the sum total scribbled on the covers. The only uncounted amount was the household expense set aside in the folder. In it were thousand-rupee notes, five hundreds, hundreds, and twenties and tens. Meena pulled out one hundred-rupee note and one twenty-rupee note. "We have to get you and Pirti out of here, my sack of sugar," she said. "You two have to go to a nice solid place and get a nice solid education for your minds. All this pinching-sinching and whatnot will not do for you. Where is that sister of yours anyway?"

She replaced the folder into the safe and Adi scrambled the numbers back to nine-zero-two. Then he ran off into the television room.

From the door Meena watched Sridevi's husband suddenly stumble upon his wife dancing before a dozen men, her eyes and hair wild like a madwoman's, the flare of her white skirt sweeping the floor, and the husband, disoriented and angry, slapped his wife across her face because he understood nothing. Meena flinched but thought the husband justified. Why keep such secrets? How was he to understand the precarious world he lived in if his wife treated him like a child? He did not even know he was actually a dead boy brought to life by his wife. Without her, he would not be. And now he had come home to find his wife dancing like a slut before a dozen men who looked more like demons and less like men, and now, confused and bewildered, he had slapped her. Now he was unjust and cruel and Meena did not know what to do.

"Eh, Aduli," she said through the window, "do you think your father does not know about our robberies? He does, my lovely. But he is a man and men will not give you anything if you ask nicely for it. You have to just take. Men, I tell you, they are all donkeys."

"I'm not a donkey," Adi said.

"Not you. Only your father."

Meena came to the door and pulled another sari from the clotheshorse and stood before the dressing table. Here, she changed from her drab yellow sari into a bright parrot green. Could it really be that Manmohan did not know about the money that disappeared? She took only small amounts.

"A couple hundreds from this folder," she said, confident Adi could follow her train of thought. "A couple from the briefcase, a ten-rupee note from his shirt pocket, a few coins from his pants. It is never significant, never five hundred. It is not much at all."

Meena dabbed her lips with the lightest of pinks. She dipped the tip of her ring finger into a sindoor case and the tip came out red as a flower and she carefully dotted her forehead with vermilion. She tied her hair to a high bun, and over her sari she wore a complementing pink-and-white cardigan that she left unbuttoned to show the embroidery on her blouse.

Meena worked steadily, not bothered anymore with Sridevi. Besides, the movie was almost at its end. She redusted the furniture and polished the mirrors with newspaper. She threw open the curtains, letting the ample sun illuminate the dust floating in the rooms. In the television room, while Sridevi twiddled her thumbs, Meena changed the cushion covers and straightened the crafts on the wall. She pushed the horse back into the bedroom. There wasn't a wrinkle on the bed after she replaced its sheet with a rich maroon one. She burnt an incense stick at a corner and slowly the house smelled of roses, ready to welcome kings.

The lights went off suddenly, ten minutes before the movie ended, and with the lights Meena's disinterest in Sridevi also vanished. Meena wanted desperately to watch the end now. She was more and more angry with Sridevi. She wanted Sridevi's powers stripped, wanted to see her turn into an ordinary woman, one who had no secrets to guard, one who dreamed, like all women did, of another world in which she did indeed have powers. Now, with ten minutes left of the movie, Meena wanted a normal, ordinary life, where when a movie began, it ended, too.

Adi stared at the empty TV as though shocked by its silence. His face, deprived of the colors on the screen, was suddenly dull, his eyes wide. He waited, still like a statue, for the television to flicker on, then he jumped off the chair. "I am going down to play, Ma," he said.

Meena stayed in the chair. The bed, smooth and wrinkle-free, was too grand to sit on. In a moment, it was one. The clock Preeti had won in a musical chair competition ticked steadily behind the TV. In another moment, it was two. At two thirty Meena called Radha and listened to the phone ring at the other end. She walked about the room, looking at the clutter she had gotten accustomed to—a pen holder, calendars with gods, the fish, the flowers, the parrot, the heavy curtains, the wooden ceiling, the dull and faded carpet, the bed pushed against the wall. At three thirty, she lay on the bed and fell asleep.

When she woke it was not yet four, but the power was back, and Meena played with the remote of the television until the screen showed King Birendra, smiling, a simple man in his daura suruwal and Dhaka topi. "The load-shedding," he announced, "is temporary. Everything will come back to normal soon. Please be patient."

Meena wondered what the king was talking about. She turned the television off and packed her green suitcase with a few clothes and walked out the rooms and the doors. She locked the entrance behind her and went down the stairs, to the main gate.

Outside, the sky was overcast but it had not rained yet, and a few children were on the lane, fiercely bundled by their mothers and ready to face sickness and death for an hour of play. They stood before their houses, their cheeks scrubbed by the chill. Their eyes were hard.

Meena stepped through the gate and onto the lane. She was leaving. She was not coming back to this jungle, this place that had sucked her like she was a stalk of sugarcane. This time, after she reached Darbhanga, she would not return. Her mother's house at Darbhanga was three times larger than this house in Kathmandu and there would be a place in it for her and her children forever.

She called to one of the children. "Have you seen Adi and Pirti?" she asked.

"They are behind the shop, playing Pen Fight," the child said and Meena walked to the spot to find her children, so at ease with the world and its inhabitants. For a while she stood at a distance watching the strange games her children played, wondering. Then she put the suitcase down on the ground and called to her son and daughter.

"Come, my lovelies," she called out to them. "We are leaving."

LEAVE-TAKING

The autorickshaw started suddenly, bumping once into a pothole and Meena felt her heart jump sharp inside her. Then the auto bumped all the way to the bus terminal.

At one bend, a one-legged cobbler sat under a big, black umbrella, both his wooden toolbox and his wooden spare leg protected by the umbrella. He looked up and saw Meena looking at him and Meena watched him as though mesmerized. Despite the bleak sky, the needles in his toolbox sparkled as the auto left the cobbler and his tools behind. There was a cart in which two boys were eating momos off leaf plates. There were the students of Rose Primary English Boarding School in blue shirts and gray pants walking hand in hand on the footpath. There was the Krishi Bikash Bank where Bindu Jha worked and talked all day behind a rust-colored window.

There was a bhaiya standing before the embassy, slicing pineapples for customers. Then at another bend was the window canteen, which sold biscuits and tea on weekdays, but momos on Saturday mornings. The momos were so famous people drove down from Bhaktapur for a bite. The rickshaw turned and Meena could no longer see the momo line. She sat back straight again and became conscious of Adi's fingers curled around Preeti's, and her own fingers curled around the green suitcase. Without Manmohan in her life, Meena could live again. She could play music on the National Radio at a high volume. She could loll on the bed with her children until hunger forced them out of it. She could watch movies in the cinema hall and not worry about what her husband thought of her.

"The king is going to Delhi next week," the man sitting across from her said to everyone. "The trade treaty between India and Nepal is coming to an end. The king is going to renew it."

"Oh, you have information about everything, don't you," said the man sitting beside him, laughing good-naturedly.

"What trade treaty?" another man asked.

"It is our misfortune that we are so landlocked, so dependent on India for everything. And India is all swollen like a balloon with self-importance."

"I would like to teach that country a lesson or two, but what is to be done. This is the misfortune of being landlocked."

Meena's throat was dry and she longed for a drink. She longed also to become deaf, to no longer hear conversations around her, to simply sit in a vehicle and be carried to destinations. She looked away from the men. Outside a petrol pump a gang of young boys were gathered. They held a banner above their heads that said they demanded that the exiled be brought back to the country. Meena wondered what that meant. Who had been exiled? When? How could these young boys, so vulnerable and fresh, expose themselves this way on roads?

Finally, the rickshaw pulled into the bus station and came to a stop. "What is good and what is bad," the man across from her said before getting off, and once he was off the rickshaw he continued to talk to the passengers who followed him out as though he was imparting a secret. "Everything is always mixed-up."

Only once all the passengers had gotten off the rickshaw did Meena realize she did not know where she was taking her children. She had no place to go. Kaveri was dead. Bilash was dead. And without mother and father there would be no one in Darbhanga to welcome her and her children. There would be no room for her and her children in her childhood home.

The driver looked through the bars separating the driver's area from the passengers and coughed for attention. "Not getting off, didi?" she asked.

Meena shook her head. No. But almost immediately started to get off.

"I can take you back home," the driver said.

Again, Meena shook her head.

"Last week," the driver said, "I watched a movie and there was Meena Kumari in it. So tragic. When Meena Kumari cries, I always cry also. She does it so nicely, all the crying scenes. In this movie also, she was leaving like you are leaving, then she did not leave. You look just like Meena Kumari. So pretty."

Meena stared at the driver. She was a small woman with two long plaits hanging over her checkered kurta and for a second Meena was surprised to find a woman driver, though she had traveled on many autorickshaws in Kathmandu that were driven by women. This could never happen in Darbhanga. Women in Darbhanga could not drive strangers around the city.

"So tragic that Meena Kumari is," the driver went on. "And in black and white she is even more tragic. I am always waiting for her to start crying because I know she will cry so nicely, and then I will cry also. It is like that only, between Meena Kumari and me. We are like sisters, crying over the same things, ditto." She turned fully now to look at Meena. "You look like her," she said. "Same pretty and sad face. You should be in the cinema, but I am sure your husband will break your leg if you join the films. My husband wants to break my leg because I want to be a taxi driver. Four men will get in your taxi and you will be everybody's wife after that, he says. It is true, too. You know what four men will do to a woman. In the rickshaw there are many people, but the rickshaw is all open from everywhere. Everyone can see everything, even from the roads. You are safe in a rickshaw. Not so much in a taxi. In that movie Meena Kumari was in a taxi once, and she was so scared because it was the middle of the night and she was alone with a strange man in a closed taxi. Now, had she got into a rickshaw, she would not be so scared. That is the thing with rickshaws. They are made for women."

"Which movie was it?" Meena asked.

"Who knows? It was on TV. Do you watch Doordarshan on Sundays? Nice old movies they show on Sunday evenings."

"I have watched every Meena Kumari movie," Meena said.

"There are many Meena Kumari movies," the driver said. "You might have missed this one."

"My father manages cinema halls. I have watched them all," insisted Meena. She looked at the driver and added, "My name is Meena Rani."

"No, no. Meena Kumari," the driver said.

"My name," Meena said. "My name is Meena Rani."

The driver came close to Meena's face and frowned, and when Meena chuckled, the driver laughed. And Preeti and Adi, who had been quiet the entire trip, laughed too. There were passengers beginning to board again, those who needed to be taken back to the place Meena and her children had forever left, and they asked her what she was laughing about, and the driver answered each time, "Her name is Meena Rani and she looks just like Meena Kumari, no? Just like in that movie where Meena Kumari wants to leave and does not leave."

So people looked at Meena and the green suitcase she held between her knees. "What movie?" they asked but everyone agreed Meena looked like Meena Kumari. "Is your name Meena Rani? Really?"

"Really," said Meena, laughing.

Then finally she got off the rickshaw with her children. She pulled out the fare but the driver would not take the money.

"You are a nice star, Meenaji," she said. "I will not take money from you."

"But I am not Meena Kumari," Meena said, laughing again.

"But you are," the driver insisted.

There was a giddiness inside Meena, and she wanted to thank the driver for making her laugh. She wanted to tell the driver how pretty she was, too, and how brave to be driving an autorickshaw and refusing fares. Will your husband not break your leg? she wanted to ask, but the driver kept talking, making small comments until the passengers said, "enough, enough," and Meena waved goodbye to the driver and the rickshaw rattled away.

From the footpath where the autorickshaw dropped off Meena and her children, Meena stared at the green and red buses swaying like pregnant women on the undulating, unpaved field. She had known, even as she was leaving, that she was only going out the way people go out for a change of scenery. She had known she was leaving only to return, and yet, now that she had decided to return to Manmohan, she could not gather herself. She was tired after a day of waiting, of planning a departure, of knowing she was headed toward nothing. In traveling toward Kaveri, she traveled toward a vacuum. Even if Kaveri had lived, Meena could not have gone to her. Kaveri was no longer her mother. She had stopped being her mother the day she had given her away to Manmohan.

Meena's trip to the bus station, her packed suitcase, which she kept slightly lifted off the ground so its base would not scratch against the concrete, were experiments to test her abilities. She had once, during those months when the ghosts of her dead babies had haunted her the most intensely, set herself experimentally on fire. She had stood beside a bucket of water and struck a match. The orange fire had licked her sari up toward her hips. It had lasted no more than a few seconds. The fire had turned blue every time it hit a pattern and was orange again. Then she had felt the singe of its heat. It had touched a point on her thigh and scalded it so Meena had thrown two mugs full of water upon her body and changed into another sari. The fire, the scalded spot, the small minute of death, each had given her the strength she needed to face a world that refused to change for her.

It was cold despite the sweaters and Meena ushered her children into one of the tea-momo stores lining the footpath. There were men sipping tea from steaming glasses and two men waiting for their share. It was not a clean stall. It was long and irregular and nothing fit well within it. Meena smiled at the man behind the crowded counter, the one making tea, and he looked at her questioningly. She headed with her children to the bench where the men were sitting and the men pushed against each other to make space for them at the outer edge. Adi was unusually quiet and held Preeti's hand. The counter man got Meena a cup of tea and two cups of milk for Preeti and Adi. They held their cups with both hands, the warmth soothing their cold bodies, as they watched the station fill with more buses.

For an hour after that Meena bought snacks and sweets for her children—peanuts, a Coca-Cola, fritters, mixtures with so much chili on it Preeti wept. When the spice got unbearable, Meena bought two bottles of water. She had never bought water before but it seemed appropriate to buy everything now.

More and more buses left before them. "We should call that father of yours," she finally said.

"I am cold, Ma," Preeti said. "I want to go home."

It was getting darker. The stall was warm but the wind outside had the trees lisping and whistling softly. Meena went to the counter and spoke to the stall-keeper. "I have to use the phone," she said and the man pushed the phone toward her. Meena dialed and when Manmohan picked up at the other end, she looked at the stall-keeper long enough so that he left the counter and turned away to boil more tea.

"Are you watching from the window?" Meena asked Manmohan, and inside the house Manmohan jumped back in surprise.

Manmohan had returned home to find the house locked and had had to go Doctor Singh's house to get the extra key. In the bedroom he had found the dramatic note Meena had left on the dressing table. "Leaving forever," and Manmohan had felt rage begin to spread through him like a deep rumbling.

He spent the evening sunk in a chair before the television, the anger building. He had not thought Meena would leave. She had always threatened to leave but had never left, and now she had, just like that, without caring for the house and the things within it that were hers. If the rain came, the cane chairs on the veranda would soak and rot, but she did not care. She thought he would follow her to Kaveri's house and beg her to return, but she was wrong. Eventually it would be six, and then seven, and then eight, and then ten years would pass away. He would rather have every piece of furniture in the world decay and decompose, have his head fall off his body without his six o'clock tea, than follow Meena to her dead mother's house.

On the television, the king's portrait came upon the screen: King Birendra smiling, silver cape waving, silver plume trembling so slightly, chin high. The national anthem played but Manmohan continued sitting. It was ridiculous how his friends stood every time the king's picture came upon the television. In the presence of these friends Manmohan rose, too, but he would not rise now, in his own house.

The portrait and the national anthem gave way to the news, and there was that news again, recycled for the tenth time, about the minister's wife who collapsed at the bathroom door and died. She was a fat buffalo and Manmohan was sure she would have lived longer if she had not eaten like a pig, but she had and now she was dead and the news was clogged with reruns of her big face smiling at him. The entire world was in a state of gluttony and disrespect.

Manmohan remained in his chair. He had forgotten to put his feet up and a small ache brewed at the base of his neck. No one ever looked after him. He was a self-made man. While his brothers still lived in the village, farming and never setting a leg forward to see the world, Manmohan had come to the capital and made an auditor of himself. No one helped him; not his parents, not his wife, and after all these years of living and struggling, Manmohan felt fatigue climb up his feet and travel to the rest of his body. He longed for a cup of tea but could not move. Outside, the clouds were immense and thick. He would put that Meena Rani Chaudhary in her place. Yes, sir. And that was when the phone rang and Manmohan jumped up in surprise.

"Are you behind the curtain?" Meena asked.

"It is my curtain if I want to be behind it," said Manmohan.

"I am not coming to that house of yours tonight," she said. "And if you hit me when I come, I will poison you to death and I will set myself on fire. You understand?"

"What do you mean you are not coming home?"

But Meena hung up. She turned toward her children. "Let your father jump around a little, no?" she said.

"It is getting late, didi," said the shopkeeper. "What bus are you taking?"

"No bus. We are going home now. Ready to go, my lovelies?"

Three buses pulled into the terminal and a group of people stumbled out the doors. The wind was sharp and they huddled together, pulling tight their shawls and sweaters. Children ran for cover. Men and women ran, too, suitcases and bags in hand.

"It will rain any moment, didi," the shopkeeper said. "And the autorickshaw stand is almost empty. These people will take the last one away if you don't hurry. Give me forty rupees and go on."

Outside the stall the grass and the weed at their feet trembled, swaying to the right, to the right, and Meena and her children swayed, too, to the right, as they hurried toward the auto stand. There was only one rickshaw standing in it. The sky sagged above their heads and Meena's sari clung to her legs. Preeti's teeth chattered. A dozen young boys got into the last rickshaw and there was no place in it for Meena and her children.

"You better get to the sanjha-bus stand, didi," said the driver. "A storm is on its way and I don't think there will be any other rickshaw coming here now. Get to the sanjha-bus stand."

Adi and Preeti stayed close to their mother. The suitcase, light at the beginning of the journey, was heavy now, and Meena thought her arms would fall off her shoulders if she did not put her weight down. Her own teeth began to chatter as she walked toward the sanjha-bus stand at the other end of the road, against the darkening wind.

The sanjha-bus stand was a small, canopied structure with a bench for waiting passengers. Once she and her children got there, Meena put the suitcase down and pulled in long breaths. Her palms were calloused and her head pounded slightly. Once under the canopy, she reached out for her children and held their hands. Their hands were like early morning water, chilled, and Meena shivered violently upon touching them. She looked at her daughter and noticed the chapped cheeks, the thin line of blood upon the cracks of her lips, the red nose, the puffed eyes, and Meena felt the same pain she had felt the day she had almost aborted her daughter. She felt the same pain she had felt when she and Manmohan had walked into that clinic and talked about "dropping the thing." Three babies had died already, and the fear that this one would die, too, had kept both Meena and Manmohan awake at night. Besides, after her third miscarriage, the doctor had warned them against further pregnancies. It's not good for her body, it's not good for her mind, the doctor had said. And then Meena had gotten pregnant again and the doctor had been angry. How could you get pregnant again? he had asked. Did I not say one child is enough? You have one child. It is enough.

And so, when Meena was pregnant with Preeti, Meena and Manmohan had visited a gynecologist in Kathmandu and proposed abortion, not so much because they did not want another child, but because they were afraid that this time, too, the child would reach a certain term and then die. This time, they feared, it would be too much for Meena to bear. Perhaps, this time her body would give away. Perhaps, she too would die and leave Manmohan alone with a child to raise. Perhaps her mind would collapse under the burden of grief. Not worth the risk, Manmohan explained to the doctor. Better have it dropped now, when Meena was still healthy, than wait for too long and risk her health and life.

And yet, the fear of death and ill-health was not what had brought Meena to this small, dreadful place. Meena had come to the clinic to punish herself for the terrible curse she had put upon herself when she had first gotten pregnant. I hope this child dies, she had said, and all her children had died. A part of her waited for Adi to die, too, suddenly and without warning. Meena had come to the clinic because she did not want another Adi, a child who would tease her with living, and then die suddenly, without warning. She had come to the clinic to preempt the dreadful fate she knew awaited her.

But now, looking at Preeti, at the line of blood upon her lips, Meena felt her own curse come rushing back to her. She looked at Preeti's dry lips and felt horror. What was she doing, she asked herself, out in this cold? Was she killing her children?

The clinic had been cold too. The bed the doctor had assigned to her had had steel rails. And may the gods protect that nurse who had said, again and again, like a prayer, like a chant, Don't do it, sister, don't do it. This will haunt you tomorrow. What god takes away is for god to consider, but what you take away will haunt you forever. And this time, the nurse had insisted, You will have a daughter, sister. I can tell by the way you carry her. It is a daughter in you. Very strong she is. When you have her, she had said, you can name her Preeti after me, sister, so you should have her. I would like for your daughter to have my name. And Meena had climbed off the bed and gone back home with two Preetis inside her—one in her womb, one in her heart.

Meena let go of her daughter's hand now and knelt upon the cement floor of the sanjha-bus stand. Her sari bunched up under her feet and she almost toppled over, but she pulled Preeti close and held her against her breasts until she knew neither of them would fall. She felt her daughter beginning to cry and parts of her body grew both warm and wet as her blouse soaked in Preeti's tears. For a second Meena could not differentiate between her body and her daughter's, and Meena was helpless, like a murderess who wanted to undo her murder. She held her child like they were lovers, unable to let go, feeling the madness and destruction of love. She felt love's demented feet climb her nerves and make all her reflexes its own. She pushed her child gently away and looked at her face. "You are so quiet," she said, and fell in love with her child's quietness.

She wiped her daughter's face with the ends of her sari and knew she would never set herself on fire again, never again experiment with life, never again have the courage and strength for death. When the sanjha-bus showed up, she straightened and waved for it to stop. "To Ganesh Basti," she shouted, and as the bus pulled in before the stand, the first gush of rain fell, and everything came alive with the sudden sound of water upon the world.

BOOK SIX

HIS MAJESTY THE KING

DAZZLE-BADAZZLE

Just before His Majesty left Kathmandu for Delhi, his government announced a citywide load-shedding in Kathmandu. There wasn't enough electricity for everybody and load-sheddings or power outages were scheduled throughout the city. It was scheduled for Wednesdays in Ganesh Basti. In Chabahil, load-shedding was scheduled for Thursdays. Near Sundhara, for Fridays. Along the Bagmati, behind Pashupatinath, on Saturdays. Darkness, like a patchwork quilt, suffocated Kathmandu.

Then, before the city could adjust to its sudden blindness, His Majesty King Birendra left for Delhi to discuss the renewal of the Trade and Commerce Treaty that existed between India and Nepal and returned home, stunned, angry and helpless, with an embargo in his bag.

The prime minister of India that year was a man named Rajiv Gandhi who was neither Hindu nor Muslim nor Christian. He was everything and nothing, though it was known that his wife was a Christian and a foreigner. Upon marrying Rajiv Gandhi, Sonia, his wife, had left Italy, her country of birth, to live in India. She was very pretty and wore saris in the most proper way. In the year 1988, just before Preeti had stood with Sachi watching the Royal Procession, Rajiv Gandhi and his wife had visited Kathmandu, and as was the case with every person who visited Kathmandu, the couple had wanted to pay their respects at the Pashupatinath Temple. The Pashupatinath Temple was the most important temple in Nepal. The lingam around which the temple stood was given to Kathmandu by the gods themselves and until the humble cowherd and his beautiful cow had discovered it, it had lain buried deep in the ground like a smiling seed.

Once upon a time, before any country was a country, there lived a hardworking cowherd. Every day the cowherd took his cows to the large fields around his hut and set them loose to graze. The cows grazed all day and every evening gave the cowherd buckets and buckets of milk. All was wonderful in the cowherd's household, all except one particular cow who was stubborn and ungrateful. Unlike other cows she did not amble around the field, eating first this piece of grass, then that. Instead, once in the fields, she stood at the same spot every day for hours and nibbled at what grass she could get without moving around too much. The cowherd thought her most lazy and sometimes hit her with a thin branch, but nothing could coax her to move. What was wondrous, however, was the fact that though the cow insisted on eating from the same spot daily, the grass on the spot seemed never to thin. The grass grew lush and fresh upon the spot, and indeed, the cow, for all her laziness, was as healthy as her other sisters, and so the cowherd was not overly worried about the cow's grazing habits. What worried him, however, was the cow's milking habits. Like her sisters she, too, had udders full of creamy milk, but this milk she would not give to the cowherd. Every evening, before the cowherd made his way back to his hut with all his cattle, this recalcitrant cow drained her udders dry at the spot where she munched her grass. The cowherd was exasperated by the cow's behavior and tried every form of punishment to get the cow to comply, but with no gain at all. Ultimately the cowherd gave up on the cow. What else could he have done?

However, as the months went by, the cowherd began to get curious about the spot where the cow grazed and drained her udders. There was something magical about the spot, something that drew him, too. It was the grass for sure, nurtured to a luminescent green with all the milk the cow fed it, but it seemed to the cowherd that there was something more to the spot than just its soft green grass. The spot seemed to breathe. To be alive. Some days the cowherd was frightened by the spot and stayed far from it. But on other days he was consumed with curiosity and sat under a tree at some distance and watched his obsessed cow. How at peace was this silly cow of his. How lacking in ambition and desires. Some days he wanted to stop being a cowherd. Some days he wanted to be a cow.

And one day, while he sat under the tree and watched his silly cow, he had the oddest sensation that his cow, so mindless and beautiful, was calling out to him. Baaaan . . . baaan, she hummed, and the cowherd was sure that in her cow language she was saying, "Come here, Father, come here." Hypnotized, the cowherd went to his cow. Having pulled him here, she continued to graze, though the cowherd was sure she was smiling a cow-smile. The cowherd sat beside her. The ground beneath him was cool, and upon touching it the cowherd felt a serene joy wash over him. He felt that he had indeed become a cow, that he was no longer a man with greed and ambition tied to a world of shadows. He felt suddenly a desire to weep, the way he sometimes wanted to weep when the sun set and burned the sky.

From that day on the cow and her cowherd sat on the spot for hours. He was no longer angry with his cow for draining her udders here. Instead he felt an intense delight. He wanted all his cows to drain their udders here, but the other cows were not as serene, as joyous as this silly cow and they carried their heavy udders home every evening to his cowshed, where the cowherd's wife emptied their udders for them. Earlier, when the cowherd's wife had scolded the silly cow for returning home empty-uddered, the cowherd had joined his wife and doubled the chastising. But now he urged his wife to keep peace. What do we know about her? he asked his wife. What do we know about the secret lives of animals? The wife, overworked and tired, shook her head and tried to keep what peace she could.

And so days and months passed. More and more, every day, the cowherd felt he was no longer a part of the world in which existed his wife, his cowshed, his house, his buckets. The only reality for him was the light green, velvety grass upon which his beautiful cow sat and munched. The cowherd was now part cow, or so he felt. Some days he felt he was the grass. Some days, the soil beneath the grass. And some days, the distant sky. And one day he was overcome with a desire to burrow himself into the ground. To dig, to sleep like an earthworm, to wrap his body with moist earth. The desire was not simple. It consumed him. Night after night he dreamt of his body of clay become clay again. And one day he brought along with him a kodalo and began to dig the ground. He dug mindlessly. He was seeking nothing other than the earth itself. He was a root digging deep for nourishment. As he dug he found at his feet secrets he could not decipher. Pots of gold, streams of silver, cups full of sweets, but he dug past them. He dug until he found the moistness he had dreamt of, the clay, the nourishment. He found god. Black, gleaming, four faced, bare torsoed, and the cowherd fell back in terror.

It was the terror all mortals feel before the immortal. The terror of the unfathomable. The terror of pure beauty, of intimacy, depth, and death. Falling at the feet of his god, the cowherd wept. What else could he have done? How else could he have fallen in love? Afraid of appearing ugly to his god, he kept his eyes away from the statue he had dug from the ground. He faced the walls of the hole in which he stood and wept.

It was his cow, bovine, all wise and giving, who once again called him out. Come, Father, come, she said to him, smiling, and hypnotized as all fathers are by their children, the man finally climbed out of the hole where he had remained for two nights. When he emerged from the hole, the world was a different place. His cows were scattered and lost. They had crossed the river, gone up hills, and become desolate rocks. His wife no longer lived in the hut he had built for her. There was, indeed, no hut at all. No cowshed, no buckets of milk to sell to the market. The cowherd was a man without possessions. He was cow. He was grass. He was moist earth.

It was as earth, as grass, as cow, that he left his village in search of the world. In the world lived kings of rich palaces. They had the means to build temples with silver gates, large copper bells, and gold ceilings. To this world went the cowherd with his smiling cow. He sat outside the palace and told the story of his gleaming god to all those who passed, and so it was that the news of the god reached the king.

And so it was that the temple of Pashupathinath was built.

And it was this temple of silver gates and golden ceilings that the areligious Indian prime minister and his Christian wife wanted to visit in the year 1988. It was to this temple that Rajiv Gandhi and Sonia Gandhi were denied access. How could a temple, discovered as it was by a cow, allow a cow-eating Christian within it?

≈

It was in 1988, too, after Rajiv Gandhi and Sonia Gandhi's visit to Kathmandu, that His Majesty King Birendra Bir Bikram Shah decided to begin load-shedding as a measure to counter the increasing shortage of electricity. He distributed the power outages democratically, ensuring no neighborhood suffered too long from these shortages. And it was true, initially there were no complaints against the outages. Citizens took it in their stride. Nepal was a poor country.

These kinds of troubles were minor and could be handled with candles and good cheer. Then His Majesty visited Rajiv Gandhi and returned with an official ban on trade between India and Nepal.

Prime Minister Rajiv Gandhi made it clear to King Birendra that the embargo was India's way of warning Nepal against its growing friendship with China, but an immediate rumor involving Rajiv Gandhi, Sonia Gandhi, and Pashupatinath began circulating in the capital. It became known to everyone that Rajiv Gandhi had imposed the ban because his beef-eating wife had been denied entry into Pashupatinath. How atrocious to take this denial personally, people said to one another. How atrocious to not understand that no cow-eating Christian, no matter who she was, could be allowed entry into the temple?

Overnight Nepal's equation with India, with goods and commodities, with electricity, and with King Birendra changed.

Kathmandu, locked like a pearl by tall blue mountains, and sharing no porous borders with India, suffered the most from India's strangely Christian wrath. For nearly a year after the embargo came into effect, long queues formed before grocery stores. People waited in cold and rain for small amounts of household goods. The price of potatoes went up by five hundred percent. Spices became impossible to buy. Salt was so steep, women scarcely curried vegetables, and food, bland already without spices, sat lifelessly on tongues. Long, weary lines moved slowly outside shops from early morning to late in the evening. There was no kerosene, no gas, no needles or thread. Shopkeepers—harassed and harangued—sulked as they handed packets of available rations to tired, angry customers. All hoped to buy what rice could be found, what carton of noodles was available, maybe wheat, maybe dried fish—though not all could bear the smell of dried fish—hopefully lentils, soap. There was little hope for salt or kerosene. These were hardest to get.

Anger simmered. It simmered under the surface. It simmered in Kathmandu. It simmered in Pokhara, in Janakpur, in Biratnagar. It simmered through Nepal, and paradoxically, it simmered in India, where some Nepali citizens, dissatisfied by the monarchy, had fled decades ago, or where those exiled by earlier monarchs had taken refuge. Too many of these men, now old, wrinkled, and hairy-eared, lived in small one-room apartments, doing small one-room jobs, waiting patiently, impatiently for the day when they would be able to return to their own country and bring to it the democracy they dreamed of. Most of these men were exiled when His Majesty King Birendra was still a child, when his father, autocratic and charismatic, had ruled the nation with an iron fist. King Birendra's father had undertaken the difficult task of bringing order to a chaotic land, and this had forced him to make difficult decisions. He had imprisoned thousands who had opposed his rule. He had murdered families. As children, these old men had heard stories about the Brahmin woman who had drowned herself in protest against monarchy. A hundred or more Brahmin women, all clean-shaven, had plunged into the river after her, following her drifting body in protest. Together, their bodies had floated like lilies on the river, their white saris billowing like the rise and fall of music. The old men remembered other stories, too. There was a banyan copse and from every branch had hung dead men, like dangling roots of the gigantic trees. Vultures had eaten through these men. The old men had heard of other men who had been exiled before them and had died in exile. Then there were those who, in the land of exile, had given up on their dreams of return and had adopted India as their own. Traitors, these. There were many others, who, gnawed by nostalgia and disillusioned by loneliness, had abandoned their longing for democracy, of education for all, of smoking industries and green fields, and asked the king for pardon. Those who sought pardon under the auspices of King Birendra were granted pardon, for King Birendra was kinder than his father. Those pardoned had assimilated into His Majesty's government. They hoped to bring change, to do good, from within. There was so little they could have done from India. But there were others, like these old men living in single-roomed apartments in India, who were waiting, now for decades, for the opportune moment, and the moment came with the Indian embargo, with the humiliation, the poverty, the desperation that the embargo pushed Nepal, and more specifically, Kathmandu, into.

These men met in rooms in the country that was both their friend and their foe and discussed the state of their nation. The monarchy is compromising Nepal, they said. The king is spineless. He cannot stand up to India. He is merely a decoration and little else. The world beyond is changing, and Nepal, unchanging, will either fall apart like a brittle book rotting upon an ancient shelf of tradition, or continue stagnant like an increasingly fetid lake. Out there, in the world without monarchs, there is education, free market, movies and books and stimulating conversations only free minds can engage in. We, exiled decades ago by kings and their prime ministers, must now come out of our hiding. We must rid our homeland of the canker of monarchs. Monarchy has doomed us to eternal exile. Let us return!

But these men were the "underground" voice, the "out there," the "outside." There were many others who were not angry with the king. Granted, His Majesty could have handled affairs better. Granted, he could be more worldly-wise. But wasn't his naivete, his innocent boyishness, his inability to deal with national affairs also his appeal? Wasn't India, with its arrogance and bossiness, to blame? Which country cut another off of daily necessities simply because it could? India was full of rhetoric about Indo-Nepal brotherhood. What kind of brotherhood was this?

Sitting on terraces under gloomy skies, citizens grumbled. "Are we cattle," some were beginning to ask, "that we must eat dinner in darkness? Are we animals that we must walk miles and miles to work? Can the king not manage a thing? Is his palace ever dark, cold, and hungry? It is all India's doing. Are we India's servants that we must suffer this ignominy in silence?"

After a few months, the load-shedding stretched to four hours a week, and ultimately, four hours a day, then longer and longer, like the strangling hands of a ghost.

Once the sun set, there was nothing at all to do but sit on the terrace, if the weather was not too uncomfortable, or sit in houses dimly lit by candles. Once the sun set, a brooding quiet fell over Kathmandu, an impossible frustration that muted and dulled the senses.

It was Kathmandu's cold and unheated evenings, its hungry and growling afternoons, its brooding mornings that ultimately created the riot against Vivek Rahane, the Indian Bollywood star who had until recently charmed the citizens of Nepal with his boyish looks and out-of-the-world dance moves. What was there to do without electricity, without salt, without diesel and petrol, but create riots? In this starved and suffocating world, children performed poorly in schools because they could not stay up late into the night to learn their lessons. When these children were caned by irate teachers, their sobs of protest against the tyranny echoed the sobs of protest the adults kept locked in their hearts. These adults, simmering, brewing, went about their day either spiritless or consumed with restlessness. Men returned home sooner than usual from their works. Dark offices were not conducive to work. Nor were markets and bazaars the men had liked to loiter in before. Cooped in their dark houses, men expected entertainment from their wives and children and were invariably disappointed. The youngsters, those who spent their evenings sitting on stairways of various stores, had nothing at all to do now, now that stores pulled their shutters down before streets got too opaque. Women burned with anger. There was no peace at all. No quiet place to hide in.

The Rahane riot flared suddenly, like a sharp scream running and puncturing the streets, and then it died, just as suddenly, leaving the city sore, like an infected throat. Once the riot subsided it became apparent that Vivek Rahane, the dance, dazzle-badazzle Bollywood heartthrob who lived in Bombay, had never said anything anywhere about hating Nepal and all people Nepali. He denied having ever mentioned Nepal in any capacity, good or bad, and would not bow to the allegations made against him. "Why would I?" he asked in interviews later aired by television channels and carried by newspapers. "My chef is a Nepali. My assistant too. My friend of fifteen years. Why would I?" Though his father was an actor and producer and had been associated with the Indian film industry for several years, Rahane himself was a newcomer, having made only three movies when the riots broke out in Kathmandu's streets. He looked flabbergasted by the accusations and stared with an expression of hurt at his audience in the interview that was released soon after the Kamala Krishna Cinema Hall was set ablaze by an angry mob for showing one of his films.

The toxic rumor detailing Rahane's anti-Nepal sentiments spread rapidly through Kathmandu's streets and within minutes of its outbreak, the Kamala Krishna Cinema Hall, Nepal's first multiscreen cinema complex, and fifteen minutes away from Manmohan's house, glowed orange under the fire started by a group of young boys. The fire alarm rang and the screen upon which Rahane was wooing his audience went blank. The audience, unaware of the rumor, interpreted the blank screen as another power outage and booed good-naturedly. Even before the load-shedding, such blank-outs in cinema auditoriums were not uncommon. Such blanks darkened screens despite owners' efforts to keep movies running on generators, and viewers secretly enjoyed the sudden disruption, the excuse to whistle and howl, to misbehave. And so, even on this day, when Rahane suddenly vanished from the screen, as though he were a magician, the audience rose in a roar and hooted loudly, laughing at their own childishness. Aaaaay, aaaay, they booed. But then someone shouted Aago! Aago! Fire! Fire! And the fire alarm wailed. *Taaawaaa, taaawaaa, taaawaaa,* like a police siren. A hush fell before the stampede.

Outside the cinema hall, where the momo stalls were, where the ticket counter had already been shut down, a band of boys set a Vivek Rahane effigy on fire. Blue flames leapt to the sky from Rahane's head, making his boyish face look genuinely roguish for once. The newspapers never carried pictures of this burning boy, but those who witnessed the burning remembered him later as dreadfully handsome.

Inside, the Kamala Krishna auditorium filled with vandals. They ripped off seats and set the Dolby sound system aflame. They howled as the print of the film burned. As they slit and tore, they shouted. Saale dhoti! Fucking Indian! Their voices carried through the corridors to the front of the theater and those watching the burning effigy took up the slogan with happy gusto. Fucking Indian! Fucking Indian! Fucking Indian!

On the bridge that connected the Ring Road to Kamala Krishna, and under this bridge, where an emaciated and viscous river slugged on, smoke, solid as the river's viscosity, pushed toward the sky. A car stood burning in the middle of the road, and burning tires turned the air to acid. A few kilometers away, at the Durbar Marg, students of Tribhuvan University threw stones at someone named Pooja because she looked like she could be from India. But she was not. She was from Janakpur, but it was impossible to tell where she came from simply by looking at her. One stone hit her back and she broke into a run, terrified of the men who followed. At New Road, another group of students stoned the Haldiram Store because it was owned and run by an

Indian-looking merchant. A man, dark brown, paunchy, balding on the head huffed as he ran from a gang of light brown, straight-haired, small-size citizens. Within no time there was graffiti on walls—*Madhise Chor, Desh Chor!* Madhise Thieves, it's time he leaves!

By the end of the day, four Indian-looking men were dead. One of them was the man who ran Mr. Kajra's restaurant at New Road.

For three days after Kamala Krishna was burned, Manmohan did not leave his house and while Preeti's and Adi's friends continued to go to school, they stayed home.

On the third day, while Vivek Rahane was shooting in Europe for another Bollywood sensation, he issued an apology to the people of Nepal, "Though I have not said a word against Nepali people. Why should I? My chef, my personal assistant, my friend of fifteen years . . . but I still apologize. I hope I can visit Kathmandu soon, perhaps shoot a movie there," and the vision of Vivek Rahane, his fair, gaunt face, muscles like bricks on his chest, his eyes dreamy, the vision of him dance-dazzling in Kathmandu, melted even the cruelest of hearts and he was forgiven, that easily. The straight-haired, small-size, superangry Kathmanduite patted the Indian-looking on their backs and shook their heads. "Unfortunate events," they said, "but you know how it is. Sometimes the wrong people pay the price. Now, not all Madhesis are India lovers, obviously, but even they end up paying the price. But really, India should not be doing what it is doing. All this embargo and whatnot."

Men returned to their jobs. The Indian-looking returned to stores that stood confused beside roads; shelves and ceilings charred with fire, glass triangles sharp on floors, sweets and fruits decaying. They applied Boroline on their wounds and tied gauze where required. Kamala

Krishna Cinema Hall fixed its upholstery and painted its walls all colors modern—very mint green, very blood red, very burnt orange.

On the day Manmohan returned to his office at Sundhara, Mr. Kajra called to say he was selling his restaurants in Kathmandu. "Swaroop is dead, Manmohan," he said, his voice tired. Swaroop was Mrs. Kajra's brother. "Metin sits here like a ghost, thinking I don't know what. Swaroop was a brother to me, too, and now he is dead. Over a film actor, Mohan? Over an actor born yesterday? I cannot come there anymore, Mohan. I tried all these years. I tried for Metin and for Swaroop."

"What about Metin?" Manmohan asked, his heart aching for the man he had come to love over the years, but also racing with fear. Mr. Kajra was an important client for Manmohan's audit firm, and his absence would be a substantial financial loss.

"What about Metin?" Mr. Kajra asked. "Now India is her home, is it not? If people are murdered this way, over film actors, does she have to go to Nepal at all? I will forbid her from visiting, ever."

"This is Metin's home, Mr. Kajra," said Manmohan, speaking gently on the phone. "You cannot forbid her from coming home."

"What about you, Manmohan?" Mr. Kajra asked bitterly. "Your wife is from India. If Indians came charging at you with stones and sticks, would you let her go? Where is her home now? With you, or with people in her maika?"

There were so many responses to Mr. Kajra, so many Manmohan thought of after he hung up the phone, but at that moment all Manmohan could say was, "I don't know, Mr. Kajra. I don't know where Meena's home is, but I don't know where my home is, either. I have never known. Sometimes I feel like a slipper abandoned on the roadside. Who knows who the slipper belongs to."

It turned out Manmohan was wrong about Mr. Kajra. Mr. Kajra did not calm down. He did not come to his senses and decide to forget the violence that is the inevitable part of all cities, and a week after his telephone conversation with Manmohan, Manmohan met the people to whom Mr. Kajra sold the three restaurants he owned in Kathmandu. "You handle the accounts, Manmohan," Mr. Kajra instructed over another telephone conversation. "And you handle the transactions."

"Will you not come?" Manmohan asked.

"No, I will not come."

GRILLES

On the day of the phone call, Meena was in the garden. Adi was with Preeti in the bedroom. Meena had turned the radio on and a Geeta Dutt song filled the room and streamed out of the window to her. Adi listened to the song and doodled on the last page of a notebook. Preeti lay on her back with her legs raised high against the wall. She tapped her feet to the beat of the song. It was an undisturbed, sunny afternoon and the meal of rice, dal, and spinach had relaxed Adi and made him lazy. In the sunlight Preeti was transparent and Adi thought that if she moved, she would first break into little pieces, then melt away into the air. One day, he thought, he would paint this moment. His mother in the garden, working with water, marigolds, and lady fingers, and sky, and pebbles; and his sister's legs like toffees upon the wall. Adi watched the world as casually as he doodled. He thought, in a casual way, that he loved his mother and his sister, and that he would like to do something spectacular for them someday. He felt vaguely that, together, one day, they would expand all things beautiful in the world. Vaguely he wished for his father's death.

When the phone rang, Adi got off the bed without much thought. Most calls the family received were for his father, but sometimes Suman Uncle or Kirti Mausi called for his mother. Only once had a call come for Adi, and on that particular day Adi had scarcely been able to contain the sense of importance he had felt. Preeti had never received a call.

Now Adi was distractedly curious. Would he recognize the voice at the other end?

When he finally received the call, Adi did not recognize the voice, and for a second, because a new song—this one sung by Lata Mangeshkar—started on the radio, he did not catch the man's first few words.

"Is this Chaudharyji's house?" the man asked, perhaps after a Namaste. "Is Chaudharyji home? No? Is your mother available? No? Then I will talk to you. My name is Jagdish Thakur," the man went on. "I called you because I don't know anyone else in the neighborhood yet. I don't know you, either, but you are from Janakpur and we are from Janakpur, too, so I thought I could call you. We people have to help each other out, no? My wife and I are in Singapore right now, and our son is in the house we just finished building in Ganesh Basti. Do you know the new, light green house, with the big windows, near the Chundevi Temple? That is our house. Our son studies in America and has just come home for vacations. We were supposed to be in Kathmandu in a week, but there has been an accident. Something has happened. Will you check on our son, please? Please, will you go to our house? We will fly out immediately, but will you check on our son, please?"

In all of what the man said, Adi was unable to think beyond the fact that he was talking to a Madhesi man who could afford to go to Singapore, and whose son studied in America. He had never met such a man before. "Uncle, my mother is in the garden," he said, the word *accident* seeping into his mind suddenly, like a fish, and thrashing about in the placid sea of *Singapore* and *America* that had filled it until a second earlier. "If you hold, I will call my mother," he said, unable to focus. He shouted out for his mother.

Meena came in with mud around her fingers and a frown upon her forehead. "You can't take care of a thing, Adikins. Your brain has shrunk and become the size of your penis," she said, and before Adi could react to the bizarreness of her sentence, she was already at the phone. Where her hand held the cream-colored instrument, she left streaks of mud.

Adi remained rooted to his spot, wondering. He felt a strong desire to pull the receiver away from her, to demand an explanation, but he was too stunned to do anything. Instead, he watched his mother. She tilted her head in concentration and finally she asked, in a somewhat confused, somewhat encouraging tone. "Aahaan ke kutcho kaam hai?" Do you have something you want us to do?

She waited again, listening intently. "I will send my son immediately to your house. His father is something of a chutiya but he himself is fast. I am slow. I will follow him. Is your son at home?"

After she replaced the receiver, she remained standing for a fraction of a second, then she turned. "Did I frighten you, Adi? How frightened I make you." She giggled. Adi waited. "And that boy is all right," she went on, now somewhat agitated. "A small injury. And his poor father. I am sure his slut-wife made this father all nervous. Slutty wives worry too much, then they make everyone else worry too. I don't know why I say these things. I truly don't know. Listen, Adi, will you not go and look into the poor bastard? He is in the new, light green house, just before the Chundevi Temple. Will you go? But better you don't go. You can be a chutiya sometimes, too. Men are bastards." She looked at Preeti who stared at her mother. "You go, my sack of sugar. You tell him his parents will be here early tomorrow. He could be dead though." She giggled again. "Poor thing. All dying all the time. How come you did not die, Adi? Your father does not die and you don't die and this Pirti does not die. It's a good thing, though. Your father would drink the blood of a pig to live. Tell the poor bastard his slutty mother would have come right away, but how does one cover distance so quickly-quickly? You run, Pirti. And you go, too, Adikins. This girl cannot run. You also go. The boy has had an accident."

"What is wrong with you, Ma?" Adi asked, his heart banging.

The light green house was spacious with large, sky-filled windows on its wide walls. It was tucked away behind other houses at the edge of Ganesh Basti. Outside and within its compound gate were men, gathered in small groups, discussing animatedly in hushed tones, and nobody took any notice of Adi and Preeti as they walked toward the house. Nobody stopped them when they crossed the iron compound gate. Behind the gate, almost lost among the gathered men, were two policemen. Adi navigated the men carefully, ensuring Preeti followed because he was suddenly worried about leaving his sister behind. What did the boy's father mean by an accident? Adi wondered. Was it a road accident? Did the accident take place in the house? Adi knew he should worry about possible blood and fractured bones, but he felt no worry, only distant curiosity.

He wondered what Ma was doing. He tried not to think of what she had said. Why do you not die? she had asked. How strange had been her words. How she had mocked him. How she had laughed at the shock he felt. Your brain has shrunk to the size of your penis, she had said.

Why, he wondered, had Ma sent him and Preeti here? Wasn't Preeti too young to witness accidents?

Adi and Preeti entered the house like two light-footed ghosts. The house was not furnished yet, though decorative pieces were already placed around the large, hollow hall. There were two metal dogs, almost as high as Preeti, sitting tall and alert by one of the walls. On the wall hung an abstract painting. The walls were a rich, goldenish yellow, and the painting's play with white and red emphasized the wall. Adi could tell the people of the house were rich. The dogs were metallic gray. A few unopened boxes lay in another corner. There were more policemen within the house, and one of the policemen came over to them.

"Why are you here?" he asked.

"This is my cousin brother's house," Adi said, lying automatically. "Uncle called to say he is not well so I came to see him."

The man looked at him quietly. "He is upstairs, in his room. You know his room?"

Adi shook his head. No.

"Up the stairs. The first door on your left. You will know."

Years later, when he was much older, Adi wondered about the policeman. Why had he allowed Adi and Preeti, two children who could surely not have helped with any investigation, and who were too young to understand murder, into the room?

When he was older, he wondered about the investigation, too. How casual everything was. People milling in and out the house. In movies they showed howling sirens, vigilant policemen, a curious crowd kept at bay, yellow tapes saying stay away, stay away, stay away, circling the scene of crime, but in the only murder scene Adi would ever witness in real life, there was none of the formality and order of the movies.

With time Adi forgot the details of the house. He forgot that he had climbed a delicately balustered staircase to reach the first floor and the door on his left. He remembered the room though, clean, capacious, airy without any beds or chairs. The body lay on a thin mattress and was covered with a white sheet. Adi could not tell the age of the body and he was bothered by this. The body, asleep, the way Adi himself sometimes slept, with the cover drawn over his face. There was nothing at all that Adi felt, other than the curiosity about the body's age. Years later, when he thought about the day, Adi wondered where he had heard the few things he seemed to have heard—that the murder was unintended. A thief had found access into the house through the ungrilled windows. The boy, only just returned from America and here only for half a month, had heard some commotion and gone up the stairs and into the carefree, lighthearted room. There had been a struggle. The boy was dead. Perhaps the servant who was in charge of looking after the house had contacted the thief. Perhaps they had expected that the boy, newly returned from America, had brought with him untold riches.

"All that anger over that Vivek Rahane," someone said. "And this boy was so dark, like a piece of coal. So Marsiya. Should have stayed in America only. Or in India. But even so, the thief should have stolen. Should have left. Haven't found the thief or the servant. The house abandoned. Only twenty-three. Poor thing."

Adi stood before the body for less than a minute. There was no blood on the sheets though the boy had been stabbed. The sheet was clean, and in the seconds that Adi stood before the body he looked only at the hand that had slipped out of the sheet and rested beyond the edge of the mattress.

It was Preeti who later brought the shirtsleeve to his attention. Throughout that day in the light green house Preeti had quietly followed her brother. She had held his hand and looked around, but she had not spoken. But at night when brother and sister had lain on the bare terrace, staring at the stars so visible during the load-shedding, she had brought up the shirtsleeve. "You were wearing the same shirt as that boy." It had startled Adi and in an instant the image of the hand strayed from the body had intensified within him.

At unexpected times the dead boy with whom Adi had spent less than a minute, whose face he did not see, whose name he eventually forgot, entered his conversations. In these conversations they always wore the same shirt—blue, long sleeved. A year later, when he left Kathmandu for his education in India, Adi and the dead boy sat by the window in the train and watched the towns and fields passing by. Another time, after an evening spent celebrating this thirty-first birthday, he told his wife about the boy. He did not mention the shirt, or the fact that the boy should have stayed in America only. Or in India. He only mentioned the fact that the house was all complete but for the grilles, that the servant and the murderer were never caught. As he narrated he thought of the two dogs, metallic and prepared. They had failed to save the boy. "Thank god I had Preeti with me," he said. "She kept chattering and kept me distracted." Even though Preeti had been so quiet, so subdued that day.

He said nothing about Ma, nothing about her desire to see him dead.

After Adi and Preeti left for the light green house, Meena went to the window and leaned out. She could see people through the trees, floating down the lane, nonchalant, pretending not to be interested in her though they were clearly malignant, clearly in search of her. She was vaguely disturbed by what one of the women, walking away with such studied carelessness, called her—Rajiv Gandhi's lover! As though that was possible at all. Rajiv Gandhi had an Italian wife. What would he want with Meena? She found the prospect laughable. Then another woman whispered—Vivek Rahane's lover! And despite herself Meena blossomed a little. To be Vivek Rahane's lover! The blue-eyed, rakish Vivek Rahane! She was aware this was a fantasy, perhaps of every woman, and that the woman walking so casually upon the street had done nothing more than project her own fantasy upon Meena, but she did not mind. Meena dancing to songs of romance, chasing butterflies in gardens, circling trees in glee, all the while reflected in Vivek Rahane's blue eyes. The image swelled her heart.

But then one of the women getting farther away in the lane said, "She should be burnt, that slut."

And in response Meena leaned out the window and shouted out behind the retreating figures. "You should be burnt, you slut!"

Instantly, she clamped her hands over her mouth in horror. Could she have really screamed these words into the world? Then she turned to Vivek Rahane, who was sitting beside her on the bed, and winked at him.

MONSTER

My understanding of Nepal's struggles to free itself was colored by Ma's monster that scaled the insides of our house the way the ghosts of *Jaani Dushman* had roamed the cinema halls of my childhood years. But Ma was not frightened of her monster the way I had been of my ghosts. Ma loved her monster. She spoke to it in a variety of tones. Some days she was loving and free, calling it her yaar, her lover, other days she was disdainful and angry. "Go away," she muttered. "Leave me alone, you shameful slut." Some days she spoke to it in a language Adi and I could not understand, singing to it in a vocabulary and grammar that carried its own cadence. Some days she rhymed. "In the gooshy of the tooshy of the mooshy of the looshy of the whoosh." Always she was vulgar and crass, rude and dirty, reveling in her ability to make the air around her unclean and murky. We children winced at the sounds she made. "Haramkhor," she said lovingly, stroking the thick air before her. "Come sit by my side, my motherfucker."

The first day Ma spoke thus to her monster was the day Papa left for Janakpur to support the revolution now brewing in the plains. Despite the Vivek Rahane violence, a movement to support Kathmandu's anti-monarchy revolution had begun in cities like Janakpur, Biratnagar, and Birgunj, and our father left his family to be where he felt he would be better appreciated. "The nation is drowning and we have our chance at last," he said before stepping out of the house. He knew nothing of

Ma's monster. He looked at us all one last time and said, "Take care of yourselves," as though taking care of the self is easy.

In Janakpur, Manmohan knew people who knew he had been a student activist during his college days in the 1960s. Even now, when he talked about the sixties, a rush of pleasure went through him. That heady thrill, the excitement of being wanted. Even now, though he was a stable man with a stable job and family, he dreamt of a life in politics. Resistance. Speeches. Elections. Leaders. These words stirred within him. He longed to be a part of these words. Perhaps, as a student, if he had allowed the police to arrest him, or if he had emphasized the fact that he was not really a student but a political refugee in exile in Varanasi, perhaps then he would have made a stronger dent in Nepal's political metal. As it was, he was respected for his penetrating analysis of Nepal's political climate, but the respect had not amounted to seats and posts with the government.

In Janakpur Manmohan knew people who had changed their names and lived incognito because either they were children of those exiled long ago or were the exiled themselves. These people lived a twilight life between India and Nepal. They worked in the Janakpur cigarette factory or managed the upkeep of the Janaki Mandir, or ran paper shops at the Janaki Chowk, but these jobs were little more than meal tickets. What these men had always been really engaged with was the nation, with nation building, with quietly resisting the rule of the king.

In Janakpur Manmohan spent his time chatting with such men over multiple cups of tea. In some households there were fritters to be had. In these rooms new questions were being asked and the state of the nation being interpreted in new ways.

"Why should we help the Pahadis after what they have just done to us?"

"It is precisely because there is no way to take action against such atrocities that we need to support the revolution. What we have is lawlessness. What we need is structure!"

Someone went into a long, tedious rant. "They don't think of us as people, these Pahadis, but who is to blame? The king and his ancestors who began the whole pro-India is anti-Nepal slogan. A clever tool, this creation of antagonism. And to think these kings are all of Indian origin themselves! All leftovers of India's crippling maharajas. But who can say a word about that? These kings and their kin marry their daughters off to Rajasthani princes, but who can say anything? We must get these hypocritical rabble-rousers off the throne. Democracy is the way to go. If we Madhesis want equal status, democracy must come first."

"You have heard of the pamphlets being printed? In thousands, I have heard. Secretly in houses. A date is being set for something. A demonstration of some sort."

Manmohan's heart banged. This was as close as he could get to his student years.

It was the day our father left for Janakpur that Ma narrowed her eyes at the television and said, "He is setting the criminals free so they can come kill me." She, Adi, and I were watching a movie and for a second we thought she was joking, but we saw a shudder run through our mother's body and knew something strange had become real. Ma's eyes watched the air as though its particles were made of people, all tumbling toward her, and in an instant she hid under the quilt. From her hiding place she made incoherent sounds, like whimpers. When we coaxed her out, she raised her hand as though she was a warrior and began a shout: "Mai ke bhoos me ghusal hai, kutta! Hiding in your mother's vagina, are you, dog!" She charged past Adi and me, chasing the enemy. "Machodh, saale, hut! Get away, you motherfucker." Later, having chased the enemy right out the house, she sat with us on the bed.

"Your father thinks he can send goondas to throw me out of the house," she explained. "He thinks I can be cowed by such people. He does not know me, does he? I am Kaveri's daughter! I am cowed by nothing."

For four days Adi and I stayed with Ma and her monster. We had no way of contacting Papa. There was no phone in the small house he owned in Janakpur, and we did not know where our father spent his days. In those four days Ma stopped gardening. She stopped cooking. She stopped washing her hair. She listened to the radio at a volume that drowned every other sound. She frowned as she listened, her eyes always watching the air, her senses alert for all suspicious actions.

Terrified, I stayed away from her, refusing to sit too close. It was Adi who took charge, who managed somehow to take her hands and kiss them, who spoke to her. "They are gone, Ma. It is just us now," he said in a voice cracking with fear. "You should eat something. Would you like some sugar and roti? Preeti can get you some. Go, Preeti, get Ma some sugar and roti."

How gentle, how marvelous was my brother. How subtle were the things he understood. He cradled Ma and stroked her grimy hair. He tried to soothe her though it seemed impossible that he could. Ma muttered and stared. She howled to the wind. I made roti for the first time. For the first time I kneaded dough and roasted it over the flame. Adi fell asleep with Ma's hand in his, sitting upright beside the window out of which Ma stared at the world. He held it together but I could see he was terrified. I was only twelve. Adi was fifteen.

Was separation from her home the beginning of Ma's anxiety? Was Shankar, the servant boy who had lived with us for a week and molested me and whom Ma had beaten with anything and everything she could find, the beginning of her violence? Was Kathmandu's perpetual water shortage the beginning of her melancholy? Was the revolution the beginning of her aggressive fear? Was the poetry of Bollywood music the beginning of her dirty, filthy language? When was the first time she told me Papa was a bhosdi ke, he who belonged to the muck of a woman's vagina? "He sleeps with his mother when he goes to Sabaila," she said to me. "Why do you think he goes running to Sabaila? The motherfucker. He fucks her in the arse." She must have caught herself immediately. It was not frequent, these outbursts, not initially anyway. Initially, she knew what was going on. In fact, she once sat me down and explained herself to me thus:

"Have you seen a hijra, a eunuch, my sack of sugar?" she asked. "Can you ignore them when they come smacking their lips at you and thrusting their flat breasts under your nose? They used to repulse me once, but now I understand them. If a little vulgarity gets me money, what is there to it? You should see how quickly your father will shell out money the moment I let my tongue roll."

I had never seen a hip-gyrating hijra in Nepal. All the hijras I had ever seen were in Darbhanga and I was terrified of their extravagant saris and loud bangles. I could not decide whether they were born that way, or whether they were simply playing a part, acting a script. And now I could not decide about my mother.

Did her madness begin as a script, as an experiment to extract money from Papa, as a language to repay some of the abuse he had previously hurled at her? And eventually, did she simply fall in love with her own role and therefore refuse to let go? Did she decide she had to invent a hyperbolic language to be visible and then immerse herself in its cadence? Bhosdi ke, bhutni ke, chutiya, machodh, haramkhor, haramjaada, apan mai ke bhosdi me ghusal rahai chhai—her words. Some of these words I can still make no sense of. Bhutni ke? Of ghosts? What can that mean? What can it mean to be of ghosts? Is this the gibberish of madness?

It was Doctor Uncle, with whom we shared a boundary and who had once sent over a mutant cucumber for Ma, who came to our aid. He had heard Ma's howls. He had seen her stand upon the stairwell, screaming obscenities at the world. He had understood her filthy sari and greasy hair. He had watched us, aged twelve and fifteen, struggle to contain the situation. On the fifth day of Papa's absence Doctor Uncle visited our house for the first time. He was a slim, curly-haired man with drooping, sad eyes and a soft voice. He is the kindest man I know. He brought us food and he listened to Ma as she raved against Papa. "Bhootni ke!" she howled. "Laandwa!" Where had she learned these words? How did she know what these words meant? But Doctor Uncle listened patiently. Every now and then Ma broke into a roar. Her eyes went wild and white. Her pupils disappeared. She was so dirty. Where was my father? What was he doing wherever he was? I wanted to stand on the staircase and scream to him. *Bhootni ke!* I wanted to roar. *Laandwa!*

A vehicle arrived shortly after Doctor Uncle and two women came into our house. Together with Doctor Uncle the women took Ma out the house. "You both stay here," Doctor Uncle said to us in his soft, sad voice. "Your father will be here tomorrow morning. I am taking your mother to Teaching Hospital. She might not come home tonight. Will you be okay? You can stay in my house tonight if you want. Your mother will be home tomorrow. Your father will be home too. And your mother will be fine. There is nothing to worry about."

But Adi and I did not take up Doctor Uncle's offer. We slept in our own home. That night Adi and I wrapped ourselves around each other and fell into a deep, exhausted sleep. I dreamt of sounds and quickly shifting shapes. When I woke up the next morning, I knew I had dreamt of Sachi. She was riding her bicycle and as she pedaled, I could see her ankles. She wore mismatched socks on her feet and her legs flashed pink and yellow as she wheeled around my terrace. Perhaps I stood at the center of the terrace because she sometimes whizzed around me in a blur of colors. I held on to her spinning body with a thick rope, and sometimes I went round and round in an effort to keep her from flying off. At other times I stood with my arms to my side, unable to look away from her socks.

The dream stayed with me for hours after we woke up. It stayed with me as Adi and I went to Ma's garden and watered the plants. It stayed with me as we plucked some tomatoes and pulled out a few roots. It stayed with me as we made some green salad. "Ma likes potato curry and rice," Adi said and together we chopped potatoes and cooked rice. We waited breathlessly for our mother to return to us. I prayed incoherently. Let her be well, let her be well, let her be well. I missed Sachi and wanted to run to her so I could stop feeling the fear and the pain, and yet, that afternoon when Sachi came to hang out with me, I told her I could not. I said, almost rudely, that I was not in the mood. I did not tell her why. I did not give her the details of my life. I did not invite her up. I kept her in the garden so I would not have to tell her Ma and Papa were not home. She had not heard anything about Ma yet and I was too angry with her for not having sought me out, for not having consoled me, for not having known somehow that I needed her, and I was too embarrassed by Ma's animal cries to tell Sachi anything. I wonder now if that was the beginning of the separation that came between Sachi and me. If that was the break.

Ma came home late that evening. Doctor Uncle came with her. So did Papa, who had gone straight to Teaching Hospital from the bus station. Papa had called us the night before to tell us we were to sleep at Doctor Uncle's house, then he had called us in the morning to let us know he was now in Kathmandu, then he had called us in the evening to let us know they were leaving the hospital. Each time he had spoken to me because Adi refused to speak with him.

When Ma, Papa, and Doctor Uncle got home, Adi and I held hands and hung back. She was so lifeless, so hollow. How emptily my ma looked at me. Her hair was matted and stuck out in all directions. She smelled. My mother, who liked to look pretty. How clean, puffed, and vulgar was Papa beside her. I could feel Adi shrink from him. Then when Papa turned to us and said, "Didn't I ask you to stay in Doctor Uncle's house?" Adi's face contorted with an emotion I cannot describe. "Die, you motherfucker," he hissed.

BOOK SEVEN

SECRETIVE HOUSES, TIGHT-LIPPED STREETS

THE ADC GURUNG AND HIS WIFE

Had Meena considered the various events that cornered her life in Kathmandu, the Vivek Rahane riot that shook the city soon after her neighbor Radha failed to keep her afternoon appointment with Meena would not have shaken her.

Between the time that Radha failed to turn up for tea at her place, and when the Vivek Rahane riot turned up at her doorstep, Meena met Kamala Gurung, and had Meena studied Kamala Gurung with the seriousness Gurung deserved, Meena would have received Vivek Rahane with more balance and fortitude than she did. But as it was, Meena did not make the various links she should have between Radha's absence, Kamala Gurung's aggression, and, ultimately, Vivek Rahane's appearance at her doorstep.

Kamala Gurung, forty-two years old, short and squat, was the wife of the notorious ADC Gurung. ADC Gurung was often referred to as His Majesty King Birendra's right-hand man. He was His Majesty's aide-de-camp and was instrumental in securing extra income for the royal family. He assisted the royal family in running the several casinos that were the pride of the five-star hotels within which the casinos operated. He was also a consummate smuggler and owned several shops at New Road that sold smuggled electronic goods, clothes of the latest fashion, and foreign toys. Customers from India crowded before these shops for cameras, Walkmans, toasters, and radios made mostly in China, but also sometimes in France and the UK. India did not as yet have an open market, and goods common in the streets of Kathmandu were difficult and expensive to come by in Delhi.

ADC Gurung was instrumental for smuggling heroin into Kathmandu, which came in mostly from Burma via India. Then there was the gold. Lesser smugglers wore three pairs of jeans and several shirts upon their torso when they entered Nepal from foreign destinations, but the ADC brought in gold plates, gold bricks, and gold biscuits in hard-cased attachés. ADC Gurung and his short, squat wife lived fifteen minutes walking distance away from Meena's house, and it was rumored that there were bricks of gold holding up the ADC's house.

By the time Meena met Kamala Gurung, Meena had lived in Kathmandu for more than fifteen years and the garden surrounding her house was lush and green. Her trees were healthy and forceful, independent and no longer in need of her care, though they gave her bags full of apples and plums. By the time she met Kamala Gurung, Meena had let her own roots tentatively enter Kathmandu's soil, had begun to carefully, though awkwardly, navigate its undersurface and seek a place for herself in this kingdom.

Despite herself, she was beginning to grow familiar with the landscape in which her husband had situated her, while Kamala Gurung, an illiterate, village-born-and-bred wife, felt out of place and unwanted in the city. Before Kamala Gurung came to Kathmandu, she had spent her life tending to goats and calves. There was no elegance to her. She was loud, crass, indefatigable, devoid of imagination, fearless, and deeply god-fearing. In many ways she was a perfect match for ADC Gurung who was city bred, sophisticated, and like many men whose talent lie in violence, a man of society. ADC Gurung and Kamala married young and while the ADC stayed in Kathmandu to further his political career, Kamala made a home for herself in her husband's ancestral village where she took care of the ADC's aging parents, his ample fields, and the large herd of cattle his family owned.

Unlike Meena, who, despite living in Nepal's capital city, longed for an authentic city experience, village life was the only life Kamala had ever known or wanted. The Gurungs were the richest family in their village and while Kamala enjoyed working the fields once in a while, she mostly supervised the numerous workers who looked after their fields, cattle, and household, and the needs of the ADC's parents. When it became clear that she could not bear children, Kamala adopted her cows and buffaloes with a gusto, naming each one carefully, and sometimes soothing a troubled animal with songs and stories.

What Meena, therefore, met when she met Kamala Gurung was a Sawari Devi displaced from her labor and her love and pushed into the unforgiving foreignness of Kathmandu's culture.

Kamala Gurung had lived in the village like a robust and vigorous tree. She had thought of her husband as one thinks of an acquaintance, distantly and fondly. When he visited her, she found his manners, his cigarette smoking, and his whiskey drinking boring and useless. She could not understand what exactly this man did in the king's palace and though she was immensely proud of her husband, she thought there must be something amiss with the king, for why else would he want someone so lacking in skills in his palace? When the ADC visited the village, he lolled about on the veranda, or walked the gardens, surveying fruits and flowers. He talked as awkwardly with his wife as he did with the laborers working the fields, and Kamala could see he was perpetually bored. Her husband's boredom saddened her a little, sickened her a little, and though she did not know this herself, she was relieved not to be living with him in Kathmandu.

But then the aging parents died, and in Kathmandu the ADC's

friends and acquaintances began to question him about his wife. Why was she now in the village? His female friends were especially vociferous. Was the ADC so self-centered, so devoid of love and affection, that he would not allow his bride a few years of companionship? The ADC knew these friends and acquaintances were sniggering at him. They thought of Kamala as he thought of Kamala—as uncouth and boorish. A wonderful person, yes, but not meant for the city. And it was precisely because they thought her unfit that they wanted her in the capital—so they could feel superior, so they could compare and take notes. Even his mistress taunted him now and then. Bring the mistress of the house over, she said in the middle of sex and laughed. We could have a delightful threesome.

Ultimately, the ADC was not sure why he decided to bring Kamala over. Perhaps it was the promise of a delightful threesome. Or perhaps it was curiosity. He did not really know his wife but now that people were talking about her, he found himself wondering about her. Who was she? There were so many villagers in Kathmandu and they adapted to the city quite well. Perhaps she would too. And his mistress's comment had thrown him off balance. Did his mistress love him so little that she felt no jealousy at all? Did she feel no insecurity? No passionate rage? Her jokes left him both angry and lonely, and slowly, over nights spent drinking whiskey with sophisticated men, the ADC began to yearn for his simple, uncouth wife.

Kamala Gurung was not happy to leave her village; the ADC could see that. She would rather have stayed in her sprawling hut with her buffaloes and goats. He could see, too, that she felt orphaned without his parents and was startled to realize the deep bond she had shared with them. He learned something new about her. She was a tender woman, with tender feelings and strong loyalties, and the ADC felt cheated at not having received any of this strong tenderness. He brought her to Kathmandu.

In Kathmandu, things unfolded with an almost clichéd expectedness. Kamala Gurung was lonely. She was lost. She did not understand the royal Nepali in which the ADC and his friends conversed. She did not like the taste of wine, the compulsory drink for women. She could not smoke the long cigarettes everyone was perennially smoking. Her clothes, even when they were identical to someone else's, were not right. Her speech, no matter how she tempered it, was too loud, too out of sync. From the robust tree, she dwindled into a weed, unkempt, unwanted, a sore sight in an otherwise manicured garden.

Kamala tried her best to change. She hired a tutor who would teach her royal Nepali and sprinkle her tongue with a smattering of English. She went shopping. Shelves and racks filled with thin, embroidered chiffons in pastel shades. There was nothing to do but buy shoes and line the dressing table with lipsticks and perfumes.

The ADC studied her with curiosity. He liked her fine enough, but she also amused him, tickled his funny bone, and sometimes he spent time with his mistress imitating his wife. He sat before an imaginary mirror and dabbed his cheeks and chin with a brush that looked like a squirrel tail. The mistress threw her legs up in an uproarious laugh and doubled the imitation. But even so, the ADC understood his wife. After all, he was a villager, too, one who had learned the city ways. He understood her loneliness and pining for hills, jungles, and animals. And finally, after a night Kamala had spent smothering her sobs into her pillow, the ADC sat her by his side and told her about the lands they owned around the city.

"I am building an asset for us," he said. "Some land, a couple of houses." He smiled ruefully as he said this. He knew Kamala knew that these assets were not for her. These were for his two sons, none he had had with his wife, but he had decided now that perhaps she could be mistress of at least one land. "The closest one is at Ganesh Basti," he said. "Ten minutes' walk for you. We grow paddy in it and the workers are thieves. You take care of that, Kamala. You grow paddy there."

And that was how Meena met Kamala Devi. Had they met under different circumstances, as women who felt cheated by their husbands, or as women who longed to be elsewhere, away from the alienating customs of the city they were forced to live in, as women who missed their parents, who loved the smell of soils and the sight of trees and plants, they would have befriended each other. But as it was, such friendships were not possible. Their lives, separated and made alien by royalty, ethnicity, politics, and history, could not recognize that which was common between them.

One morning Kamala arrived at her field, whose borders touched the boundaries of Meena's land, and a vicious rivalry began between the women. Kamala came with a troupe of women, all dressed in saris raised to their knees and wearing high gumboots, and Meena watched them from her veranda as she popped peas and crushed garlic. Initially, Meena was filled with admiration. She appreciated the women squelching in the waterlogged land and screaming like goats until they suddenly began to work, quietly and with focus. Kamala Gurung entered the field, too, her boots sinking into the soft mud as she worked the soil. When the women spoke gently and slowly with one another, a murmur rose from the fields and reached Meena softly, but sometimes Kamala Gurung barked at the women, and Meena chuckled on the veranda. Kamala Gurung reminded her of her mother-in-law. Like a bull in shoes, she thought disdainfully.

What Kamala saw when she looked at Meena was haughty aloofness. She, too, had watched Meena in her gardens, tending to her radish and mustard seeds. She, too, had felt a stir of familiarity upon gazing at the younger woman, and more than once she had considered walking over to greet her, but she had held back. Why should she make the first move? she thought each time. Why should she be the one to change herself? To buy lipsticks and chiffon saris. Did she not work hard? Did her husband not toil and serve the nation? Why should she always walk the extra step?

Then, over the weeks, she began to spot Manmohan—dark, thin, so obviously not from Kathmandu. In fact, so obviously not from Nepal. He belonged elsewhere, and whenever it was that he had entered the borders of Nepal, he still belonged to that other, savage country. Manmohan's appearance upon the scene shocked Kamala. Before she saw him, Meena's fair skin had duped Kamala into believing Meena was a high-caste Pahadi, but now she saw Meena for who she was. An outsider married to another outsider, and living a life of comfort in the Kathmandu her husband worked so hard to keep safe and well provided for. Upon spotting Manmohan, Kamala began to resent Meena's trees, her radishes, her veranda, her life with a husband who came home to her, and the two children who fluttered around her like gold-patterned insects.

And so, one day, Kamala came up to Meena while Meena was wringing water out of the clothes she had just finished washing and demanded that she shift her trees. "Is this your father's land that you have all these trees? They are encroaching upon my land."

Meena stopped wringing the frock in her hand and let the garment drop back into the tub from which she had picked it. Here was Sawari Devi once again, with her foul language and her bossiness. Meena stood to full height, which went about an inch above Kamala Gurung and said, simply, "No, they are not."

"Your trees shed their leaves into my land. Your fruits drop and rot on them," complained Kamala Gurung.

"Well, then," said Meena, "take your land and go to your landlord. Tell him you cannot work if the land is not moved elsewhere."

Kamala Gurung glared. "I am the landlord of this land."

And Meena burst into a laugh. "Oh, you are? You look hideous for a landlord."

What Meena felt at that moment was the delicious excitement of fighting once again. This was a continuation of the fight she had not ended with her mother-in-law, a continuation of the fight she longed to have with Manmohan, a continuation of what she sometimes wanted to say to the world. *You look hideous,* she wanted to say, and so she said it to Kamala.

Kamala, the wife of His Majesty's right-hand man, froze. In Meena's words she heard all the sniggering and murmuring that went on behind her back when she accompanied her husband to parties and dinners. The essence of these sniggers was that she looked hideous for a landlord, and no amount of perfume, bags, and shoes would change that.

"You will regret this," said Kamala Gurung, and Meena, who was beginning to slip into a kind of happy madness by this point, snorted in disagreement.

It would have been easy for Kamala Gurung to complain about Meena to her husband. Her husband could easily have Meena and her family removed from this place, but a shame, deep and troubling, kept Kamala from reaching out to her husband. She stayed up until late at night fantasizing about the different ways in which she could destroy Meena if she so wanted. *The bitch!* she thought and ground her teeth.

Meena, on the other hand, dismissed Kamala. She did not know who Kamala was and therefore felt no fear. When Kamala came at her again, screaming and snarling, "Your trees are eating into my land. Your land is swallowing my land. O ho, until yesterday your land ended there, now it is ending here!" Meena shouted back, "What a cheap thief! Have some shame, you thief!"

"I am a thief? I am a thief?" stuttered Kamala. "You come into my country and call me a thief?"

And every week or so Kamala pushed her dike into Meena's land until the dikes were touching the trunks of her trees.

"Call the surveyor," said Meena. "He will testify. Our trees are well within our property."

"What surveyor?" asked Kamala. "I know where my land begins and where it ends simply by looking. I am the surveyor. Tell your trees to stay within your land. Your branches rob my rice of sunlight."

Eventually, Manmohan, who witnessed the war one Saturday, tried to placate Kamala, but this only infuriated Kamala further. "*Saale Dhoti! Saale Chor!*" she screeched at his pleading face.

Manmohan shrank from the woman's viciousness. Her illiteracy and hate filled Manmohan with dread. He knew enough about politics to imagine the terrible consequences that entangling with it could have. He imagined time in prison, imagined the pain of torture and mutilation. He imagined homelessness and poverty. He imagined humiliation and disgrace. The more Meena engaged with Kamala, the more frightened Manmohan grew. He could not sleep. He could scarcely eat without terror rising within him like bile.

Meena, on the other hand, seemed to grow a cobra's hood upon her head. "How dare she! How dare she!" she hissed. "I will go to the palace with my complaints. I will seek out His Majesty!"

"Her husband is the king's weapon," Manmohan said in disgust. "You think he is going to listen to you?"

"He will, because I will speak loudly and repeatedly. His Majesty is an honest and fair man. He knows his citizens. He will listen if we speak. I have poured sweat into this land and this witch thinks she can take it away from me? Chaudharyji, if you are half a man, you will do something; if not, you are a eunuch and nothing more! This land belongs to me and my children and nobody will come poisoning it. You are a donkey, Chaudharyji, for just standing there twiddling your thumbs!"

But Manmohan knew there was very little he could do other than twiddle his thumbs and grovel. He knew about the smugglings and the murders. He knew the king was weak and frail, too dependent on thugs and goondas to keep his country going. He knew the likes of him and Meena stood no chance against the ADC and the king.

And one day when Manmohan returned from work, when he cut through the trees that marked the boundaries of his home, he found a short, squat, square man in his compound. In the dark he could not recognize the man, but from the confidence with which he stood before the veranda, Manmohan could tell the man had not wandered in by mistake.

The man was facing away, deep in thought, and so did not immediately register Manmohan's arrival. Manmohan cleared his throat to announce himself and the man turned to look at him.

"Chaudhary?" the man asked.

"Yes," said Manmohan. "Forgive me but I do not recognize you." He went to the corner of the veranda and turned on the light and in the light Manmohan recognized ADC Gurung.

"I hear your wife has been giving my wife some trouble over our land," said Gurung, without introducing himself.

"There has been some confusion, hajur," said Manmohan. "Your wife thinks our land is jutting into your land, but this is not true. We have had our land measured by a surveyor only recently, only to satisfy your wife, and our trees and our land are very much within their limit."

ADC Gurung looked quietly at Manmohan. "Put your wife in her place," he said. "If you want to continue living here, put her in her place."

"You know how these women are, hajur," Manmohan said. "They have peas for brains."

But even as the words left his mouth, Manmohan recoiled. In his mind he saw Meena, filled with the courage to fight the world. She would never have called this short, funny-looking man "hajur." She would not have twiddled her thumbs and groveled.

"Could you make a cup of tea?" the ADC asked and Manmohan nodded.

"Of course," he said and invited the ADC into his house.

And it was over the cups of tea that Meena served to the ADC without knowing who he was that Manmohan knew he would have to sell off his land.

Manmohan sold the land, and with it its trees and grass, to a Gurkha family that had until now lived in Singapore but were making plans to return home. They were in Kathmandu and Manmohan invited them to the restaurant where he had recently conducted the transactions for Mr. Kajra and signed the required papers to transfer Mr. Kajra's business to other interested parties. The restaurant, called Daawat when Mr. Kajra had owned it, was now Momo Palace and the family praised the momos as they completed the business.

"What an excellent piece of land it is, Mr. Chaudhary. Why you want to sell it is beyond us," they said once papers were exchanged.

Manmohan smiled and nodded. He said nothing about the self-loathing that filled him. He did not tell them that he had led the ADC into his living room and asked Meena to serve him a cup of tea and a plate of biscuits. He said nothing about the revulsion he felt when he saw the cup from which the ADC had sipped sitting beside the other cups on the cup shelf.

Back in Ganesh Basti he got off the rickshaw and walked down the lane, and for the first time in his life he knew he belonged nowhere. When he reached home, he stood on the lane for a minute, startled by the beauty of the trees surrounding the compound that was no longer his. How, Manmohan wondered, had Meena managed to create such beauty in the middle of the barrenness that was their life? And suddenly, as he stood gazing at what was once his, he thought of the young boy murdered soon after the Vivek Rahane riots and wondered at how easy it was to kill people.

Manmohan said nothing about the sale to Meena. To her he only said, "Don't fight with that woman. It is not safe for our children for you to fight this way."

He spoke with the Gurkha family over the phone the next day, "Do you want us to cut down the trees?" he asked.

"No," said the family. "When we build the house, we will see what we want to do with them."

And so it was that Meena knew nothing about the sale. The day she learned she was eating apples from someone else's trees was the day the Gurkha family, despite entertaining possibilities of retaining the trees, dropped a truckload of bricks upon the land to begin the construction of their new home.

BLACK

Immediately after the sale Manmohan fled to Janakpur, the one place he felt increasingly at home. Janakpur was cold then and covered with fog. A sweater was required. A muffler. Thick socks. And Manmohan remained buried in his clothes like an animal in its shell, lumbering through the town's translucent air to emerge into the small hotels that sold meals and snacks. For the first two days Manmohan informed no one of his arrival in the city. He stayed concealed, like a dormant seed, both cold and warm, and ate his lunches and snacks privately at the hotels by the chowk. It was not so much that Manmohan was trying to avoid his friends and acquaintances but that on the very first evening of his arrival in Janakpur, he encountered a boy, no older than eighteen, in the Hotel Kailash Parbat and as he watched the boy and drank his tea, Manmohan fell in love.

On his first day in Janakpur, Manmohan took one of the cornermost tables at the Kailash Parbhat and ordered a large cup of tea to go with his plate of fritters. Diagonally from him, at the other corner, a boy jested and bantered somewhat sulkily with his friends. Manmohan could see the boy was agitated though he tried valiantly to maintain his calm and humor. His friends seemed to have confiscated the boy's college bag and were teasing him tirelessly. The young rivalry among the boys and their easy camaraderie reminded Manmohan of his days at the Banaras University and despite himself

Manmohan smiled. He watched them closely, yet with detachment, as one watches a movie.

"Your Highness," cried one of the friends, imitating melodramatic swoons, "such metaphoric angsts in such baroque sentences, Your Highness! We die! We die!" He put his hand over his heart and collapsed upon the chair behind him. There was much merriment over this drama. Manmohan chuckled into his teacup.

The friends, it seemed to Manmohan, were after a particular notebook the youth owned. They tossed this notebook among themselves and its pages fluttered like flustered pigeons in the air. The boy, who was not too robust of built, jumped up and down in an attempt to get his book back.

Don't pester him, Manmohan wanted to say, but instead he decided to extend his stay in the canteen and ordered a plate of beaten paddy and boiled eggs, and an additional cup of tea.

"Do sit, Your Highness," the boy's friends said, laughing and continuing to tease. "Do recite your words to us. Our withered minds cannot abide your standing arse!"

Manmohan quietly sipped his tea.

And suddenly, as though he had come to a decision, the boy gave up jumping up and down, and instead sat upon the table that was littered with thick glass tumblers of tea, and looking at his friends, he began reciting to them in a loud and authoritative voice.

Once upon a time there lived a cow and a tigress, began the boy's story. The cow gave birth to a sweet, soft calf, and the tigress to an orange and furry cub. While the calf grazed in the meadow and the cub rolled about in the mud, the two met each other and instantly became friends. They matched their steps and their play and refused to go anywhere without the other. It was a strange and beautiful sight—a snow-white calf and a fire-red cub in company, playing as only children can play. The parents were worried. The cow worried her calf was playing with danger, and the tigress worried her cub would grow up soft and unfit for its destination, and the parents tried everything they could to separate the younglings, but nothing would part the cub and the calf. Time passed thus and then came a month when the jungle went suddenly dry. No rain fell and water bodies shrank. Animals grew frantic with thirst and hunger. Some died, some fled. The cow and her calf lay languid under a brutal sun. At some distance the tigress watched over her cub. One day the tigress left her cub under the shade of a stone and went in search of some nourishment for herself and her child, and as she dragged herself across the arid land, she saw the cow and her calf, limp with exhaustion, lying under a skeletal tree. The tigress, too, was exhausted and in her current condition would never be able to chase an agile creature in hunt. This is it, she thought, though with some regret, and pounced upon the cow. The cow died almost instantly. The calf mooed in misery and surprise. She had not expected the tigress to attack her, and she called out to her friend, but the cub, weak and nearly dead, could not hear her cries. The tigress then swiped at the calf and ended her life. The tigress ate the calf because she could not bring herself to feed this meat to her son. For her cub she carried a hunk of the mother's meat and a cup of her blood.

Thirstily, hungrily, the cub ate the meat and drank the blood, and with every bite and sip life returned to the cub's body. In just an hour he was up and running and had forgotten the pains of hunger.

Mother, he said, where is calf, my friend? I feel I haven't seen her in weeks, and because the cub would not stop asking for the calf, and because, despite his newfound health, he looked weak and despondent, and because in his search for the calf, the cub stopped eating and drinking even though the rains fell from the sky and food was to be found in abundance, and because he seemed to have lost all will to live or laugh, the tigress finally told her son.

They died, she said. It was hot and dry and there was nothing to eat.

And because the cub was intelligent and insightful, and because the tigress looked guiltily away as she spoke, the cub knew suddenly and with certainty what had happened.

You killed them, he cried, horrified, and stepped away from his mother. You killed them and you fed me their meat. I am alive because they are dead.

And because the cub was innocent, like all children are, but was now corrupted by his mother, and because he could not mitigate his grief with logic and greed, and because with every breath he was reminded of his friend and her gentle mother, the cub found his situation impossible to bear.

"So," said the boy at this point in the story and looked majestically at his listeners. "What do you think the cub should do at this point? Should he accept his condition and understand the strength of his mother's love for him and continue to live, or should he climb the tip of a cliff and jump off its height? Should he accept that there is an order to the world and no matter how he tries that order cannot be broken, or should he challenge that order and come to the conclusion that a new world order can be established? What, my friends, do you think he should do?"

Taken aback by the sudden question, Manmohan leaned forward, as did the boy's friends, and the youth glowered at them all. Manmohan felt his blood grow warm. He could see that his friends understood nothing of what the boy meant, though, like Manmohan, they understood that in these inexplicable words was rage. They understood that the boy was angry, not vaguely, but dangerously, and though he was shy, he was fierce and capable. They were confused by this ability and this rage because while his friends were still stuck in a world controlled by parents and teachers, their timid friend, whom they loved to pester and plague, seemed to have escaped into an important and all-consuming world that nearly excluded them.

"My friends," said the boy when no one dared to break the hushed silence, "do not be mistaken! We are and always have been the gentle cow and her calf, and we will always be slaughtered by the tigress. For the first time in history the tigress finds herself cornered by her very offspring and if we do not join the cub now, if we do not fight to overthrow the tigress, noble as she might be, we will perish and there will be nothing left to show for us." Here the boy looked deep into his friends' eyes, and through his look he fed them the metaphor. His friends looked back, astonished. "Do you, my friends," asked the boy, "want to be a part of history?"

His friends, subdued by the story and the question, giggled nervously.

Manmohan, sitting behind his table, nodded though nobody paid him any heed.

"What do you mean, Your Highness?" one of the friends asked.

"The supporters of monarchy are bringing out yet another rally tomorrow," the boy said, looking precisely at each of his friends. "They will walk the city carrying large frames of the king and queen, chanting praises of the system that does not allow our growth or our freedom. As a Madhesi I am tired of the Pahadi rule over me. As a Madhesi I want equality, but before that dream is fulfilled, we must bring democracy into the country. Only in a true democracy is true equality possible. I will be there when the rally ends at the Janaki Mandir and the meeting begins. Just when the meeting begins I will tie a black bandanna around my head, and like a magician, pull a black handkerchief from my pocket. I will shout slogans against the monarchy and against the panchayat system. I will cheer for a multiparty political system."

"And Your Highness of nowhere hopes to achieve what? Your Highness will be the ruling party of the Janakpur Jail after his bandanna shows itself."

"So be it," said the boy.

The students stared. "Our poet is an idiot," one said.

"There are idiots like me all over the country," the boy solemnly said.

"Will you go alone?" another classmate asked.

"They will put you in jail," said another.

And it was at that moment that the boy looked up suddenly, and across the room, at Manmohan and said, "You can come, too, if you like. They cannot put us in jail if there are enough of us."

Embarrassed, Manmohan looked away and took a bite of the boiled egg he had ordered.

That night Manmohan could not sleep. To be young again, he thought. To be filled with such enthusiasm. To be noticed by people. To be a leader. He thought of a rumor he had heard while still in Kathmandu. He had heard protest pamphlets were being secretly written in the gullies of Janakpur, though he wondered how such an initiative could be a secret if he had heard of it across the mountains. He imagined songs and slogans being sung in alleys and dark rooms. He imagined young men, sharpened upon the rocks of poverty and neglect, burning to study subjects such as medicine and engineering but reduced, instead, to the necessity of using words. He thought of the boy and the invitation he had extended to Manmohan. *You can come too.*

The next afternoon Manmohan went to the Janaki Mandir, and despite the fact that he had expected to see the Panchayati Raj rally at its courtyard, he was surprised to find it swaying and swinging before the majestic temple. Amid the usual crowd of people, animals, and birds, the rally, a rather thin and pathetic affair under its bravado, shouted energetically. "Panchayatikal zindabad, zindabad!" it insisted. Nobody paid it much attention and around the rally people continued with their day. Vendors called out to devotees and coaxed them to buy prasad. Pigeons pecked at the ground for grain. Cows chewed on leaves and paper. Manmohan found a spot for himself upon a stool by a vendor's side and looked around for the boy. His heart raced as he thought of him. Where was he? Had he got frightened?

And then Manmohan spotted him. There he was, running across the courtyard, a white megaphone in hand. Indeed, he had a black bandanna tied around his head, and he looked like a ridiculous school student as he jumped upon a cement bench close to where the rally stood shouting its slogans and began speaking into the megaphone. He began in a rushed and agitated voice, as though he had a script memorized that he had to get through.

"My grandfather once lived in Kathmandu and tells me of the time the city first got electricity," he squeaked into the megaphone. "My grandfather and his sister would look out their window and see the palaces like ships glittering at the foothills. Only the palaces. The rest of the city was dark. Now Kathmandu glitters. But we in Janakpur are still dark. We are still the foothills. I feel fear when I say the word king or queen." A man in the rally disconnected from his group and ran toward the cement bench upon which the youth stood. The boy saw the man approaching and jumped off the bench. He ran around the courtyard in an attempt to escape the man and spoke into the megaphone as he ran. "I feel I have no rights to use such words," he nearly shrieked. "This fear I feel is wrong," he huffed. "The king, kind and handsome as he is, is wrong. His queen, haughty and sharp tongued, is wrong." People stopped in their tracks now and watched the comic scene before them. Some chuckled and laughed. The boy's words wobbled like water-filled balloons in the air. An atmosphere of hilarity took over the courtyard, and Manmohan felt anger rising within him. The fool, he thought, running like a chicken. No dignity at all.

In no time two potbellied policemen entered the courtyard and joined the rally man in his chase. "The king's brothers, smuggling precious statues out of our temples and selling them to museums in foreign countries, are wrong," the boy squeaked and shrieked and huffed, still running. "That my father lives in exile is wrong." He dodged people and cows. "That my grandfather never lived with electricity is wrong. Our king is weak." Two dogs joined the chase and joined the boy's speech by barking vigorously. "His ancestors were weak. And we are weak for not fighting them. Rise, fellow citizens! Rise!" And he was arrested. One of the policemen swung his baton and brought it down upon the boy. The megaphone dropped out of his hand. The pigeons scattered. The dogs stayed held back and watched from a distance.

Manmohan stayed in the courtyard long after the boy had been dragged away and the rally had dispersed. As the evening strengthened, the lights around and upon the temple came on and the temple gleamed like an ornate block of marble. Manmohan left the temple and took to the streets. The streets bustled with shops and vendors. Janakpur was a town of temples and lakes, but this particular corner came especially alive and temples dedicated to Sita, Ram, Ganga, Shiva, and Hanuman rang with bhajans and bells. Manmohan walked past these temples, he bowed before them, and in snippets he imagined a scenario where, instead of sitting on the stool he had chosen by the vendor's side, he sprung to his feet and chased after the rally man and the policemen. He imagined that he beat them up and rescued the boy. In another daydream, he visited the boy in jail and together they planned an elaborate escape.

It made Manmohan sick to think that the boy and his childish friends would not be in the canteen when he went there the next day, and a pining for the boy overtook him. He wondered why it mattered to him so much that the boy had been arrested. Surely, he would be released soon, and though the policeman had swung the baton at him, the boy was not in any way seriously injured. And yet, the image of the boy stayed painfully tucked in Manmohan and left him restless and morose. It was only later, as he walked past the Shiv Mandir toward Murli Chowk where he lived that Manmohan suddenly realized that the boy reminded him of Adi. They had almost the same face. They could have been brothers. They had the same eyes—large and long lashed like a girl's. And Manmohan wished he had, in reality, run across the courtyard and protected the boy from the men. He wished he had scolded the boy and said, Don't be foolish. This is no age to be risking your life. The world will take care of itself. You go, sit in a corner and finish your homework.

It was in the same canteen where Manmohan had met the boy that he met other men who dreamed of democracy and freedom. Hotel Kailash Parbat, Manmohan realized, was beloved of dreamers. Here, surrounded by men who were grown versions of the boy, Manmohan slowly lost his fears and gained a kind of inner independence.

With the men at Kailash Parbat, Manmohan opined and expounded. "Until when will we prostrate ourselves before bullies?" he demanded, and his body trembled with passion, his eyes blazed. The men listened to him with respect. "In the sixties," said Manmohan, "I was the youngest member of the Congress Party, and I lived my life as an exile, underground and invisible." Some evenings, warm after cups of tea and the company of men, as Manmohan and his friends walked back to their homes, Manmohan felt like a man doomed to run forever upon a circular road. Why do I live in Kathmandu? he wondered as he gazed upon Janakpur's vast, flat, uncomplicated landscape. Why do I not live here? And yet he knew he would never leave Kathmandu, dead as it was to him, to move into the warmth of Janakpur. Back in Kathmandu he knew a couple who had lived for ten years in America and then moved back home, and no matter how vehemently they insisted that it was nostalgia and love that had drawn them back, everyone thought of them as failures forced to retrace their steps because they had not been able to adjust to the demands of the big country. Manmohan was no failure. He had made a life for himself in the capital, amid Pahadis, amid the tigress and her cubs. He was no calf, no cow who was slaughtered to satisfy his enemy's hunger. No, he would not live in Janakpur. He would not let anyone say he had returned to a small town because he was not smart and sophisticated enough to live in a capital city.

It was in Hotel Kailash Parbat, while drinking tea with his friends, that Manmohan heard of ADC Gurung's disappearance.

"Doesn't the ADC live near your neighborhood?" one of the men asked Manmohan. "We hear he and his wife have disappeared. There are rumors they are dead."

"What nonsense," Manmohan said. "I saw them recently. How can they be dead?" But when he thought back he realized he had not seen the ADC or his wife for over a month now. Everything during the last few months had been so chaotic he had not really kept track of what was happening in the paddy fields. Besides, now that the land was sold, he no longer cared what Gurung's wife was up to in her fields.

In time he heard other rumors. The ADC and his wife were taken away during the pitch of night to a dungeonlike prison where they were relentlessly tortured.

"The guards pissed on them. They were made to eat feces."

"By whom?" asked Manmohan, bewildered. "The ADC is the king's man. Why would the police arrest him?"

"Who can know by whom?"

The news of the ADC's disappearance unsettled Manmohan. Had he really sold the land because of someone who would soon become so irrelevant? The more he heard, the more it seemed that the ADC and his wife were indeed no longer to be seen anywhere. The ADC's disappearance should have liberated him, but what Manmohan felt was humiliation and embarrassment. He did not want to return to Kathmandu. He did not want to face Meena. He did not want to explain to her that he had succumbed to fear of a man so vulnerable he could be forced to eat feces. It felt to him that in having succumbed to a man who ate feces, he had eaten something worse, something so repugnant there was no possible word for it. No, he did not want to return to Kathmandu. He wanted to stay in Janakpur where he could hide from the ADC, even though in Janakpur the ADC's name cropped up every time people gave arguments against the monarchy. "The king is surrounded by the corrupt!" people snarled. And they spoke of the ADC. "Smuggler, this ADC!"

Manmohan refrained from adding to these descriptions. What could he have said? The ADC visited my house? My wife brewed tea for him? I licked the dust off his feet?

Manmohan had come to Janakpur to reclaim some of his freedom but he felt more imprisoned than before. He had come to fly black banners and lead demonstrations but the same fear that had kept him from throwing the ADC out of his house now kept him from flying black banners in the city. He was an outsider. No matter what he did, he did not belong. He realized, too, that he was not young. He was no boy with throbbing veins and lava for blood. He realized Janakpur was not his city. He had no city.

Once one of the men thus locked in the canteen looked around at other men and said, "These are not good days for us, brothers. Even as we fight alongside the Pahadis, we must be careful. They still think of themselves as our rulers, think of us as their servants. Do you think we will suddenly be brothers after all this is over? No, no. They will still be kings and ministers, and we will still be selling bottles and papers to them. What, Manmohan? Didn't you say your son got beaten at school for being Madhesi?"

Manmohan startled. Had he said that? He often said things in the heat of the moment, not really meaning them, really saying what he did only to support a sentiment, but now he felt trapped by these well-intentioned words of support.

"He did, he did," Manmohan answered. "His mother told me they beat him because he did not know anything about Gai Jatra. I don't know much about Gai Jatra, either. It is not my festival. But if you live in Kathmandu, you have to know about Gai Jatra and Kumari and Tara, though they have to know nothing about Chhath Puja. I am worried for my son but I don't know what to do. I am thinking of sending him away to a boarding school in India. My daughter, too. At least they will mingle properly and not live this crooked, rough life they live here."

And even as he spoke Manmohan wondered why he was saying what he was saying. Adi had not been beaten at school and Manmohan had no intention of sending either of his children away to India. Education in India was no cheap feat.

"Why don't you leave Kathmandu, Manmohan? Why don't you come to Janakpur?" someone asked him.

"And do what? Open a shop?" he said with scorn, when what he had actually wanted to say was, I will consider it. I really want to consider it.

The revolution was being constructed brick by brick, though not many took it seriously yet. One rally here, one rally there did little to catch enough attention. One maddened youth here, one there. Not enough people arrested. Not enough known about what happened to those who were arrested. Manmohan wanted to know, officially, about what happened to those the police took away, but the news never made it to the papers or to the television. He looked for any news he could find about the boy, and about the ADC, but found nothing.

But even so policemen were rounding up rabble-rousers. Anyone harboring antipanchayat sentiments were being taken away. Sometimes Manmohan wondered if he ought to take to rallying and sloganing simply to court arrest, even though he no longer had the appetite for the hardships of prison. Surely, if he shouted loudly enough, he could go to jail, and once in jail, his life, his choices could possibly be justified. Waking early in windowless rooms, cleaning up by wells, cooking his own meals, reading smuggled-in newspapers, these would justify him. He could tell that mad schoolboy that the reason he had not saved him that day at the Janaki Mandir was because he was old, and because he had not expected the boy to get arrested so easily. He could say he had sold Meena's land as an act of rebellion. *I want nothing to do with the Pahadi land,* he could say. He could say he had, with a swift hand, silenced the ADC and his wife. He could seem valid to Meena.

Anyone watching Manmohan on the streets would think his day-to-day life was eventless. They would have no inkling of the thoughts that tortured him. Who had taken the ADC away? Why would the police, the force that worked for the king, arrest one of the king's men? Or had the ADC simply fled? Why? These questions surrounded Manmohan as he walked the town's length, or even as he crossed over to the Indian side of the border to buy spices and salt to take back to Kathmandu. Once he imagined he was being chased because he had crossed the border, but nobody checked his bags, nobody slapped handcuffs upon his wrists, nobody took him away, nobody noticed him.

And so it was that Manmohan engaged almost frantically in the evening conversations buried in houses and canteens.

"Shameful," he hissed. "Arresting students! If you take away the few educated Madhesis and stuff up the jails, what will be left?"

"Why should the Pashupatinath, a temple with hardly any history, be given such prominence when Janakpur is the birthplace of Sita? Why should Janaki Mandir not be Nepal's central religious site? There would be no *Ramayana* without the Janaki Mandir, no *Ramayana* without Janakpur."

"Once democracy comes to Nepal, Madhesh should ask for a separate nation. Really, are we even a part of Nepal?"

"I will not raise my children in this godforsaken place. I will send them to India where they will be true human beings!"

Manmohan was in Kailash Parbat with the men, saying things he simultaneously meant and did not mean, when a boy came to him with a message: he was to call his neighbor, the doctor, immediately. For a second Manmohan could not place this neighbor. What doctor? he wondered, then remembered the doctor with his peepul trees. Because the doctor was a well-known royalist, Manmohan's first instinct was to assume the ADC had been found, and for some obscure reason needed to reach out to Manmohan, and had asked for the doctor's assistance.

The obscurity of the reason paralyzed Manmohan and it was with great effort that Manmohan left the eatery for the STD (Subscriber Trunk Dialing) booth at the chowk from which he would call the doctor.

"Yes, Doctorji," he said with fake enthusiasm into the receiver, then listened quietly as the doctor informed him that Meena had been institutionalized for the day. "She is very unwell, Manmohan," the doctor said, "and your children have stood like soldiers by her side. But they are only children. It is you who should have been here. You must have noticed the symptoms earlier. There are always symptoms. Well, you come over immediately."

After Manmohan returned the receiver to its bed, he stood lost in thought for a while. Outside the booth another rally, whether led by the Panchayati Raj party or the revolutionaries, Manmohan could not tell, moved leisurely toward the temple square.

"I will leave immediately," he said to the empty booth. "There is nothing for me to do here."

JWALA AND AGNI

Sitting in the night bus that would take him back to Kathmandu, Manmohan clutched the edge of his seat. Institutionalized? Psychosis? Such words! But did this mean he would no longer need to have the conversation about the ADC with Meena? Was her mental disability such that she would not understand what he meant anyway? Could he use this to justify the sale? Could he, for instance, say the cost of her treatment left him with no other option but to sell the land? Had the ADC really been arrested? The ADC, a panchayat supporter, a supporter of the monarchy, why would the police arrest him? Why was this bus driver racing so recklessly?

Manmohan sat in a yellow, bug-shaped vehicle that cut through the night. What coincidence that there should be two buses, each the same yellow, the same buglike shape, each with a name that echoed the other's—one Jwala, the other Agni, both fire—each starting in the flats of Janakpur and ending in the valley of Kathmandu, each controlled by maniacs behind wheels, each racing, missing the edge after which began the abysmal plunge to death. The road, silver and ash, narrow and spiraling, weightless like wire, wrapped around mountains that went on, mound after mound, piling like nightmares. The glare of light outside the window. The sinking ravine. The chilled, unending stabs of mountains. The pain of death, Manmohan imagined, would be unbearable in such cold.

"You maniac!" someone shouted from the back seat.

The bus bounced on something. There were inches between the wheels and the edge of the road after which began an endless slope of death. In all his life Manmohan had never once been so afraid of traveling. Manmohan loved journeys. He traveled everywhere, through every weather, through everything. Once even by air, but even in that one moment when the craft had shivered like an animal in fever Manmohan had felt no fear. He had only felt adventure. Air, tunnels, bridges, mountains, rivers, foliage, rocks—these had never threatened, never seemed perilous. In buses he had always fallen asleep, lulled by the intense green outside the windows, the quiet rhythm of wheels beneath.

But today Manmohan was gripped by the imagination of death and perilous thoughts flitted in and out his head. What was wrong with Meena? Why would she need to be institutionalized? Who had arrested King Birendra's ADC? He had heard the ADC was intensely tortured, his nails pulled out and acid poured into his ears. By who? Why had "they" pulled out his nails? How did it feel to have nails pulled out? Was a plunging death easier than the pain of nails stretching off flesh? The pulp and blood? Apparently, "they" had discovered rows upon rows of shoes in the ADC's wife's closet, totaling a massive seven hundred pairs, and "they" had taken all the shoes away. Apparently, it was King Birendra's way of saying he would not stand any longer for corruption. He would not allow for such discrepancies that allowed almost all of his citizens to go without salt and kerosene while his officials arranged a thousand pairs of shoes in their closets. It was his way of appeasing the nation.

But what good was this appeasing to Manmohan?

Now that the ADC and his wife were arrested, their property confiscated, their powers stripped, it left Manmohan dizzy to think he had lost his land for nothing, that if he had fought longer, kept his fear down, quarreled and stayed, the land would still have been Meena's. The only consolation was the fact that Meena was unwell and if he played his cards well, he could come out of the situation all right.

There were other versions about the ADC and his wife. Manmohan had also heard, for example, that the ADC and his wife were killed, though kindly. The feces eating, the nail pulling, the acid pouring were rumors. The killing was true, but it was also humane—three shots of poison pushed into the veins. The first shot had made the prisoners sleep, the second numbed, and the third killed.

But someone else said the ADC and his wife were still alive and living in Hong Kong like minor rulers. They had chosen Hong Kong because there they could mingle easily. It was the king's plan. Once the atmosphere stilled, the ADC would be asked to return.

Manmohan wondered about the diversity of his knowledge. In the tight, secretive houses, tight-lipped streets, how had Manmohan heard these versions? Who was the "someone else" who always narrated alternate tales? It seemed as though the world was afloat and within the floating world were words, lifted directly from tongues and set free. These words, mouthless, were for all ears. These diffused words became information. Who knew who the informant was?

For so many reasons Manmohan wanted the ADC to return and take up his old job as a harasser and a bully. Look, he could say to Meena then, I told you, did I not? These people are too powerful for the likes of us.

He wished he was elsewhere. The seat he gripped so hard would not save him. If the bus fell, it would fall forever, and perhaps all passengers would be dead before the bus hit rocks and froze in the rivers.

"Stop," screamed the man from the back seat again and Manmohan saw a stream of vomit glide outside his window, bright yellow and streaked with mucus, like a flat fish with a transparent tail. "Stop, you motherfucker! You asshole! Bastard, stop!"

And the bus, screeching and swaying, stopped just like that, as though the insult had sobered the madman driver. A clearing of a sort, as unreal and misty as the road itself, and balanced precariously upon the edge, had opened upon the mountain and the bus made its way to it, letting the other bus, Jwala, blaze past. It sped on, honking in derision. The driver, a young man with bushy, wavy hair stuck his head out the window and hollered good-naturedly. "Saale!" and then the other bus was gone.

Manmohan kept his grip on the seat. His head throbbed. Behind him someone retched. The bus stank. A child had perhaps soiled his pants. There was no other sound but of the person vomiting. Then the driver put some music on and a drawling, ubiquitous tune of a lovelorn Hindi song grated out of the speakers. *How well have you repaid my love. You, my friend, have looted my house.*

The song's alarming poignancy, its warbling complaint against withering flowers and blistering heartaches seemed to stir the passengers, and slowly, hesitatingly, a line of shaken, shaking people formed in the aisle. The smell was of shit and puke. A mother consoled a child who started a sudden wail. Manmohan's knees shook as he stood. He clenched his thighs to keep his piss from leaking. He kept a frantic eye on the scene outside the bus.

The driver was out already and, through the windows, Manmohan saw him smoking upon a rock, staring at the stretch of road curving and disappearing behind a hill and Manmohan was amazed at how young and tousled the driver was, his hair windblown and the cigarette at an angle, like a schoolboy.

Nobody reprimanded the driver and he smoked without acknowledging his passengers. A radius had formed around him. Nobody came too close. The drop behind him was dark but his back was toward it, his eyes trained on the road. He smoked his cigarette now like a rogue, letting it dangle from his lips; now like a villager, cupping the stick with both his hands as he dragged in the fume. He wore a white shirt, the sleeves rolled to reveal his arms. His trousers were brown.

In safe distances men unzipped their pants to pee. Women went behind a rock and the two heaped bushes that grew upon the otherwise bare ground. There was a sound of peeing everywhere, like objects singing. The women strategically lifted their saris so not an inch of skin showed while they did their business. Manmohan imagined insects crawling out from the ground. The creatures were the right size to crawl into holes, into anuses and vaginas, and they administered death so painful, so prolonged Manmohan had to clench harder to keep from wetting his pants. When he finally got to the bus door he half ran, half skipped to where the men had gathered. Beside him an old man, too thin, was vomiting and Manmohan was ashamed because he could no longer hold himself, and while the old man retched Manmohan peed, unable even to stop the sighs of relief that escaped his lungs.

The bus reached Kathmandu at dawn with the moon still out. Due to a landslide in the heart of the mountains, the eight hours' journey had taken fourteen shivering hours to reach the capital.

Out on the dark road, the passengers scattered, most hailing taxis and dissolving into the misty cold. Under the streetlights, the road was littered with paper and strips of cloth. There were some bricks and stones, shards of glass, but the passengers, reduced to shaking in the cold did not care, almost did not seem to notice. Ultimately there was only Manmohan and one other man left upon the street, each waiting for an autorickshaw, their suitcases standing by their feet.

Manmohan did not know this but the man standing by his side was Lila Yadav. In his suitcase he carried bundles of pamphlets that urged the professionals of Kathmandu to demonstrate resistance against atrocities being carried out by the police. He hoped his actions would bring joy and pride to his family.

Lila Yadav's father lived in India, in Patna, the capital of Bihar. Now that Lila himself was a father of one child, he wondered at his father's ability to stay away from his family. When Lila was still a child, he had traveled to Patna with his mother for every vacation. Every vacation Lila and his mother had taken a skeletal, overcrowded train and three rickety buses to cross Nepal's border and visit his father in Patna. During these visits Lila had not run up to his father. Instead he had stood at a distance and watched, waiting for his father to call out for him, but he never did.

And now he was in Kathmandu, on an important mission, and he hoped when his mother told his father about the trip, his father would finally notice him. Standing by the road, worrying nervously about the little money he carried with him, waiting anxiously for an autorickshaw, Lila thought of his fatherless childhood, and of his thin, too soft-spoken, too impenetrable father who never called out for him. He wondered about his mother. His mother was from Patna, the city his father had taken refuge in. Her parents and siblings lived in Patna. Why then had she not stayed on in Patna with her husband? Her family in India must have questioned her. They must have made assumptions. They must have asked, why don't you leave Nepal and join your husband? They must have scolded. What about the boy? They must have asked. And yet, at the end of every vacation the boy and his mother had taken the rickety buses and the skeletal train back into Nepal. We are your father's eyes and ears, his mother said to him. You are his arms and legs. If your father's struggles are to mean anything, if his struggles are meant to win, we have to be here. We have to meet people, understand their needs. If we love your father, we have to love his dreams too. Your cousins are wonderful, she said, but they are useless. To them

Nepal is a picnic spot. Her temples bring peace, her mountains glitter under warm suns, her rivers are clean, her king is handsome and Hindu, her politics simple, her people too naive. Don't you see how they speak to you? They think you are fit for nothing but mindless jobs. Join the army. Become a security guard. Does it not make your blood boil? Aren't you tired of polite platitudes, of rolling your tongue in sugar before you speak?

Now, at twenty-six, Lila's heart choked with love for his mother. She, the daughter from Patna, a stranger to Nepal, how had she grown such patriotism? Why had she loved a foreign country? How much love did she bear her husband? He understood, of course, that despite changing nations, his mother had not had to change too many things. The plains of Nepal were in too many ways India's extensions. His mother did not have to learn new languages or new cuisines. But despite the sameness, her home had changed, and this change had gifted her an absent husband. And yet she managed so well. She invited people for teas and dinners to her simple house. Lean, serious-faced men took up her invitation. They arrived in their thin kurtas and dhotis and while Lila's mother served snacks, they discussed Nepal's prospects and within the larger framework, they discussed the fate of the plain's people, of the Teraians and the Madhesis. Through it all sometimes Lila lost himself. He thought of his cousins living in Patna. They looked like him, they spoke like him, and Lila loved them with a tenderness he could confess to no one.

It was cold and Lila shivered despite the shawl he had wrapped tightly around him. The littered street concerned him. Had the Professional People's Strike already taken place? he wondered. One of the pamphlets Lila carried urged professionals to follow what the doctors of Teaching Hospital had begun. The doctors were the first to notice flowering bullets in the bodies of victims the government had already begun to shoot at in deep corners of Patan and Bhaktapur.

Flowering bullets were internationally banned because they burst inside the body and caused extreme trauma to victims even as they died. The doctors meeting these victims upon their surgery tables had been horrified and ultimately gone into a protest outside the hospital building. They had worn placards around their necks. Stop shooting unarmed civilians. Stop the use of flowering bullets. Stop. They had tied black cloth around their arms.

Lila's pamphlets urged other professionals—teachers, lawyers, bankers—to follow suit. Protest against government atrocities, they said. But the black strips of cloths on the streets made Lila believe that some groups had already begun demonstrations.

There was no autorickshaw in sight and as Lila and Manmohan stood in wait their breath was white and smoky and mingled with each other's. Had Manmohan known he stood beside a revolutionist, a man who would soon be jailed and questioned, a man who would be quarantined in an unknown building at the foothills of the Himalayas because his mere presence gave impetus to the revolution, he would have started a coded conversation. He would have asked him about the "them" and demanded the truth about ADC Gurung. But Manmohan did not know Lila and therefore did little other than watch their mingling breath. His mind was far away. He did not notice the debris on the street with the same intensity that Lila Yadav did.

Standing on the isolated road, Manmohan felt like a ghost. The ADC was now gone; if not dead, then he was at least away in another country, at least for some time, and there was a possibility that Manmohan's family was free. But this morning Manmohan felt more bound than ever before, more confused by his situation.

"People like you and me," Lila said suddenly to Manmohan, "we will make this fight our fight, but nothing will change. We will always be Madhesis, always traitors and outsiders. Why we are fighting? Who can tell? Tomorrow they will say, this is not your country, saale dhoti. Why we are fighting?"

And just like that, while he stood with a stranger on a cold, foggy day, all of Manmohan's struggles became futile.

BOOK EIGHT

THE MONKEY

A DOT OF INFINITY

I missed Adi. I missed lying down on his arm and listening to the horror stories he sometimes made up to frighten me just before we fell asleep. I missed the exciting fear I felt in the security that Adi would ward off the ghosts as easily as he brought them in. I missed our battles and skirmishes and was frightened by the focus with which he now tried to live his days. In Ma's absence Adi took over the house. He woke up early, and after Papa left for his morning walk, began the preparation for our lunch, which, despite its meagerness, took up his entire day. The rice, boiled in the pressure cooker, inevitably browned at its base, and the daal came out bland and too pale no matter how he altered his recipe. For the first time Papa did not complain about the salt or the consistency of the vegetables he was served. We ate dutifully, biting down on half-cooked potatoes and rubbery brinjal. I helped, and some days Papa helped, too, but mostly Adi washed the dishes, swept the floors, washed the clothes, filled the water filter.

A quiet slime took over our house. The plates we ate off grew slippery with grease and the collar of my school shirt was brown with thin streaks of sweat and mud that looked like my veins had jumped off my nape and attached themselves to my clothes like roots. I wanted to tell Adi that he could not clean, that despite his work the house was dirty and unkempt, but I knew from the disciplined and determined way in which he worked that I could never tell him.

Every once in a while he insisted that he and I attend school and ushered me out of the house. "We cannot become uneducated, can we?" he insisted. He held my hand as we walked down the Ring Road. We no longer took the lane, though the lane would take us faster to school. Two brick shops had sprouted almost overnight at the turn of the lane. These shacklike shops, built of bricks piled one on top of the other to create unstable, uneven walls, supplied bricks, cement, and sand to the new buildings that, despite the revolution, seemed to be constantly under construction in Ganesh Basti. Two boys each manned these dusty shops, and from within their confines, seated on unsteady chairs, they took orders for their merchandise or ogled at girls passing by. All day they listened to songs coming from radios placed on wobbly stools. At midday and on days of shutdowns, when constructions had to be suspended, they placed their chairs upon the lane and settled down to chat and play games of carrom, snakes and ladder, or Chinese checkers. Sometimes they sat lethargically behind their board games, legs extended before them, digging their noses, meditative, absentmindedly contemplating the sticky guck they shaped into balls with their fingers.

And so, Adi and I avoided the lane. Instead, we took the main road and from its pavements watched jeeps of young boys with red bandannas tied around their heads speeding off with cries of *Panchayatikaal murdabad*. Death to the panchayat system. *Janatantra zindabad.* Long live democracy. Closer to our school, we read the posters pasted on walls appealing people to join protests and demonstrations. *Help us oust monarchy,* they read. *Freedom and Dignity!* they proclaimed. Once Adi and I read a poster advertising adaptations of *Hamlet* and *Macbeth* being played out in the National Theatre. Both productions, the posters said, aimed to look at the role of kings in nations. Kings can be devious. Kind and virtuous kings could suffer regicide. The plays aimed to generate discussions. Though I knew of a William Shakespeare, I did not know anything about *Hamlet* or *Macbeth* and could make no real sense of what the posters intended.

Some days we reached school only to find out it was closed for the day or the week and we returned home feeling strangely empty-handed. On days we found it open, I sat in the classroom and waited for time to pass, unable to concentrate.

But most days Adi and I stayed home, cooking, cleaning, watching over Ma. Ma sat on her bed, or we took her to the veranda and sat her down behind the green teapoy. From her seat she stared upon a spot on the floor like it was an alive and pulsating dot of infinity. I was not always certain she could see the spot, because her eyes were always empty and meaningless.

I suppose Adi no longer lulled me to sleep with horror stories because Ma's blankness was more frightening than anything else we could experience or imagine. We knew she no longer lived with us. She lived elsewhere, in her own country with a different sun and moon and a different set of children. She had no interest in Adi or me. Her body, sinking in our world, was alive elsewhere. Here, she focused on the minute—a pebble, a stain, a leaf on the space before her—as though these were portals she entered to escape us. What she left for us was an empty body we were responsible for maintaining. Sometimes I wanted to leave her in peace, to not constantly force her back to us, but I was afraid if I looked away for too long something drastic would happen and I would be to blame for it, so I sat beside her even as she looked past me, and in desperation and fear mimicked Adi's gestures. I held her hand. I kissed her cheek. I called out to her, softly, like Adi had taught me to. "Ma, it's me. Pirti. Your sack of sugar," I said, terrified she would shake out of the death the medicines had sent to her and snarl and roar like an animal at me.

In my dreams she looked at me with large eyes and talked to me in strange gibberish. Sometimes she stayed in the background, a hazy replica of herself, and I felt myself grow dry and brittle before her.

Papa watched the news with a feverish religiosity and ran a constant commentary alongside the anchor. "This time the king is done for," he said. At other times he chuckled. "But what will we do without a king? Are we ready to be responsible for ourselves?" As though we were at all interested in such questions. Papa was nervous. He had returned from Janakpur to a house that no longer resembled the house he had lived in until recently. He was afraid of Ma and kept an eye on her from a distance. Most of the time she was drugged and dull and he was safe, but once, when the fog of drugs had momentarily lifted, Ma had spotted him and charged with a suddenness that had Papa stumbling back and banging against the steel cabinet in the bedroom. "Randi ke beta," she had roared—son of a whore—loud enough for her voice to travel through windows to neighboring houses. He was afraid of her dilated eyes and nonhuman voice. He fled to the television room and locked himself before the news anchor the way one would before a deity.

It was Adi who cared for Ma, who took her arm and sat her down, forced her to swallow the medicines that shoved down her anger and pushed her into a mist that eradicated everything. Only when she grew thus inert and invisible did Papa emerge from the news, his own source of mist, and came to us armed with information.

"After all this, is he blaming his cabinet ministers for what is happening to the country? Do you know he has dissolved the current cabinet of ministers and not even appointed the next one yet?" he asked us.

Apparently, His Majesty's statement in April of 1990 that he was dissolving the current cabinet of ministers, instead of heeding the nation's demand that he give up the throne, had sent shock waves across the country. Within hours people had gathered like puddles in marketplaces and come together like streams in New Road, Asan, Patan, and

Chabahil. One time, while giving Papa his food, which he ate before the television, I caught a glimpse of people gathered at Indra Chowk, the intense blues and reds of woolen shawls sold upon the steps of Indra Chowk hidden by the crowd of human bodies. It seemed like the kind of crowd that would gather for festivals—restless, excited, purposeful, and I was arrested by the fact that while a stillness had come over our own home, the streets of Kathmandu were overtaken by activity and chaos. I imagined these people flowing sluggishly through the narrow roads of Asan. I imagined them before shops that sold brass and copper lamps; I imagined them spill into the expanse of the Asan tole, disturbing the vegetable and flower vendors. Or perhaps, there were no men and women selling nuts and fruits and potatoes in Asan's square any longer. Perhaps all of Kathmandu had poured into the stream that moved so viscously toward the Narayanhiti Palace. Perhaps, in the palace His Majesty sat on the Sheshnaga throne, the plume of the paradise bird decorating his head, and watched the news on his television with wonder and confusion. These were his children. They were pelting his palace with stones. Some were throwing shoes at it. At the crossroad stood a sculpture of His Majesty's grandfather, and there were boys spitting at it, others trying to topple it down. That man, mumbled His Majesty, is the one who freed the palace from the Ranas and restored the Shahs to their rightful place. But perhaps it did not matter to the men and women shouting for blood. A Rana ruler. A Shah ruler. Perhaps it was all the same to the crowd now. Perhaps it had only really mattered to him.

Despite her absence, Adi tried to keep Ma updated. "The king has locked himself in his palace," he told her. "The Communist Party and the Congress Party are working together against the king. This is a new phase of unity in Nepal." He spoke to Ma's blank face without fear or anxiety, and I tried to hold his hand as he spoke.

At other times he told her about her plants. He gave her reports of the new lady finger that had dipped out of a stem, the sudden length of chilies, and the mint that grew around the hand pump like scented grass.

A day before the baby monkey came into our neighborhood, the weather was paradoxical. There was thunder and lightning but very little rain. Adi and I stayed close to Ma because we worried the thunder and lightning would frighten her. Now that Ma was not well Adi and I thought of Ma as someone younger than we were, as someone easily frightened and easily consoled. But Adi and I were wrong. Now that Ma was not well, nothing mattered enough to her. She sat on the bed watching the guava tree outside the window shimmer under the lightning with an expression neither of us could read.

And the next morning, on our way to school, we saw the baby monkey. The boys manning the hardware stores had adopted it and they kept the animal tied to a post beside a heap of bricks swelling like smoldering coal between the two shops. Beside the heap, two delivery trucks painted in psychedelic patterns of blues, greens, and oranges stood ready for delivery. On the isle created by the bricks and the trucks, the monkey, small and alienlike with large eyes bulging out of its angular face, stared at us. Adi and I stood still, struck by its sudden and pathetic presence, and unable to understand what this frail, frightened animal was doing amid the dust and grit of concrete. If it moved, the rope around its neck chafed its skin and so it stayed as still as possible; only its dark saucer eyes moved in their sockets. Then, two days after the boys adopted it, the monkey began a protest, screeching and chattering in discomfort. All day it picked at its rope, trying to get it off its sickly neck. The boys remained in their shops, listening to folk songs.

Every day for a week after the boys brought the monkey into the neighborhood Adi forced me out of the house with him. He fed Ma her breakfast and her medicine and put her down for a nap. He then took my hand and forced me out of the house. He frowned as he walked, his steps brisk and angry, and he stood upon the pavement of the Ring Road and stared at the pathetic animal until I sometimes feared he would begin to cry.

It was I who gave Adi the push he needed to talk to the boys. "I will come with you," I said and the two of us went recklessly into one of the shops. As always a song played on the radio and drowned out the monkey's pleas. *Oh, beyond the river lives my beloved,* the radio warbled. *Oh, it is a sweet village from where my beloved comes to fill her pitcher with cool river water.*

"Is that monkey yours?" Adi asked and the boys nodded without looking up from their game. "You should let it go. The rope is hurting it."

They looked up then, and I felt my stomach tighten.

"We will let it go if we can have your girlfriend instead," one of the boys said smacking a kiss at me and the two of them laughed.

"No," said Adi. "You really should let it go."

"Saale dhoti," said the other boy. "We should let you go. Marsiya mora. Now get lost before I bash in all your thirty-two teeth."

I stiffened. I had expected a fight, a scuffle. I had not expected this verbal attack.

The boys returned to their game, nonchalant. I could see that Adi had made no impact on them. They were not perturbed by him. His request that they let the monkey go had stirred nothing in them, nor had the fact that they had just abused us. Having shown us our worth, the boys returned with ease to their game of ludo, and for a while Adi and I continued standing before them, trying to come up with a response, then Adi turned and exited the shop and I followed him out.

He walked ahead of me and I trotted to keep pace with him. When

I reached him, I saw he was crying. "How do they know I am a dhoti?" he asked, his voice flat and without emotions despite the tears in his eyes. Then he looked at me and stopped. "How come no one ever calls you a dhoti? How are you so completely comfortable? How does nothing bother you ever?" I wanted to tell him I was not at ease. I had not escaped anything, but my brother was crying. "Why doesn't she snap out of it?" he sobbed. "The city is full of animals, all starving and injured. What is one monkey in a city of limping dogs and flea-infested cows? And if Ma wants to live like she is already dead, I don't care."

That evening, while making omelettes for dinner, Adi said, so casually, "If Papa dies, Ma will be okay. She will outlive him by a hundred decades if he dies. But he will not die first. She will die first and you and I will be orphans." Then he flipped the omelette on the pan.

The day the psychedelic truck painted green, blue, and orange came into our land and dropped its first load of bricks on it, I was with Ma on the veranda. The truck waddled into our ground and I stood up swiftly, momentarily transfixed as I watched its throbbing blue body. Just before the truck had entered our land, I had had a thought. I had thought Ma looked better. I had felt she could see more than just one blade of grass or just one dot of some pattern. I had a fleeting sense that she knew me. Earlier that morning Adi had coaxed her into eating a banana and until the truck entered our land this had felt like a triumph. But then the truck came.

I listened to its growl and could not speak. It moved languorously, like a mythical elephant on our land, and upon its gorgeous, muscular body trembled a heap of bricks, flesh colored and vibrant. I watched, unable to make sense, as the beast began to retch fleshy bricks upon Ma's spinach and garlic. For a few mesmerized seconds I assumed the truck, an ancient animal gone astray, had lost its way. It had wandered around the globe and stumbled into our world, accidentally, destroying my mother's delicate greens. By the time I rushed down the steps, a pile of bricks had crushed the moist leaves of spinach. Several succulent stems of young garlic were broken and squashed, and they hung at mutilated angles. I began to scream. "What are you doing? What are you doing?" I demanded as I ran, but the truck, like a creature too sick to comprehend me, continued to vomit. Ma stared apathetically, as though she lived in a stale, dense, green bottle and had nothing to do with us. "Ma!" I cried but she didn't move.

"Watch out for the plants," I shouted. "What are you doing on our land?" I hurried to the driver, a young boy, not more than five or six years older than I was, his mustache a hazy line above his mouth. I recognized him instantly. He was one of the boys who had adopted the monkey. Once, while I was returning from school by myself, he had asked me if I had started wearing a bra yet. I stopped before him now, suddenly conscious and awkward of my body. But the boy looked at me hesitantly and I realized he did not know who I was. He thought I was a stranger, someone he had never spoken to before. He registered my distress and was arrested by it. He pulled out a piece of paper from his shirt pocket and inspected it. "This is the address," he said, showing me the piece. I looked at the paper with our address on it. I called out for Adi, though I knew he was not home. He had accompanied Papa to his office for some errand. He had left the house, sullen and uncompromising, after feeding Ma the banana. He had stepped out stiffly, unwilling but forced to walk beside Papa. "Adi!" I called futilely. Then I turned to the boy-driver. "There has been a mistake, brother," I said. "If you only wait a minute, I will call my father. He will tell you. Will you not wait?"

"Is that your mother?" the boy asked. I nodded. "Well," he said, "she will know," but even before he completed his sentence he shook his head. "She is not well, is she? She has that terrible disease. My mother has it also. It is a terrible disease."

"She does not have a disease," I said. Then I took in a breath and said, "But will you not wait, please?"

The boy hollered to the two other workers, his accomplices in digging noses and catcalling girls. "Stop for a while!" he said, and I ran into the house, my legs tangling in my hurry.

Adi received my call at the other end and I told him quickly and breathlessly. "There is a truck on our compound. They are unloading bricks on our ground. They killed all the spinach. Right on our vegetables, all this rubble. Tell Papa to talk to the people. Tell him to come home."

I heard Adi tell Papa what I had just said and I heard Papa as he responded. "I told you all," he said, "or did I only tell your mother? Your mother can be so irresponsible sometimes, not telling the children anything. She worries, I think. She wanted the land sold off. She got terrified of the Gurungs. She just could not deal with it. What hooligans, those Gurungs."

I listened, perplexed. Finally, I replaced the phone and went back to the veranda. Ma watched the truck with a straight face. I sat beside her and nodded to the boy. He hollered, "Get back to work!"

Over the week our land filled with piles of red bricks, heaps of fine sand, small hills of pebbles, and sacks of cement. They grew like noxious weed among Ma's struggling plants. Then some men came and chopped down our trees.

Around us the revolution intensified. People attacked police stations. They smashed windows and punctured wheels of police vehicles. They set motorcycles on fire. Two policemen were dead, Papa told us, and three protesters. The families of the protesters waited for their bodies, but the hospitals were unable to give the bodies to the families because the police would not allow the handing over. Doctors were threatening to go on a strike again. They were threatening to never treat a policeman if a policeman was brought to their door. There were graffiti on walls that called the Royal Nepal Police murderers.

"It's not so bad the land is gone," Papa said. "There is so much uncertainty, so much violence. Who can say what tomorrow will bring. The other day I looked out the window of my office and saw a man bleeding from his head. Someone had thrown a brick at him. Must be a royal supporter. Nothing is safe. And it is a struggle to maintain so much land. How much work your mother did, day in day out, weeding, sowing, cutting, watering. It is no small achievement, all this work. And in Kathmandu it is impossible to get any domestic help. Look at what has happened to our house in just this much time. It is a pigsty! Property is not easy to maintain. And everything is a mess here."

Another day, between bites of a quick meal, he told us that Adi and I were soon to leave Kathmandu. "Your mother and I were talking about sending the two of you to India anyway," he said. "India is a very good place for education. Look at how things are here. Your school is shut half the time. What education will you get here? Illiterate buffoons are what you will become. Your mother is too ill to look after you and I have work to keep the house going. I cannot sit at home, can I? We want to send you to the best school in India and that costs money, does it not? Even before your mother fell ill she had suggested we sell the land so we could get the money for your education in India. She has a big heart, your mother."

"Ma wants us to go to a hostel?" Adi asked.

"Well, both of you are growing up and your mother is not educated enough to teach you things at home. In a hostel you will be taught well. Besides, everyone is sending their children to either Darjeeling or Dehradun. Mr. Swaroop's children are in Dehradun now. His wife thought it best to send them there because she cannot handle them alone. I am thinking of Dehradun for you."

"But Ma said that? She wants us to go?" Adi asked.

"The city is not safe."

"But Ma said that to you?"

"Yes. And I want you to go too. I cannot handle the two of you."

"She has not said a word to us about any hostel," Adi insisted.

Something sat inside my rib cage and pushed down, down. Like Adi, I did not believe Papa. I wanted Ma to wake up. If Ma woke up, I was willing to go anywhere, even a hostel.

Some days I wondered if Ma had perhaps taken off, as Adi sometimes did now, to explore possible streets and neighborhoods within herself. Perhaps the world was getting too crowded and loud for her and she needed a quieter lane. Some days I wanted to ask Ma where she lived when she visited that other country. How did she navigate the boiling streets of her own geography? What did she see in those squares of light and spots of leaves? Who was it she spoke to when she uttered those lilting, rhyming sentences made of grotesque, ugly sounds? What was the name of her new language?

Perhaps Ma had deliberately turned away from us and stepped into a personal landscape where burning bricks and withering kings, and budding breasts and choking animals, and psychedelic trucks and dying stumps of trees did not exist. She had abandoned us. Without her Adi and I were orphans, now at the brink of homelessness.

Some days, when no one was looking, I whispered deep into her ears. "How selfish are you?" I asked. "I hate you," I said. I imagined my words stumble like rocks into the tunnels of her ears. From there they went into her other world, rolling down black hills, black roads, black, burnt-up forests.

In my solitariness, I spoke to Sachi. I imagined myself describing the condition of my house to her. I told her in whispers that I was embarrassed by its condition, embarrassed by the filth that had begun to accumulate in the nooks and corners of its rooms and furniture. I confessed that I hated how swollen yet lax Ma's body had become with her medications. I told her I was ashamed of Ma's vacant eyes, her repressed anger, her detached and inconsolable loneliness. I wanted to shake her out of it, I said to Sachi. I wanted her to become beautiful and playful again. It's like living with some ghost.

In my solitariness, I traded Sachi's flesh and blood and turned her into a wraith that like a genie came to me when I needed her. I abandoned the girl I had known and fastened myself to the fluid, smiling, forever subservient person in my mind. In school, during recess, I stayed away from the areas Sachi tended to hang out in. I rarely left home other than to run errands and so did not have to meet her corporeal self in the evenings. Once or twice, when Sachi rode her bicycle to our house, I met her body with curt responses and cut short her visit with whatever excuse I could think of. Eventually, she stopped coming over. Sometimes I saw her in school, looking questioningly at me, but I never returned her look, and perhaps, eventually, she stopped looking too. I found it all very funny, because the more she kept her distance from me, the more she lived in the gullies of my mind. She was always there, around the corner, within earshot, and when I called out, she always arrived.

And yet, I thought of the flesh-and-body Sachi constantly. I wondered how she was doing. I wondered if she was angry with me, or if she had forgotten me entirely. I daydreamed about her. In many of these daydreams I imagined her with some terrible sickness, something that meant death, something that was repulsive and incurable. And I imagined myself taking care of her. I imagined surrender and selflessness. I imagined a kind of mingling with her. My heart ached with intense love, and with the fear I felt of losing her. In my fantasies I ran around, sometimes aimlessly, sometimes with intense focus, always responding to the pain in me, always looking for a cure for my dying, fading friend. Sometimes I sat by her bedside and tried to explain myself. I had to go away for a little while, I said, but now I am back and you will be fine again. And then, sometimes, she was well again, and sometimes she died, and sometimes I got so mad at her I screamed at her face and called her ugly.

I sat next to Ma, holding her hand, and longed for Sachi. My heart banged, and sometimes my fingers felt numb because they had not touched her for so long.

And so, when one evening during dinner Papa brought up Sachi, I almost dropped the roti I had brought from the kitchen for him.

"So your friend is leaving, too, is she?" Papa asked, and I knew he was talking about Sachi though he had not yet named her.

"Leaving?" I asked, carefully placing the roti on his plate.

"I met her father this morning. He said she is moving to Darjeeling for her studies. Everyone is leaving. This country is no country for children." I stared at Papa. I had heard of Darjeeling but had no geographical understanding of where the place was. "Anyone who can afford to is going to India now," Papa went on. "It's a good time for Adi and you to go, too."

I returned to the kitchen where Adi was making rotis for the rest of us.

"Where is Darjeeling?" I asked him.

"Somewhere," he said. He flipped the roti on the pan. "In the middle of India somewhere, maybe," he said. "Why?"

"Just asking," I said and worried about how I would reach Sachi when she fell sick. How would I care for her when that terrible illness came? How would I convince her that though I had left for some time, I was back now and we would be fine again? How could she be leaving without telling me? How could I hear of something like this from my father?

Perhaps the boys could no longer handle the monkey. Perhaps its protests, increasingly feeble, finally stirred them, or they got tired of feeding an animal that did little other than squeal and yell, and just like that, after holding it captive for nearly a month, the boys untied the rope that held its neck and let the monkey go.

Adi and I watched it from the Ring Road. For many days it did not leave the place of its captivity and spent its first few days of freedom on the backs of the trucks. Occasionally, it hovered about the shop, possibly awaiting food, unsure of what it was supposed to do, now that it had been as unceremoniously abandoned as it had once been kept roped. But after a few tentative days it left the confinement area and jumped into the neighborhood.

All at once the neighborhood burst into hysteria. A madness came over it. The monkey was everywhere, destroying everything it could. We could hear screams of children from the new building that housed eight families in its four stories, and we often saw the monkey emerge from its third-floor window. The children ran up to the terrace, screaming and waving at the monkey even after it was nowhere in sight.

Windows could no longer be left open and grilles designed to keep out thieves proved hopeless in keeping out the agile primate and it entered rooms and spaces only to leave them in disarray; vases and picture frames shattered, pots of curry toppled over, clothes poked through.

The four-storied house residents secured their rooms by nailing chicken wire upon their windows. The Gurkha House, as we called the house now coming up on our land, became the monkey's home, and Doctor Uncle's peepul trees its private jungle. Our house, situated within this whirlwind, was the eye of the storm, the calm curiously untouched by the turmoil. The monkey didn't wreck a thing that belonged to us. It was a strange silence from which we watched screaming children and shuddering trees.

Then one night a storm woke me up. A door banged and banged somewhere. I lay in bed, listening to the shrill whistle that ran through Doctor Uncle's trees. The guava tree, the only one left of our trees, knocked upon my window, and rain and wind rushed outside. I wondered about the monkey. I wondered how it protected itself from the storm. When the morning came, crisp and clean, I looked for it from the terrace. It was nowhere and I never saw it again. Maybe it died in the storm. Maybe it ran off.

A SLOW RETURN

Ma's unreachable emptiness did not last forever, though it remained a part of her and visited her every now and then for the rest of her life. But even so, she returned to us, bit by bit, partly the same, partly altered, stunned by her journey. Her travel to and away from her unreal landscape meant that the landscape outside her also took on something of unreality. When she emerged, it seemed to us she was not entirely sure what she really had visited and where she really lived now. She did not know for sure where she belonged, and that uncertain, questioning, somewhat bewildered look remained with her forever. She loved us—we knew this from the way she suddenly reached out to touch Adi and me—but it seemed like she loved with some detachment, as though learning for the first time that she did not own us, or indeed own anything at all. She did not own her own self, either. Her self was independent of her. It had its rules and could, when it wanted, cast her out. But even so, she returned, and for this we were grateful.

Slowly, and hesitantly, Ma went back to cooking, cleaning, and caring for our daily needs. The doctors advised that the sooner she reclaimed her old duties, the sooner she would be better. She was to be monitored during these tasks, but she needed to begin doing them. Papa hired a girl of around my age to help Ma with the tasks. "Your mother will need someone once you are gone," he said. The girl's name was Rita and she and I stayed in the kitchen supervising Ma as she practiced making cups of tea and boiling rice.

Some days Ma stood on our star-mosaiced veranda and took in the house that the people from Singapore had built upon the land that had once been ours. It was more than half constructed now. She looked at our shrunk, broken garden. Where Ma's constant turning of the soil had once yielded soft, brown, fertile ground, the construction of the new house had riddled the land with pieces of broken bricks, tiles, glass, hardened cement, and chipped wood. Adi and I stood at the door with our breaths held, but Ma said nothing. Initially I was afraid she would never garden again, but she did, eventually. Eventually, she cleaned the little patch of land left to us and grew herbs on them, but she asked us nothing. She did not inquire after the house that had dwarfed ours and robbed us of sunlight and of the view of our beloved lane, or the lost trees, the brinjals and potatoes. Adi tried to tell her but she never seemed interested enough. Even Papa tried to tell her, but she nodded absently and left. It was not as though she was trying to avoid the conversation. Adi would have understood the avoidance. It was that she was not interested. She did not care that we were trapped behind a pink-walled, slant-roofed house, that everything we loved was gone. It left Adi desperate and confused, and in his confusion he lashed out. "Papa is a rich man now. He sold the land for lots of money," he said. "You are rich too," he said. "You can get yourself new clothes now. You can buy a few more servants. Papa wants to send us to a hostel in India," he said, staring at her as she ground daal to smoother consistency. "Ma, do you hear me? I don't want to go anywhere. I want to stay here, with you and Preeti. I don't want to go to India. Ma, you have to do something." But she did nothing. She did not fight for us. She did not interfere as Papa made phone calls to narrow down possible cities and possible schools. She watched TV—always with that distracted attention—as Papa verbalized pros and cons of this place and that place, this possibility and that possibility, as he went on, jubilant and filled with pride. Forever, after Papa sent us away, he would tell everyone of his great sacrifice. “I put a stone on my heart and sent my children away to the best Indian school so they could get the education I could not have dreamed was possible.” Forever we would have to be indebted to him. Even when we were thirty and forty and fifty, he would bring up the school. “I could have lived a comfortable life with drivers and cars had I not sent the two of you to Carman School,” he said. “Your education was more important to me than my own comfort and happiness.” But Adi and I saw the education for the farce it was. We saw it when we were children and we saw it when we were adults, but we could never call out his bluff because our mother had not fought for us when she needed to. She pushed her fingers into her ears and turned away while we thrashed around for help.

FAREWELL

In an hour it will be seven and every citizen of Kathmandu will voluntarily turn off their lights for an hour. The city will plunge into darkness. The king, sitting in his lighted palace, will receive, yet again, the black message of the drastic gloom that awaits him. It is all dark for you, Mr. King, the city is telling him. We will not be placated, Mr. Majesty, the city is warning. We will snuff you out, Mr. So-and-So.

I am walking toward Sachi's house.

It is almost two months since Papa told me Sachi is leaving for Darjeeling, and now there is only one week left for her to leave. If I don't see her now, I might not see her again for a long time, maybe even forever.

Within me, I have visited her daily. Sitting on the veranda with Ma I have told Sachi every detail about my life. I have assumed she can hear me. I have assumed that when I can talk again, she will understand my reasons, and we will go for walks and sit by the gorge. The fact that she has told me nothing about leaving Kathmandu makes me nervous because it makes me feel like we are not connected. It makes me wonder if she did tell me about Darjeeling and I did not hear her.

I am visiting Sachi to tell her that the blackness of seven p.m. frightens Ma. I am excited by Ma's fear. It means she finally understands the difference between light and dark. It means she is slowly returning to us. I am visiting to ask Sachi not to leave. I am visiting to say, stay. We will come out of this.

I have thought of all this very carefully. Very carefully I have crafted my images and sentences.

When I ring the bell, Sachi's mother opens the door almost immediately. I can hear voices of guests behind her and recall that today is Friday and Sachi's house is full of relatives gathered for games and dinner.

"Is it raining?" Aunty asks incredulously.

"Just started," I say.

"You are muddy already. We haven't seen you in so long. Sachi is in her room. Run up quickly and wash up before you meet her."

In Sachi's house the main door leads directly to the living room. Unlike our house there is no corridor here and despite Aunty's instructions that I run up quickly, I stay awkwardly before her for a few long seconds, feeling like a stranger in the house I have entered so often before. Behind Aunty, relatives are gathered for a game of carrom and the board has been placed at the very center of the floor. Everything else has been put directly on the floor, too—drinks, tidbits, glasses, shawls for those who are cold, cushions and pillows, packs of cards, just in case. I take in the bodies sprawled upon the floor, spread out like melted butter. Somebody murmurs a welcome at me but mostly the game and the conversation go on.

"He has no right being a king! His people are starving. There is no electricity in the country, no market, no education—"

"You have plenty food, electricity, and education in this room, Ajitji. What are you complaining about?"

The same conversation. But I am mesmerized by the sight. This sight is not possible in my house.

"Hurry, darling," Aunty says to me. "Run up. You are wetting the floor." Then she turns to her husband and adds, "Ajit, my lord, bring out the whiskey! Tonight your wife is going to topple the queen!"

How do women talk this way?

Sachi is in her room and on her bed are piles of brand-new towels and sheets, and on the sheets are bottles of perfumes, shampoos, oils, cakes of soap, tubes of toothpastes and creams. She is packing to leave, and here I am, firm in my belief I can stop her.

When she sees me, she is holding a bottle of lotion and she puts it down immediately. I have flustered her and she looks strangely aghast, like she could not comprehend how I had appeared at her door.

My throat is dry. "It started raining so suddenly," I say.

"You are wet," she says.

My heart is pounding. I haven't seen Sachi for weeks, and her presence heats my body.

"I got a bottle of paint with me," I say. "Will you paint my nails?"

She continues looking at me in surprise. "Paint your nails?" she asks and I nod, though I feel foolish and awkward. Then she shrugs. "Okay," she says. "Sit on the sill."

I let go of the breath I have unconsciously been holding. She will paint my nails. I can sit on her sill.

I enter the room and walk to the window by her bed. I sit on the sill and Sachi settles at my feet. She takes the nail polish from me and unscrews the cap. "How is Aunty?" she asks.

"She is better," I say.

She starts painting my toes.

My script has run dry and I don't know what to say to her anymore.

She is wearing the T-shirt I gave her a year back. I had stolen it from a store and it appropriately reads RISK. I had gifted it to her for a Wednesday. "Happy Wednesday," I had said. Now it sits casually upon her body and before I can stop myself I say, "Give me back that T-shirt. I don't want you to have it anymore."

Sachi stares. "Are you mad?" She pulls my feet toward her. "Your nails are so funny. Mine are shapely and oval. Yours are so small you can hardly see the ones on your small toes. The smallest toe is a dot. It's hilarious."

"You should have studied," I say, desperate to hurt her. "It's no good if you don't study. People go to school to study. Everyone else in your class passed. I heard you failed three subjects. No wonder your parents think they have to send you away to a boarding school. A few slaps you will get from those people and you will begin to study. I guess Springdale is not right for you and it's a good thing you are leaving. Springdale is a tough school and just because your sisters are intelligent does not mean you have to be intelligent too. Not all people are the same. Not even siblings."

Sachi paints my toes as I speak and my toes are little polka dots of orange at the tip of my feet. Once she finishes painting she closes the bottle and tosses it to the bed. It mingles with the other bottles, its color like fire against the blue sheet. "Can I take this polish with me? I like the color," she says.

I love Sachi's room—the set of blue sheets with matching pillowcases and blue-and-white-checked blanket upon the bed. I love the feel of my body on her mattress, love our bodies together under the soft blanket. How many afternoons have I fallen asleep on it, my thighs resting on hers, our hands lost around each other? Some afternoons I kissed Sachi before we fell asleep and if I woke up during the nap, I kissed her again. Always Sachi kissed me back, sometimes on my brows, sometimes on the tip of my nose, on my neck, on my lips, on everywhere. At this moment, on this day, Sachi is only a year older than the age my mother was when she married my father. Of course, I do not think about this now, watching my orange toes. I think about it later, when I can understand my love for Sachi. Later, when I look back, I don't just see children in Sachi and me. We are young girls, alive to each other, as Ma must have been alive to Kumud, as Ruby must have been alive to her neighborhood boy. I understand Ma's love for Kumud only after I understand my own love for Sachi, and it is even later that I understand what Ma meant when she said to me once: A woman must love a woman first. There can be no other way. And in men, too, it is the woman in them we love.

Did Ma say that? Could she say it? Am I imagining she said it because this is the kind of thing I imagine I would say to my daughter, had I had a daughter?

When Sachi moves away from the floor and pulls out a suitcase from under the bed I continue sitting on the sill, half watching the construction of the Singapore House that is visible from Sachi's windows and half watching Sachi. The suitcase is a big, expensive baggage, the kind carried in airplanes, the kind that will not endure the roughness of buses or trains. On buses and trains its fleshy skin will be sliced open by the sharp blades of thieves and robbers. Even without the thieves, the suitcase will not survive the rigors of the journey. The gentle sway of the commute will graze and shred its leather.

The rain is still soft but the sky is suddenly rough with gray clouds and I stare out the window fatalistically. The smell of wet earth is unbearable. My rage is over. I can see individual strands of rain upon the leaves of the tree that grows a little way away from Sachi's window. In the distance I can see my own house, pushed back by the new construction that has taken away Ma's flowers and trees. I imagine rain upon the half-built walls of the house. I imagine rain upon its bare window frames, its unhinged doors, rain upon its unplastered walls. Then I see the cart. Sachi looks out the window too.

"You know," I say, "when I build my own house it will be small and wooden. There will be a library, tall burgundy shelves with books, and a bar at one end."

"But you never read and you don't drink," Sachi says.

"So what? They are gorgeous, yes or no?" I say. "I will build my house on a mountain and raise sheep."

"Witches live on mountains, in claustrophobic cottages, and drink sheep blood," says Sachi.

"I wonder what would have happened to Indira if she had fallen onto the concrete instead of the marigold bushes," I say.

"She would have died."

"There's the monkey," I point. "Look, on Thapa Uncle's roof."

Sachi looks then starts laughing. "Thapa Uncle is furious with the monkey," she says. "It has been getting into his water tank and swimming in it. Apparently, it opens the lid to the tank and goes right in. It never bothers to put the lid back on. Every morning Thapa Uncle shuts the tank and every morning he finds it open. He has only just found out it is the monkey. He was so angry when he told us. He kept saying, 'I should leave a towel for him, should I not?'"

"Maybe your parents should not insist you study," I say. "Maybe you are not meant for studying at all. Maybe you are made for something else, like basketball, maybe. You are good at basketball. You are damn good at basketball, aren't you? Or maybe you should get yourself hired at some hotel and do housekeeping. You are fucking Miss Spick-and-Span anyway! Why the hell do you need to line your suitcase with newspapers? Who does that?" I shriek the last sentence, angered by the precision with which Sachi goes about clearing her bed.

"Shut up, Preeti," she finally says. "You will get my entire family here."

"You are a good basketballer, aren't you, though? The best? The very best."

"Yes. All right? Yes. I am a very good player. All right? Now stop yelling."

"This is why your parents are sending you to India. What basketball will you play in Nepal? Which school plays anything here? They are sending you there because you are dumb at studies and maybe you will be some good at playing ball. Maybe then," I go on, my voice rising despite myself, "maybe you should join this school I have heard of. Savitri School. Have you heard of the school? They take in all basketballers. Flunkers or no flunkers. Do you know Binita Shah? Do you know her? Binita Shah? Binita Shah?"

"Why?" Sachi asks at last.

"Binita Shah flunked school four times. She was a dumb idiot. Only dumb idiots flunk a class four times, but she was a swell basketballer so Savitri School took her in. This Savitri School is in Rajasthan, though. It is not in Darjeeling. Tell your parents to send you to Rajasthan. I hear Binita Shah will play for the state championships one day. They are more interested in producing state champions at Savitri than in producing scholars. You should try it there. Tell that to your mother. Maybe you won't even have to repeat your classes there. And why do you have so many things? People in our country are out on the streets to make things better and you are running off to India with your bottles of perfumes and nail paints! You have so many things. A profusion. A profusion of perfumes, a profusion of cassettes, a profusion of clothes! What is your sister doing now? Not Siksha? The older one? Prateebha. What is she doing?"

Sachi sighs. "Medicine."

"She must be smart as hell, no?"

"Very."

"How come you are so dumb then? How come you are so ugly to look at and your sisters are so beautiful?"

Sachi stares at me. "Where the fuck were you all these days?" she asks. "You don't even look at me anymore. And now you care whether I stay or go?"

Heavy drops of water bounce off the window and settle mistily upon Sachi's short hair. A few unreal drops sit on her lashes and she is unreal, like a sequined angel. I have never seen anyone so beautiful and for a second when I look at her oval face, her perfect skin with the little scar above her left eyebrow, I cannot stop looking. "I don't care whether you stay or go," I say. I feel uprooted. Like Ma's trees.

I tell Sachi I am waiting for Ma to notice the fact that our bountiful land of fruits, vegetables, and dreams of badminton courts are gone. "She notices nothing," I say.

I tell her Adi and I are leaving too. "We are going to some place called Dehradun."

"Tell your father to send you to Darjeeling," Sachi says. "How does it matter? Dehradun or Darjeeling?"

"We have admissions in some school in Dehradun."

At one point she says going to Darjeeling is no big deal. "I am not really going to India," she says. "Darjeeling is in Nepal only. It has fallen accidentally in India."

"That is the biggest bullcrap I ever heard," I say. "Darjeeling is as much India as Janakpur is Nepal, but that does not ever matter, does it? Darjeeling is conveniently Nepal and Janakpur is conveniently India how and when it suits you! I don't think I want to be friends with you anymore." Such brave words.

And then it is seven and Sachi turns off the lights and begins to light candles in the room. The carrom game in the room below us seems to have ended and there is a momentary hush in the house. I think of Ma. I think she loves plums more for their shock of white flowers than for the fat fruits that attract fat flies during the season. I think that I miss them, now that the flowers are gone, and the flies, and the prickly caterpillars that appear suddenly every summer like they have been transported upon the trees through magic. I think of Adi, so angry, so sullen, so absent from home at all times. Where does he go? Does he not want to spend time with Ma? But I can see, too, that he is angry. I am not angry with Ma. I know with certainty that one day Ma will take my hand, turn it palm side up and kiss it, and with that kiss all distance will dissolve. I know I have to be patient. A day will come when we will once again become mother and child, indiscriminate, buried into each other, but I have to wait. But Adi does not know this and so he is angry.

What does it matter to me where Darjeeling and Janakpur are? What do I care about such elusive geography?

By the time Sachi has lit the two candles in her room, my clothes are almost dry and I hop off the window and push away whatever hostel paraphernalia of creams and clothes are left upon the bed. I lay on the bed and stare at the ceiling. In the candlelight the room is golden. When Sachi joins me, we watch the patterns the flames throw upon the roof and are quiet.

I ache to feel Sachi in one undivided length, to crush her into myself, to knead every part of her with my hands, but I hold back. She is leaving. Though right now this room is golden, everything else is dark inside and outside of me. I know I stand on a cliff and if I take one false step I will fall. Besides, despite our kisses and our naps, I do not know what I mean to Sachi. In this world of same-sex friendships, all girlfriends fall asleep together, everybody loves their best friend passionately, every girl navigates the edge of the cliff. Ma's withdrawal within herself has sharpened my cliff, but even before Ma fell sick I walked the edge of this precipice with caution.

I have hugged and kissed and loved Sachi as one hugs and kisses and loves a best friend. I have bought her cards and gifts of stolen T-shirts as one does for best friends. I have spent whatever little money I have had on her. I have invented secrets to entertain her with. I have stayed up all night doing her homework and completing her projects. I have shoplifted for Sachi's amusement—stolen pastries from bakeries—and passed them on to her giggling hands. I have written letters and in these letters drawn pictures of us together. I do not know how to draw eternity, or else I would have included the vastness of eternity in these pictures. It has always been all right. But even so I have never known what Sachi feels.

"Papa says Ma has gone mad and will always stay mad," I finally say.

Sachi turns to me more fully then. "I don't want to go, Preeti," she says. "I don't know what I will do."

And perhaps because we feel so homeless, so alone, so lost in this new, dark, golden world, we decide to cut each other's names on our arms.

In this quiet, disturbed, dark evening Sachi and I sit on the floor of her room and carve each other's names upon our arms with the tips of safety pins. Sachi heats the needle of the safety pin on one of the candle's flame and we scrape the pin upon our arms, up and down, digging for blood, hunting for ways to hold on to our worlds.

"We will wear each other's names," Sachi says before we begin the carving. "We will exchange blood. We will become blood sisters." With each proclamation my skin heats. I am surprised I have not fainted, have not died of the frightening joy I feel. "We will mingle," Sachi says.

In that first-sharp-then-blunt pain of the needle piercing my skin, I find for the first time a language for the ache I feel for Sachi. I marvel at the discovery, the serrated, stinging alphabets of love. I marvel at Sachi, head bent in concentration as she writes herself on my forearm. And somewhere in that moment I think of Ruby and her slashed wrists. Only pain can compete with love, I think with naive, jubilant ecstasy.

"You know," Sachi says without breaking her concentration, "my house, when I build it, will be a red and gray, neat as they come. I hate birthday cake and wedding dress houses. The rooms will be large, the walls made of glass, and there will be huge ventilators for lots of fresh air. The inside walls will be all glass and all white, except maybe the bedrooms. The house will be by the sea. The sitting room will be big, very nice and comfortable. There will be two guestrooms, a dining room, four bedrooms, a store, a kitchen, four toilet-bathrooms, and—" She stops uneasily.

"And?" I ask, scarcely able to breathe.

"And a room for you," she says, in a hurry.

A wonder, the kind that comes with listening to music, the kind that melts everything else, fills me then.

Sachi lifts the safety pin off my arms and looks at me, suddenly verbose. "I don't want the future to separate us," she says. Her voice is trembling. "I don't want anything to be the end of us. In all my futures I will keep a room ready for you. I'll have fresh sheets on the bed, slippers on the mat, toothbrushes and shampoo and soap in the bath. There will be nightsuits and everything else in the closet. You will come to me every time. You will never have to pack. I know you don't like going places because you don't like packing. I never want you to not like coming to me." It is not true that I don't like to pack or don't like to go to places, but it becomes true just then.

How brutal are the demands of our skin, the tenderness of our words. The future, so brittle. Separation, I think, is never possible after this. Whatever separations have already happened between us are sealed by the laceration of our skins. Sachi etched upon me, I bleeding on Sachi's arm. What I feel at this moment is an endless hunger, one I fear will never be satiated. What I feel without knowing it is slow death by hunger. What will satisfy would be a meal of Sachi. Well cooked, well served, in large quantities. This cutting of the skin is insufficient.

"I want to run away with you," I croak, my voice a saw in my throat.

But separation comes to us so soon after that golden night. In May,

Sachi has left for Darjeeling, fifteen days late for her semester but gone nevertheless.

What I remember most strongly is the solitariness of my life in the years that followed. It seems to me now that for years I could taste nothing, love nothing. With every person I met I tried to re-create what I had lost with Sachi but no one ever matched. Once I reached my hostel in Dehradun I roamed with packs of friends, always hiding in groups, always longing for single friendships but finding the notion also repulsive and impossible. How deep, how poignant was my grief. It is still there, thirty years later. Even after my love for Sachi, the person, has faded. Or not faded. It is always there.

BIRTHDAY PARTY

Neither Meena nor her siblings, nor anyone else from her childhood days, knew their dates of birth. They had tentative memories of months or seasons, of how hot or cold days were, or what event had pulled people out of their homes and into streets or temples or into the homes of their neighbors. Like all parents from the days when Meena was growing up, Kaveri, too, marked the days on which her children were born with events surrounding them.

The day Suman was born a snake fell into the water tank behind Kaveri's house. From the windows of the darkened room where Kaveri labored, Kaveri and her sister-in-law watched the gold-skinned snake. It was yellow and brown, rolled out like a blade of grass, and shining brilliantly in the sun. "Just goes in and out the pool like some majesty," said Kaveri to her sister-in-law just before another round of contractions began.

When Suman was born, Kaveri held him in her arms and scowled. His hair, like feathers on a chick, were nearly golden. It was a full year before it turned black.

The day Kirti was born, the papaya tree in Kaveri's garden bore its first fruit. "It was also the day Madhu from our neighborhood got married,"

Kaveri told Kirti every time she re-created the day of her daughter's birth to her daughter. "I had to miss the marriage because of you," she complained.

The day Meena was born, a large, bumbling bird perched nervously on Kaveri's terrace. It held an impressively long twig in its beak. Kirti and Mansi were little girls then, playing on the terrace, and when they saw the bird alight on the parapet they shrieked in half delight, half terror, but the bird sat on, confused, as though wondering what it could do with the twig in its beak.

"This gentleman," said little Kirti to little Mansi, "is a workaholic. He has a big enough nest but he still looks for twigs and sticks. What does he need it bigger for? Must be his wife!"

"It looks like a cow," said Mansi, watching the silly bird with amused curiosity.

"A cow?" repeated Kirti, glaring at the bird. "Yes, yes. It is a cow. But it is wearing very woolen socks." The girls stared at the bird's heavily down-feathered feet and nodded in satisfaction. "No wonder nobody is respecting it," said Kirti.

"Who is not respecting it?" asked Mansi, startled by this piece of information.

"The parrots, the crows. Not even the sparrows. Nobody is respecting it. It is just a cow in socks. How can it go hunting? His wife must be doing all the hunting. Ridiculous bird!"

Then the bird flew away.

Meena's birth was marked by the arrival of a henpecked, workaholic, bumbling peregrine falcon that was nothing but a socks-wearing cow.

The day Shanti was born, the day was still. A quiet, like a cool glass of water, stayed in Kaveri's labor room, and Kaveri decided to name the child that was soon to be hers, Shanti, if it was a girl, and Shant, if it was a boy. That her girl was born deaf, was born into a quietly trembling world, seemed therefore inevitable, almost miraculous.

Like Kaveri had, Meena, too, marked her children's birthdays with events. "The day you were born," she told Adi, "big pebbles of ice fell from the sky."

The hail had drummed on the roof of the room Meena was in and distracted her from the pain. The storm had come and gone, and from the window behind her bed, Meena could hear the excitement of children as they ran out their homes into the streets. From her bed Meena imagined the children collecting ice in tumblers and bottles. She imagined them eating the ice, wincing as the chill pierced their teeth. "Your aunts must have eaten ice too," Meena said to Adi. "We always ate ice on the rare, rare occasion of hail."

A week before Preeti was born Meena's father hired a VCR and treated the family to a marathon of movies, and the day Preeti was born, the family watched the superhit film *Amar Akbar Anthony*. While Meena labored later that night, the family paced about the house and loudly sang:

My name is Anthony Gonsalves, yea!
My heart is as empty as my home
And only a girl of courage shall live in it both.

"That Suman created such a ruckus, shouting about the house," said Meena to her daughter. "There was no peace at all. And for almost an entire year he called you Anthony Gonsalves, as though that is any name for a girl!"

All this Meena told Adi and Preeti. All this to make them understand why she did not know the exact date and time when her children were born. You were born on special days, she told them. "You were born and the world was full of treats and songs." But despite the stories, despite the joy Meena felt when she recalled those days, her children longed for dates. Which day? they demanded, always meaning which month, which date, which year. For some years Meena was able to fend the questions away. Specifics of birth dates revealed too much about individuals. Birth dates, like lines on the palms and creases on the forehead, guarded futures—jobs, marriages, children, death—and were best left hidden in dusty trunks, under heavy, forgotten swathes of silk and velvet, and removed only for momentous occasions. It was better to forget birth dates than to distribute them among reckless friends and strangers who could then glimpse into your future and interfere with it.

To stave off her children's questions Meena constructed dates and months for them from memory. The day Preeti was born had been colder than the day Adi was born, and this despite the hail. It was after Makar Shankranti—Meena remembered not being allowed to eat the til-ke-laddu because sesame was too warm a food and could be bad for the baby she was carrying. So, Meena calculated, Preeti was born after mid-January and before March. Preeti was born in February.

"You were born in June," she told Preeti.

"When in June?" Preeti asked. Meena thought. When? She tried to locate a possible day.

"Twenty-fifth," she said, somewhat wildly, almost biting her tongue. "You were born on the twenty-fifth of June and your brother was born on July twentieth."

How exciting, how strange were these fixed, impersonal, fabricated dates. She had weaved time into fine baskets to hold her children in. These false dates revealed nothing about them–neither the secret joys that lay before them, nor the sorrows. These dates that Meena had created were for shallow events—for parties and exchanges of gifts.

But now that her children were leaving, Meena thought often about the day hail had fallen from the sky, and the song her brother had yelled so crudely at her infant daughter's face. Now that her children were leaving, Meena wanted to give her children something real, something they could hold on to secretly, something that would belong only between her and them. They would continue to be children of June and July for the world, continue to fill forms with fake dates and respond to wishes with fake thank-yous on hot, rainy days. Only Meena and her children would know that they belonged to spring and fog and flowers, that they belonged to February and March. It would be their secret, something they could get under the quilt and whisper about, something they could take comfort in as they sipped hot cups of tea. And so Meena called her children to the kitchen one morning.

"You were born on the twenty-sixth of February," she told Preeti, "and you," she said to Adi, "were born on the eighth of March, but you can never tell anyone these dates. This is our secret and before you leave we will celebrate a combined birthday on the thirtieth of June just to fully fool the world. What do you say?"

Meena could tell from the way her children stared at her too long before responding that they thought she spoke from a space of insanity. They did not believe her. They thought they were children of heat and rain, children of the season of mangoes. They thought her season of berries and flowers were fake. A sense of fear and defeat overtook her then, but even so, Meena waited for her children to respond.

Then Adi nodded. "Yes, Ma," he said. "Let's have a party." But he said it the way he said everything of late. A little distantly. A little wearily.

Preeti kissed her hard. "Let's cook all your favorite things," she said.

It wasn't that Meena did not remember her madness. She remembered it clearly, like one remembers bites of chilies taken to enhance the taste of bland food. She remembered the heady, almost intoxicated taste of curses and foul words upon her tongue. The sudden freedom it had granted her to push Manmohan away. She remembered grabbing her breasts and charging at Manmohan. Die! Die! She remembered the ecstasy of aggression. She remembered, too, the intensity of her anger and the abyss of the sudden fears that gripped her. She remembered the day she met Kaveri in one of these abysses, and she remembered how, with her mother, she fell and fell, unable to reach anywhere. I am just like you, she said to Kaveri during the fall. What else will you be like? Your neighbor? asked Kaveri. Meena also remembered the confusion that came with the falling, the confusion of not knowing who was who, who lived and who had died, who stayed and who had already left. Are you real? she asked Kaveri. Are you real? she asked Vivek Rahane who joined them during the fall. Are you real? she asked His Majesty whom she also met along the way. She was most surprised at meeting His Majesty because she had never met him before. Are you real? she once asked Adi, and immediately after the question she clamped her mouth shut. How could she have asked Adi such a question? How could she have forgotten?

She remembered the bright intensity the world had taken around her. The relentless glow with which everything had burned.

The fire was gone now, and so was the heat of chilies from her tongue. There was only a hazy fog where there had once been outrageous color and blinding phosphorescence. Sometimes, when she sat on her bed, studying magazines that showed pictures of smiling families in conical hats gathered around happy children cutting special birthday cakes, Meena almost missed the blinding clarity of her madness. Though she studied these images for inspiration for the birthday party she was planning, they left her numb. How had she lost her children?

But despite the transparency and freedom of mania, Meena did not really wish her madness back. The bright well of madness had charred her children. From its glare she had not recognized her son. From its rude shimmer she had asked him if he was real, and now her son, briefly forgotten by her, had forgotten her altogether. Meena had not spoken to Adi for months and now he did not speak to her, not even when he watched her prepare for the party. He held his silence behind his teeth, like cold, hard ice. He stayed away from her and the house, walking in late, always distracted, always with that demand she could not fully understand.

"Do something," he said, his eyes brittle with anger.

"Do what?" Meena asked, confused.

She tried to do as he wanted. She tried to talk more, to do things that were real. She tried to cook meals with more meticulousness. She tried to cut out patterns from magazines with more accuracy. She knew, even as she cooked and cut, that this was not what Adi wanted, and so, now and then, when the world took on that delicious radiance she recognized so well, she tied down her tongue and her limbs and tried to not stare too longingly at the fire burning scarcely five steps away from her. She tried to dull her senses, to clip the scattered pages of her mind.

"Talk to him, Ma," Adi said, and Meena tried to talk to Manmohan, though his smell repelled her. Some days she had to clench her jaws and tighten her fists to keep herself from lifting her sari and from screaming a curse at him. She had to keep herself from galloping like a goat and bleating out songs that ricocheted among the pillars holding in her brain. *Sun Ré Dulha, you will blush at my shamelessness.* But she tied herself to a post and spoke evenly. "You cannot send my children away," she said. "I cannot live without them."

Her children were leaving. They were taking autorickshaws and cycle rickshaws. They were boarding buses and trains. They would hear the hollow of bridges under the wheels of their shivering vehicles. They would cross unknown villages marked by single benches and ancient banyan trees. She imagined her children looking out the barred windows of trains, their hair swept back by the wind, their eyes squinted as they took in the landscape, their elbows poking out like arrows pointing to a world Meena could not follow them to. Her children were leaving and she had a party to throw, like a handful of colored rice into the wind, each particle small and flung, incapable of coming back into her palms again.

"You cannot, you cannot, I cannot," she murmured in her dreams. In her dreams she asked her friends for help, but they remained locked in luminescent glass rooms. His Majesty, especially, was helpless. He was surrounded by walls made of noise and no matter how loudly she spoke, he looked at her in bewilderment because he could not hear her. She asked Kaveri, but Kaveri sniggered. "Where were you when your father was chasing me round and round the streets, eh?" she demanded, oiling her dry, wrinkled legs. Then she looked slyly at Meena. "All children leave. You left the moment you could with your Romeo, and look what a bakwas place you got yourself into."

"Do you think I can live without them?" Manmohan asked. "You have left me no option but to send them away."

"I am sorry," said Meena. "I will be good now. Now I will not do anything wrong."

"For how long?"

"Forever."

But Manmohan did not believe her.

Sometimes Manmohan held her hands and stroked them. "You are not well, Meeni," he said. "You are not fit anymore. It kills me to send them away, but it is for their good and it is for your good."

"How can being away from me be good for them?" Meena asked. "How can their absence be good for me?"

"It is, it is, Meeni," Manmohan repeated softly.

When had he started calling her Meeni?

"It is, it is," echoed Kaveri. "It is, it is," said Rahane. His Majesty said nothing because he seemed to have forgotten how to speak.

Then Adi came home one day and shrugged. "I am glad I am getting away from here," he said, staring at the two metallic trunks that had appeared miraculously in the room. "I hate being here anyway."

It was only then that Meena noticed there were things in the house now, like the metallic trunks, new and unknown to her. The trunks had Adi's and Preeti's names written in black, calligraphic letters on them. She went to the trunks and gingerly opened their lids. Locked in these trunks were neatly folded sheets, towels, pillow covers, pairs and pairs of white socks, new underwear, new tubes of pastes, cakes of soap, unopened toothbrushes. Meena trembled before these objects and when she extended her hands to touch them, they burned her with their fire. And now Adi was glad. And perhaps Meena started to cry, because Adi said, from where he sat, that it was all right.

"It's okay, Ma," he said, sharp edged. "We will come home for vacations."

Meena focused on the colors in the magazines—purple, hot pink, dark orange, ruby red, yellow—and asked Preeti to buy broad sheets of tissues from the gift shop at Ring Road. "I will make streamers and chandeliers with them," she said. "I will throw you such a party you will forget everything."

When her children were away at school during the day, Meena sat with the foot-long wooden ruler all schoolchildren were required to own, and used the width of the ruler to fold these sheets into breadths of one and a half inch. Later, she cut out the folds and rolled the strips into soft wheels. She had to be gentle. The sheets were fragile. They crumpled and bruised and tore so easily. She segregated the strips, keeping the yellows with yellows and oranges with oranges. When it was time for her children to come home, she put away the sheets and the strips in the green suitcase she had taken with her so often every time she had thought of running away and waited for them. Here, too, she had to be careful. She did not want to be too excited about the fake birthday. She did not want it to get lurid and gaudy. She did not want her children to think she did nothing but prepare all day for something that was not real. She had to balance it carefully. She had to fool everyone, her children included. She thought of what Adi had said—*we will come home for vacations*—and the cruelty of those words cut deep into her.

A day before the party Meena boiled wheat flour over medium heat for over half an hour and a sticky, glutinous gum sat ready for her in the bowl. She was not mad, though she longed for madness. When she closed her eyes and imagined barefoot women on streets with matted hair and filthy layers of assorted clothes, speaking to trees and cars, and shouting belligerently at the sky, Meena longed for madness, but she was not mad. Meena was not mad because madwomen could not stand before fire for so long. They could not boil wheat and plan parties.

In the afternoon Preeti sat with Meena and prepared smaller strips of paper for chain links, pom-poms, alphabets, and such.

"Your birthday is when you can have a birthday," said Meena. "When you go to your India school, you can cast it again on whichever day is good for you. You don't have to stick to June and July. Just don't tell anyone about February and March."

All afternoon Meena and Preeti cut and glued. The alphabets spelled "Happy Birthday, Adi and Preeti" and the fiction in the sentence had Meena giggling. The pom-poms went on corners of windows and doors. From the center of the roof curved spirals of colorful paper that hung and went up again in thick curls and looked like a large chandelier. From the center of this chandelier hung several pom-poms. Not all sheets were cut into strips; some were cut into smaller squares and circles and these were shaped into flowers and geometric patterns of snowflakes. Preeti stuck them on windowpanes and walls and at the ends of the sentence announcing the birthday. Some hung from the doorframe.

"Can we celebrate my birthday every June?" asked Preeti, looking around the transformed room.

"We can," Meena said.

"Can we decorate the room every year?"

"We can, but you remember our secret, don't you?"

"I do," said Preeti.

For the rest of the afternoon, as they prepared for the party in the evening, Meena described the journey to Preeti. "It will take you three nights," she said. "You will ride all night from here to Birgunj and from Birgunj you will take a cycle-rickshaw to cross over to India. In Raxaul you will get into a narrow gauge train to Gorakhpur and in Gorakhpur you will switch to the broad gauge to Dehradun. Three nights, four days. For three nights and four days you will gaze out the window at unknown ponds, rooftops, streets, and shops. Three nights and four days of dozing off and waking up farther and farther away."

"You know, Ma," Preeti said while they were in the kitchen adding finishing touches to the cake they had shaped out of suji halwa and decorated with cashews and raisins, "Sachi is gone too."

"Where?" Meena asked, confused by the sudden violence with which her daughter began to cry. "Is she dead?" Meena asked, gripped with fear.

"No," said Preeti. "Not dead, Ma. Just away." And yet she cried as though her friend was dead, and not just away.

Meena gently rocked her daughter. "Even the dead don't die, my bird. Even the dead visit when the distance gets too much. Your grandmother visits regularly. She comes to me on the staircase, sometimes alone, sometimes with a monkey, always chattering about this and that, telling me what to do and how to live. Your Sachi will come too."

But the next day, just before Meena began heating the food for the guests she had invited to the party, she accosted Kaveri at the staircase.

"It is the same thing, isn't it?" she asked her mother. "Not dead, just away. Not gone, but home for vacations?"

Kaveri shrugged. She was walking with the thin, ugly monkey and now she looked at the monkey and said, "You don't leave me alone, ever. You are a whiny, clingy thing." To Meena she said, "I was twelve when I married your father and went from here to there. I did not go all crooked thinking this and that. I just went from my mother to that mother, and that was that!"

"And you missed nothing at all?" asked Meena. "You wanted nothing at all?"

"Want-shwant," said Kaveri. "I only know what I did not want. Your father, I did not want. I wanted him dead, nice and proper." So far the monkey had walked patiently beside Kaveri, but now it jumped and sat up on her shoulders. Kaveri shrieked and Meena almost fell down the stairs in a fright. "Want-shwant," said Kaveri and patted the animal.

"Can I go too?" Meena asked Manmohan after her conversation with Kaveri, because even though she admired Kaveri's lack of want-shwant, Meena still wanted to see the lakes and rooftops her children would doze and wake up to as they traveled away from her.

"Go where?" asked Manmohan, but he understood her question right away and shook his head. "You are too unwell, Meeni," he said. "You don't want to be unwell during a journey. Here you can rest. Take your pills and you will be fine. And I will be here too. I cannot go. What will people say if I go? I have asked Mr. Dinesh to take the kids along when he takes his own children. I cannot go right now. What will Doctor Singh say if I go?"

"Is Doctor Singh my whore?" asked Meena. "Will both of you warm my bed now, one this side, one that side?"

"You did not take your pill," Manmohan warned.

"You did not take your pill," mimicked Meena, sniggering.

"If you behave this way, how will the children go?"

"If you behave this way, how will the children go?"

"Shut up."

"Shut up, *madarchod*," Meena said and lifted her sari.

So many people came for the birthday party. Kaveri came with the monkey and Meena ordered the monkey out. "It will destroy everything," she said. His Majesty came, too, and was his usual melancholic self. He bored everyone with his woes. "I feel centuries old," he said. "I feel like an old man whose bones, exposed constantly to history, have rusted and whose muscles have shrunk against the continuous movement of time."

"What is this nonsense way of talking?" Kaveri asked. "You learn this nonsense in some King School, is it?"

"What I want," His Majesty went on, unable to engage with Kaveri, "is to pluck myself off this tree on which I am just a helpless fruit and set myself rolling down a hill and plunking into a river."

"Ohoho," said Kaveri, losing all patience. "Can we throw this man out? Can we have our party now?"

And so Meena ushered Adi and Preeti to the table where the halwa cake was set and surrounded with flowers and confetti and paper cone hats. Her children wore the hats, too, and looked delightfully ridiculous in them.

"Live long," blessed Vivek Rahane.

"Live happy," said His Majesty in his most melancholic tone.

"Live free," said Kaveri.

At some point the ADC's wife, Kamala, joined the party in her squelching gumboots, and Meena immediately pointed her to the door. "You cannot come," she said, and together with Kaveri, she pushed the short, bulky woman out the house, while the woman cried in agony. "Let me stay for the party. Let me stay for the party."

Once the ADC's wife had left, everyone handed over the gifts they had brought with them. Vivek had brought along a thin, angular doll. The doll wore a green dress and had yellow hair. His Majesty brought a chubbier doll who had blue eyes and sat on a globe. His Majesty's doll could never be pushed around because no matter how hard one pushed him, he always sprang back to his sitting position. Kaveri brought a key-operated bear that beat the drums, and an inexplicable dog in a pink-red frock. Then Vivek Rahane performed a little dance for everyone. It was splendid. It was spectacular. It was better than birthdays in magazines and cinemas.

Later Kaveri said she missed the monkey and insisted the entire party move to the terrace to look for the simian, so they moved the party to the terrace. They found the monkey straightaway in the compound of the new house. The monkey was riding a dog like a horse and the dog ran round and round the compound. The dog barked, the monkey screeched, and everyone cheered. "Look, Ma. Look, Ma." Preeti pointed. "I am not going anywhere, Ma. I am staying right here with you," Adi said, also pointing and laughing. How delightful it was to watch from the terrace, with Adi and Preeti and Kaveri and Rahane and His Majesty. Who else could Meena want? It seemed to Meena that the dog and the monkey knew they were being watched and enhanced their performance. They knew people were kinder to animals, beggars, the sickly, the old, and the dying who were entertaining and fun than they were to animals, beggars, the sickly, the old, and the dying who asked for care without offering any pay in return.

"I will only age and sag upon these branches," said His Majesty, morose and gloomy. He was quite insufferable, the poor thing. "One day I will fall off the branch ungraciously and burst open upon the ground, much to the delight of worms."

"There you will be," said Kaveri, tsking her tongue, "an overripe carcass and a bountiful feast for the flies. Some use at least you will be of."

"Here," said Adi, suddenly looking very serious. "Take your pill." And because Meena never said no to Adi, she took the pretty pink pill and gulped it down with water.

Want-shwant, want-shwant, the pill went in her head, scratching against the edges of her skull and giving her a dull ache. Only after she had taken the pill did she understand that had she not taken the pill, want-shwant would have opened her head and exploded into the room, screaming like a monkey on fire, but the pill kept the creature cold and bouncing like a watchful eyeball within her.

At one point Meena woke up with a start. The house was hushed with only a sound like fire burning in her head. "Where are my children?" she asked the empty house.

Was it in a dream that the monkey entered the living room and shredded the chandeliers and paper chains? It ripped the flowers and beat the cake into its mouth. Ke-ke-ke-ke-ke, it said, dancing around the room. Preeti shrieked while Adi chased it around the room with a stick. Kaveri sat with Meena and laughed, slapping her thighs for emphasis. "Thwack it! Thwack it!" Kaveri said, clapping her hands.

Through it all Meena was happy because none of this was real. This was June and July, while the real thing lay deep below the earth, unharmed by pills, monkeys, and ghosts, in February and March.

EPILOGUE

THE WOMAN WHO CLIMBED TREES

When the barber's wife started the mehendi on Meena's palms, she also started the first story she would tell Meena through the evening and the night. "Such was the night that the wind howled," she said.

Such was the night that the wind howled. A roguish wind slapped against windows and houses, and at some distance bamboos shrilly whistled. The water in the lake behind Laxmaniya's house came alive and jumped like a maddened animal, and bundles of thatch from roofs took wings and hurled into the sky. Everywhere there were sounds—otherworldly and dreadful. And yet Laxmaniya, a barber's daughter, slept, unaware that a storm whirred through the village, strong enough to haul the girl and fling her against walls.

It was Laxmaniya's father, the barber, who heard the knock upon his door, definite and narrow, like a woodpecker's beak, and woke from his sleep. He stayed for some time on his cot, unable to orient himself. The mirror upon the wall glistened and threw the barber's face back from its surface. And the knock on his door went on. The barber moved slowly. An unusual fear seized him. He wanted to secure the door and protect his sleeping daughter, though he did not know what from.

The barber and his daughter were poor people. There wasn't enough to eat. There weren't enough rooms in the house, and the father and daughter slept in the same room—he upon a thin, coconut-roped cot, she upon the wooden bed. Laxmaniya's mother had died at childbirth and the barber had raised his daughter as only a mother can. He had not remarried. All this he thought as he stared at his stirring daughter.

The barber watched his daughter and noticed things about her he had not seen before. He saw, for the first time, that his daughter was no longer a girl. She had, somehow during the howling night, become a woman. Her blouse had come undone and her breasts were gentle hills with nipples like flower moles upon her. As he stared, the barber felt a tingle in his loins and his balls bunched to become a mass of thick skin, and a shame, more terrible than the storm, burned a permanent crack within his chest.

And all this while the knocker banged upon the door and finally woke the daughter.

Who is it? the barber and his daughter asked together, and a small, flutelike voice answered from outside.

Come out, clipper of nails and hair, said the voice.

Laxmaniya muttered angry words under her breath and stepped off the bed. She tucked the ends of her yellow sari into her waist and asked, What do you want?

I have a job for you, said the voice.

At this time? asked the daughter.

It is a job you will not regret. Open the door, clipper of nails and hair.

And so she opened the door and a soft breeze entered the room. The barber was amazed. Where was the raging wind? Had the sky swallowed the storm? Had he dreamed it all—the whistling bamboos, the snapping trees? He stared at the suddenly hushed night and at the withering, walnut-faced woman standing before them. Upon her bony body she wore a white sari. There was a large moon dripping from the sky, big and luminous, and the old woman's clothes gleamed under its light. The village was lit like a lantern behind her. Under the moon everything was in place—the trees obedient, the thatch settled, the wind buried under the ground.

What do you want? asked the barber.

There is a wedding in our village, said the old woman, and our village barber has died.

What is the exact job? asked the barber.

There is no one to clip our bride's nails, no one to outline her feet with color, and no one to put mehendi on her.

But it is already late at night. This is not an auspicious hour. Daughter, you go back to bed. This is no job for you.

Laxmaniya walked back to her bed, but she did not lie down. She sat at the edge and listened curiously to the conversation between the old woman and her father.

If you don't come, the old woman said, your business will crumble. The new saloon that stands at the bazaar will steal your last few customers and you will starve without dignity. There will be pain and suffering in store, and even if you ask, there will be jobs no more.

You evil woman! cried the barber. And if the new saloon is so attractive to you, why have you come to me? Why have you not gone to the new saloon?

The old woman grinned. I have not come to you, she said. I have come to your daughter. Only a woman can clip our women's toes. That is the custom of our people. She stretched her neck and looked at Laxmaniya sitting at the edge of her bed. The more you take, the more you leave behind. What is it? she asked.

Footsteps, said Laxmaniya.

Ah well, said the barber. She could not take the job even if she wanted to. The hour is inauspicious.

Again the old woman stretched her neck and talked to the daughter. What can a bag of gold buy? she asked.

Potatoes, said Laxmaniya, and lentils. Beans, rice, spinach, wheat. New clothes for my father. A slipper each for his feet. New scissors, boxes of alta, brushes and combs, mirrors, powders, pom-poms, creams and oils. A new roof perhaps. A hundred cows. A thousand goats.

If you come, said the old woman, there will be a bag of gold and silver.

The daughter pinched the ends of her sari and nibbled at them. The barber, too, bit his thumb. They had not seen a decent meal since the town-trained barber had set up his saloon at the bazaar. The saloon door, made of glass, had a big, red WELCOME with yellow outlines painted upon it.

Father and daughter stared at the ground, one chewing his thumb, the other her sari, debating the inauspiciousness of the hour and balancing it with the auspiciousness of the reward. A new roof. Perhaps, a new room with a glass door upon it. The barber thought of a new blouse for his daughter, a new sari. Finally, he harrumphed. Stay here, old mother, he said. My daughter cannot go with you this late, but I can. I will collect my tools.

The old woman grinned. No, she said. We cannot have strange men touching our bride.

But I will be like a father to her! the barber protested.

The old woman grinned wider. You are not like a father to your own daughter anymore, she said. How will you be a father to ours? And the barber, defeated by his shame, let his daughter go off with the old woman.

"Is this a ghost story?" Meena asked the barber's wife who told the tale. "I don't want to hear scary stories one night before I marry."

"Not all ghost stories are scary," said the barber's wife, laughing at Meena. "Besides, we have a long time before us, and stories are baskets to carry time away in."

Laxmaniya followed the old woman and together they crossed the village. They crossed the glittering lake, then they moved on, walking through fields where grains shone like silver on wheat stalks that caught the moon. The old woman sang through the journey, sad and bony, describing objects and events Laxmaniya could make no sense of. *You can dream of it over tea and toast*, she sang. *You can follow its path as it hunts. It glides along the languorous coast, and frolics the water for fun.*

Where are we going, Grandmother? Laxmaniya asked, but the old woman would not answer.

Finally, they reached the bleached grounds of a clearing before the village river, and here the old woman stopped and waited for Laxmaniya to catch up. Once Laxmaniya was close enough, the old woman pointed to the ancient banyan tree that was older than the village itself. It stood large and wide upon the ground, like a planet of leaves and gnarly roots. This is our destination, said the old woman. Climb it.

Immediately Laxmaniya was gripped with fear. Had she come along with a mad, senile witch?

Who are you, Grandmother? she asked.

Your sari is wet, said the old woman, suddenly giggling. And so is your blouse. Right here, she said, extending a skeletal finger to show Laxmaniya where her blouse was wet. Laxmaniya pulled away and rearranged her sari, and slowly, very quietly, she felt the eyes of the universe upon her wet sari—the deathless moon, the water gurgling before her, the tree like a gigantic mountain.

The old woman sang, *O, the heart is never your own, my darling; it is but a bird on a tree.* Then she looked at Laxmaniya and said, You must climb. When Laxmaniya refused to move, the old woman said, If you do not climb, you will die.

But I have never climbed trees, cried Laxmaniya. I don't know how to climb trees. And there will be cobras and owls and a hundred insects on the branches.

If you return home without having climbed the tree, a curse will befall you, and you will spend the rest of your life unable to move from this spot. Even as you live within the walls of your house, you will be stranded here, forever wondering about the tree, said the old woman in a nasal voice. You have very little time. You must climb while the moon is still large. And remember the reward you will receive. Enough gold to build a hundred huts.

Then the old woman put her hands on her ears and listened to the wind. Do you hear? she asked.

No, insisted Laxmaniya, gathering herself stubbornly against the old woman, though indeed, she could hear a faint persistence of shehnai coming from somewhere. *Pipiripippi-pipiripipi,* went the instrument. Laxmaniya listened. And there was rhythmic drum. There were cymbals. And Laxmaniya, well acquainted with jewels even though she owned few, heard the *chhum-chhum* of anklets and bangles.

Climb, said the old woman.

"Oh," cried Meena, "is Laxmaniya going to die? I don't want to hear the story if Laxmaniya is going to die."

"You have to let the story tell itself," scolded the barber's wife. "You cannot be impatient with a story."

Eventually, Laxmaniya climbed the tree because she was too afraid to disobey the old woman. She hitched up her sari and tucked it between her legs. She secured her pallu around her waist. She retied her hair into a tight bun. Then she caught hold of one of the hundreds of roots dangling from the ancient tree and hauled her body up. Laxmaniya's palms, unaccustomed to pulling the weight of her body, immediately bruised and began to bleed, and Laxmaniya wept in pain. She turned once to look at the old woman but it seemed to her like the old woman was drinking the night, and becoming curiously like the night, like a moon behind clouds, vague and shapeless and freckled. Her nasal voice came from farther and farther away. Laxmaniya continued to pull herself along the length of the root. It was easier once she reached the first branch. Other branches were closer together, and Laxmaniya went from one branch to another, cautiously reaching out with unsure feet. She was enclosed within a thick green vegetation, and she could see nothing of the world she had left far below. At one point she stopped and called for the old woman. Grandmother! she called, but there was no response, and Laxmaniya continued her climb. The *pipiripiripi* of the shehnai grew louder now, and it was this sound she followed. Later she heard laughs and talks of people, and still later she heard wedding songs sung to the beat of dholaks. *The heart will not sit quietly beside you, my darling, as you slurp your roti and daal.*

Higher and higher Laxmaniya climbed until she reached the very top, to a strange world supported by barks and leaves, and set to light by the melting moon. Laxmaniya stood at the edge, dizzy from her climb, washed by the moon, unable to understand her journey.

Upon the tree, seated on leaves, were women everywhere, milling about, singing, weaving, cooking, accounting. At one end a few women sat on a wide leaf and smoked cloudy bidis. At another end girls with saris worn like dhotis played hopscotch and skipped ropes. At the center were the singing women, keeping time with their dholaks. Laxmaniya walked gingerly toward these women. There were women in this world, and there were birds—grumpy parrots, woolly legged falcons, pigeons with rainbow capes around their necks. There were squirrels, and monkeys, and a few dogs sleeping with their bellies exposed to the moon.

"Your mother is here too," said the barber's wife to Meena. "Do you see her singing with the women? She has a dholak pinned under her legs, and she is beating it most lustily."

Meena laughed. Indeed, she could see her mother, small and compact even here among these women. She could hear her too. *O, the heart is never your own, my darling,* she sang with the women. *It is but a fraudulent bird on a tree.*

Laxmaniya went to the women and introduced herself. I am here to beautify the bride, she said, overtaken by a coyness she could not explain. Immediately a hue and cry ran through the top of the banyan tree. The beautician is here, went the news, rustling leaves and shaking branches. The parrots flew off grumpily. The pigeons complained.

Only the falcon, put to task by its mate, continued to build his nest. Is the bride ready to be made ready? went the question.

Efficiently, but without any hurry, Laxmaniya was led to the bride waiting to be made pretty.

"And that bride is you," whispered the barber's wife to Meena. "There you are, sitting on a leaf, surrounded by your girlfriends, hair still wet from your bath, skin glowing, joking about this and that."

"Am I not shy to be joking a day before my wedding?" asked Meena.

"Women are only shy around men, and there are no men in this world."

"Who am I marrying then?" asked Meena, amused.

"Who knows? Perhaps the group of smokers? Or the group of singers? Or the group of cooks? Or do you want to marry the accountants?"

"The group playing hopscotch," said Meena. "I can beat them in no time."

"Then you are marrying the group playing hopscotch," said the barber's wife.

Laxmaniya styled the bride with strips of leaves and curls of roots. She painted her feet with the juice of hibiscus. She lined her eyes using the tip of a feather. The bride's girlfriends passed a basket of flowers to Laxmaniya, and these she fashioned into bracelets and pendants. What do you think? she asked the girlfriends once she was done with the bride. She is a rival to the moon, said the girlfriends, gaping at her.

When the women on the treetop saw the bride, they too gaped. They praised Laxmaniya for her skillfulness and said they would always call for her if she so wished. Only here are you allowed to show how truly skillful you are, they said.

May I stay for the ceremony? asked Laxmaniya, intrigued by this strange marriage.

Stay, stay, said the women, and Laxmaniya stayed.

Perhaps the bride was married over the night, but Laxmaniya could make nothing of it, for the bride, decked in flowers and leaves, played hopscotch, jumped ropes, smoked bidis, cooked a meal, did some accounting, sang some songs, chatted with her girlfriends, walked about the tree, put on eyeglasses and wrote something in a notebook, knitted a scarf, and then, exhausted by the many activities she had participated in, fell into a deep sleep.

You have done your work well, said the bride's mother, upon whose shoulder now sat a monkey and a parrot. Here is your bag of gold and silver.

So engrossed had Laxmaniya been in this new, mysterious world, she had forgotten all about the promised gold, and she received the bag from the mother with a little surprise. She peered into the bag and was amazed to see that it indeed shone with yellow gold and white silver.

I don't really need this, said Laxmaniya, stammering before her wealth.

Don't be silly, said the mother, somewhat distracted by the animals. All promises must be kept. But now the moon is almost set and the sun will be out soon. You must return home before the first rays of sun.

What about you? asked Laxmaniya.

We live here, said the woman.

And so Laxmaniya returned home. She climbed down the tree, and with every branch she left, she felt her heart grow heavy. She wanted to grasp a root and swing herself up again, but the thought of her father awaiting her in their hut kept her from returning to the treetop. She walked back, passing the river, the fields, the lakes, the cows, the huts. She wondered where the old, vaporous woman was, and where she had been all night, but she could not see her, and Laxmaniya walked on, carefully protecting her bag of gold and silver.

The closer she got to her hut, the lighter the sky grew, though it also lost its magical silver luster. Soon the sky was purple silk. Now the clouds were orange, now pink. Her hut came before her, slowly, and Laxmaniya walked toward it with hesitation. With hesitation she knocked upon its rotting door. What was this feeling she felt? she wondered and knocked again, loudly and with feigned confidence.

Hah, said the barber when he opened the door and saw her. Then he narrowed his eyes and looked. Are you thirsty? he asked.

Yes, said Laxmaniya and stepped into the hut.

How much smaller the hut was. Her bed against the wall was small too. She could not believe her father fit on that cot. They needed a larger hut, larger beds. They needed better food, stronger clothes.

I got the money, Father, Laxmaniya said when the barber returned with a tumbler of water. He was smaller, too, shrunk in body and with thinner hair.

But first tell me about the wedding, said the barber.

Laxmaniya tried to describe what she had lived. It was a different universe, Father, she said, on a tree and full of women. It was a strange ceremony I attended, a marriage without a groom, and festivities without men. Everyone lived on top of trees.

The father frowned. He could not understand a word of what his daughter detailed. Finally, he shook his head. Show me what they paid you, these idle, singing women.

They paid me in gold and silver, said Laxmaniya, beaming with pride. They said my work was beautiful and the reward just.

Again, the father frowned. No one had ever paid him gold and silver for his work, and he could not understand what would make his daughter's work worth gold and silver.

Let's take a look at the bag, he said finally, and Laxmaniya handed the bag over to him. It was lighter than he had expected and when he untied the mouth of the bag he let out a shriek. What catastrophe is this? he demanded. Where is the gold and silver?

It is right there, said Laxmaniya. I saw it myself when they gave it to me, and checked it again, once, on the way home. But when she peered into the bag her father was holding, she too shrieked. There was no gold and no silver in it. There was instead, only ash and mud. This cannot be, shouted Laxmaniya, and snatched the bag from her father, and in her hand the contents of the bag were gold again. Look, Father, look, said Laxmaniya, showing the jewels in the bag to him. Again, the father took the bag from her, and again in his hand the gold turned to dust.

This is witchery, said the father, staring deep into the bag and taking steps away from his daughter. You have consorted with witches.

I have not, Father, said Laxmaniya, her heart banging with fear. And I only went because you sent me. I did not want to go in the middle of the night with a strange woman to a strange land. You forced me to go. Look, Father, said Laxmaniya, taking in long breaths and calming herself. It is still gold in my hand. You let me hold on to the bag, and you let me spend it for us. I will take a piece to the market and exchange it for tools for our kit, and a door for our shop, and new mirrors for its walls. Together we will run a such a business. You and I.

The father looked at his daughter with fear and suspicion, but the image of a shop with mirrors and doors, the image of new tools in his old kit, filled him with dreams. But you mustn't tell anyone about what has happened, he said. Then he frowned. Look at you, he said, you are so thin I can almost see through you.

I have been working all night, said Laxmaniya, frightened by the way her father looked at her.

You should not have gone. Which girl goes off in the middle of the night?

Laxmaniya said nothing.

The next morning the father and the daughter went to the market with the bag. Through the journey, the father held the bag to keep it secure from thieves and looters, but when they reached the shops selling mirrors, he handed the bag to his daughter. Immediately, the bag grew heavy. The father and daughter selected the mirrors they wanted, and Laxmaniya reached into the bag and pulled out a silver coin.

Here, brother, she said, offering a coin to the shopkeeper.

Thank you, said the man, and received the coin, which, in his hand, turned to stone.

What joke is this? asked the man and hurled the stone out of the shop. He stared at Laxmaniya, confused. He was convinced he had seen a piece of silver in Laxmaniya's hand, but it was stone in his. How could that be? It had to be a mistake. Get away from my shop if you only have jokes to make, he said and pushed Laxmaniya and her father out.

Quietly, with feet of dread, the father and daughter left the shop, empty-handed. What use was this gold and silver that turned to dust and stone?

At one turn, as they returned home, a woman sat behind a large kerchief upon which she sold roasted peanuts, and in a moment of uncertain inspiration, Laxmaniya bought a cone of peanuts from her. Here, Mother, she said, and handed the woman a small piece of silver. The woman took the silver from Laxmaniya and gazed in amazement at the shining circle upon her palm. God bless you, daughter, she said, and pushed the silver between her breasts. Laxmaniya's father stared at his daughter and the woman. For the rest of their way home, he said nothing, and a sickening dismay filled Laxmaniya.

You witch, the father screamed, charging at his daughter the moment they got home.

Laxmaniya cowered against the wall. But think of it, Father, she said, breathlessly. This works between women. This is currency between women, Father. We will buy from women, and build our world. Father! Father! she wept.

And which whore-woman sells doors and tools and mirrors? And am I to tell everyone I have built my world with goods and money made by women? the father roared.

That night Laxmaniya took the bag of gold and silver and flung it into the lake. The lake opened its mouth and drank it in. The money had destroyed her life. It had taken away her father from her. He had never scolded her before, and now he would not look at her. Laxmaniya stood upon the bank a long time, staring at the ripples upon the lake's belly.

When she returned from the lake, she sat softly beside her father. Father, she said gently, I have drowned the bag into the lake. Let us not think about it anymore. There was no bag yesterday, and there is no bag today. We live like we always have so far. Father, she said, will you not give me something to eat?

Thrown the bag away? echoed the father in disbelief. You threw away the bag that could have got us at least rice, at least vegetables? You threw it away?

I did not want you so angry with me, said Laxmaniya, stunned by the hate she saw on her father's face. This is not my fault, Father, she cried. How was I to know what that marriage was, and what the money meant? Can we not forget it all? Can we not?

But it was not just that the father could not forget. It was that

Laxmaniya could not forget either. Over and again, in her dreams, she returned to the banyan tree and climbed its gnarly branches. Over and again she reached the treetop and sat smoking and singing and cooking with women. Over and again she built things with her hands—huts, scarves, conversations, bracelets, and anklets of flowers. With every passing day, even as she pushed the memory of the gold deeper within herself, dreams of a moonlit treetop where girls played and women sang washed her body. Her life with her father began to take on a dull, frightening sheen, though she struggled against it. She served her father his meals, though he scarcely spoke to her with civility now. He seemed in equal measure to hate and fear her, and yet she swept and tidied his barbershop, fighting the resentment that overtook her. Her money, a reward for her skillfulness, lay at the bottom of the lake, rubbing against fishes that swam by.

On the eighth night since the wedding at the treetop, Laxmaniya heard sounds outside her window, and when she looked out she saw men with burning torches marching toward her house. Father, she called out, then saw her father, too, leading the men. She stiffened.

Quietly she exited her room and went into the courtyard. Quietly she ran out the back door that led to the fields. Quietly, in the cover of darkness, protected by tall stalks of wheat, she ran. She ran past the lake where her gold and silver lay, she ran past other fields, she ran past sleeping cows and roosters, she ran to the river, beside which the ancient banyan stood like history. The old woman was there, waiting for her. You must climb the tree, she said in her vaporous, nasal voice, or else you will die, and without being told again, Laxmaniya took a knotted root and heaved her body up. Her palms hurt less this time, and her feet were surer. Up and up she went, leaving behind her treacherous world. Up and up, until she reached the very top. And the moon was large, and there were women on the leaves, very official today, because there was no scheduled marriage. Everyone was industrious, writing books and reading papers, producing cloth and painting walls. Girls still played and some women sang and others smoked. One of the women turned and said, There you are, and clapped her hands.

≈

"Is it my mother?" asked Meena.

"Who else would it be?" laughed the barber's wife.

≈

Laxmaniya smiled and stepped into the moonlight.

≈

"Am I still on the tree?" asked Meena.

"There you are," said the barber's wife. "Do you see yourself, sitting on a branch, hair loose upon your back, your feet naked and swaying under you, humming a song as you plan your next chore? Do you see your mother walking to you, agile like a monkey on the branches, all the parrots perched on her shoulders? She sits by your side and you sing together."

"What do we sing?" asked Meena, looking at herself.

"You sing this," said the barber's wife, and sang the song to Meena.

Gé mai, the clouds will drop down balls of butter
And the wind will give me milk they say
But I will not fall for these promises again
And I will not get on board today.

Meena smiled. She remembered the song from the story and sang along with the barber's wife.

Give me a world where you stay, gé mai
And my aunts and sisters and girlfriends too
A man will give me love they say
But I will not go to a man today.

And the sweet song filled Meena with mighty ambitions. She sat upon a silver branch, under a silver moon, watching a silver river flowing at her feet, and sang noisily with Kaveri. Behind them, the women of the trees burst into a choir.

Mai gé, my heart is no fraudulent bird
That will flit off your branch so easily

Finally, exhausted, Meena fell asleep and Kaveri took her head upon her lap and hummed softly into her dreams.

Give me a kingdom of women, gé mai
And its wonders that I have dreamt today.

ACKNOWLEDGMENTS

Any writer's first book is a dangerous journey—it might or might not begin, let alone end. And if it gets written, it is often touched by many, many people. I thank most sincerely the many teachers, mentors, and friends who have, over the years, helped me find my voice and develop a style. Thank you, Manjushree Thapa, Wayne Amtzis, Sridhar Lohani, Padma Devkota, Prateebha Tuladhar, and Annie Zaidi for those early years when you not only provided, but sometimes created platforms from which I could read and write. My immense gratitude to Samuel Delany, John Kessel, Wilton Barnhardt, and Elaine Orr for your workshops, feedback, and wisdom. There is so much I learnt from you. Of the many peers who helped me grow, I have to especially mention Paul Seth (I wish I knew where you are now), Emily Howson, Laura Giovanelli, and Josh Eure. Special thanks to William Badger, Rashmi Palkhivala, Jehangir Palkhivala, and Jerry Pinto, without whose love, openness, and generosity this book might not have existed. Thank you, Jerry, for getting me in touch with my agent, Kanishka, who is now a friend I feel comfortable calling at all hours of the day with the most inane of questions. Thank you, Maria Dahvana Headley, for reading my draft and for getting me in touch with Stephanie Cabot, who helped me chisel the book and found The Woman a place in the wider world. A big thanks to Rahul Soni, my fabulous editor, for always keeping my preferences in mind. Thank you, Daniella Wexler, Ghjulia Romiti,

Ajitha G.S., and Karthika V.K. for your insights. Conversations with you helped me get over many roadblocks. A special thanks to my students, Riana Shah, Aria Panchal, and Asmita Gattamraju, for being so happy for me, and for reading my early, early draft. How well you used the skills honed in our literature classes! I am a very, very lucky teacher, indeed. Thanks also to Cyrus Vakil, the principal of Bombay International School (BIS), Mumbai, and to Supriya Atal, head of curriculum development, for giving me the space, time, and support I needed through the years I was writing the book. Not once did you deny me my requests for leaves, part-time situations, or rants in your office. Your care and help have made it possible for me to wear the several hats I do as a writer, educator, and family person. If all bosses were like you, the world would be incredibly rich. And thank you Ananya Priyadarshi, my partner-in-crime at BIS, for taking time out to read the story. I am more than a little intimidated by how smart and how well read you are and your appreciation, therefore, means that much more to me. I should not forget also to thank the library committee at the Tata Institute of Fundamental Research, Mumbai, for letting me use the space in their library. One has to be a Mumbaikar to understand what a huge service this is!

I reserve the biggest thanks for my family. Thank you, Papa, for celebrating every phase of my life with such joy. Thank you, Mummy, for loving me so fiercely and adamantly. I miss you more and more every day. This book is, in most parts, an expression of my love for you. Thank you, husband, darling, Ravindra Venkatramani, for not just the romance you bring daily to life, but also for so sharply correcting my grammar and vocabulary, and for knowing exactly what I am trying to say but not being able to. And thank you, my sweet, sweet son, Arya Ravindra, for all the material you provide just by being around. You are my favourite story.

ABOUT THE AUTHOR

Smriti Ravindra is a Nepali-Indian writer. She is a Fulbright scholar and holds an MFA in creative writing from North Carolina State University. Her fiction and journalism have been published globally including the US, India, and Nepal. *The Woman Who Climbed Trees* is her first novel. She currently resides in Mumbai, India.

30 Years *of*

HarperCollins *Publishers* India

At HarperCollins, we believe in telling the best stories and finding the widest possible readership for our books in every format possible. We started publishing 30 years ago; a great deal has changed since then, but what has remained constant is the passion with which our authors write their books, the love with which readers receive them, and the sheer joy and excitement that we as publishers feel in being a part of the publishing process.

Over the years, we've had the pleasure of publishing some of the finest writing from the subcontinent and around the world, and some of the biggest bestsellers in India's publishing history. Our books and authors have won a phenomenal range of awards, and we ourselves have been named Publisher of the Year the greatest number of times. But nothing has meant more to us than the fact that millions of people have read the books we published, and somewhere, a book of ours might have made a difference.

As we step into our fourth decade, we go back to that one word – a word which has been a driving force for us all these years.

Read.